T0145999

CLICKBAIT

CLICKBAIT

A NOVEL

HOLLY BAXTER

HARPER  PERENNIAL

NEW YORK • LONDON • TORONTO • SYDNEY • NEW DELHI • AUCKLAND

HARPER PERENNIAL

HarperCollins books may be purchased for educational, business, or sales promotional use. For information, please email the Special Markets Department at SPsales@harpercollins.com.

FIRST EDITION

Library of Congress Cataloging-in-Publication Data has been applied for.

ISBN 978-0-06-337576-5

24 25 26 27 28 LBC 5 4 3 2 1

For Edmund,
who always asks the right questions

I'm afraid you'll have to take up art. Art is the only work open to people who can't get along with others and still want to be special.

—Alasdair Gray, *Lanark: A Life in Four Books*

ONE

I ENTERED THE YEAR OF MY DISGRACE AT ROCKAWAY BEACH. I WAS thirty-five and divorced for the worst reason, a reason that had imploded my career and the lives of pretty much everyone around me, a reason that had even made the newspapers. This was not good, especially for a reporter. The first thing they tell you when you begin your training is never to become the news.

Together, Joe and I had saved toward the down payment on a brownstone in Brooklyn, where we hubristically imagined we'd deposit three healthy, glowing kids. It was a brownstone that existed only in our minds: a spacious stoop on which to enjoy our morning coffees, tall windows and dramatic doorways, palatial ceilings with cornices. We'd get one for a song in Brownsville. We'd volunteer for local initiatives. We'd feel conflicted about gentrification. It was the ethically dubious New York transplant dream.

Then I embarrassed us both, irrevocably, on the world stage. We split the meager cash we'd accrued fifty-fifty, the same way it went in; avoided divorce courts; filed for a quickie separation. An entire world, painstakingly built by two people, ended with all the ceremony of a two-pump fuck.

Instead of taking my half of the cash and doing anything sensible with it, I'd gotten myself a mortgage on an ugly, salt-caked little place in a nondescript high-rise two blocks from the sea in Queens. On the fifth floor of six, I had a slice of an ocean view off to the left, only partially obscured by a down-at-the-heels bodega whose flashing sign perpetually announced GREAT BREKFEST. The floors creaked incessantly, and although a realtor had promised hardwood floors underneath smoke-laden, graying carpets, I hadn't bothered to pull them up to check. The kitchen was small but functional; two bedrooms faced each other at the back, equally depressing, with once-white walls.

On the day I moved in, it was mid-February, peak season for winter depression and desolate self-pity. Nobody was on the beach, not even Lycra-clad joggers with branded water bottles or drug dealers who hadn't yet graduated to blacked-out SUVs. I unpacked at sunset and pretended to myself that I liked it. *Why wouldn't I like it?* A sliding door led out onto a worn, grimy rectangle of balcony that I soon realized blew sand and debris straight inside, with wind so freezing that it made me gasp. Below me, a pregnant woman passed by the building in a coat that made her look like she was being eaten by a caterpillar. She stopped at the corner of the street for a moment and put a protective hand over her huge belly. I rolled my eyes. Like, *yeah, we get it, you had sex recently.*

What if I leaned so far over the balcony I fell? I shook the flimsy-looking railing, with its half-peeled white paint, and it shuddered a little. Maybe it was structurally unsound. Maybe one day I'd balance myself on it to yell bitter insults at pregnant passersby, lose my footing, and plummet to the sidewalk below, smashing into a thousand red watermelon pieces. Everyone who currently hated me would have to come to the funeral, and in death I'd be absolved of my sins. People would leave trite messages on my social media pages: *Gone too soon! Fly high, little bird!* (A little insensitive for someone who ended their life in pieces at the bottom of a tall building, but still.) They'd memorialize my LinkedIn page. My mother's small-town friends—the type who get a grief boner every time someone dies and gives them something to talk about over dinner—would send her flowers for weeks. She'd find a new spot for each bouquet and tell my sister the house had never looked better.

As I stood there contemplating the details of my own funeral with some satisfaction, another gust of wind displaced some papers on top of the unpacked boxes in the living room, and I decided today was too cold for my untimely demise. I braced my foot and pulled the stiff sliding door closed behind me.

My friend Ellie had promised to come over the next day and help me to screw the various parts of the easy-assembly bed together. There was no point trying on my own; I lacked a sense of coordination and couldn't even ride a bike until I was seventeen. Ellie, on the other hand, was my pragmatic counterpart, the yin to my yang. She knew a Phillips screwdriver from a flathead and a fuckboy from a marriageable man—that's why we'd stayed friends for so long. If I did meet my maker falling over the balcony while yelling insults at pregnant women, Ellie would turn up at the funeral and say something magnanimous yet unapologetically honest, like, "Natasha was my best friend and a shining star. And she died doing what she loved: making other people feel bad to avoid addressing her own insecurities." The gathered masses would nod and agree, respectfully and mournfully, that I really should have done more therapy.

So, no bed frame tonight. I flipped my new mattress off the side of the bedroom wall where the movers had left it, grabbed a sheet from a box marked "Linens," then pulled out a thin comforter my husband and I had never used because he hated it. It had an aggressively fecund-looking purple flower print. Now that I saw it through different eyes, removed from the joking context of my marriage—"Honestly, *I* love it!" I'd said to Joe as he went on a comedic rant about its demerits—I realized I hated it too.

My phone lit up with an incoming call while I was crouched by one corner of the mattress, attempting to pull the sheet taut. *Mom.* The only person who called me these days. I picked up and paced around the darkening apartment as I told her about how great the place seemed, how easy the move was, how well I was doing. She wanted to make sure I was still planning to visit. "So we can keep an eye on your *mental health*," she reminded me brightly. I imagined her sitting in her living room in Nantucket, eyes on the deck, perhaps an early deer nibbling at the apple tree, a veritable Garden of Eden from which I had exiled myself.

"Yeah. I haven't booked my flight yet, but I will."

"How about you do it before you go to bed tonight?"

"I said I will."

We talked about how I might decorate, where I'd put the big lamp and the small sofa. There weren't many options. I'd brought her to see the apartment just after I'd put in the offer, and since I was already committed, she was uncharacteristically polite. Pinching her lips, she said, "Well, you could probably do something with it." Then, "Maybe you can rent it out as a vacation spot later." She'd minded her words but hadn't bothered to disguise her tone.

After we'd exhausted the back-and-forth about furniture over the phone and I'd poured myself a suspiciously cloudy glass of water from the kitchen sink and announced I really was going to bed, she got around to saying what she really wanted to say. "Have you heard from him?"

"Which one?" I said, with a vague laugh.

A pause. "Your husband, Natasha, obviously." She still referred to Joe in that austere way, as if she had a leg to stand on where relationships were concerned.

"No, I haven't heard from Joe," I said, conversationally dehusbanding him, and his name hung between us for a second like the crack of a whip.

"Don't even tell me if you've heard from the other one," she said eventually. "I don't want to know. I'm just glad I never got a call from his parents."

THE NEXT TIME MY PHONE RANG, IN THE WHITE SLANT OF THE NEXT morning, it was the junior news editor of the paper. Mere weeks ago, this chinless, self-important man hadn't been above me in the newsroom hierarchy, but today he was more than glad to let me know that times had changed. We were no longer equals.

"You'll take a digital card from the list, follow the link, and re-write the story so it's different enough that we don't get accused of plagiarism," he said, his boredom seeping through the phone. "If someone's been killed, confirm with the local police. If someone's been arrested—"

"I know the basics, thanks," I cut in.

"Just making sure," he said, after a pause. I could imagine the smile spreading across his self-satisfied face.

Under the terms of my "reduced return," as it had been euphe-mistically termed by HR, I was expected to do the job of a junior news reporter for the morning. If all went smoothly, I'd get the chance to continue with the demotion full time. It was supposed to be better than being fired outright: better for me—a person who needed a job to live—and better for the paper, a show of capitula-tion to the social media rabble who still called for my head daily.

I logged in and cast my eyes down the list of digital cards assigned to me. They'd already been given prospective headlines.

Gory Scene When Friends Check on "Beautiful" Prom Queen in Deserted House

Last Words of College Student Stabbed While on the Phone with His Mother

Beloved "Talking" Puppy "Deliberately Run Over" by Psycho Neighbor

Asteroid Hurtling to Earth Could Wipe Out All of Humanity

The Corn Snack That Some Psychologists Say Can Get Rid of Your Anxiety Forever

I considered that imminent apocalypse was probably the most urgent, so I clicked on the card about the approaching asteroid and found a link to a story from a site called 911BigNews. The copy read like it had been written by a bot, but there was a college astrophysics professor quoted ("My job is basically to make sure the space debris that naturally surrounds us doesn't cause disaster. And this one, in terms of our solar system, is very, very close") who really did work at the University of Texas, according to their staff directory.

Despite myself, I felt my pulse quicken. *Very, very close?* I pulled up the CNN home page to see if there was anything about humanity's impending doom. I trusted CNN. CNN would tell me if the world was about to end. I scrolled past news about senators arguing over universal childcare and nope, no asteroid news at all. Presumably this was one of those "only missed us by ten thousand light-years!" stories that told the reader she wasn't about to die in a fiery hell in the thirteenth paragraph. Besides, if the apocalypse was coming, it probably wouldn't be announced first by 911Big-News, a website whose current top story was "DOES ELON HAVE A SECRET CYBORG SON????" Underneath another article on their home page entitled "What It's Like When Your Girlfriend Cheats with Your MOM" was the article about the asteroid. I had to assume that, if the editors of this site really believed we were all about to die, they might have bumped up the headline, at least above Oedipal love triangles.

Once, I was given space to pitch my own ideas in meetings where people listened like I might have something important to say. Now I'd been kicked back down into the news aggregation mine, where poor saps straight out of college rewrote barely legal, un-fact-checked stories so the site could rake in ad clicks. *The money for all that expensive reporting has to come from somewhere. Got a problem? Let me know when you've come up with your own profitable news model.* I couldn't really complain. Everybody knew I deserved this.

Just a year ago, I'd been packing my bags for London and drafting the requisite social media announcement: *Some personal news! Over the moon to say I'm moving to London next month to start a multiyear stint as the paper's senior UK reporter. I'll be reporting on our precarious geopolitical moment—and also getting the chance to interview all the fascinating British celebs you're curious about, from Phoebe Waller-Bridge to Prince William (okay, that one's a stretch, but a girl can dream!). Let me know which British issues you want to hear more about!* So many exclamation marks it makes me cringe now.

"I'm the one who's taking the big leap of faith here," Joe had joked as we loaded up our suitcases on the uneven floor of our Crown Heights rental. "You already come from a rainy island, while I have a high baseline expectation of vitamin D." I was a transplant to the city from a tony part of Massachusetts; he was a San Diego native whose parents and sister still lived by the beach. Every winter, he'd moon over photos of his sister hiking in the sunshine in a T-shirt and jeans, and I would cajole him into *learning to love* the snow, repeating that East Coast mantra: "You just need the right shoes!" He'd never quite taken to duck boots.

On the plane to London, we'd hit turbulence above Ireland, and Joe had taken my hand. He knew I hated rough air. "Just think," he'd said, "we're only an hour away now. I bet we'll be able to review some restaurants. I've heard the French food is incredible." When that didn't calm me, he'd offered: "*Or* we can go to a terrible Mexican restaurant and talk about how much fresher the guacamole is at home." This effort made me smile. Joe knew I loved being obnoxiously opinionated in public.

Within six months of that flight, I'd shown him how wrong he'd been to expend any effort on me at all. And now I lived with the consequences, starting with 911BigNews.

I shot an email to the astrophysics professor at the University of Texas and waited for a reply while I wrote up the parts of the asteroid story that made any sense. *Asteroid will come closer to Earth than any other space debris in the past ten years. Anxious readers shouldn't worry, however, as it'll still pass us by at a cool 4.7 million miles.*

Twenty minutes later, I got an alert from the paper's internal messaging system that the junior news editor had written me: *Everything okay?*

> *Yes, thanks! Think I'm getting the hang of the work-flow.*

> *I wondered because it's taken you a while to do that card.*

I looked at the clock. *Thirty mins?*

> *We're aiming for a quick turnaround here.*

> *Sure. Just waiting for the academic they quoted on 911BigNews to get back to me and confirm.*

> *Not necessary. An asteroid isn't going to sue us.*

Oh right. I sat on the floor of my shitty apartment, the wind intermittently rattling the balcony doors, feeling like I couldn't move. What was the next action again? Eventually, I typed out: *What do you want me to do?*

The answer was curt. *Set it live.*

I uploaded my semiplagiarized words into the content management system, pulled a generic picture of an asteroid from the image library, and published the piece under the edited headline: "Asteroid Hurtling Toward Earth Is Coming 'Closer Than Any Other Debris in the Past Decade.'" Within seconds, the card with my name on it had been taken off the list and moved into another area of the board marked AUDIENCE TEAM: TO TWEET.

What do I do if the professor gets back to me?

You can update if you want. But don't let it get in the way of doing the next card. Lots happening today.

Cool, okay.

The list of news items to aggregate got smaller as a team of junior reporters like me took them, rewrote them, published them, and then grew again almost instantly as members of the audience team dropped in suggestions.

Serial Killer on the Loose?: Woman's Body Found with "Mysterious Symbols" Scrawled on It

Toddler "Nearly Decapitated" by Pit Bull at South Carolina Farm

"I Served so You Could Insult Me": Airline Told Breastfeeding Veteran to "Put Her Tits Away"

Backlash Against Gym-Goer Who Filmed Man "Raping" Her "With His Eyes"

As I hovered over a card on the list marked "Sorority Hazing Gone Wrong," another message from the news editor appeared.

Hey . . . the one you wrote earlier has a bit of a weird tone.

It does? I'm sorry.

Yeah, try to avoid that.

Gotcha.

And can you go back in there and change miles to space miles? Gives it a bit more jazz.

Is "space miles" a technical term?

Readers aren't stupid. They know what we mean.

I went back into the system and changed *miles* to *space miles* then picked up the hazing story, which was about a woman being sexually assaulted with a Corona bottle by a group of freshmen outside a sorority house in Kentucky.

What a metaphor for the 2020 pandemic lol, wrote the news editor. I didn't know how he could possibly construe the story that way, so I just added a thumbs-up emoji to his message and moved on.

Two hours and five news articles later, I received an email back from the astrophysics professor at the University of Texas:

Hi Natasha,

Thanks for reaching out. That's actually an old story and the asteroid passed by some time ago. If you're interested in talking more, though, I'd be happy to set up an interview sometime this week. It's fascinating what's out there in the solar system, particularly the astronomical (no pun intended!) levels of space junk we've got floating around in our immediate vicinity . . .

I deleted the email and logged off for lunch.

IN THE EARLY AFTERNOON, I WAS HEADING OUT FOR A WALK WHEN I saw my upstairs neighbor Mrs. Konstantin near the entrance of the building, rattling her arthritic hands around the flimsy metal of her mailbox.

"Need any help?" I said cheerily. The only reason I even knew her name was that the realtor had knocked on her door on our first visit to ask for the spare set of keys she kept for the old guy selling the apartment. "Mrs. Konstantin," he'd said. "This could be your neighbor!" She'd been dressed in the same ratty brown jacket she was wearing today when she'd handed over the keys, had looked me up and down and said, in accented English, "I don't like noise." I wanted to grab her by the shoulders and say: *It's nice that you've looked at me and deduced I'm the kind of person who might play loud music and have friends over and maybe even enjoy rambunctious, ceiling-rattling sex with my handsome boyfriend. But I just want you to know that there's no danger of that happening. If you prefer quiet, beg the owner to accept my offer ASAP. I'm a black hole of silent self-loathing! I promise!*

Today, my question to her hung in the air, and it took her a moment to acknowledge it. Then: "No, no," and she gestured with her hand as if to shoo me away. Her little dog was with her, on a worn-out red leash. I'd assumed, from farther away, that it was a chihuahua, but up close I guessed it was actually a mutt. Some of the hair on its back had come out in tufts, and one of its teeth was definitely longer than the other.

"Aw, cute. I can walk her sometime if you want," I said, pointing to the dog and then the door. I don't know why I said that. I didn't want to walk that ugly-ass creature, and Mrs. Konstantin definitely didn't want me to either. She looked back at me in wordless horror, like I'd asked if she'd ever considered attending the annual Yulin Dogmeat Festival.

I shrugged it off, waved goodbye, and made my way past her in the narrow hallway, through the building's front door, and onto the street. The wind was barreling along the sidewalks, disturbing candy wrappers and abandoned innards of deli sandwiches. As I turned to walk toward the beach, I noticed two used needles in the road next to a sewer grate. *Lucky bastards*, I thought. If only I had a drug habit. It would be such a better excuse for what I'd done. *Sorry, everyone, I was on heroin!* My friends and colleagues would've made a show of standing by me, "helping me through this," and maybe I wouldn't even have gotten demoted because, *hey, I have a disease and that's discrimination!* Yes, if I was wise I really would've started street drugs before causing an international scandal, but I suppose the moment had passed.

When I reached the boardwalk, I sat down on a bench in front of the railings and pulled my sherpa coat around me. It had been an impractical gift from my mother, and it soaked up the salt air like a sponge, becoming damp and cold in seconds. Periodically, the wind would throw up a gust so powerful that it whipped sand into my eyes.

I'd heard that sea air was good for serotonin levels—another reason why I'd convinced myself buying the place was a good idea—so I sat there, freezing and breathing it in for a while. *People in Manhattan pay twenty dollars an hour to sit by a salt lamp in a basement room and you get this for free*, I told myself. When I watched my tiny square of shoreline the day before, I'd imagined myself a poignant and solitary figure in my own internal movie, taking a walk down the beach and perhaps crouching over a divot in the sand to pick up a tiny shell. Instead, my sneakers became caked with heavy, wet sand as soon as I ventured from the bench to test a foot off the boardwalk, and I retreated back. I couldn't even properly satiate my own self-pity.

"Nobody feels sorry for you," Joe had said when I was packing up my stuff in London.

"I know," I said, pushing a shoe into the corner of the suitcase.

"This decision was yours alone. You just forced me to react to it," he added. I nodded and folded a shirt. "And you'll lose your job, probably, too."

I looked back at him carefully. "They haven't decided that yet."

A couple of minutes went by as I continued to pack under his gaze. Then he sat down at the kitchen table and started to cry with great, ugly, unrestrained sobs. Garbled, incomprehensible words came out of his mouth, and it was only when he repeated himself that I could understand what he was saying: *"Why did you even do this?"*

It was a conversation we'd had over and over again during the preceding forty-eight hours, and we both knew there wasn't anything more to add to it. Four salient facts sat on the table in front of us, like unwelcome condiments: Our marriage was over. It was my fault. He had ended it. Neither of us wanted it to end.

I knew better than to take the bait again, but I knew I owed him some acknowledgment. "I mean, I told you why . . . in terms of not knowing why myself," I tried, but he got up off the chair he'd been crouched on, told me to shut up, and left, slamming the door childishly behind him. Joe had never been childish; he'd always been the steady wooden beam in the house of our marriage, the one standing wryly in the corner of a party while I regaled our new British friends with exaggerated tales of American life. He could hold his own in conversation, but he was also careful to support me when I wanted to take center stage, never one to cut in and chide me for telling lies. "Well brought up," as my mother, and indeed any mother, would put it.

Digging my nails into my fingers against the cold on Rockaway Beach, I realized that one day Joe would go home with some other woman and her mother would call him well brought up too.

Despite his humiliation and broken heart, I maintained that Joe had gotten the better end of the deal. Of course he loved me, but he hated me too, and that hate would be his saving grace, guiding him through the slimy, cloying darkness of our divorce and pushing him up for clear air at the other side. I was left without any of that self-righteousness; I had not been wronged, I was not the victim. I was left with myself as punishment, along with the unbearable knowledge that I really did wish him well. When my plane hit turbulence flying back into JFK in January, as I sat next to a sleeping teenage boy with a beanie pulled over his eyes rather than the man who used to be my husband, for the first time I felt no fear. I had nothing left to lose.

ELLIE STOPPED BY AS THE AFTERNOON CRESTED INTO EVENING, THE sky above the sea slowly mottling into spores of sunset.

"This is pretty bleak," she said, gently kicking the baseboards with her foot to test their strength. Ellie was one of the few friends I had retained after the divorce, first, because she'd always belonged to me—we met in college, sitting together in Deontology 101—and second, because she didn't shy away from saying what she really thought. Other friends, mortified by my behavior, melted away rather than ever associate with me again. Ellie called me at 4:00 a.m. London time, and we spoke through the early morning hours about what had led me to self-destruct so spectacularly. ("Though really, I wouldn't say it was self-destruction," she said, when I offered that explanation. "You destroyed someone else, and I think we have to be honest about that.")

Now, eight months pregnant, she inspected the apartment with a wrinkled nose. She pointed out the blossoming mold behind the kitchen cabinets and the flakes of lead paint peeling away from the window frame in the living room. "Better wash my hands after touching that," she muttered, wiping bits of debris from her hands onto the shirt straining over her belly.

Ellie had a no-nonsense approach to furniture construction that echoed her no-nonsense approach to life. When she saw my bed frame, she literally rolled her sleeves up and got to work. I sat on the floor beside her, a useless, beached blobfish, handing over screws every so often or propping up a wooden leg while she tested the slats under the mattress.

"Did you not get self-conscious, with him being that young and all?" she asked, when the bed was fully made and we sat together on the dirty carpet, me cross-legged and her in a wide, weirdly gymnastic pose, legs out either side of her bump.

"A bit," I said. "But then I figured he didn't have as much experience as me so it wouldn't matter."

"What was it like, then? Did he act all grateful?"

"Ellie, come on."

"No, I mean it. I want to hear it. Do you know how irritating it is to be the size of a whale and horny all the fucking time? Just give me something to remind me of single life."

I shot her a look. "I am not doing that."

"Just tell me. Did you really not go all the way?"

"I already told you everything." I got up, looked out the window from my bedroom down at the bodega. The neon lights of GREAT BREK-FEST weren't on yet. Two disheveled men in the street below looked like they were having an argument, one pointing at his compatriot with an accusing finger, the other unsteady and clutching a filthy sleeping bag. I looked back at Ellie and said, "I sucked his cock. That's all."

"Yeah, but was it big?"

I thought about it, my head to one side. "I guess it was average. It wasn't really about that."

"What *was* it about? Power?"

The question unnerved me, so I shot back: "Let's talk about *you*. What's it like to screw with a full-size baby in between you? Do you worry Jake's going to touch it with his wiener?"

She threw a pillow she'd just wrestled into a sham at me. "You're a sick fuck."

"That's what they say."

"But for real, though, it's weird. Jake can't really bring himself to do it anymore. Every time we get going, the baby gets jazzed up and starts to kick . . ."

"Oh, fucking hell." I put my head on the heel of my palm. "I really wish I didn't know that."

She shrugged. "Play stupid games, win stupid prizes."

I TOLD MYSELF THAT AFTER ELLIE LEFT, HUGGING ME GOODBYE IN her familiar-smelling sweater at the entrance to the A train, I'd take myself out for dinner, sample the local delicacies. I'd try to make my life *nice*. In reality, all I found was street after street of fried chicken shops and the occasional Ukrainian diner that couples looking for something "off the beaten path" tried on a fourth or fifth date so they could call themselves adventurous. As soon as Ellie disappeared back toward Park Slope, I realized I didn't want to eat sad pierogies in a booth by myself near the sea, my solitude reflected back at me by oversize windows in the darkness. This wasn't a fucking Noah Baumbach movie. So I retreated back to the apartment—taking the stairs because I didn't trust the ancient elevator and securing the worn yellow deadlock behind me once inside—and ordered Vietnamese food on an app.

Thirty minutes later, brisket pho on my lap, I sat on my newly made bed and scrolled with one finger through social media. My laptop screen was the only illumination in the room; something creaked repetitively in the walls, but otherwise there was no sound. I'd seen a small cockroach in the bathtub earlier but elected not to do anything about it. I knew that small cockroaches were the worst-case scenario: their presence pointed to a nest, a mother with hundreds of cockroach babies, while a big cockroach was usually just an isolated adult dropping by. I hoped the cockroach family would realize soon enough that my cupboards were bare and move on. I didn't want to have to take decisive action against them.

Just to press on the bruise, I decided to methodically make my way through the online presence of every man I'd ever slept with. Chopsticks in one hand, I shuffled myself into position on a couple of pillows to get properly comfortable for this masochistic investigation. Ben from middle school was married with two kids, I learned, as I popped a noodle into my mouth. He'd gone to seed and had a dad paunch now, but he looked pretty happy. Daniel, my college fling, had moved to Australia and mainly posted shirtless beach pictures, looking way more cut than he'd been when I knew him. It seemed like he was dating a model too. I should probably take that as a compliment.

Paul, whom I'd met on a dating app, was also married—very recently, it looked like, and at one of those fake Elvis chapels in Vegas that seemed to be having a renaissance among "I'm quirky!" types. Still, multiple images confirmed Paul had also stayed legitimately hot, especially when dressed in a tux. I thought about masturbating but couldn't work up the energy. Instead, I moved on to Zach, the one true claimant to breaking my heart. He'd done it with spectacular nonchalance, a year before I'd met my future husband.

I knew looking him up was a stupid idea, obviously, but I clicked onto Zach's profile anyway. A close-up of his face stared blankly out of the grids of Instagram, overlaid with the words: *Party animal (complete introvert & misanthrope) looking for a room in NYC, ASAP. Moving to pursue my lifelong dream of being an admin assistant. Let me know if you hear of anything.*

He was still as attractive as he'd been six years ago, when he'd told me that he wasn't actually looking for anything serious.

"It's been ten months," I'd said desperately, as if I could get him on a technicality.

"Yeah, no, you're right," he'd said. "I probably should've broken it off earlier."

I'd cried in the shower, cried when I had sex with someone from an app to try to get over it, cried during a commercial showing a couple Christmas shopping together. Then I'd briefly, desperately, tried to convince him I didn't want anything serious either. That led to an excruciating text conversation where he told me he was "into polyamory" but it was still better we didn't see each other anymore, because I was "fundamentally too conventional for the radical reimagining of a previously monogamous world."

Three months later, I'd met Joe and thrown myself into the relationship with the dedication and discipline of an amateur jogger training for a marathon. Hoping that sex would be a magical hormonal fix for my lingering feelings for Zach, I did it with Joe three or four times a day. And you know what? It worked. Anyone who says you can't get over a man by getting under another one hasn't tried hard enough, and maybe needs to switch positions. My affections slowly but surely transferred onto a man who actually wanted to be with me.

There was no way I could live with Zach. I knew that, even as I read his Instagram plea for a room in New York City. Well-established rules of time travel state that no matter how tempting, you can't interfere with the past to try and fix the present. So instead, I screenshotted his post and sent it to Ellie, adding: *Shall we go back to 2018?* as a joke. Just a joke to underline how I would never even consider it.

Her response came in seconds. *Don't you dare.*

I wouldn't!! I replied. Then I closed my laptop and got up to pour Drano into the bathtub, apologizing out loud to the insects I hoped it would liquidate.

This is where you are at thirty-five, I thought to myself. *Crouched on the filthy grout of a bathroom floor at Rockaway Beach, committing cockroach genocide and begging for forgiveness.*

TWO

OVER THE NEXT FEW DAYS, I REALIZED THE APARTMENT HAD A SERIous insulation problem: I heard the popping of pipes and the shuffling of my misanthropic neighbor above as often as the crashing of the waves on the beach. Mrs. Konstantin moved like the surf up and down her own apartment with her mutt in tow, tapping its nails on the floor so they beat out a bizarre little rhythm together: shuffle, bang, click-click-click, repeat. The woman muttered to herself, too, adding to that incessant percussion with a vocal accompaniment about the economy. The word "Reaganomics" floated down from the flimsy ceiling one day when I was in the bathroom, picking a pimple in front of the small mirror. And it was clear the noise pollution was a building-wide issue: The banging of a broom on my floor came every time I dared to move across the kitchen with my shoes on. Whenever annoyance rose in my throat at this cacophonous conveyor belt of neighborly bad feeling, I reminded myself that I had forfeited the right to judge anyone. These were my people now.

While tethered to another aggregation news shift, I kept one eye on Zach's Instagram. His New York post had gotten a fair amount of traction, with lots of people I didn't recognize—mostly women—commenting with emoji hearts and promises of: *I have a cousin in the area, I'll ask her if she knows anyone!* They were all written in the noncommittally supportive language of the unbothered acquaintance, and I could tell he hadn't thus far been successful in his search.

I moved on to his other accounts, scouring through them until I came to a tweet about taking his mother to a chemotherapy appointment. It was some wry comment about the American health-care system, illustrated with a clear bag of fluid marked CYTOTOXIC.

His mom has cancer, I texted Ellie. *Don't you think that creates a moral imperative for me to contact him? I have a spare room just sitting here.*

You know what I'm going to say. It's a bad idea.

A ping from the newspaper's internal system reminded me that I still needed to write up a piece the audience team had tentatively headlined "Man Who Went Viral for 'Screaming About Immigrant Ghosts' on Plane Had Just Received Vaccine," so I logged in to take care of it. An article I'd written the day before—"Pope Breaks Vatican Protocol by 'Secretly Declaring' His Super Bowl Team Through 'Coded Gestures,' Says Behavioral Analyst"—had an alert on it: twenty new reader comments, an unusual amount of engagement for a simple news piece. I scrolled down to read the comments.

"Trash"—two thumbs-up icons. "Boring"—one thumbs-up. "Maybe a bit of deflection from Natasha Bailey, drawing attention to OTHER PEOPLE'S lesser wrongs, no??"—five thumbs-ups. "Six months ago, Natasha Bailey wrote a VIOLENT piece about a young boy who she probably sexually assaulted. Still SILENCE from her editors. And now she's writing this kind of shit? It beggars belief. Natasha Bailey should be FIRED, yesterday"—fifteen thumbs-ups.

AS FEBRUARY LOLLOPED TO ITS DULL END, I GOT ON THE PLANE BACK to Nantucket. Perhaps I should have felt embarrassed, retreating to my family home in my mid-thirties because Mommy had told me to, but I'd lost all sense of personal shame.

I landed on the island during a late-afternoon rain shower on a Friday; it was a few degrees colder than New York and the humidity increased the chill. Mom picked me up in her battered SUV. "You look tired," she said, as she opened her arms to embrace me.

"Thanks a lot. I'm fine," I replied, slinging my backpack over my shoulder. I planned to stay only a week, so I hadn't checked any luggage, instead overstuffing a duffel bag I'd had since college. Mom took a sideways look at it as I threw it in the back seat and said, "Didn't you have anything better?"

"Who am I here to impress?" I responded and put my feet up on the dashboard.

We drove past the usual stores on Main Street, the houses of childhood friends I'd once regularly haunted. As was her habit, my mother pointed to each one: "There's Lily's place. What's she doing these days?" and I answered, without emotion, "We never stayed in touch." After we'd done the same routine for three in a row, she turned to me and said, "Maybe that's your problem. Staying power."

"Keep your eyes on the road," I replied.

"You need to be able to accept criticism."

"Thanks for the feedback."

"You and your sister both, you know, you've always lacked that little bit of . . ." She paused to pull into our driveway. "I mean, you're both smart. That much was obvious from a young age. Do you know that biology teacher, Mrs. Clay, she said to me about Miriam, she has a *natural talent* for the sciences. Very similar to what they said about you with humanities. No doubt I had two smart girls. But the staying power, I think it's something both of you need to work on."

I exited the car wordlessly, laden down with my impractical bags. It was gray on the island, small spots of white only occasionally filtering through a blanket of low-hanging clouds. Mom continued her lecture on resilience as we made our way up to the front door of the wood-paneled house.

"Are those lights new?" I asked to change the subject, pointing toward a new constellation of fairy lights by the front door.

"Oh . . . yes. I got those because I thought I might start renting out one of the bedrooms. If people arrive at night, I want them to be able to see."

"That's a good idea," I said, simply because I thought a steady procession of guests through the door would disturb my sister, and that gave me a twinge of satisfaction.

I loved Miriam in the way every woman loves her sister: a complicated way. She was twenty-nine, six years younger than me, and had never really bothered to leave home, with the exception of two attempts at college that had flamed out pretty quickly. Miriam was not troubled by the fact that our mother had spent her rapidly dwindling life savings propping up her failure to achieve any notable qualifications. She'd moved back into her childhood bedroom after the second college didn't work out and occasionally took a shift at one of the seasonal ice cream shops on the island, claiming that she was "working on a novel." In a way, I admired the way Miri had so conspicuously given up on life before it began, while I flailed away like a fish keen to please the line it was hooked on.

"Well," said Mom as soon as we got inside. "Glass of wine on the deck?"

"Not really the weather for it, but sure." I left my duffel and backpack in the living room and went to the kitchen to grab two glasses. "Is there a bottle in the fridge?"

"I'll get it." She waved me out of the way and bent down to grab a bottle of Pinot Grigio from the cabinet. "It's cold in here anyway," she added, "but I'll bring some ice if you want it."

"I'm not fussy."

I walked quickly across the living room to the back door that led out onto the deck, to deny her the gratification of knowing I'd heard her retort: "That's news to me. I better bring the ice!"

As we sat on the deck in our jackets—the deck was Mom's pride and joy, and we were going to see it on every possible occasion, even if we both silently and stubbornly froze—we talked about Miriam as a way to avoid talking about me.

"She's finding her footing, you know. I'm proud of her. It looks like things are falling into place. She's seeing a nice boy on the island," Mom said, swirling the wine in her glass.

"That doesn't count as a career."

"Oh, Natasha, come on." She sighed, then added, "Not *every* woman gets a comfortable life through hard work. Sometimes other avenues—"

"Mom."

"She's a very pretty girl, Tasha. I mean, I looked just like her at her age. If a nice man can take her under his wing, I would celebrate that. She takes such good care of her hair." Miriam's hair had always been a subject of fascination and pride to our mother. I was shockingly pale with frizzy but flat hair in an unreflective dark brown; my sister's rich mahogany mass of glossy curls fell down her back like she was a fucking Disney mermaid.

"You got along fine without marrying a rich man," I said. "Maybe have a bit more ambition for Miri." What hung in the air was the truth: Mom managed because she was the only one left with the Bailey name, the recipient of a free house and a very healthy inheritance. She'd made sure to piss that away so we couldn't sit around doing nothing like she had—or at least both of us couldn't. Truly an act of astonishing benevolence.

"Oh, your grandfather would *much* rather I had married well," said Mom. Both my grandparents had died before I was ten; they existed in my memory as friendly blurs. "Lucky I didn't care much about his approval."

"You didn't?"

Mom looked over my shoulder at the trellis, her eyes following a bird I could hear rustling within it. "You know, Natasha," she said, "I brought you girls up to be free from the pressures I had foisted upon me. You'll never know what it was like being raised as the daughter of Big Deal parents. It was a life of crushing expectations.

When I told my father I wanted to go to art school, he said only one thing to me: 'What a terrible waste.'"

"Did he have a point?"

She looked at me sharply. "No, I don't think so."

I pressed on. "But do you feel like you fulfilled your potential?"

"He wasn't worried about my potential, Tasha. He was worried about his reputation. He wanted a daughter who went to law school or became an MD." She sipped her wine, put the glass down delicately, her eyes still trained over my shoulder, and added: "Well, that's not entirely true—what he wanted was a son. But failing that, he wanted a respectable daughter who kept the money pouring in. Just below that on the list was marrying well, and I didn't even manage that."

How noble of you, spending the family fortune instead, while selling animal paintings for pocket change, I thought but didn't say. What I did say was: "Sounds like Grandpa was hard on you." Her father was a lawyer who'd spent half his time helping evil corporations hold on to their money and the other half of his time assuaging his conscience through pro bono work for disabled veterans. A true American, a capitalist and a patriot. My grandmother lived in the beach house mostly full time while Grandpa shuttled back and forth from Boston; she wrote the gardening section for the local paper in Nantucket. But not for money, of course. That would've been vulgar.

"I'm just glad you girls didn't have to live with that kind of thing. I worked so hard to make sure you had a different childhood," Mom added, finally looking me in the eye.

"Thanks, Mom," I said without emotion.

"You never want to acknowledge that I worked at giving you a wonderful life—a free life."

"Mom, minutes ago you were extolling the virtues of Miriam marrying a rich dude. Sorry if I don't exactly see how you managed to break free from Grandpa's restrictive expectations."

She pursed her lips. "He wasn't wrong about everything." Then she downed the rest of her wine in two gulps and tapped her fingers on the wooden table, returning to form. "The last few boys Miri's gone out with," she continued, "they keep breaking it off. She comes home and there's tears, drama . . . It doesn't make any sense, does it? With *her* looks? There's got to be something . . . maybe psychologically wrong. Do you think there's some issue she doesn't feel she can talk about with me?"

"Maybe they're just people whose relationships don't work out," I said, irritated. How many times did we need to state Miriam's incredible beauty while I sat here, disgraced and average?

"I just hope this new guy sticks around. He's got a chemical engineering degree, you know. They'd be a perfect fit."

"What does Miri have to offer some guy with a chemical engineering degree?"

"Honestly, Natasha, you can be a real bitch sometimes."

So there it was. We sat in silence for a few moments, then the self-pity began. "I don't know what I do to deserve this," she said, pouring herself more wine. "Two capable adult women, and all you can do is tear each other down, and me with you. You know, I remember the day I stood at your high school graduation, and thought to myself, my life is going to look a certain way in a few years' time—"

"Okay, spare me the monologue," I said. "It's Miriam's latest boyfriend not *King Lear.*"

"Well, sorry I don't have a PhD in Shakespearean literature."

"Neither do I, but that wasn't the point."

"Okay. Look, I just want us to get along." She stirred the loose ice cubes with her finger. "That's always what I want."

"I want that too."

She paused and swallowed. "So Joe hasn't reached out at all?"

"I told you he hasn't."

"I was thinking about checking in with his mother. Nothing big, just an olive branch kind of thing. Oh, don't look at me like that, Natasha, you know how much we connected at the wedding. It's not just you who's been hurt by this divorce, you know."

I sipped my wine and said quietly, "Sorry for the inconvenience," but she went on loudly: "I've never accepted this New York individualism bullshit. Like, 'do your own thing and nobody gets affected.' Be brave enough to own your mistakes, is what I say. Deal with the consequences. Something happens, everyone gets hurt. That's the reality."

"I am owning my mistakes, Mom," I said. "Who else do you think is dealing with the consequences right now? I got demoted at work. I live alone. I've lost basically all my friends."

"And he definitely won't take you back, will he?" She paused with her glass halfway to her mouth, the bottle almost completely drained.

I looked back at her steadily. "I didn't ask, and I don't intend to."

She shrugged. "It's your funeral." *If only, Mom*, I thought.

LATER, SHE CAME UP TO MY BEDROOM—A TIME CAPSULE OF MY LATE teens, with glow-in-the-dark plastic stars on the ceiling, a corkboard by the bed covered in Polaroids of high school friends, and a closet full of clothes that were just about coming back into fashion—with a freshly laundered set of towels and a cup of ginger tea. "Give me a hug," she said, and put her arms around me. I reciprocated awkwardly. I'd long ago stopped letting my guard fully down around her.

"Look," she said as she pulled out of the embrace, keeping an arm around my shoulder. "You know I love you more than anything in the world. I just hate to see you hurting. And I'm so glad you're here. We're gonna have a great week, the three of us."

"Yeah," I said, noncommittal. "I'm sure we will."

"You know I can't get on my high horse when it comes to men. We've all made mistakes. But the important thing is that we're family and we're here for you."

"Yeah. I know."

"*Yeah. I know.*" She imitated my monotone back at me. "Chin up! Maybe tomorrow we can go shopping? Or get a pedicure? We can go down to Alberta's and get that special hot chocolate too. Let's make this whole recovery period *fun*. And be nice to your sister. She loves you too."

"I always am," I said.

She smiled. "I know you are. Mostly. Goodnight."

"Goodnight."

She paused in the hallway while turning out the light and said again, "Love you!" before disappearing into the darkness. I put on my bedside lamp, pulled the sheets over me, and started reading about the world's worst plane crashes on Wikipedia on my phone. Then I pivoted onto the r/IncelExit subreddit. Frustrated young men who used to be blackpillers and now wanted to rejoin society were swapping tales about how not being able to fuck supermodels had almost turned them into murderers. They vacillated between ranting about how hard it was being short or underpaid or having unimpressive jawlines and self-flagellating about how they'd almost become misogynist terrorists because of their own oppression. "I have an imaginary gf and Idk what to do" was the title of the latest post, written by a young man who had long concluded the best kind of woman was a life-size body pillow. There was deep reassurance in knowing that there were people out there who'd been, or still were, in situations objectively much worse than mine. At least I wasn't about to plunge to my death in a fiery wreck or make a public commitment to bed linens.

Before I turned off the light, I clicked back onto Zach's Instagram account, the male tragedies of lifelong sexual rejection still reverberating in my mind. Six more people had commented on his post about moving back to New York. One, a woman whose profile said she did "artful wedding photography," and whose location was "Somerville, MA," had left a series of kisses and a red heart. Another had said: *I know why you're really leaving lol.* A final profile, which looked like it had been created for the express purpose of commenting on this post, had written: *literally, fuck you.* I guessed that she had literally fucked him.

In the morning, I checked and saw with a stab of vindication that the comment had been removed.

MIRIAM AND I WERE TECHNICALLY HALF SISTERS, THOUGH OUR mother had long forbidden us to tell other people that. She forbade us from saying a lot of things while we grew up, not under the threat of violence but rather of "breaking her heart." That's also why, when I was seven years old and watched her loading up the shopping cart with bottles of midrange wine, I got chewed out for saying the word I'd recently learned at school: "alcoholic." Mom was functional, after all. And the worst things that came out of her mouth were not due to the wine so much as facilitated by it. She was just as capable of character assassination over iced coffee as she was over Chardonnay.

She was the mom who let us bring back beers to the house in high school, and the mom who picked me up from a night out gone wrong and rubbed my back while I barfed out the window of her car. She looked after our dog until he was a cancer-ridden mess and took him to the vet to euthanize him when I was at college, holding the phone up to his ear so I could sob my goodbyes. She'd packed up Miriam's boxes for college, twice, and unpacked them at the other end, twice, while Miri cried about her own self-inflicted inability to get an education. She helped arrange the shipping of my possessions back from England after the divorce and reassured me that the public would move on from my cancellation, and I would find love again. In fact, her attitude during a crisis was almost always impeccable. The fact that she couldn't sustain this leadership during peacetime was something we'd all stopped bothering to mention.

Miriam and I had names themed around men we'd never known: our fathers. Mine was Stan, a Russian immigrant who worked in construction: a great, pale slab of a man with wide shoulders and a kindly smile, at least according to my mother, who'd gone out with him only a few times in New York. She'd never told him she was pregnant. She had ideas about becoming a full-time artist and owning a studio off Union Square where she could paint in flowing skirts with a baby at her hip. That plan had lasted until I was six months old, and then she'd admitted defeat and moved in with her parents. Being old-school East Coast wealth, they plugged away at their own marriage to the end, obstinately failing to divorce while maintaining an existence meted out in separate bedrooms and separate vacations. My mother—their pampered only child, the free spirit whose freedom had come with too many downsides—got a fully paid-for nanny for me. Then Grandma passed away when I was three, followed by Grandpa a year later, and we moved to their old summer place on Nantucket with the inheritance, where Mom occasionally sold locally commissioned portraits of dogs and babies, and during the tourist months, paintings of exaggerated sunsets over the local beaches. This was her low-key rebellion against the gilded cage—not exactly Bolshevism.

Mom got pregnant again when I was five and a half, though I only remember it in snippets: pressing my hand on her expanded belly to feel a kick; telling my kindergarten teacher I was going to have a sister. Miriam's father was Israeli: a long-haired, brown-eyed hippie spending the summer on the island with friends from some prestigious college, different from his preppy compatriots in their boat shoes and red shorts, hanging back from the crowd serenely with his guitar on his shoulder. Zeke. I didn't remember his brief appearance in our lives, though apparently he'd built a sandcastle with me on the beach. He told my mother he was too young to have a child, and she agreed, and said she'd probably get an abortion. He didn't return the summer after that.

I guess Mom's choice of names for us was supposed to give us each a sense of history or legacy, some way of placing who we were. Natasha is the nickname for Natalia in Russian, where Sergei becomes Serozha and Nikolai becomes Kolya. It's a language that frankly doesn't give a fuck about the logic of its diminutives. A crash course in Russian nicknames had made reading Dostoyevsky easier as an undergrad, but it hadn't made me feel any closer to a faceless man who worked on building sites all day, laying bricks and directing cranes, and then knocking up my mother. And honestly, it made me nauseous thinking about how quickly and easily Mom could throw away her own identity. How could she carry a baby for nine months inside her own womb and then name it for the culture of an absent father, as if she didn't have anything to give us but incubation? Was her own sense of self so flimsy?

I LOGGED INTO WORK THE DAY AFTER ARRIVING IN NANTUCKET, pulling up the card list and the in-house messaging service, and opening up the paper's curated news feeds, which allowed us to see what every other website was publishing every minute of the day. My cheap work-provided computer strained audibly under the pressure of loading all the ads on our site's main page. Whenever the advertising team agreed to sell off another inch of space to a client, my laptop took another hit; today, it sounded like a jet engine taking off.

Morning, said the news editor on the messaging service.

Hi, I typed back.

> *School shooting yesterday. Could you do a bit of a social media trawl and write up the juicy stuff from grieving families etc? One of the other reporters was saying there's a tribute from a sister somewhere with a good pic.*

> *Can we use that?*

> *Yep. Public domain once they've shared it on social. Plus the kid's dead so it's all good.*

> *Cool.*

I started gathering together tributes, scanning them for key words or headline-worthy phrases. Within fifteen minutes, I had a piece ready to go, with the headline: "'Hope You Didn't Suffer Too Badly, Bro': Tributes from New Mexico Families Torn Apart by Shooter."

In the group chat for reporters and editors, someone I didn't know piped up: *Should we say "disturbed" shooter?*

Not sure, replied the editor. *Do we have confirmation he was mentally ill?*

Some school counselor claiming she was concerned.

How about "deranged"? someone else suggested.

Love that, said the editor. *Has more texture. Natasha, can you jump in and change?*

Sure, I said. *I'm 90% sure all the tributes in here are real btw. A couple I couldn't confirm.*

Proceed until told otherwise, said the editor. *At the end of the day, the message is the same. People losing kids is really fucking sad. And if you can get a pic up top of one of the moms crying or something, that'll really hit home.*

Is there one available in the pics system?

Should be soon. We have a photographer down there in NM outside the room where the parents are being told if their kids made it.

Wow, said another reporter.

Yeah, said the editor. *Really tragic stuff.*

Super tragic, I typed back.

"I brought you some fresh strawberries!" Mom barreled into my room without knocking, carrying a small bowl. As she set it on the desk beside me, she peered over my shoulder at my screen and said, "What even *are* those?"

"The pixelated corpses of children," I replied flatly.

"Oh my God! *Why?* Is that for work?"

"No, Mom, it's how I spend my leisure time." I turned around in my wheeled chair and gave her a look that said: *Please get out and stop invading my privacy*, though it had never deterred her before.

She shook her head. "I just think working a job like that can get to you mentally."

"Well, it can sometimes."

"You got in all that trouble because of that job, and now you let them do things like *this* to you."

"Mom. Reporting the news is the basic function of a newspaper."

"I remember when you were interviewing senators. If I'd known you'd end up staring at photos of dead babies all day—"

"Then you wouldn't have been able to do anything about it," I said, finishing the sentence before she had a chance. "Because it's my choice."

AS I WAS LOGGING OFF FROM WORK, MIRIAM CAME BACK FROM HER new boyfriend's house and flopped onto the end of my bed.

"Hey, stranger," she said, all bright-eyed and bushy-tailed. Her hair was looking irritatingly good. Whose hair looked good in cold, drizzly weather? I noticed she was wearing pink eyeshadow, which complemented her skin tone. I would've looked like I'd just been punched in the face.

"You're wearing a lot of makeup," I said.

She laughed. "Do you like it?"

"I guess. It's more than I'm used to seeing you in."

"I also got bangs, you know," she said, unclipping a section of her hair at the front. "But I can't wear them down yet, 'cause of the weather."

"Give me a break. Your hair is practically weatherproof."

"No, no, *honestly.* It's just the conditioner I use. I'll lend you some."

"Yeah, sure. Is it DNA-unraveling conditioner?"

"New York has made you such a skeptic." She jumped up off the bed, light on her feet, and stood in front of the vanity. "I got a new hair stylist and he's a guy."

"How exotic," I said sarcastically, closing my laptop a little too hard.

"No, seriously, I know it's not groundbreaking, but I think you should try it. Like, all this time I've had women doing my style, and I had this revelation, like, men know what men want, you know?"

"Sure." Why would I bother to challenge that horrifically anti-feminist assumption at this point?

She teased the front of her hair easily back behind her ear and clipped it into place. I watched her fingers work though the slippery strands, so utterly different from my fine, brittle ends. Our similarities were in facial structure: wide cheeks, small chins, broad foreheads, big eyes. But the minor details were enough to give Miriam a clear edge: the hair, skin that tanned versus skin that burned, her D-cup boobs and skinny, tapered waist versus my "athletic figure," the clothes-store euphemism that means you go straight up and down with only the tiniest detour at a couple of pinprick breasts that struggle to fill out a B cup. "A perfect handful" is what Joe had kindly called them. I didn't mind their size, but whenever we walked down the street, I noticed the way men's eyes bounced straight off my body and then undulated like gently melting glue down every inch of hers.

"Mom says you're still 'grieving your divorce,'" Miri said, turning away from the vanity so she could do air quotes with her fingers.

"She does, huh?" I said evenly, bringing one foot into my lap.

"Yeah. But are you, actually?"

I sighed. "I don't know. Is it bad if I say no?"

"Not really. I got over my breakup with Dan after, like, a shower. I mean . . . I know it's not the same. But you and Joe weren't actually *together* together that long."

"It was two and a half years."

"Yeah, but I mean. It could've been longer."

"I'm not broken, if that's what you're worried about," I said, choosing to proceed in good faith. "And I'd rather Mom didn't go around saying that I'm grieving or whatever."

"No one's expecting you to feel great after a divorce, so I wouldn't worry about it."

"I don't *worry* about it. Like, my reputation on the great island of Nantucket isn't on my mind all day, every day. But I'd like the chance to keep some things to myself."

"Then you know what the solution is," said Miriam, perching on the end of my bed. "Don't tell Radio Mom."

"I never do. But it doesn't stop her from deciding how I'm feeling, clearly."

"Hmm." She made a noncommittal noise and started messing around with her hair again. I thought about Mom's pronouncement that with looks like hers, Miri didn't need a career.

"Stop it," I said suddenly, more forcefully than I'd intended.

She looked back at me, surprised. "Stop what?"

"Just . . . showing off." I waved a vague hand toward her.

"All right. Jesus." She got up off the bed and padded out toward the hallway, muttering something under her breath.

"What was that?"

"Nothing," she said brightly, poking her head back around my bedroom door. "But can you get in a better mood by dinner? I want to try the burrata at Bob's Pizza and Mom only takes me out when you're home."

THREE

HEY, I TOLD YOU YOU'D MISS NYC, I MESSAGED ZACH LATE SUNDAY
night, after three beers in the living room with Mom. I regretted
it in the morning, thinking of the time stamp, ashamed at what
I'd revealed about myself, but it was too late: he'd clearly seen it,
because he'd replied.

Did you? Well, better late than never.

Don't pretend like you don't remember, you asshole.

It was 9:00 a.m. on Monday, my fourth day in Nantucket. I
had the day off from work because I'd taken the Saturday shift. My
presence was no longer a big deal in the newsroom; I clocked on for
aggregation work, clocked off, rarely had to travel to the office. I had
no adoring fans or irate detractors emailing me about the content
of my investigative features. Nothing I wrote ran on the front page.
My worth was measured in numbers of cards on the list cleared
during my allotted eight hours, my byline now only attached to
aggregated articles of two hundred words apiece.

I saw Zach was online and was seized by the need to write
something more, to elicit another reply. *Yeah, I guess so. I actually
live in Queens now.*

His own reply came fast. He was generally unbothered about
how he appeared—eager, absent, interested, casually cruel—and
had never cared about my impression of him. *Thought you went
to London.*

I blushed, alone with my humiliation. *That's over now.*

He didn't ask for further details. *Ah right. Well, welcome back to the US of A.*

Ha. Thanks. You know, I do have a spare room at the moment, if you're still looking.

I saw he was typing, then pausing, then typing again. *That's kind. How long is the room available? I'd only need it short-term.*

I didn't want to say anything that implied closeness, like *As long as you need,* since we hadn't technically stayed friends after he'd dumped me. So I went with: *A couple months, maybe up to six. I'm just working a few things out. It doesn't exactly come fully furnished, but it's got a bed. I'll warn you it's all the way out in the Rockaways. So you'd have to be prepared for beach living!*

A minute passed. Then he said: *Ah. Not ideal.*

I sat against the headboard of my childhood bed, deflated. There was no reply I could craft that wouldn't make me feel like a complete loser. I put my phone down.

MONDAY BECAME A GOOD DAY, MOM-WISE. WE WALKED DOWN TO Main Street, where we ran into one of my childhood teachers on our way to get pedicures. Mom bragged about me to Mrs. Fletch, even though there was little left to brag about. "She's a journalist in New York, you know. And she's just arrived back from an assignment in London."

"I always knew you'd go on to do big things," said Mrs. Fletch. It was so clearly something she said to everyone, but Mom couldn't stop mentioning it as we continued down the street, repeating that "everyone felt you girls were destined for big things, you know, and I still believe it."

"Come on, Mom," I said as I pushed open the door of the mani-pedi place. "I'm not sure she even recognized me."

"Oh, stop it! I don't know why you say these things."

We sat next to each other on pleather chairs, and when the pedicurist proffered her samples, I chose a loud red. "Prostitute red," said Mom, and I thought about being as disapproving as

I'd have to be if someone said that in Brooklyn, but then I just laughed. We graduated into gossip about people I'd been to college with and people she met up with in Nantucket, who'd had an ugly grandchild and who had never had a boyfriend, whose IVF had failed and who recently got their third abortion. You know, girl stuff.

While my pedicurist got to work on the dry skin of my heels, I said, "Do you remember Zach? He's moving to the city."

Mom turned toward me and almost kicked her pedicurist in the face. "The one you cried about on the porch? Right before Joe?"

"Yeah." I shrugged. "I don't know how I feel about it."

"He's the one who didn't want anything serious?"

"Yeah. Well, you know. We were young."

"He sounded kind of messed up."

"Only as messed up as anyone at that age." I didn't know why I was getting defensive on behalf of a man who had treated me like shit, but somehow I was.

"Well, it wasn't exactly a decade ago! But still." She gave me a meaningful look. "You never know what happens when old flames meet again."

"I don't know what you mean."

"Mm-hmm. Sure." We both laughed, then she added, "Is he single?"

"I think so. But Mom," I said, giving her a meaningful look, "Dr. Reese said I need a break from men." I couldn't help it though: my internal voice chimed with what she'd said, two siren voices united in an a cappella harmony.

WHEN I'D FIRST COME HOME UNDER THE SHADOW OF DISGRACE, Mom had picked me up at Logan and driven me all the way back to Nantucket, quietly parking the car on the ferry during the final leg of the journey and biting her lip every time she stole a glance at me, as if I were dangerous cargo, liable to explode without careful handling. Neither of us mentioned what had happened in London.

I slept off my jet lag most of the day after we arrived home, but she woke me up the following morning with a cup of coffee and the news that she'd booked me an appointment with a therapist. "Just try it," she said. "You've been through a lot. I asked the women at pickleball, and Brenna said she's an expert."

"You told the women at pickleball?" I said, but it was a hollow kind of anger I felt, an indignant echo from miles away. I didn't really have the strength to care.

"I didn't tell them," Mom lied lightly. "They read about it in the newspaper."

We drove to Dr. Reese's in silence, although I found out by the plaque outside her door that she wasn't so much a medical doctor as a "qualified counselor" with a PhD in geography. "This is what passes for psychiatry outside New York City," I muttered, because I knew it drove Mom crazy when I went all urban elite on her, and she took the bait, snapping back, "Well, no one else here on the island has managed to make the news for violating a young athlete."

That was me: the violator, the destroyer of worlds.

Mom waited in the car while I went in, which made me feel uneasy, like she was standing sentry at the gates of my consciousness. But then again, I guess everyone brought their mother to therapy in some form.

"Call me Diane," Dr. Reese said as soon as I sat down on her half-collapsed sofa.

"I'd prefer not to," I said. "I'm working on maintaining distance with people I work with."

She didn't laugh. "Do you think you have a problem with boundaries?" she asked instead.

"You know what?" I said. "I think my whole family has always had a problem with boundaries, and I've worked my entire life to convince them that boundaries are a thing. And now, I make one fuckup and everything wants it to point to some fatal flaw inside of me. But if I'd swept it all under the rug or if people on social media weren't hell-bent on destroying other people for sport or if my husband had cheated on me at the same time as I'd done it to him, then we wouldn't be here digging for my hamartia. We'd say that something unfortunate had happened, and you'd just think I was a person."

"We're all just people, Natasha."

"Obviously," I said, picking at my nails irritably.

"Think of this as a safe space," said Diane. "We can explore what happened, or we can leave it by the wayside for a while and talk about other things. Either way, everything that's said here is totally, one hundred percent between us. And don't worry about shocking me—I've seen and heard the full spectrum of human experience."

"It didn't even cross my mind to be worried about shocking you," I said. "I assumed you'd be professional."

"Well, I'm glad."

We sat in silence for a while, then she said, "So. Shall we talk about what happened?"

"Dr. Reese—Diane—whoever you are. Respectfully, you remind me of my mother. I don't know how graphically I can describe oral sex to you."

"Perhaps not all the gory details, but how you felt about them."

"But that's the thing, Diane," I said, leaning forward. "It was all *about* the gory details."

When my hour was up and I crossed the parking lot, Mom looked up at me with an encouraging smile and paused the audiobook playing too loudly from her car speakers. "How did it go?" she asked. "Brenna said she was really good. Very solid. She helped her a lot with menopausal rage."

"For sure, she seemed great. She said it all happened because of my fucked-up childhood," I said, pulling my seat belt across my chest. Mom's face went stony in a cartoon instant, so fast that I began to laugh—sardonically at first, then it turned into real throaty, childish laughter, and before I knew it, it was crashing in waves across my rib cage, dragging me down onto the dashboard, leaving me gasping for breath. At that point, Mom had the charity to join in. We laughed until tears were streaming down our faces, until she grabbed me by one shoulder and said, through her laughter, "Stop—stop! I have to start the car!"

To be perfectly honest, it was clear to me that Dr. Diane Reese was a fraud, but she was a nice fraud. She regurgitated all that life-coach bullshit about needing to love yourself before you can love anyone else, about how you can't hope to be happy in a relationship if you aren't happy single and how the body keeps the score. I felt like she'd watched too many YouTube channels hosted by people who thought you could get cancer from bad vibes and cure it with crystals. But there was something comforting about hearing her trot out her truisms, like we were gathered around a bonfire, toasting marshmallows with our bras off. I knew that in real life, people in functioning relationships hadn't managed it because they'd first become the Platonic form of "happy, independent woman." I knew plenty of hot messes who'd jump off a bridge if they were single but were transformed into functioning members of society simply because they were willing to settle for the dregs of a dating app. Sometimes, relationships really are the cure for the disease, and the disease isn't always "I forgot to write in my gratitude journal today." But we all like to pretend, and pretending with Dr. Diane Reese was its own kind of ritual.

"I'm still moving back to New York," I said to Mom as she drove us back to the house after the therapy appointment. "I've decided. I just can't stay here. It'd feel like I was going backward." I conceded, however, that I would visit regularly, allowing my mother to keep an eye on me as I focused on rebuilding my fractured psyche.

When we made it back, Miri gave me a hug so tight I was genuinely shocked. We'd never been hug-it-out close. But something about how I looked after Dr. Reese's session seemed to have touched her, and she grabbed me by the kitchen island and clasped me close, her hair tickling my cheek.

"I'm so sorry, Tasha," she said into my shoulder.

"What about?" I said, because her reaction was so intense that I genuinely thought something terrible must have happened while we were out—like maybe she'd heard that an old friend of mine from high school had walked into the sea, or maybe she'd destroyed one of my favorite dresses.

She looked into my face a little searchingly and then said, confused, "About everything that happened. The divorce and . . . all the other stuff. I just think it's so unfair."

"Oh right," I said, stepping out of her embrace. "Yeah. That. Well, you know. Everything will probably be okay."

That was in October. Everything was still very much not okay.

ON THURSDAY, ELLIE TEXTED ME TO SAY SHE'D GONE INTO LABOR, three weeks before her due date. *We're trying not to panic,* she wrote. *The doctors say everything looks normal so far and the heartbeat is strong.*

I sat on my bed and wondered whether I should get an early flight back to New York. I'd been planning to stay through the weekend, but the more I thought about it, the more I wanted to leave the suffocating embrace of this idyllic island and get back to my shitty apartment. I wanted to walk along my untamed patch of sea at the Rockaways, where the wind was so strong you could barely catch your breath. Nantucket was beach huts and gentle sand dunes and quiet dog walkers in three-hundred-dollar Moncler jackets; Rockaway Beach was Eastern European asceticism and bad deli sandwiches and anonymous neighbors who avoided your gaze. I felt far more suited to the Rockaways, like I might calcify into something else if I stayed on Mom's deck too long, drinking just one more glass of wine, absorbing one more barbed comment, only to come around to an "I love you" again in the morning.

I texted Ellie. *I'm getting an early plane back. Let me know if you need anything. Could bring PJs/stuff from your apt?*

Jake's got the baby bag, she said. *Don't cut anything short for me. They don't allow visitors right now anyway.*

I wondered if that was true, or if she just didn't want me to come near her during her most vulnerable hour and contaminate her with my bad luck. It would be an understandable position. I typed back: *No prob. Just keep me updated!*

It was hard to get my head around Ellie becoming someone's mother, the person who replied when a living child said, "Mom?" Her being pregnant had felt natural to me, like ticking off a life stage on a chart, but being beholden to an actual child felt different and confusing. In some backwater of my mind, the idea raised its head: *What if the baby dies?* I imagined the silence and then the sad text, the way she might become the person in crisis instead of me. I imagined myself stepping in to help her get over the big tragedy, supportive, resilient, just the right kind of quiet. Maybe her marriage would fall apart. Jake could never imagine the kind of grief that chokes a woman who has carried a baby inside her for nine months only to leave the hospital with an empty car seat and a suitcase of still-folded onesies. He'd say all the wrong things, end up driving her away. I could shield Ellie as she crouched to pick up her boxes and take them out to the moving van while her soon-to-be ex-husband looked on. He'd stop me at the door and say, "Natasha, please, you don't understand. Grief touches us all in different ways," and I would turn to him—staunch, stoic—and say, "I think it'd be best if you stay inside while we load the truck. I don't want anyone to say anything they'll regret."

I'd get invited to parties again. People would tell me in hushed tones how Ellie hadn't been the same since the stillbirth, that they were impressed by the way I'd managed to reach her when others couldn't. While she spent some time on a bougie mental health ward for people with the less scary psychological illnesses, I'd bring her flowers and rearrange them slowly by her bed. She'd stare out the window and I'd take her hand gently in mine and say, "Hey. Look at me. We're gonna get through this."

She'd maybe write a memoir about the whole thing a decade later, when she was happily remarried, and the inscription would read: *For Natasha. You know why.* We'd get back on the dating scene together, and later we'd have pregnancies at the same time. She'd need extra support, of course, considering what had happened, but she could lean on me for that because we'd already been through everything together.

I CALLED DOWN THE STAIRS TO MY MOTHER: "ELLIE'S IN LABOR!"

"Oh, good!"

"No, it's not good. It's three weeks early."

"Well, that isn't so bad," she said. "I'm sure she'll be okay."

"Yeah, I guess. But you never know."

"Are you worried?"

"No. But I'm allowed to say that you don't know it'll all work out for sure."

It occurred to me that my last text to Ellie might have seemed a little too flippant or not positive enough, all things considered. I added a follow-up: *Everything's gonna be fine. You got this! I can't wait to meet Baby!!*

I thought about the way we all reassured one another all the time that everything will be fine. My aunt used to have a saying spuriously attributed to John Lennon on a poster on her wall, Helvetica superimposed over a yacht at sunset: *Everything will be okay in the end. If it's not okay, it's not the end.* What a stupid phrase for any member of the human race to latch on to, considering that death comes for everyone, that the very definition of the end is not being okay, and that there's absolutely nothing we can do about it.

Mom hauled herself up the stairs and leaned on the wall by the upstairs landing. "Is she at the hospital?"

"Yes, obviously."

"Then she's in the best place she can be."

"Yeah. I'm going to move up my flight, though. I think it'll be reassuring for her to know that I'm nearby."

Mom tapped her fingers on the wall and gave me a quizzical look. "Do you really think she needs you that much?"

FOUR

I MET THE SWIMMER WHO WOULD BRING ABOUT MY DOWNFALL ON A routine reporting trip. It barely even counted as a trip, really, since I got on the Victoria line at Brixton station and got off minutes later at Pimlico, meeting him in a Caffè Nero, where the drinks routinely tasted terrible. The British had imported everything from tikka masala to shakshuka and blithely passed them off as their own over a long colonial history, but a simple drip coffee setup was beyond them.

"I'm sorry," I said to the swimmer when I winced at the cappuccino. "I just can't get used to the coffee situation in England."

He nodded sympathetically. He wasn't one of those British guys determined to prove that America didn't live up to the hype. These men—many of whom had never left their parents' eighteenth-century houses in upscale commuter towns surrounding London—perpetually wanted to lecture me on gun violence in flyover states or the military-industrial complex. They fell over themselves to tell me that Joe Biden was *never* a liberal in global terms," adding with self-satisfied smirks that "the fact that anyone even thought Ka-MAH-la would deliver serious justice reform with *her* policy background is frankly *incredible!*"

I'd been standing in someone's converted warehouse apartment in Haringey when a man with halitosis and shoulder-length hair presented his opinions on American chocolate. That was a new one.

"Is there anything you miss about the States?" he'd asked, leaning against a cabinet with a pint glass of vodka and Sprite in his hand.

"Not too much. Apart from my family," I lied. Getting away from my mother had been one of the major bonuses of my transatlantic move. "But I do crave a Hershey bar every now and then. It's weird, really, because I never bought them when I had the choice."

The long-haired man smiled the smile of a hunter who's just spotted a turkey with a limp. "You do realize they taste of gone-off milk?"

"Oh." I shrugged. "Well, each to his own."

"No, no, you see." He tapped his finger against the refrigerator impatiently. "It's an objective fact. The chocolate used to be shipped over from Britain, and by the time it reached American shores, it had all gone off. The milk dried out and went bad and every American got used to eating this rancid, half-chocolate stuff. Then they tried to reintroduce actual chocolate to the country and people basically revolted. They'd been conditioned to like a lesser product. Hershey's actually put the spoiled milk taste *in* as a flavoring these days." He paused, a little gleefully, then added, "It's like a metaphor, really, for a fallen empire."

I smiled weakly. "What a history lesson."

"I just find it funny," he said, hopping lightly from foot to foot. "It's like, you've literally baked in the bad taste in America. It's generational!"

Someone who'd been standing near us broke out into forced laughter, trying to get in on the conversation. I laughed too. Everything was fake.

BUT THE POINT IS THAT HE WASN'T LIKE THAT, THE SWIMMER. INstead, he was the kind of wide-eyed, self-effacing, docile type often produced by type A parents with *plans* for their children. Before I was sent out by the newspaper to write a long-form profile about him—his world-record-breaking success, his impossible youth, his

alluringly meme-able good looks that meant he'd accrued a following of crop-topped teenage girls and even some famous TikTok
MILFs—I researched by watching videos of his training. For long
hours into the night, I sat in front of YouTube, glued to playback after playback of his slick, hairless, triangular body slipping into the
water and gliding out again. He had a certain way of doing things,
treading water calmly after he'd won a race, not following the group
who were hauled out by their trainers and immediately swaddled
in microfiber towels before shuttling off to the changing rooms.
Instead, his innocent blue eyes would scan the immediate area before he lifted himself onto the tiles, a little ungainly but impressive
in his strength. He'd wave away the first trainer to proffer a towel,
instead choosing to take stock on the side of a pool for a second. I
couldn't decide if what he was doing was Zen and ritualistic and
proof of that sweet, naïve interior, or if it was egomaniacal and nar-
cissistic and hypermasculine, reveling in the attention of the win
while affecting modesty.

That was the first question I asked him after I winced at the
taste of the cappuccino. Which one is it?

"Oh," he said, with a half smile, and stared over my shoulder
into the middle distance for a second. Then he said, "You know, I
suppose it's a bit of both."

Despite myself, I laughed. "That's a nonanswer."

"I don't know." He lay one of his long, veiny arms across the
back of the chair next to him. I thought about what he'd be like in
bed. He was only just twenty. Could he still be a virgin? He was
gorgeous and semifamous, so probably not—but then aren't young
athletes, like young actors, often coddled by their coaches and representatives, kept away from the real world? He'd ordered a green
tea fifteen minutes earlier. Everyone knows green tea strongly cor-
relates with a lack of sexual activity.

There was a pause that lingered before he picked up the thread
again with a languid echo of his poolside manner: "I honestly don't
know enough about myself to deconstruct that. It's just something

I've always done. Maybe because my mum was always rushing me out, you know? Not in a bad way—she's absolutely my biggest cheerleader—but she always wants to get you from one place to another. Maybe waiting around at the edge of the pool, with no real point to it, is my tiny bit of rebellion."

"No other rebellious urges, then?" I asked, catching his famous eye, and he shook his head.

When we wrapped up that first session, I switched off my recording app and we chatted to fill in the awkward moments while I gathered my journalistic paraphernalia.

"How do you find the UK, really?" he'd asked. "Now you're not on the record."

"I like it," I said automatically, then: "Well, most of the time."

"Most of the time?" he prompted, as we got up to walk out the door. I knew then that underneath his innocent demeanor was a man who enjoyed a bit of controversy. We had that in common.

As we made our way down the street—him on a search for the number 73 bus, me looking for the Tube station—I told him about the long-haired man and the Hershey bars. His verdict was succinct: "What a cunt." I still found myself a little taken aback by the British tendency to curse so casually, and I'd gasped for a second then laughed out loud.

THE SECOND TIME I MET HIM WAS MORE RUSHED. THE BRITISH SWIM-ming Championships—a necessary precursor to qualifying for the Olympics— were only months away, so he was training hard, and asked me to meet him at a café in the same complex as the pool where he was practicing his entrance dives. "Start strong, finish first," was his favorite coach's mantra.

I was surprised that his training ground was a community pool owned by the local council, where mothers lined up with rowdy children clutching floaties at all hours of the day. The whole place smelled like chlorine mixed with stale tea and old pastries, and we sat at a small table with a window that overlooked the water.

"No fancy membership-only facility for you, then?" I said as I sipped my drink. I'd learned to tolerate black tea by then, since a good cup of tea was better than a bad cup of coffee.

"This is truly the best facility around," he said. "Honestly. They made it up to the exact dimensions for the Olympics—there's nothing better." I knew from my Google Alerts for his name that he used to train at a secluded pool owned by a fancy private school, but the school came with a slew of adoring teenage girls who hung off the fences outside and cheered when he emerged. Eventually, after one of the students managed to breach the security system and approach him in the showers to beg for his autograph, his coaches had decided it was better for him to stay under the radar, and these days, he rotated among unglamorous local pools. I found it cute that he didn't mention any of this, and instead chose to focus on the delights of British infrastructure.

"You're a lot less fussy than American athletes," I said, although I didn't really know enough about his US counterparts to know if that was true. I just wanted something to say, preferably something complimentary.

"Britain's a socialist country," he replied, teasing in his voice. "We like to chuck everyone in together. Schools, hospitals, swimming pools . . ."

"Ah yes, socialism," I said, gesturing to the women sweeping crumbs off the floor of the café, kids fighting over goggles, and the vending machine in the corner populated with Yorkie bars and salt-and-vinegar Chipsticks. "Truly, am I in the UK right now, or on the shores of Venezuela?"

"You Yanks are always willfully confusing socialism and communism," he said, flashing a half smile. "You know very well it's not the same." I was allowing a twenty-year-old boy to talk down to me, albeit flirtatiously, and I reveled in it because I knew how many other, hotter, younger women would have died to be in my place. Knowing that a young girl with her whole life ahead of her had broken into a shower just for five seconds of access to this man—

the same man I could meet with and greet casually at his place of work—made me feel powerful, relevant, attractive by circumstance. I'd struggled with the idea of becoming an invisible person in my thirties, of losing the youthful femininity I'd been warned was a currency and a curse. Now here I was, the envy of a million screaming fans. I should have known they'd tear me apart. But of course, I had a WASPy American habit back then of presuming everything would always turn out all right. I shared the disposition of my foremothers, one founded on the surety that I wouldn't ever really be held to account for anything.

I leaned over my elbows on the table and watched a woman in the pool below, her long braids spilling out the sides of a tight swimming cap and a black Adidas one-piece that meant business. She did a fast lap of the pool in butterfly stroke, hit the side triumphantly with her hands, then turned around and began another in less time than I'd have been able to get down the ladder and into the water. "What a pro," I said.

"Who, her?" He followed my gaze. "Very fast. Bad form, though."

"I don't dare to think what you'd say about mine."

"You should get in the water with me some day. Come down and get changed at the end of my training." He said it like it was the most natural thing in the world, and I gave him a look in return that said: *Wouldn't that be a little inappropriate?* I'd gone to work with interviewees before, but always fully clothed.

"No, for real." He slapped his hand on the table. "There's nothing weird about it. Don't you know I spend all day, every day around half-naked people? I don't think of it like that."

"You're the one who brought up being half naked." I shrugged exaggeratedly, and he rolled his eyes.

"Now you're looking for reasons not to do it. What is it, you don't know how to swim?"

"Of course I know how to swim! Come on!"

He gave me a very earnest look, the kind that made me picture him in bed, young and lithe and eager to please. "Listen, I'm being serious here. I do a lot of community outreach classes, and if you don't know how, it's nothing to be ashamed of." I knew how to swim just fine; in fact, completing a lap of the pool was a graduation requirement at my high school. But that was the first time I thought to myself, looking back into his square, open face: *My God, I want to fuck you.*

When I went home later, Joe was chopping vegetables for a stir-fry in the kitchen. I'd texted him to let him know I was on my way back, and he'd started on dinner.

"How's the swimmer?" he asked as he poured a bowl of chopped onions into the pan and flicked on the fan over the stove with the other hand.

"Oh, fine," I said, taking a seat at our fold-out kitchen table. "He said he wants to teach me how to dive." It was the least weird way I could think to communicate the swimmer's offer.

"Ha! Imagine." Joe opened the fridge, pulled out a bag of fresh noodles, and started manipulating them out of their plastic casing and into the pan in front of him. We both went quiet as he stirred them in, added a handful of defrosted shrimp, stirred again. Then he turned to me and said, "You're not gonna do it, though, right?"

I shrugged. "Could make for a funny part of the feature. Like, I open the first paragraph describing myself flailing in a pool while an Olympic athlete rolls his eyes at me."

"I guess." He sounded unsure, but he was always good at biting his tongue.

I opened the recording app on my phone, emailed myself the audio file from that day's meeting, and started transcribing the interview on my laptop with one earphone in. As I did so, I realized that a lot of the conversation had been borderline flirtatious. I became aware that I didn't want to play it with Joe nearby, and I closed the tab rather than examining that feeling further.

A couple of minutes later, Joe plonked a plate of noodles, vegetables, and shrimp in front of me, and I closed my laptop and started to eat. My mind was on the swimmer.

"You're not in the room, are you?" said Joe.

"I am, sorry," I said. "Just a long day at work. And then the extra interview in the evening—it was a lot."

"Yeah, I get it," he said. "Listen, if you want to do the diving lesson, then go ahead. He's just a kid anyway, right?"

"He's twenty," I said, "but that doesn't matter."

"I'm kidding. If I was insecure about you hanging out with attractive men, I'd have kicked up a fuss when you went to the Oscars."

"Or, even worse, the Senate," I said, smiling. "Anyway, I'm just trying to find an interesting way in, you know? Something that isn't a reiteration of all those dumb TikToks. I just need a way to make him my own."

THE NEXT THREE TIMES I MET UP WITH THE SWIMMER, I TOOK MY one-piece and my sexiest bikini just in case he insisted on taking a look at my butterfly stroke. I figured I'd decide in the moment whether I wanted to come out of the changing room in a serious, athletic-looking swimsuit or a push-up bikini. "Oh, stop, it's the only thing I have," I imagined myself saying, when he raised an eyebrow at my getup. "I bought it in the Florida Keys years ago. It's not like I spend my time wild swimming in the Thames like *some* people."

But I never got the opportunity. He didn't invite me to swim again, and the next few times we met up he wanted to talk about Olympic logistics, conversations that often bordered on the obsessive and boring. We couldn't get food because he was on a strict diet dictated by an athletic nutritionist, so instead we'd sit in front of endless teas and coffees until neither of us could absorb any more caffeine.

I wanted to sit on a street corner outside a burger van with him, or to share a steaming packet of fish and chips while kneeling in the damp grass of a small London park. I wanted to tap my can of West Country hard cider against his and say, "Cheers to that!" a little drunkenly, before he leaned over and kissed me on the cheek, then apologized and blamed it on the booze.

But the reality was green tea, glaringly lit cafés, snatched bits of time outside pools, conversations that were cut short with, "Damn, I'm sorry, I really have to go. Coach says I need ten hours of sleep."

Then, eventually, a week before nationals, we had our final meeting. He was leaner and more muscular than he'd ever been, but his face was a little withdrawn. There were soft, dark bags under his wide-open eyes.

"I'm stressed," he confided when he came out of the changing rooms to meet me, smelling like fresh deodorant and Head & Shoulders 2-in-1 shampoo, his hair still wet.

"I know it's against the rules," I said in a stage whisper, "but should we go to the pub?"

He looked at me for a second, raised his eyebrows, smiled, and leaned back in his chair. Then he said: "Wait until the coaches leave."

We sat in the plastic café seats in the leisure center and shot the shit until both of his coaches emerged. One gave him a quick, single-handed wave before leaving through the automatic doors, a waterproof drawstring bag on his shoulder. The other—a wiry, people-pleasing man who always gave the impression of repressed energy—stood fidgeting at our table for a bit, reintroducing himself to me and reminding the swimmer that it wasn't long now to the big day, to behave himself, to work on his timing like they'd practiced. Then he gave me a friendly wink and sidled off too.

It was 9:00 p.m. The center was closing up, kids were being chased into clothes and out of showers, and the man behind the counter was looking at his watch pointedly. "Well, I just haven't got everything I needed yet for the feature," I said to the swimmer, smiling, "so that's a real shame. I guess we have no choice . . ."

"To the pub!" He got up with happy purpose, his sports bag under his arm, and as we stood I realized how much taller than me he was. I'd thought of him as a teen when all I could see was his smooth face across from mine, but he felt like so much more of a man when all six foot two of him towered above my five foot five.

We went around the corner to a pub called the Cat and Mutton. "I can never get over these pub names," I said. "It's one of my favorite things about the UK."

It flashed through my mind that if we were in America, he wouldn't have even been able to accompany me into a bar. It was the first red flag, and I forced it back down.

He insisted on paying, a chivalrous gesture that felt both quaint and telling at the same time. Then he set my lager and his IPA down on the table triumphantly and said, "Well, I don't know about you, but I've had a hell of a day."

"Me too," I said. "I think we've earned our pints." I thought about texting Joe to say I'd be home late, but I didn't.

After I'd drunk half my first beer and he'd downed one and ordered a second, I confirmed a few nominal quotes on my laptop with him, so we could both pretend this was work. Then I said, "I've gotta tell you, I'm actually going to miss our time together."

"Yeah," he said. "Me too. Do you think you'll get tickets to the actual championships? I could meet up with you there."

"Sadly, I think our media passes are reserved for the sports reporters," I said. "And I happen to work mainly in politics and lifestyle."

"Politics?"

"I mean, the feature about you will run in the lifestyle pages."

He laughed. "What does that say about how newspapers see swimmers?"

"No," I said. "Like, obviously the sports reporters will be writing straight-up news reports about how you do, your results and your medals and everything." At "medals," I made sure to knock on the wood of the table in front of us. "It's just that the longer features tend to go to reporters. People on the ground who do a mixture of interviews and long-form content, like me."

"I see," he said, with the air of someone who didn't see at all.

I ordered another beer. We talked about nothing and everything, and for some reason I found myself saying I was proud of him.

"I'm proud of you too," he said.

I laughed. "For what, exactly?"

"Well, first of all, for sticking at it with such a heinous subject. That's a tough job you've got there. And second of all, because of the fantastic, life-changing feature you're going to write about all my many positive attributes. We can split the profits when I sign that multimillion-pound deal with Nike."

"For sure," I said, smiling, and I caught his eye, and we held each other's gaze. We weren't going to see each other again. It was now or never. I leaned across the wooden table and kept my eyes on his. Then I said, quietly enough so I knew no one else could hear, "You ever had a blow job?"

He blushed—he actually blushed—and then he said, "I mean . . . of course . . ."

"You're single right now, though?"

He began to look confused. His eyes bounced quickly around the room, behind my head and back onto the table, as if he were looking for some hidden device. "This is on the record or something? Is this a trick question?"

I smiled wryly and then, in an even lower voice, said, "Do you think I'd say I wanted to suck your cock on the record?"

Now I could tell that he was no longer focusing on anything in the room except me.

"If I could do what I wanted right now," I said, "I'd have you follow me into those bathrooms and I'd run my hand over your jeans while I kissed your neck, and then I'd pull out your dick just as it was getting hard and caress it like it was the only thing that mattered to me in the world."

He swallowed a little too loudly, and I could see his breathing was getting shallow. Was it my imagination, or did he take a very quick look at the wedding ring on my left hand?

"I'd take you into my mouth and run my tongue all the way

along the length of that hard cock," I said, speaking quickly and without pausing, "and then I'd hold your warm balls in my hand while I took every inch of you down my throat." His pupils dilated, his eyes fixated on my lips. "I'd sit there on my knees in the bathroom stall with your cock so far into my mouth you couldn't help but face-fuck me," I said, "and I'd be so fucking wet for you, you have no idea. My panties would be soaked right through. And I'd steady my hands on your perfect ass and keep letting you face-fuck me until your cum was shooting down my throat. All I'd want is to taste all that cum, dripping through my lips and all over my face. That would be enough."

"Fucking hell, Natasha," he said, releasing a short breath. "How am I ever going to stand up?"

"The bathroom's that way," I said, inclining my head toward the opposing wooden doors that read GENTLEMEN and LADIES in gold cursive. "Your call if we go in together or one after the other."

"Okay," he said. "Okay. Give me a second. Jesus Christ. This is a lot."

THE FIRST TWEET THAT PEOPLE STARTED SHARING IN THEIR HUN-dreds, then their thousands: "So just to be clear, when a grown-ass woman writes this about a vulnerable young boy we're okay with it?" Attached was a screenshot of the most damning paragraph of my article, the part that made Joe put his head in his hands.

"Every inch?" he kept repeating. "*Every inch?*"

I know it sounds unlikely now, in the debris-strewn aftermath of the Category 5 social media storm, but it hadn't occurred to me then that what I wrote was that bad. It was a long, involved piece, one that I'd opened with a description of how the swimmer had overcome his difficulties with the butterfly stroke in order to finally master it and use it to his advantage. I talked about the strict exercise regimes; the treadmills and the weight lifting outside the pool; the endless meals of chicken, rice, and beans; the pressure of the Olympics, his family background, and the fact that he'd unexpectedly become an object of adoration for thousands of young female fans. I talked about Britain pinning all its hopes on this one, world-record-breaking, globally popular, ridiculously attractive young man, who was experiencing the kind of pressure a middle-aged Goldman Sachs CEO might endure but was only on the brink of his twenties. Sensitively, I addressed how his coach had been accused of sexually assaulting two of his best friends on the swim team when he was a young teen, and how the swimmer didn't know how to talk about it, making some allusions that implied he might also have been a victim. "All I know is that I was in a difficult position," he'd told me. "I was the star—I don't want to sound arrogant but that was the truth—and here was this man who was very nice to me, and who held my future in his hands. It all felt fine at the time. You look back and you realize what was actually going on."

In the penultimate paragraph, I came to a payoff: that he now spends one hour a week teaching the butterfly stroke to promising young athletes at underprivileged schools. And followed by that was that final paragraph, the one that got screenshotted again and again by men's rights activists and tomato-throwing tweeters and laughing TV personalities during quick asides after the main news of the day:

> So what's the reason for all the social media adoration; the hordes of teen fans clutching at fences to catch a glimpse of his chiseled cheekbones before he's even won the promised Olympic golds; the way women seem to melt around a man who, in his own words, likes to keep to himself? Well, when you're sitting opposite him in a romantically lit London pub, all I can say is that it becomes pretty obvious why. The taut yet burly figure with those shockingly blue eyes; the way he chooses his words carefully, then deploys them with a lopsided grin; the talent that's bigger than his well-defined muscles (and his muscles are pretty

big). All of those add up to something pretty tantalizing, a shockingly sweet taste that lingers. All I can say is that after spending the past six weeks following this young man around on his pre-Olympic tour of the UK's most low-key swimming pools, I'm going to find it very hard to forget him—every inch of him.

When I sent the article to the editor on duty, he hadn't mentioned any concerns. He'd corrected a minor typo in the first two paragraphs and published it without paying much attention, because at that point my profile was one in a long assembly line of pieces waiting to be signed off on and sent to the social media team. I had a feeling he'd stopped reading after the first few sentences.

For hours, there was silence. Then someone with a big social media following called me a pervert, and suddenly everyone—the editor in chief, the junior reporters, the audience team, my own husband—was clamoring to chime in that they'd thought it was suspect all along.

"I DON'T MEAN TO KICK YOU WHEN YOU'RE DOWN, BUT IT'S NOT EVEN good writing," said the editor in chief when he called me at the end of my workday in London. It was lunchtime in New York, where he was based, and I could hear people bustling around him, murmurs about sandwiches and putting on a pot of coffee. I felt humiliated that he hadn't even booked a private room for this conversation.

"I don't know what you want me to say to that," I said. I was in a meeting room in the London bureau, listening to other reporters clock out and shout their goodbyes to members of their team. The local news editor had shaken his head at me and said, "Listen, I think you'd better talk it over with New York," when I'd tried to start a tentative conversation about the enraged readers flooding our website and dragging my name across 4chan. No one in London wanted to grab this particular nettle by the leaves, and I'd had to wait a long few hours to take the call at the EIC's earliest convenience. By then I'd received multiple emails from men with email addresses specifically made for the task of calling me a "stupid whore."

"Whatever. That's not the main point, not by far," the editor in chief continued. We called him BR behind his back: Bald and Repressed, generally considered to be his two most notable attributes. He was a suit-wearing old-school sexist from a legacy publication. "Whoever signed off on this shouldn't have done so, clearly. But everyone's got a lot of work and you're supposed to be one of our most trusted reporters. The buck stops with you."

There would be no examination of the nonexistent editing process in the organization after this; no acknowledgment that "editors" had stopped engaging with most submissions over five hundred words after the assembly line of aggregated news cards about femicides and five-dollar miracle creams and Earth-destroying asteroids got too much; no uploader or copy editor was asked why they hadn't sounded the alarm. The real truth was that no one would have seen anything wrong with it if Twitter hadn't gotten involved, especially as the audience numbers ticked up. But now everyone had to pretend like I'd come out as a cannibal at a work-sponsored event or something.

"I'm sorry," I said, because I couldn't think of what else to say.

"But I'd like to know what you're sorry *for*." I could hear BR walking through the New York office now, sequestering himself in his cube-shaped glass office and closing the door. The background noise came to an abrupt halt. "I'd really like to hear it. Because my deepest concern here is that you don't realize the gravity of the situation."

"No, I understand," I said quickly, "and it won't happen again."

"You've embarrassed the entire organization. You talk about this young man possibly having been abused by a coach, and then you write about him like you're a salivating deviant in a sex-toy emporium. I hope to God you didn't violate our ethical standards and do anything . . . untoward with a minor on top of all that. Actually, don't tell me if you did."

"He's not a minor," I said, quietly.

"Excuse me?"

"I just . . . I mean, he's over the age of consent."

BR was silent for a few seconds in a way that communicated disbelief that the thought had even crossed my mind, then he said, "The issue is that he's your interviewee. Have you read our code of ethics?"

"Of course." I hadn't. I wasn't even aware it existed.

"And the PR damage." BR made a noise that sounded like he was being physically tortured. "Did you see it made Fox News? Hannity's talking about the liberal media elite's secret plot to take down masculinity, for God's sake."

"Well, I hardly think that's fair," I said. "If anything, you could say I was very . . . admiring of masculinity."

"If that's a joke, I'm not laughing."

"It's not a joke." I had thought it was a logical retort. In all my years of working for the paper, of lapping up praise from editors and having my copy waved through, I'd never felt so out of my depth. My brain had ground to a treacherous halt.

BR sighed. I could imagine him wiping his dry right hand across his greasy, lined forehead. "We're talking about our reputation in the industry here."

"I understand that," I said. "I do. And like I said, I will put in ten times the effort to make sure this never happens again. I've already got a list of features ready to deflect attention from this—women's rights in rural Northern Ireland, the renewed push for Scottish independence, an investigation I'd love to get to work on right away about the shocking state of council housing in inner London boroughs . . ."

"Natasha, I'm going to stop you right there. We just can't have you as a reporter on our books at the moment. It's not going to work."

"You mean you're firing me?" I said, and I felt like I was saying it from the halogen lights on the ceiling rather than from steady ground. Was this derealization?

"We're not going to fire you," he said, after a pause. "We've had some long conversations with HR. You're going to be redeployed. Junior news reporting—aggregation—until further notice. Back in New York, on the same time zone as people who can oversee what you're doing. The newspaper will put out an apology and pull the article from the website—obviously, it's too late for the print edition. We're going to implement some training on appropriate workplace relationships, and needless to say your attendance will be compulsory. Now, when we're considering your compensation and benefits in light of this change of role . . ."

As he reeled off all the various career implications of a few sentences I'd written while intoxicated with a twenty-year-old, I considered the pins-and-needles feeling in my left arm and wondered whether I was having a heart attack. *Please be a heart attack*, I thought. I imagined the ambulance coming, the worried faces of Joe and my mother and Miriam peering over me in bed, the way the newspaper would rally around me. BR might get someone to send a bunch of flowers. The news editor would sort them out and add a comedic note: *Bad writing isn't worth dying over, Tash.* The social media sympathy gauge would swing, and people would start talking about how I shouldn't have been driven to the brink of self-destruction from stress. People would laugh. The swimmer—who hadn't been in touch since the article had come out, who hadn't replied to the jokey text I'd sent during the social media firestorm, and then, when I tried to contact him in a fit of panic a few hours later, rejected my call—would text me back with something reassuring and casual. *Sorry, just been busy but loved the piece!* He'd later do a TV interview declaring that he couldn't see what all the fuss was about, and that I was the most professional, compassionate journalist he'd ever had the pleasure of working with. A tongue-in-cheek petition would come out demanding that I go to the Olympics. Perhaps BR would even allow it, because it would be good for audience numbers. Maybe even Hannity would change his tune and declare me a victim of cancel culture. Yes, a (nonfatal) heart attack right then would've been an absolute blessing.

But it wasn't a heart attack. I realized that as I put down the phone and then stayed for a few minutes in the meeting room, the scene melting then reappearing then melting again before my eyes. I tried to catch my breath but couldn't, and then I panicked because I couldn't catch my breath, and then I couldn't catch my breath because of the panic. That's when I knew what it was: a regular old anxiety attack. I knew I just had to live through it then take the Tube home, where Joe would be waiting to demand whether I'd done anything with the swimmer, pleading with me, desperate for me to lie.

When I turned the key in the door to our flat, I was still convinced that my marriage would be okay. Joe, sweet, clueless Joe, was pacing around the living room—and when I caught his questioning eye, I was worried about us for the first time. He didn't want to believe what the world was saying on social media. He wasn't even a social media guy. Yet his photo was now all over the internet—scraped from his LinkedIn profile, of all places—by people hell-bent on knowing everything about me so they could take it away.

Joe didn't want to believe the red-pill YouTuber who was calling him a "beta cuck" and urging him to "leave that bitch behind." He started off half laughing about it, in that crazy-eyed, desperate way people do when they want something not to be true, because surely this was just your run-of-the-mill cancellation that I'd bounce back from within a respectful time frame, and we'd dust ourselves off and one day share a joke about how a load of anonymous online accounts took everything the wrong way and piled on. And then, as I sat there at the kitchen table with my eyes downcast, unable to bring myself to laugh along with him, he started to realize there might be something in it, and his words became increasingly aggressive and panicked. I could never keep anything from Joe.

So eventually I'd cave and admit it: a sordid five minutes in a pub bathroom, my kingdom for a BJ. The transgression I'd convinced myself my affable, trusting husband would never suspect—and if he did, he'd surely overlook. The hall pass I'd allowed myself to believe didn't really count. And Joe would look at me through his fingers with an expression I'd never seen on him before and tell me to get out.

FIVE

BACK WHEN THE SWIMMER ARTICLE RAN, ELLIE HAD BEEN PREG-
nant. Not that I knew it. She'd called me a few weeks later and told
me she was twelve weeks in, and the first thing I thought was: *You
know the last thing my husband said to me before he filed for divorce,
but you kept a pregnancy from me for three months?* I knew all the
stats on miscarriage. I knew it was customary not to announce a
pregnancy to everyone until an ultrasound tech had confirmed at
the twelve-week scan that it wasn't just a tumor with hair or whatever, but I thought I was exempt from the "everyone." Apparently not.

I had felt jealous then that Ellie and Jake had lived in their
own smug little cocoon of knowledge for so many weeks. And that
jealousy returned now, as I got on the plane from Nantucket back
to New York to watch them enter the hallowed halls of parenthood
together. Struggling through the narrow aisle with my carry-on,
I wondered if Ellie had given birth yet. I hadn't heard from her
in twenty-four hours, not since her original texts. Was the baby
crowning, a nurse poised over my poor friend's vagina with episi-
otomy scissors at the ready? Or were doctors running around and
shouting about emergency caesareans? Was she in pain, shouting
for morphine, or was she dozing on a recliner, hooked up to an
epidural IV? Was new life screaming forth from the depths of her
razed womb or was it pulsating under the surface, put on mute
until the final scene by spinal anesthetic?

I took my seat at the back of the plane and sent her a text: *Officially on my way back to NYC! Update me when you can. Thinking of you all!* Then I slammed the window shade shut and turned on my headphones. My favorite thing to listen to since the demise of my marriage was house music from the early aughts, the kind that had a sad edge to it, like tragic lyrics or a backstory that made it upsetting in retrospect. The promise of happiness and the undercurrent of sadness made me feel like it was probably the genre that spoke to the human condition most authentically, far better than a thousand calculatedly sad songs sung by beautiful people holding guitars or happy pop tunes brought into existence by label-sponsored focus groups. Avicii was a prime example: a young, talented DJ and global music sensation who ended up killing himself in Oman at the age of twenty-eight. I'd toyed with the idea of suicide after everything happened with the swimmer, of course, but I just wasn't the type to go through with it. I guess my mother was right: I lacked staying power.

The pilot started speaking over the loudspeaker, and I turned my music down just in case he was saying anything important, like: *I've decided to take you all hostage and plunge you to your fiery deaths.* I always like to assume that's at least a possibility.

"Ladies and gentlemen, this is your captain speaking. Welcome to this Embraer 190 direct flight to New York," came the announcement. "We're expecting a flight time of one hour and eleven minutes, getting you on the ground at JFK around four p.m. local time . . ."

I stopped listening and turned the music up until it started a ringing in my left ear. *Love you!!* I texted Ellie again. She didn't reply, of course.

I'D ALREADY BEEN BACK AT MY APARTMENT FOR TWO HOURS, VEGE-tating in the cold, damp-smelling living room, when I got the email. It had clearly been sent around to a bunch of people; we'd all been bcc'd.

Our baby girl was born this morning at 6:54 a.m., weighing in at 8 lbs 9 oz. Mom and baby doing well, Dad traumatized but expected to make it! Thanks everyone for your messages and well wishes. We'll be in touch to arrange visits very soon, once we've had a little time to bond as a family and recover. For now, here's a first look at our perfect little munchkin! (Name TBC!)

That's what I was to her, then: a bcc, the ultimate insult among friends. The munchkin looked like an old man who'd been run halfway through a meat processor. I didn't reply.

I went down to check my mailbox, though I wasn't expecting anything special. Mrs. Konstantin was there, without the dog, having a back-and-forth with a neighbor who lived three floors up with his wife and kids. They turned around and looked at me like they'd been caught in the act, and as I opened up my mailbox with the little key, I heard Mrs. Konstantin mutter under her breath, "What I mean is people like her."

"Good evening!" I said, turning around. "How is everybody?"

Mrs. Konstantin looked affronted.

"Very good," replied the man abruptly.

"No dog today?" I said to Mrs. Konstantin, who recoiled as if I'd propositioned her. The woman was so determinedly miserable that she ignited some kind of contrarianism in me, summoned sprightliness from the depths of my depression.

"Dog walker's out with her," she said, when she'd recovered. "I can't take her on the beach at the moment. Because of my leg."

My eyes involuntarily went to her legs, then I realized that was probably rude. She noticed and added, "Diabetes."

I nodded. "Okay then," I said, and brought my hands together like a kindergarten teacher announcing nap time. "Well, as I said before, let me know if you ever need someone to take her out. I'm more than happy to do it!" There was nothing in my mailbox, but I felt humiliated going back upstairs empty-handed, so I grabbed a couple of fast-food flyers from the nearby windowsill as if that's what I'd come for and took the stairs two at a time.

Back inside the apartment, I sat down and opened a text message I'd been avoiding reading since it arrived a few hours prior. There were only so many times I could unpack my suitcase, rearrange my drawers, and check for nonexistent mail. The text was from Joe's sister, Megan. When I was leaving our London place for the final time, Joe had told me that any attempt of mine to contact him directly would be seen as an "act of cruelty driven only by selfishness." The solution was using Megan—who I'd counted as a casual friend, someone I could swap online recipes and safe jokes about her brother with on the family group chat—as a middleman, an awkward situation to which I acquiesced because I was the idiot who'd ruined everything.

Joe and I weren't even yet officially divorced. We were "legally separated" while the paperwork made its way like treacle through the clogged pipes of the New York City administrative system. From a bureaucratic point of view, we were in limbo, but logistically we'd divided up everything we could. After the speech about acts of cruelty, I'd tried my best not to write or call him, even though I couldn't bring myself to actually delete my own husband's number. I'd texted him only once, to tell him I was withdrawing my half of the money from our joint savings account and that he should feel free to change it into his name and do whatever he wanted with the savings he'd contributed. He'd replied with a single emoji thumbs-up, suspended insultingly in its own message box.

Joe's lack of social media presence meant that I'd only been able to keep up with his movements through occasional photos that popped up on other people's Instagram accounts. One, posted by our once-mutual New York friend Ben, showed Ben visiting Joe's new London apartment, the pair drinking kitsch cocktails out of plastic pineapples in Peckham with two attractive women younger than me; another of Ben's photos featured Joe at a climbing wall, his head turned, a wry smile at the camera. Ben and Joe had gone to college together, and we'd all hung out pretty regularly for the two years before we moved to London, but when I messaged Ben asking if he'd like to remain friends after the breakup, he'd never replied. That was a pattern in my life these days. Like Michelangelo's painting of man and God on the ceiling of the Sistine Chapel, I was stuck in place, eternally attempting to reach across a tantalizingly small divide. Yes. Michelangelo would've understood me.

Time to rip off the Band-Aid. I sat down on my half-collapsed sofa and opened Megan's text.

We'd appreciate it if you could return the chest of drawers. That was it.

The chest of drawers was one of the only things of ours I had loved. It was an antique with different-colored drawers—one a bottle green, another a mustard yellow and most of the others plain oak—that we'd spotted on the sidewalk outside a secondhand-furniture store one Saturday afternoon in Brooklyn. I'd noticed it but kept walking—we were running late to his coworker's housewarming drinks—but Joe had turned to me and said, "Hey, did you see that? I thought it was really nice," and eventually convinced me to go back with him. We'd arrived at the housewarming lugging the piece of furniture between us, laughing, and our hostess had rolled her eyes and said, "That's so you two." We'd left it on its side on her welcome mat then drunkenly staggered back home with it in the dark later, occasionally taking breaks on the warm sidewalk.

The one we had in our Brooklyn apartment? I texted Megan. *That's not available.* By "not available," I meant: It's in my apartment right now and I don't intend to give it back, ever.

Joe said you put it in storage.

I did. Then I brought it to my new place in Queens.

It's Joe's property, so if you tell me a convenient time, I can have a friend drive down and pick it up.

I sat and looked at the message for a minute. What did she mean? Had Joe paid for the piece? I honestly couldn't remember. I was the one who'd convinced the guy in the store to sell it to us for a third off the sticker price, but it was possible Joe had had his wallet more readily to hand. And what need did he have for it now? He'd stayed in London and moved into a fully furnished rental near Clapton Pond. Maybe he'd promised the chest to his sister or another relative, or maybe he wanted it for sentimental value. But it had been in storage for months anyway, and it made no sense for me to relinquish it.

I'm sorry but I'm not giving you my address, I replied. That was the last weapon in my arsenal, and I was going to deploy it without shame. *Hope you understand. As a woman living on my own, it's a safety issue.* It was bullshit, but plausible bullshit.

I sat on my hands, heart beating in my ears, waiting for her eventual reply: *Don't be an asshole, Natasha.* I felt the raw satisfaction of having goaded her into casting the first ad hominem stone. Megan wasn't the type to use the word "asshole"; she and Joe came from a Nice Family, the kind that had ironic-but-not-ironic photos on the walls of themselves dressed in matching holiday pajamas. Throughout Joe and Megan's childhood, they'd had a family dinner every evening and watched movies each Friday night with homemade popcorn. Megan had married her high school boyfriend and lived down the street from their parents. Their lives were all so goddamned *easy.* I observed their paint-by-numbers life and their camaraderie with one another with the fascinated, forensic eye of a wildlife photographer.

We're done here, I texted back.

I got up, poured myself a glass of water, and sat back on the sofa, busying myself with unspooling wires from various bits of electrical equipment I'd brought along in assorted moving boxes. I wasn't entirely sure whether I was liberating a headphone jack from a spare piece of the coffee grinder or an old laptop charger from the cord of a defunct smoothie maker, but at this point it didn't matter. What mattered was the regular movement of my hands, the soothing knowledge that I could achieve something, however small, by repeatedly tugging at the tangled mess in front of me. The wind blew at the balcony door, and it rattled against its hinges then settled again, but then a plaintive creak ran across the arteries of the ceiling. Everything was connected, and everything was falling apart. I heard Mrs. Konstantin open her door upstairs, have a short conversation with someone I presumed to be the dog walker, then lock up for the night. The dog began scratching her floor, my ceiling.

Just before I went to bed, I saw Megan had messaged me one final time, an hour after my last text to her. *We used to be friends.*

In the wedding album I'd buried at the bottom of a box I never intended to unpack were pictures of me, Joe, and Megan, her with an arm hooked through mine, standing alongside the other brides-maids. She was always a little too sororities-and-bridal-showers for me, while I was probably a little too feminist-book-clubs-and-sarcastic-asides for her—but she'd always made the effort. They were make-the-effort people. Joe's father had once gamely grilled me a steak-size slice of halloumi cheese when I was briefly a vege-tarian, during a barbecue in their yard. He hadn't said a thing when I'd refused the sausages, had just quietly left in the car and returned from the store with something I might prefer. When, after eighteen months of dating, we'd announced we were get-ting married, his parents had sent us a bottle of champagne and asked how much they could pitch in, while my mother couldn't stop complaining about everything moving too fast. But I wanted fast. I wanted Joe's lack of generational trauma, his uncomplicated support; I wanted a family who wallowed in the unctuous mud of normalcy. I wanted to win at dating, and I wanted everyone to know that I'd won.

I extracted an old T-shirt from the chest of drawers at the cen-ter of tonight's firestorm and got into bed. To distract myself from the guilt of what I'd done to Joe's family, I went back to Zach's

Instagram. His latest post: *I'll be speaking on a panel at the Old Bostonian Cigarette Factory about futurism, the limits of our consciousness, and whether a certain Icelandic folk tale–inspired film will make waves at Sundance (directed by our very own @LiliBelleFilmsStuff!). Catch me in town before I move to NYC!*

I messaged him: *Hey, so you found a place?* He left me on read.

A WEEK AFTER SHE GAVE BIRTH, ELLIE DEIGNED TO SEND ME A TEXT.

Can't believe I ever let anyone suck on my tits voluntarily, she wrote. *Seven days in and ready to wean ASAP. Do you think I can feed steak to a newborn?* Attached was a photo of the baby, taken from above. It was settled into the curve of her body, its eyes closed but its mouth firmly clasped around her nipple. Ellie's areola looked impossibly big and strangely cracked, like dry lips in a bad winter, and her boob looked stretched and veiny. Off to the side of the photo was a plate with a steak on it and what looked like steamed broccoli. Apparently Ellie was eating like a bodybuilder these days.

I've heard steak is good for hungry babies, I replied. *Even better might be a burger. All that growth hormone can only be good for something that small.*

Bonus antibiotics too! Perfect for a maturing immune system! she texted back. *Btw, we came up with a name for her finally. Charlotte Louisa.*

It was boring. I was disappointed. But instead I said what I knew I was expected to say: *Aww so cute!! She looks like a Charlotte! So when do I get to meet her??*

SIX

I TOOK THE A TRAIN INTO BROOKLYN A FEW DAYS LATER TO MEET Charlotte Louisa, the subway car clattering through the tunnels while some guy in a GULF WAR VET baseball cap and a stained shirt three sizes too big wandered up and down, ranting about how he'd built this country and someone was going to have to pay for it. I watched the stations pass me by with little interest: Euclid Avenue, Broadway Junction, Utica. Maybe the guy in the cap would stab me. Maybe he'd demand money and produce a knife when I couldn't deliver, and then Ellie would have to come to the hospital and collect me and take me home to her apartment too. Maybe she and Jake would take care of me at the same time as Charlotte Louisa, like I was also their baby. By the time I changed trains in downtown Brooklyn to double back into Park Slope, the guy in the cap had just wandered into the corner of the train and pissed himself. Seven minutes later, I emerged near the Barclays Center into a surprisingly sunny afternoon.

At their apartment, Jake held a finger to his lips when I walked in. Ellie had already told me that I should text when I was outside rather than using the buzzer. "Sorry," Jake said quietly as I took my shoes off at the door. "It's just, you know, once we get her down . . ."

I nodded and followed him inside, where Ellie was reclining on the sofa. She looked like shit. She had a blanket covering most of her stomach but I could see that it was still swollen, only about a third of the way deflated from when I'd last seen her. Her eyes were small and red-rimmed, and her boobs were halfway out of her stained top. I remembered having the kind of confidence to look that unkempt in front of Joe. It felt so unlikely that I'd ever have it again.

"Hey," Ellie said, in a half whisper. "It's so great to see you."

"It's so great to see *you*!" I said, and pulled her in for an awkward hug, trying to avoid the boobs and the stains and the swollen stomach. "I brought you a bottle of good Merlot, now that you can officially drink again."

"Oh, amazing." She smiled and then looked at Jake. "Just put it in the top left cabinet. Yeah, up there." I'd hoped we might all have a drink together, but I guessed not.

"So," I said, crossing my legs and turning to face her. I didn't really know what to do now that the baby wasn't available as a prop; I'd sort of expected it to be out and ready for me, dressed in its Sunday best. Instead, Ellie looked slightly disoriented and Jake looked shell-shocked. He placed a mug of black coffee in front of me, having failed to ask what I wanted. Eventually, having realized no one was going to respond to my "so," I asked, "How's parenthood?"

Jake gave a sort of coughing laugh, and Ellie shrugged. "It's wonderful," she said. "I mean, *she's* wonderful. But of course, we're very tired. And I'm feeling a bit . . . touched out. Like, I have this thing attached to me all day and then the last thing I want is my husband's arms around me at night. Not that I'd get the chance anyway, since we're sleeping in shifts."

"You make it all sound so romantic," said Jake, but not in a snide way. They reached out and squeezed each other's hands.

"No, he knows what I mean," said Ellie.

Twenty minutes of chitchat later, the baby began to whine and Jake brought it out of the darkened bedroom, saying, "Time to meet your aunt Natasha!"

"Oh, isn't she beautiful?" I said as he placed the infant into my arms. That's the kind of thing you have to say when people you know procreate, even if your own life recently fell apart.

"Just hold her head . . . yep, that's it . . . you got it . . ." Ellie guided me. I could see her trying to contain her nerves, to pass off her complete lack of trust in me as motherly tenderness and enthusiasm.

"Hello, baby. Hello, baby Charlotte," I said, in the dumb little voice people use for their loved ones' kids. I felt the warmth of her body and wondered how easily I could crush her, not in a psycho way but more of a way that considered the evolutionary inadequacy of human beings. Giraffes are born knowing how to walk, and we get these mewling potatoes.

Charlotte looked up at me with searching eyes. Could she see me? Did her vision extend that far? Had she only just opened her eyes, or was that puppies? Ellie directed me to put my pointer finger in her palm and Charlotte clasped her own little fingers around it.

"That's too cute," I said.

"You know, apparently it's just a reflex," said Ellie, "but it's a heck of a crowd-pleaser."

I held the baby until she started to fuss, and then Ellie sighed and said, "This little monster is boob-obsessed," and started breast-feeding. While she sat there with the kid sucking on her, Jake talked to me about the big rush they'd had to get to the hospital, the concern about the baby coming too early, the relief when she was born "so big we were grateful she didn't get to full term in the end!" The story went on for an interminably long time and included useless, boring details, like how they'd had to take a towel for the cab so Ellie didn't leak amniotic fluid all over the seats. Then, even though she was early, Charlotte Louisa came out at nine pounds nine ounces, screaming the house down! Could I believe it? The doctors all thought she'd only be six pounds! *And it's not like she came out through the sunroof!* They both laughed at that, and I laughed along at first but then stopped when I realized I was effectively commenting on the size of my best friend's vagina. I waited for them to ask about my love life, my mother, my job, really anything, but whenever there was a pause in conversation, one of them filled it instead with more idiocy about the anesthesiologist who applied the epidural or the friendly nurse who had taught Ellie how to use her breast pump while regaling them with stories about raising her own eight kids.

Charlotte Louisa fell asleep on Ellie's boob, and my coffee sat, cold and untouched, on the table. Then Ellie turned to me and said, "Look, I might have to kick you out now. Nothing personal. Just that as soon as she's had her final feed, we try to go to bed ourselves. The joys of newborn parenthood." It was barely six o'clock.

"Oh yeah, of course," I said. "Don't apologize." And I got up and said my goodbyes, thinking of my Merlot in the cabinet.

Before I got on the subway home, I stopped in at a bar Ellie and I used to go to together and ordered a glass of house red. "Anyone joining you?" said the bartender, and I shook my head without making eye contact.

The sun set as I sat there, nursing the wine. It was an unexpectedly large glass. I finally felt it take effect on the fourth sip, like a chain dragging me gently out into a warm, dark sea. I considered what it meant that I hadn't felt anything when I held Charlotte Louisa. Did it point to some fundamental flaw in my womanhood, or did it mean I was one of those Cool Girls who didn't like kids? Maybe I could start calling them "crotch goblins" while leaving snarky online reviews about how they ruined the five-star hotel experience by running around screaming during the breakfast buffet. Maybe I could complain about how I shouldn't have to pay for their schools with my taxes. I could go to adults-only meetups and say things like: "When are we going to get to the point where breeders take some *responsibility* for climate change?" It was seductive. It was tempting. But I didn't think I hated kids, really. I was neutral in the face of Charlotte Louisa, which in some ways felt like the worst response of all.

I finished my wine and walked slowly to the subway station, wondering if it was too late in my life to rebrand. Maybe I could cut my hair and try out pansexuality. Maybe I could tell people I was born after 9/11. Maybe I could act like my adult life was only just beginning and make it come true.

.   .   .

IT WAS STILL DARK. I WAS IN MY APARTMENT. I WOKE UP AND LOOKED at my phone: 5:12 a.m. I wondered why I'd woken up so abruptly, then I heard a bang from above. It sounded like something had fallen heavily against a radiator. Then there were what sounded like a couple of staggering footsteps, and another bang.

I lay in bed, wondering about the right thing to do. Was I morally obliged to get up and knock on Mrs. Konstantin's door? Should I call the police? Should I make sure my chain was on in case there was a murderer loose in the building? Was this a time for heroism or self-preservation? Mrs. Konstantin was old, old enough to have a diabetic leg. She'd had a good life. Surely I could, in good conscience, allow her to be murdered by an intruder if it allowed me to go on living at the age of thirty-five. From an evolutionary perspective, saving Mrs. Konstantin probably wasn't worth it. I still had about seven years left in me of the capacity to procreate—maybe even ten with the wonders of modern technology. What if I was destined to give birth to the next Einstein?

I stayed as still as I could, but there wasn't any more noise. Eventually, I affirmed that I couldn't reasonably be expected to put myself at risk, so I turned over and went back to sleep. Just before I drifted off, I thought I heard a dog whine, but then silence reigned again.

When I next woke up, it was 9:08 a.m., and I had a news aggregation shift that started at eleven. I had a quick shower and dressed in tracksuit bottoms and a loose T-shirt, then took the stairs up one level and knocked on Mrs. Konstantin's door. No answer. I knocked again, a little more insistently. The stairs were cold under my slippered feet, and the door was freezing when I pressed my ear against it. I could hear the March wind making its way around the building, insinuating itself into the cracks in the concrete, whistling slightly as it penetrated the panes of the communal window facing onto the floor Mrs. Konstantin shared with the inhabitants of three other apartments. I strained my ears but

I couldn't hear anything from inside her place, then knelt to the floor for a second to see if there were any pools of blood forthcoming. Eventually, a neighbor opened their door and looked out at me accusingly through the chained gap. I decided that I'd return at lunchtime.

Around 1:30, I tried again and there was no answer. I texted Ellie: *Hey, weird q but do you know what to do if you think something bad's happened to a neighbor??* She didn't reply.

I went back up at five, knocked more insistently, got no response. I sent Ellie another message: *Hey, I'm a little freaked out. Just wanted to know if you'd ever experienced something like this??* Silence. Was I making something out of nothing? Mrs. Konstantin could be out of town; the noise could've been weather, or pipes, or the elevator breaking again. She wasn't my responsibility, anyway. Or was she? What if something terrible had happened and I was held responsible? No one on social media would believe I hadn't done it.

I was two thirds of the way through my news shift, and I'd been tasked with writing up a particularly graphic description of a teenager's murder at the hands of her high school boyfriend. Headline: "Montana Student Shot in Murder-Suicide by 'Kind, Quiet' Boyfriend of Six Months." Subhead: "'He was the type to help little old ladies across the street and look after your pets if you went out of town,' says 'confused' neighbor." I could have been murdered three times over by that guy and Ellie wouldn't have even texted me back. Or I could have experienced severe trauma, soon to be complex PTSD, by discovering the body of my beloved—yes, *beloved*—upstairs neighbor inside her apartment, bludgeoned and brutalized. Did anybody care?

The paper's internal messaging system pinged, announcing a new message in the channel reserved for discussion among aggregation reporters and the audience team.

Man arrested for having sex with his Labrador (source: Rushin-NewsBang). Maybe one for @NatashaBailey? wrote an audience team member whose job was to scour the internet for certain keywords, mostly to do with deviant sexual encounters and/or murder.

Seriously? wrote another reporter. *A Labrador? They're so loyal! You had another breed in mind?* I replied.

> *I'm just saying . . . It makes it especially tragic, imo. They're just big fluffy bundles of love.*

I don't know if I love the idea of a terrier getting railed by its owner either, I wrote.

Lol Natasha. So crude, the audience editor jumped in. *I'm thinking headline for this one could be: High school grad arrested for raping "loyal" family dog.*

> *Does it matter that he graduated high school?*

> *The ceremony was last week. It's notable. I'm not talking about his credentials.*

> *Okay, because you're making it sound a little like a fucked-up résumé header. "Dog Rapist with High School Diploma Seeking New Position."*

Silence for a few seconds, then I received a private message from the same audience editor I'd been conversing with: *Just a heads-up. Maybe don't make too many jokes like that in a public channel.*

> *Oh. Sorry. I thought gallows humor kinda went with the territory.*

> *I mean, it does but . . . people screenshot things, you know? Stuff can go public.*

> *Sure. I can appreciate that more than most!*

Yeah, so on the official channels we just try and keep things a little professional.

Gotcha.

Off the back of that dog rape story, we can see there's a huge amount of interest about the specific details btw. Incoming search traffic from terms like bestiality, etc. So if you could knock together a separate piece that'd be great: "In which states is bestiality legal?"

Does that sound like we're giving people tips?

Natasha, you know I love your humor more than pretty much anyone. But it's also a virtue to know when to stop.

I sighed out loud. It hadn't been a joke. *Of course,* I typed. *I'll get going on the article.*

AS SOON AS I LOGGED OUT OF WORK, I WENT BACK UPSTAIRS AND banged very loudly on Mrs. Konstantin's door, until a man came out of the opposite apartment and asked me what I was doing.

"Have you seen her?" I asked, pointing at Mrs. Konstantin's apartment. "Did you hear the banging last night?"

He shrugged. "I don't know, lady," he said. "I keep my business to myself."

At ten, I texted Ellie one more time. *I'm really not okay here. I seriously think something bad might've happened to the woman above me. Can you at least answer me??* At eleven, I followed up with: *????*

She replied, eventually, at one in the morning. *Tash, I get that you're freaked out but I'm gonna have to set some boundaries here. I can't be at your beck and call right now—Charlotte's needy, I'm sleep-deprived, etc etc. Jake says if you really think something bad's happened, he can stop by your place after work tomorrow. Let me know.*

I looked down at my phone and felt like I'd been slapped. *Forget it*, I wrote back.

MY MOTHER CALLED. "HOW'S THE APARTMENT NOW THAT YOU'RE more settled?"

"It's great." I sat down on a box I hadn't unpacked. Actually, I hadn't unpacked most of them, except the one with the kitchen utensils and another filled with bathroom necessities. "This time I'm going for minimalism."

"Good idea. And have you met any of the neighbors?"

"One or two. I don't know. I'm slightly worried one of them might be dead." I said it nonchalantly, like it was kind of funny.

"You *what*? Natasha, don't joke about things like that."

"I'm serious," I said, overdoing it now to get her back on my side. "I heard a huge bang late last night, not the normal kind from pipes or whatever. Then, nothing. No sound from her or her dog—the dog is always whining—and then I started smelling something weird . . ." The smell was sort of an invention, but I needed to give my story extra legitimacy now, and I was burned by Ellie's implication that I was imagining it all.

"Oh, Jesus Christ." I could picture Mom putting her head in her hands. "Hang up now, and call the police."

Shit, I'd overcorrected. I backtracked. "Look, Mom. It could be as simple as someone cooking a particularly pungent stew."

"You know, I always said this. I always thought just taking all that hard-earned money out of your bank account and throwing it away on some slummy apartment was a terrible idea. You weren't in your right mind then, and to be perfectly honest, you aren't now. Living on the edges of that dirty, crime-ridden city, a place most people have *left* by their thirties because it's completely unsuitable for married life and kids . . ."

"Well, I'm not married anymore," I interrupted her. "And I don't have any kids, as you well know. So can we cool it?"

"I'm sorry that I'm saying things that are hard to hear, but that's the point. You never listen to anybody, Natasha, because you always have to know better than everyone else. And then you look down on me, but guess what? *I* had children by your age. And I owned a *family* home."

"You're engaging with a fantasy Natasha in your head again," I said. "Are you drunk?"

There was a pause, then: "How can you be so unkind? After everything you've put us through, and everything I did for you. You know, I saw that sixth-grade art teacher from camp the other day in town, and she said to me, out of all the mothers, you were the most dedicated. Your girls wanted for *nothing*, she said. And I spent *hours* with you, every evening—science projects, volcanoes made out of baking soda, all those quadratic equations you couldn't handle, and you *always* had food on the table and clean clothes, properly ironed—"

"Some people might call that the bare minimum," I interrupted.

"Oh, go on, get on your high horse again. Too much for your mother. Your mother, who stood by you when everyone else was *horrified* by what you'd done."

"Let's remember I didn't kill anyone, Mom," I said. "Anyway, goodnight."

"Well, goodnight if you're going to be like that," she said, and hung up before I could. I stood in the kitchen, looking through the dirty windowpane at the clouds hovering above the ocean, and thought I should probably work out how to use the oven, or at least plug in the microwave.

SEVEN

I WENT UPSTAIRS TO KNOCK ON MRS. KONSTANTIN'S DOOR ONE MORE time for the night. The man I'd seen talking to her by the mailboxes walked out of the elevator as I did and I stopped him to ask if he'd seen her.

"I don't know anything," he said, holding both his hands up in an absurdly defensive position. I felt like no matter what I tried, people always reacted as if I were trying to do the worst thing they could imagine.

The next day, I started a vigil outside Mrs. Konstantin's door, crouched on the floor with an oversize scarf wrapped around me against the chill. I sat with my computer balanced on my lap, within range of my apartment's wi-fi, sending suggested headlines to the audience editors so they could shoot back custom URLs for news stories: "California Schoolmates Reveal What Prince Harry's Kids Are Really Like in Class" traded for prince-harry-meghan-markle-archie-lilibet-school; "Scarred Face of Brave Teen Attacked by Four Vicious Wild Hogs Finally Revealed" traded for hogs-attack-big-reveal; "'Kids Need Protection from Porn,' Says Former Adult Star" traded for porn-kids-famous-sex. After that one, I went back to the editor who had sent it.

Do you think that makes me look bad?

Why would it make you look bad?

Well, cause it's my byline on the piece and the url looks kinda weird. Like, porn and kids next to each other.

It's all fine in context.

Mind if I make it longer or something? Like porn-star-warns-kids-famous-sex?

Longer urls can affect where we place in search.

Ah ok. Maybe we can brainstorm alternatives?

It's really important we get thru this list quickly.

I looked back at the screen, wondering if this was one of those hills worth dying on. I'd lost all perspective, though, and all the hills looked the same size to me. Eventually, I typed out *No prob* and published, before moving on to the next card: "South Carolina Woman Who Championed 'Used Sex Toy Giveaways' Becomes First to Make $1 Billion on OnlyFans." All day I churned out aggregated articles about sexual deviancy, but somehow I had lost my real job because I said I liked every inch of a swimmer. If I'd sold my own used vibrators below the Mason-Dixon Line, I might've elicited a little more sympathy.

In the late afternoon, I immersed myself in a self-help article on LinkedIn about how to leave a job you hate and manifest the job you deserve. There was no mention of what to do if you'd already manifested the job you deserved. While I considered that, I realized someone was clanging and shuffling up the stairs toward me—and as the figure rounded the corner, I saw that it was Mrs. Konstantin, carrying her ugly little dog in a bag slung over her shoulder, trailing her bad leg behind her.

"You're here!" I said, jumping up.

She looked confused. "Yes?"

"I . . . I was worried." I couldn't exactly say: *I thought you'd been brutally murdered in the dead of night and I elected not to intervene, but I did crouch down next to your front door to check for bodily fluids.* That could be construed as a little intense.

"You worried about me?" she asked slowly, her eyes narrowed.

"Yes," I said, closing my laptop and standing up. "I heard this weird bang in the middle of the night—a couple nights ago—and I was just . . . I thought you might need help up here or . . . something. I've been knocking on your door every day. To check on you."

"I got an early train on Thursday," she said. "Had some medical appointments." I guess what I'd heard was simply her packing up and leaving the house.

We stood looking at each other for a few seconds before I understood that she wanted to get past me and into her own apartment. "Sorry," I said, moving out of the way. "I don't know what I was thinking. I guess, you know, better safe than sorry!"

I thought I saw her crack a half smile as she reached the door then pulled a comically oversize bunch of keys out of her bag. I think she was repeating "better safe than sorry" under her breath.

"Sorry again," I said for some reason, and I almost did a little bow, something I'd never once done in my life but apparently had decided made sense in this moment.

"No problem," she said, waving me away with her free hand and half closing the door behind her. Then, after I'd turned to leave and was walking back down the hallway, she opened it properly again and said, "Hey, girl. I don't dislike you."

I caught her eye just before she shut herself back inside.

"I don't dislike you either, Mrs. Konstantin!" I said loudly. Someone new failing to dislike me was a pretty big deal at that moment, so I had to make sure I reciprocated the sentiment.

I heard rustling and clicking and dog noises from inside the apartment—probably her taking off her coat and the ugly dog's leash and hanging them up in the entryway—then, through the door, the reply came, brusque as ever yet also strangely heartening: "Call me Olinka."

BACK IN MY APARTMENT, I SET MY LAPTOP ON THE TABLE AND SLICED open another moving box with a pair of scissors. As I removed the microwave and struggled to set it up on the kitchen counter, I saw a notification pop up on my phone. A text message from Zach. I savored the feeling of knowing that the message was there, but not opening it right away—a pathetic social edging.

I took my time unraveling the microwave's wire and plug, placed it on the counter, and arranged some mugs inside a cabinet above. Then I sat back down in front of my computer and saw that I'd been assigned a news card titled "'Totally Unacceptable' Video Game Based on Actress's Gang Rape Goes Viral." I opened the link but couldn't concentrate on the content. The edging had gone too far; I had to see what Zach had said.

You around for a call some point this week? Other plan actually fell thru. Looks like I could use your place after all. I hugged the phone to my chest, a little victory beating inside me. I'd make him wait for my reply like the prick-tease I was.

JUNIOR NEWS REPORTERS WEREN'T REQUIRED TO COME INTO THE OFfice that often—just to show their faces every couple of weeks or so—but I was called in the Monday after I discovered Mrs. Konstantin—*Olinka*—hadn't tragically died. The office was right by Penn Station, in perhaps the most congested part of the city, where some unsuspecting commuter seemed to be pushed in front of a subway train every other week. Before I'd left for London—in the days when I was still a respected national reporter—I'd happily stepped over the pools of piss and walked past guys shooting up in the corners of the station because I was delivering copy that might go on the front page or attending Very Important Meetings with editors who read my work with interest. These days, the journey didn't feel remotely worth it.

Unfortunately, I couldn't exactly ignore a request from the editor in chief. *Would be nice to see your face on mon,* BR had written on the internal messaging system while I was working on a story about UFO conspiracy theorists in Roswell from the comfort of my own home. It was an order wrapped up in the cheap gift wrap of a suggestion. BR always communicated meetings this way: he would fit you in at some point during his Very Busy Day, and he expected you to be on-site to accommodate that. But he'd make it sound like he just missed you.

I took the subway in and arrived eight minutes late for my shift, sweaty from an hour inside a coughing sardine tin of people in my winter-to-spring transition clothes. New York was simultaneously humid and freezing in a way that brought back unwelcome memories of England. I had a light wool sweater pulled on over my navy pinstriped jumpsuit and a dark green raincoat over that; it was an outfit that I thought made me look ironically corporate, like a tongue-in-cheek journalist rather than someone who took the job too seriously. To BR, I imagined, it would look like I'd dressed up; my other colleagues would think I was fashion-forward and subtly sardonic. Perfect.

But as I caught a look at myself in the mirror-lined elevator on the way up to the office, I realized I looked like a mess. The raincoat was sitting uncomfortably on the sweater, which was falling off my shoulders, and the bottom half of the jumpsuit looked almost like sweatpants. I'd put on a few pounds since moving to the Rockaways and it showed mostly on my hips, stretching out the pin-striped fabric in a way that looked almost obscene from the back. My hair was static and frizzy in the humid air. Under the harsh elevator light, I noticed that my tinted moisturizer had stopped just shy of the end of my nose and I had grown four new gray hairs at the crown of my head. Each one of them stuck up in a different direction, like a compass announcing that my ovarian reserves were depleting by the second. By the time the elevator reached the twentieth floor, I felt thoroughly demoralized.

"Morning," said the news editor, a man who never missed an opportunity to let me know he was my boss.

I nodded at him, pointed at a desk, and said, "Mind if I sit here?" He got up and made a show of checking a laminated piece of paper with a bird's-eye view of the desks sketched on it, presumably making sure nobody more important than me was scheduled to come in that day, before eventually conceding that I could set my bag down and unpack my laptop.

As soon as I logged in to the group messaging system, the same news editor posted in the channel for reporters: *Just making sure everyone understands the protocol for when you come into the office. If you're doing your required days per month or have decided you'd prefer to work here, you are expected to be *seated* and *in place, ready for work* by 9 a.m. (or 11 a.m., 2 p.m., or 9 p.m., if you're on the second, third, or final shift).* The message prompted lots of sycophantic little emojis of thumbs-ups and green ticks. I didn't acknowledge it. He could kick me when I was down, but I was hardly going to get up off the floor and beg Daddy for more.

A couple of hours later, while I was balancing my cell phone on my shoulder, the news editor sent me a direct message. I'd been on hold for twenty minutes while trying to confirm with animal control in Rhode Island whether or not a jaguar had really been spotted by a member of the public.

Hey, can you get a pic of that woman who gave birth in the airport toilets at the top of yr article from earlier?

I looked over the open-plan office at the top of his head. He had very straight, mousy brown hair cut into a sharp, short style and pomaded in place so it stayed as still as concrete while the rest of his head moved. He was also wearing a beige linen shirt. The whole effect was very Hitler Youth.

She said on social media that she didn't want those pics republished, I replied, typing furiously while two reporters beside me talked about whether or not an "Ozempic and all-beef" diet being promoted in the lifestyle section could really give you kidney damage.

Well, ha, she's not in control of our newsroom, he replied.

It's my byline on there. She'll come after me.

I don't mean to be rude but you're getting overly obsessed with the byline stuff atm. People don't look at bylines on news stories.

The people who the article is about might.

If you get any trouble from her, then we can discuss.

But I don't want to provoke the trouble in the first place. I looked up again, furtively, from my position behind my laptop. The news editor coughed slightly and then clicked his knuckles in a way that I imagined he thought asserted dominance. What a sad little life.

There was a long-enough pause that I wondered if I'd accidentally typed out my own thoughts or been terminated from the company effective immediately. But eventually the reply came: *Leave it then. If you could just move on to the story about that guy getting sucker-punched by a veteran for saying the N-word at a football game, that'd be great.*

AROUND LUNCHTIME, A MAN IN AN OVERSIZE BERMUDA SHIRT AND baggy slacks came over to introduce himself. He looked to be at least ten years younger than me. "Bryce Taylor," he said. "The new director of the audience team? Looking forward to our catch-up later today." He had a vaguely Australian-sounding upward lilt at the end of his sentences combined with a Valley-Girlesque vocal fry, a potent combination.

"Natasha," I said, shaking his outstretched hand. "I didn't actually know we had a meeting scheduled, but I'm happy to attend."

"Oh yeah, with BR?" he said.

"Oh. Great." *That's what BR brought me into the office for?* I noted that this new guy had already ingratiated himself enough that someone had told him the boss's nickname.

"Yeah," he said, "and listen." He bent down beside my office chair and started bouncing on his Stan Smiths in an unsettling way. "A piece I thought you could grab before that meeting, if you're down for it? I don't know if you saw that YouTuber who died kind of tragically this morning? Carly Lovesprings—she's a yoga teacher. Or she was."

"Oh," I said. "No, I didn't."

"Yeah, kind of a crazy story. She snapped her neck doing that new thing that everyone's trying—the hummingbird pose? We've had a note from the lawyer representing her family, and he wants to respect the family's privacy, you know the drill. Obviously restricts what our photographers can get from the scene. So if you could just mine her social media a bit, get some nice photos of her doing squats in her Lululemons or whatever, and see if we can get a local yoga studio to say whether they think she was being reckless? There's just *so* much interest in this story today from the readers. Search traffic numbers are through the roof. Understandably. She was like, huge." He paused. "In terms of followers, I mean. Like, she was super skinny."

"Sure," I said, with a pointed lack of enthusiasm.

"Oh, and!" He clapped his hands, and almost fell out of his own squat from the effort. "I forgot the craziest thing. Her *dog* found her."

"Her dog?" I looked at him with open reproach. Did this man think animals could now report deaths to the police?

"Yeah, I mean, like it was whining and barking, and so the neighbors requested a welfare check, and that's how she was found. Poor puppy, right? So anything about the dog—the name, the breed, whatever, maybe a canine psychologist talking about the

effects that finding an owner fatally injured can have on them—
would also be a great way to capitalize on the interest."

I thought of Mrs. Konstantin and her long-toothed mutt. "Totally," I said.

"And if you could get that done before our two p.m. catch-up,"
he added quickly, pulling himself out of the squat and standing up
to what was actually a pretty impressive height, "that would be *fantastic*. Like, I would really appreciate that. And I know BR would
too." He gave me a friendly little pinch on the arm before he strode
off to harass some other member of the junior news reporting team.

I finished the article about the football game sucker-punch and
got up to make myself a coffee while ruminating on the tragically
flexible demise of Carly Lovesprings. I felt oddly responsible for
her death, like maybe I'd accidentally transferred Mrs. Konstantin's
fate onto her by keeping my anxious vigil. But fate, or whatever was
operating instead of fate at the moment—Satan, malevolent grem-
lins, whatever—probably didn't work like that.

Standing at the coffee machine, I sent Zach a message back:
*Sure, I'd be happy to chat. How about tonight or tomorrow, say 6 p.m.
after work?* That put him on a timeline, meant he had to reply soon.
Then I realized that might make me sound like I completely lacked
a social life, so I added: *Got lunch stuff so won't be able to do sooner,
unfortunately. But can def squeeze you in during an evening.* That
would do it. I felt powerful. Carly Lovesprings was dead, but I was
alive, baby!

I went to pour myself some more coffee and only got half a
cup because the pot was almost empty. In the spirit of my new
lease on life, and as a gracious, community-minded individual, I
decided to make a new one. I reached into the cupboard for the
coffee grounds, spooned them into the right compartment, and as
I stood at the kitchen cabinet waiting for it all to brew, I opened the
newspaper's website on my phone and clicked on the latest travel
article: "Haiti Is Where You'll Find Your New Favorite Beach." The

piece had been written by the deputy travel editor, and the main image was of her on a speedboat, Gucci glasses obscuring most of her face. From the angle, I could tell she'd taken the picture using a selfie stick. She was wearing a low-cut one-piece swimsuit in orange and looked irritatingly poreless and tanned.

> Just a few short miles away from the sad, unsightly poverty of Port-au-Prince, this beach resort is everything burnt-out office workers who desperately need a break from reality dream of: semideserted, chock-full of cheap deals for food and drinks, and basically undiscovered. It's had its problems, but Haiti is now welcoming tourists en masse—and its new foray into five-star luxury gets our enthusiastic thumbs-up! No more tossing toilet paper in the trash can and brushing your teeth with bottled water, not when you're ensconced behind the highly impressive topiary of the American Beauty Hotel! Read on for tips about how to find the most authentic food and where to spend a night on the town.

"Taking a break, Natasha?" said BR, breezing past me. I jumped.

"Oh! No, I mean, just making some more coffee. Being a good citizen." I tapped the pot with my finger to underline my point.

"Teamwork!" he said, flashing me a smile that didn't meet his eyes. "Well, I'm looking forward to our meeting later on. Some very important things to talk over."

"Absolutely," I said. An hour earlier, a meeting time had finally appeared in my calendar from BR's assistant, titled simply "Talk." "And I caught up with Bryce Taylor earlier—he said he's coming along?"

"Oh, yeah. Lots of people are. It's a sort of refresher thing. Great for your career. Listen, I've gotta run."

He was out the door before I could say anything else, but I don't know what I would have added anyway.

•   •   •

"NATASHA. I'M SO GLAD YOU COULD MAKE IT." THE TIME FOR "TALK" had arrived, and BR was seated in the middle of a long table with six people, all of whom appeared to be part of the audience team. It was like a Last Supper for clickbait. I noticed he was looking even more bald and repressed than before, if that was possible, and a stray piece of dry skin on his cheek was gently undulating in the breeze of the office AC. Why was his skin always so dry? Probably because presiding over the violent death of journalistic integrity was draining his life force. I imagined what it was like to be his wife, peeling off his stained old briefs and trying to pretend he was still sexy, his balls stringy and pendulous from the natural effects of gravity over the years. Did she pumice the dry skin off his heels? Did she fake her orgasms? Did she buy him expensive brands of moisturizer in the hope that her ossifying husk of a husband might reanimate thanks to the healing effects of aloe and royal jelly?

"Sure," I said, taking a seat on the other side of the table. Bryce Taylor seemed to realize how odd the whole thing looked, because he moved over to my side as I did so.

"We just wanted to talk traffic priorities for the next quarter," BR said. "But I'll let Bryce explain more thoroughly."

"Of course," said Bryce. "And Natasha, I just want to say, we all know you've been through a hard time? So don't take this as, like, added pressure or anything. Think of it as more like a clarification."

"Totally," I said. Apparently there were no secrets from the audience team. Lucky I'd maxed out on shame long ago, or such public declarations about my mental health could've been embarrassing.

"So we've just been hearing from your managing news editor that sometimes you're not totally happy following audience team priorities?" Bryce continued, speaking over me. "And I guess we just want to get to the bottom of that?"

I opened my mouth to reply, but BR cut in: "Now I know what you're going to say, Natasha. You're used to being a reporter-at-large.

I know that you're not as familiar with the slightly lowlier workings of us . . . jacks-of-all-trades. But at the end of the day, this stuff is what keeps the lights on."

The absolute audacity of the editor in chief describing himself as a lowly miner pickaxing his way through coal was apparently lost on everyone.

"This is an opportunity," said Bryce. "A really great one, I think? Hard times behind us, and some cool stuff ahead." I'd read his Instagram bio on my way to the meeting: *Award-winning journo/ audience analyst helping newsrooms report on our dystopian moment. NYC via Wisconsin. ADHD (self-dx'd). RTs and opinions all someone else's.* After seeing it, I'd immediately fired off a LinkedIn message to the editor of a local Brooklyn paper, asking if he might be available for a coffee because I was "potentially open to new roles."

"I haven't been through a hard time," I said, louder than I'd intended. Everyone on BR's table looked down at their open laptops. Two of the young women on the team looked at me with deep and undisguised sympathy.

"That's neither here nor there," said BR hurriedly. "Natasha, I'm going to level with you. Those . . . comments from the news editor aren't going to look very good on your annual review. We'd hate to have to . . . Well, we just want you to know that when you get good audience numbers on your news articles, it keeps you a lot more secure in the publication. It can only look good."

"I understand that," I said, although I didn't. But I was beginning to realize that I was the subject of this meeting, and that it was definitely not a casual catch-up.

"We've got a list of things we thought you might want to look into?" said Bryce. "You know, maybe when you're on the long train home or something—where is it you live again, Jersey City?"

"The Rockaways."

"Right, right. So you're on your way back to the beach and, you know, that's the perfect time to, like, maybe explore something you could bring to us as a news writer. Like, something extra. And I'll leave Eliza to read out the priorities we thought you could concentrate on specifically." Each member of the audience team around him, eyes glued to their laptops, huffed the drug of newsroom algorithmic software constantly, filling spaces in the conversation with extra hits.

One of the young women who'd been looking at me sympathetically jumped up like she'd been handed the mic on a game show. She had purple hair and a septum piercing. "Yeah, so," she said, "one that did *numbers* for us last week was 'Woman Bedridden by Chronic Psoriasis Cures All with $8 Cream from Target.' That kind of thing lights up *so* quickly. So having a look at skincare forums can really pay off, reading about people's experiences. You can write this down if you want. Also, backstreet abortions—those are really making waves. So, like, if we can get a girl in Texas who almost bled to death or something, that's superpowerful. With pictures. And helping to commission first-person written pieces is also such a big win. One article we've been thinking about, and I think everyone here agrees"—she gestured to the team around her who nodded in unison—"is a piece from someone who tried the four-day workweek and saw that it wasn't what it seemed. Headline: 'I Tried the Four-Day Workweek and It Ruined My Life.' People love a contrarian take."

"Isn't that kind of . . . bad for society?" I said. "I don't want to be all holier-than-thou here, but the four-day workweek is gaining a lot of traction in some high places and we could end up possibly doing damage to a movement with actual potential. I've actually seen some research about how it positively impacts gender equality and opens up opportunities for disabled people."

There was a silence, and the purple-haired girl pursed her lips. Eventually, BR said, "Would you like a four-day workweek, Natasha?"

"Me . . . personally? I mean, no."

"If you're looking to go part time . . ."

"I'm not at all. *At all.*" There it was again, the feeling of being a thousand miles away. I reminded myself to breathe. "I was just approaching things from . . . every angle."

"I see." BR took off his thin-framed reading glasses, rubbed the bridge of his nose, and put them back on. Another line of dry skin announced itself where he'd just touched his face. "Now, I understand everything can get quite ideological when you're a reporter-at-large. I know there's sometimes even a *distaste* for what goes on behind the scenes, for the people who do the work to make the publication profitable, churning the wheel all day so others can go out and about on their fun little reporting trips. But, for better or worse, here you are."

"It isn't that at all," I said weakly.

"You can't say you haven't been told," he continued, ignoring me. "Bryce is here to help you. Eliza too." The purple-haired audience team member gave me a little wave. "This whole team is now here to help you. So bear that in mind."

This felt like a show trial, but I wasn't entirely sure what the aim was. Perhaps to create a paper trail so they could eventually fire me without any legal ramifications. Or maybe they thought I still had enough juice left inside me that they could squeeze out before discarding me like an orange peel.

"I'm going to get Eliza to send you the ranking of the reporters," said Bryce, placing a kindly hand on my shoulder. "We do a list showing who's pulling in the best numbers every Friday? I think that will really motivate you."

"It's important for us to be transparent about what we do," Eliza added. "And when you can see the numbers and everything—and with this neat program, you can actually even click through and see each article the reporter wrote and how they sold it and how it did so well—that just shows what success looks like."

"Sure. Thanks," I said.

"You might be wondering how you can *improve* your ranking," Eliza continued, clearly on a roll. "And writing a headline that disrupts the browsing flow is a craft we're really encouraging among news writers at the moment. I can do a training session with you."

I looked at her. "Disrupts the browsing flow?"

"You know. Creates a bit of a gap there. An abyss of intrigue. It leaves you wanting more. Like"—she gestured around with her hands for the perfect image—"imagine you're a fish and there's a hook there, just dangling a nice piece of—"

"—bait?"

BR jumped in: "Not *bait*, Natasha. You've really got to try to break out of the negative mindset."

"Sorry," I said. "I understand what you mean."

"We're hoping to train everyone in the newsroom in these headline heuristics," said Bryce Taylor. "Because, like, we're publishing fifty articles every hour now? And the audience team can't be expected to do it all?"

"This is one of the things Bryce was passionate about in the interview process," said BR. "And why we hired him. He thinks *big*. This is business-wide strategy right here—ambitious stuff. We encourage that around here. And at the end of the day, that leads to cost savings."

"For sure," said Bryce Taylor.

"Get every news writer up to date on how to generate that *little bit* of breathing room where a reader can allow their imagination to run wild," BR continued. "And then, before you know it, we won't even need every single audience team member to run themselves into the ground reacting to every problem."

Eliza was starting to look a bit unsure. "But the audience team wouldn't be . . . shrinking, right?" she said.

BR and Bryce Taylor exchanged a quick look before BR said, with overdone enthusiasm, "Of course not! I mean, even if it did, you wouldn't be first on our list. You know how much we value you, Eliza. In fact, here we are, yakking away and preventing you from doing that incredibly important work that makes this whole news organization go round! Why don't we let you head back to your desk?"

"Sure." Eliza's mouth was a thin line as she began packing up her notebook and laptop. Maybe she wouldn't be sending me an invite to a meeting about disrupting the browsing flow after all. Once she'd left the room, BR gave me a little headshake, as if to say that Eliza was becoming a bit of a diva.

"The people who fix the ship don't always get to stay on board once it's seaworthy," he said. "That's just a sad fact of economics. We always have to factor an element of streamlining into our decisions, and we will until readers want to actually pay for the news. I think we found that when we got rid of those dinosaurs in the fact-checking department, it really worked out for us—financially, yes, but also operationally."

"We still have *some* fact-checkers, though, right?" I said, trying not to sound panicked.

"We have a small, specialist team of two that we can deploy here and there if anything looks particularly legally difficult," BR said quickly, in a manner that sounded rehearsed.

"I see," I said. "I mean, that's small, I guess, but if it works . . ."

"We can't have fact-checkers for every single article, Natasha," BR said. "We do rely on the idea here that our journalists actually know what they're doing."

"Oh, I get that," I said.

"I mean," BR continued, "the people in this newsroom were hired because they're top-notch graduates of some of the most expensive schools in the country. You're telling me they can't tell fact from fiction? Having a fact-checker for every article is a level of hand-holding I think most seasoned reporters would find insulting."

"The Billie Eilish incident, though," I said. Earlier in the week, an intern had accidentally published an article announcing the death of the young pop star, who was very much alive.

"That was an entirely different situation," said BR. "Someone should've been monitoring the Facebook page more closely. Audience team error." The article had accidentally appeared on the newspaper's public Facebook page for three hours, during which time thousands of boomers had informed their children that the singer had apparently passed away, and Eilish's agent had been inundated with calls. The agent eventually called BR himself—and by all accounts, was not very friendly.

"Why did we even have an obituary ready for Billie Eilish?" I asked. We usually didn't add new articles to our prewritten obituary section—known internally as Death Watch—unless a celebrity was seriously ill or seriously old.

BR shrugged. "I think someone saw a clip of her and thought she looked a bit sickly." Then he began to performatively stack up his papers and tap his pen on the table, to indicate he wanted the meeting to be over. "So you'll get those training sessions with Eliza and Bryce in your calendar?"

I had to shoot my shot. It was now or never.

"I wonder if one way to preserve jobs and to retain our . . . excellent reputation," I said, over the sound of BR scraping his chair back, "might be a subscriptions model. We could run really hard-hitting investigative features in it and maybe expert comment? I'd be happy to work on that, even to oversee it entirely. I could edit at first, taking a step back from reporting but still using my skills—maybe move into writing again at some point in the future when we've got it off the ground."

BR looked at me, halfway standing. "That's a little above your pay grade," he said.

"Oh," I said. "I apologize."

"I just find things work better when everyone knows where they stand. We have job titles for a reason," he said. "Anyways, I'd love to go on but—well, Bryce can elaborate for you. Unfortunately, I'm in high demand today. Great to talk!"

Now everybody stood, and for some bizarre reason I found myself opening the door for BR, then walking down the hall at his side. Before he marched off to another conference room, he turned to me and said, "By the way, Footsie called me the other day."

"Oh," I said. "Cool." The ringing started in my ears.

"She asked me how you are. I told her you were getting back on your feet."

"Yeah. Thanks."

"You should give her a call."

"I know. I'll reach out to her this week," I lied, just like I'd lied to myself for months.

Surely BR knew that there was no way I could ever speak to his friend Footsie again. I wasn't even ready to think too hard about what had happened at her eye-wateringly expensive London townhouse after the swimmer article had been published. Every time I closed my eyes and an image of her defiled Highgate guest room floated into my mind, I clenched my teeth and forced my brain to change channels. What was once vengeful, misdirected anger had crystallized into the kind of deep shame that makes you want to erase the person you mistreated rather than even attempt to make things right.

BR stalked off, and I went back to my disappointing, windowless corner of the newsroom to get to work on some further aggregation. As I sat back down on my wheeled office chair, I saw an alert for a LinkedIn message from the editor at the local Brooklyn paper I'd messaged just before the meeting.

> Hey Natasha, good to hear from you! Always interested to talk to people who work at publications like yours. Admittedly have only done a quick scan just now, but your résumé certainly looks impressive. Time for a coffee next week?

Of course. I had all the time in the world.

EIGHT

FOOTSIE DALMATIAN WAS AN ABSURD NAME BY ANY OTHER METRIC, but completely normal within the sphere of British women's magazines. BR—who had professed himself "unsure" about my transfer when my editor initially suggested me for the London role—set me up on a coffee date with her not long after Joe and I landed in the UK.

Despite myself, I wasn't someone who didn't care about the approval of old white men. I'd tried to win BR over with a number of "brand-safe" ideas I'd had for transatlantic features: articles about post-Brexit Britain and the steady rise of the UK's far right, or lifestyle pieces that introduced our American readership to the British megastars they didn't yet know existed. The pieces I'd written in New York did well with readers, I reminded him, by which I meant they provoked letters of interest and occasionally got discussed on podcasts. I had no idea how well they did in terms of per-minute audience numbers because, in that prelapsarian world, I was insulated from such things. I think I only met a member of the audience team once, and that was in passing in the communal kitchen.

In our final one-on-one meeting before I moved to the UK, BR told me that I should remember to "be culturally sensitive in another country" and that "you can always ask a second editor to look over your work, just to be sure." He'd had less to say when we sent a recent college grad male reporter from Connecticut to the front lines of the war in Yemen. I thanked him in a tone sarcastic enough to satisfy myself and sincere enough to satisfy him. As long as the newspaper was sending nonexperts to do expert jobs, then I figured I should benefit from it at least as much as the next man with family connections and an unwrinkled passport.

On the plane to London, Joe at my side, I began my first assignment as a UK reporter. It was a suitably clichéd "Goodbye to New York" personal essay. We were at the height of the period when people were leaving the city for a house in the exurbs and repackaging their experience as a revolutionary choice, and the newspaper wanted in on that orgy of overprivileged confessional writing. On hour five, I was putting the final flourishes on the article, which I felt was going pretty well:

> Living in New York is kind of like having an emotionally abusive but really hot spouse. You know you shouldn't stand for the gaslighting, the way he hates all your friends, the nagging suspicion that he's texting women from work, the way a rat once ran over your foot when you were in an open-toed sandal on a summer's evening in Brooklyn, but you keep going because those moments when it all comes together are truly magical. You and your asshole boyfriend once stayed up all night trading personal philosophies over microdosed molly and light beers, and it changed your perspective on life. You once found an underground bar on your way home from a friend's party in Stuyvesant Heights, made friends with a table of circus performers, and watched the sunrise together over the river, and you'll remember it forever. New York gives you the lightning flashes, and you're afraid that everywhere else there's just rain. But then you remember that rain is vital for life on Earth and people die when they get struck by lightning.

Surely this stuff was genius. I was getting ready to compose the final paragraph when an email came through on the interminably slow wi-fi. It was from BR.

> Hi Natasha—delighted you're heading to London. Meantime, I'd like to introduce you to a longtime friend of mine, Footsie, cc'd. She'll be a great ally for you in England and you should certainly set up a coffee as soon as possible. She has all the contacts you'll need for success over there.

"BR wants me to meet up with some woman called Footsie," I said to Joe, who was diligently working on a new coding language on his laptop. He was an unfussily talented software engineer, one who had been able to wrangle an international transfer easily and who had accepted the inevitable pay cut without question, because he supported my career wholeheartedly. I liked to think that we looked like a power couple, casually tapping away on our computers as we traversed the Atlantic.

"Oh?" he said. "Well, does she sound good?"

"I don't know," I said. "Actually, she sounds like a spy from BR. And her name is *Footsie.*"

"Well, BR's not in London," said Joe mildly. "You can get whatever you want out of her."

That was Joe: unruffled, pragmatically optimistic. Minutes later, he packed away his laptop and pulled up a Marvel movie on the in-flight entertainment system. He liked to give himself regular, unostentatious rewards for his own hard work—he was self-facilitating, psychologically robust—and he encouraged me to stick on the straight and narrow too.

I never allowed myself to miss him.

YET FOOTSIE TURNED OUT TO BE A BLESSING. SHE BARRELED INTO our lunch date at the Ivy in Kensington—her choice—wearing leopard-print pants ("Remember to say trousers, my dear, or you'll get yourself in all *sorts* of trouble") and a magenta top under a yellow feathered jacket. The overall effect was both eccentric catwalk model and Big Bird on crack. When she opened her mouth, that effect didn't change. "Hello, hello, Natasha, *wonderful* to finally meet you, really *wonderful*": eccentric catwalk model. "Listen, love, I'm going to pop out and have a fag before the salad arrives because I've been gagging for one all morning. As the actress said to the vicar!": Big Bird on crack. "Look, this industry is full of shills and fakers and you just have to make your way through the meat grinder without being turned into mince": eccentric catwalk model again. Or possibly mafioso. She had that emptied-of-buccal-fat-then-stretched-taut-by-fillers look that made her ageless in an uncanny valley way, but a quick Google had told me she was in her late forties.

"Oh, I knew your boss back when he was popping Ecstasy at festivals," she said over a plate of spaghetti del mar, teasing a mussel out of its shell with her fork. "We loved him. We'd call him the Token American. He got a kick out of it, I think."

"It's hard to imagine that," I said, and stopped myself from adding any more.

"Oh, I know, he's boring as fuck now," she said, waving her hand around with such force that she almost tipped over her Pinot Grigio. "But, listen, you can't go around acting like a wild child if you're going to head up a newspaper. Really, I feel sorry for him. My job positively *encourages* debauchery."

Footsie was the fashion editor at a lifestyle magazine, which essentially made her top dog. The editor in chief was just there to push paper around and make sure images were placed nicely on the page, she said. Everyone knew it was all about the catwalk.

"I started off running around as a little intern at *Marie Claire*," she explained, then took a big gulp of wine. "Back in the days when you had to pay your dues and work your way up. And luckily my mum's friend got me that internship, and I stayed at my parents' pied-à-terre in London while I slogged away every bloody hour that God sent, making cups of tea, photocopies, running messages between models on photoshoots and their *unbearable* agents and the editors who really thought they knew their shit. I got to know a lot about the industry there. Held me in good stead." Despite her complete lack of self-awareness, I liked her.

Over the espressos we'd ordered just to prolong the conversation, she asked me, "How's your love life?"

That struck me as an intrusive question for someone I'd met professionally, but then Footsie was hardly a paragon of professionalism. "Well, you know, I got married three months ago, just before we headed over to London," I said. "Partly because it made the visa situation easier." I said this a lot in the days before and immediately after we moved to London—*we just did it for the visa!*—because I preferred the responses I got. People stopped questioning me about how long we'd been together; they stopped commenting about how traditional it all was, in comparison with the way I was raised. In quieting those comments, I could quiet my own internal anxiety about whether Joe and I were truly compatible 'til death do us part.

She leaned over the table. "And is he a really good shag?"

Despite the fact that I often spoke to people that way, I blushed. There was saying it to Ellie and Jake and then saying it to *strangers*.

"He's a very unselfish lover," I eventually settled on, intending it to sound a little overdone and humorous, but it came out like I was being uptight. It was true, though: Joe had always been generous in bed, going down on me for a long time before even thinking about penetrative sex, asking me if I "wanted something extra" if he finished quickly. I'd never really been with a man like that before, though I'd heard about them from other women as if they were rare and possibly mythological creatures. The gold standard, Ellie and I had agreed, was her ex-boyfriend, who'd responded to "I have my period" with a gallant and enthusiastic, "Guess we should do it in the shower, then."

"You just *always* have to make sure he's good in bed," Footsie said. "I didn't learn that lesson until after my second divorce. Went that long thinking that love could solve all problems. Ha! You poor Yanks have it even worse with your purity rings and your evangelicals, sending so many young girls off to an orgasm-free fate before they've even had a chance to get fingered. Should be illegal, really. Anyway, let's get this bill paid up because I'm dying for another fag. Addiction, isn't it awful? No, no, put that card away, don't be ridiculous. This is all going on the expenses budget, anyway."

Outside the Ivy, it was raining lightly, and she escorted me the short distance to the Tube because she had an umbrella. "If you need anything, here's my number," she said, pressing her digits into my phone. "And I mean anything. Don't be a stranger."

"Thank you so much," I said. "I really appreciate you taking the time."

"Oh, Americans are always so formal!" she said, before pulling me in and giving me a messy kiss on the cheek. As her sloppy lips connected with my skin, I smelled her perfume, and wondered what it would be like to be one of her ex-husbands. Maybe one of them had been a photographer's assistant and they fucked in the models' changing rooms after they'd left, the photoshoots their foreplay. I imagined Footsie's divorces being amicable because neither partner had really cared to know the other in the first place. She'd just chuck her multicolored sex toys in a cardboard box and kiss her ex-husband on the cheek the same way she'd kissed me, then stride off into the sunset, on her way to the next good shag.

THE NEXT TIME I SAW FOOTSIE WAS AT AN INDUSTRY AWARDS CERE-mony, and she seemed drunk out of her mind. After a barely coherent conversation where she kept pressing her hand into my arm and saying, "I just *love* Americans. Honestly, I do," she led me to the ladies' bathroom, where she handed me a rolled-up twenty-pound note and asked me if I wanted a line.

"Ah . . . probably shouldn't. That stuff's expensive," I said, smiling, because I was there with some new colleagues, and I didn't really know the etiquette. I'd only done coke once before, at a party in Bushwick where I wanted to prove to a guy that I was fun and spontaneous. I'd barely felt anything.

"Oh, don't feel that way," said one of Footsie's middle-aged friends who had followed us in, overly sincere in the way drunk women often get in ladies' rooms. "Honestly, we want you to have a great time."

So I ended up doing half a line with them, bent over in a disabled stall in the basement of a Hilton. A mixture of cocaine, whatever rat poison they cut it with, and my own mucus slid down the back of my throat as I made my way back out of the bathrooms and into the bar. It tasted like detergent. The drug hit me properly as I grabbed another glass of champagne from a passing waiter. Soon, I was passionately lecturing one of the British news reporters from a rival publication about how Austin is the only truly liberal enclave left in America and New York is dead and over, so ideally Europeans shouldn't even visit, except perhaps to pay their final respects. Only people who are scared of the real America live in New York, I added. Texas was where it was at. I didn't believe any of it, of course, but it was fun to make the argument.

Buoyed by adrenaline, I stayed at the bar until they started closing up. At one point, I picked a fight with a tabloid reporter who'd won "Scoop of the Year" for a piece about a politician wearing women's lingerie in his spare time.

"Real public service there," I said sarcastically. "Your Watergate moment."

"Well, I thought so," he said, refusing to engage. He was a softspoken man with a receding hairline that he seemed to think nobody else had noticed. It was hard to see the vicious news-gathering attack dog that his colleagues proudly described him as when they'd come up to the stage tonight to accept their joint award for his pointlessly intrusive story.

When I left the venue at 1:00 a.m., I caught Footsie outside the rotating doors of the hotel having a cigarette with the woman from the bathroom who had encouraged me not to feel bad about partaking in the coke. "This is my *favorite* foreign correspondent in the whole of the United Kingdom!" Footsie announced grandly, staggering toward me on her stilettos.

"No photos today, paps," I joked, putting an arm around her shoulder because the drinks and the drugs had loosened me up. "It's been wonderful to see you, Footsie. I'm gonna get a cab now."

"No, come here before you go." She drew me in and pointed to her phone screen. "Look at this! Have you seen it?" It was a screenshot of a TikTok video featuring the swimmer, his innocent smile beaming. His body was half submerged in water, but you could clearly see the definition of his wide shoulders and the beginning of his six-pack. I didn't know who he was, but I sensed I was supposed to.

"Very nice," I said, laughing.

"No, really," she said, with urgency. "My stepdaughter and her friends are *obsessed* with this boy. He does these little dance routines and he's expected to medal at the Olympics—and isn't he just *gorgeous*? He's about to become a big thing, you know. My friend at Burberry said they're in talks with him about a collaboration."

"Wow," I said. "Good for him."

"Listen . . . Listen!" She poked me with one of her long nails, leaving the shadow of a dent on my bare shoulder. "You're the one for this story! You're young, you're talented, you're absolutely fucking beautiful—isn't she beautiful, girls?" The woman beside her nodded in enthusiastic assent. "You seriously have a good chance of landing the first big profile piece about him. He's about to become the next Harry Styles, I'm telling you! I've got his agent's contact details. Fuck it, I'm emailing her now."

On my way home in the taxi, I opened my inbox and saw that Footsie had been as good as her word: a surprisingly well-worded and forceful email was sitting there, cc'ing me and the swimmer's representatives. It ended with: *Hugs and kisses! Footsie xxx*

How did you navigate the world with that amount of confidence, I wondered? Was it just a case of doing so many things that eventually one of them paid off? Did the people you pissed off just fade into the background? Did you calculate who was likely to do that and who was likely to make you pay for your behavior?

When I got back into our dark apartment and crawled into bed beside Joe, he murmured, half asleep, "How were the awards?"

"Boring," I whispered. "Stupid and boring." Then I lay in bed, staring at the ceiling, willing my chemical heartbeat to slow down so I could get some sleep.

AFTER MY FIRST MEETING WITH THE SWIMMER, I'D TEXTED FOOTSIE: *You were right. He's gonna be big.* I doubted she would need any context, and that was confirmed when she replied almost instantly: *Swimmer boy? Told you. He's a phenomenon.*

Before my second meeting with the swimmer, the Burberry collaboration was announced, which confirmed something else: that the story I'd pitched to the newsroom was a very good idea. Footsie gave me a heads-up and told me to mention it to BR as evidence of my journalistic intuition. "Don't say I connected you," she said over salad in a café near the office. "Take this victory for yourself. You deserve it."

When I mentioned, during my monthly features Zoom with the New York team, that I'd scoped out an up-and-coming British celebrity and secured a series of exclusive interviews with him, BR nodded. His head was suspended inside a square on my computer screen, his shirt buttoned tightly against his permanently expanding neck. "Sounds like a good one," he said, in a very bored voice. "I'll look forward to reading it." He'd never indicated that he'd read anything I'd written, but at least he was still making a show of stating that he would in front of others.

When I started developing some weird and complicated feelings for the swimmer, I stopped messaging Footsie about him. Once, she texted me—*Still all good with swimmer boy?*—and I experienced a rush of irritation. What did she mean by that? I had a paranoid moment of wondering whether the whole thing had been set up because she owed a favor to his PR person. Then I felt guilty about the fact that I was ascribing malice to a woman who'd been nothing but warm and helpful since I'd met her.

All great, I replied. *Really looking fwd to writing this up!*

When the feature was published, Footsie sent me another text: *Read the piece. omfg. brilliant.* I didn't reply right away, because I was basking in the glow of a successfully completed long-read article. That was before the social media warriors had begun their crusade, coming out in force that night after they'd had time to peruse the day's journalistic offerings and sharpen their pitchforks. For a few hours, I thought it might be a flash in the pan. But then it continued, on and on and on. Once other papers started doing meta-analyses of the issue, I knew I was screwed.

Twenty-four agonizing hours of uproar passed before I texted Footsie back, desperate for some scrap of approval: *Did you really think it was good? Lots of controversy online haha. Sure it'll die down soon.*

She didn't reply.

AND THEN EVERYTHING FELL APART. JOE TOLD ME TO LEAVE, SO I DID. My friends—almost all of them in New York, multiple time zones away—were either lukewarm in their sympathies or mysteriously unavailable. My Twitter account (who really called it X?) was relentless: *Fucking feckless cunt. Did u really think you could get away with this?* an account called Proud Neckbeard said. *She should be fired for this,* one poster opined, to which another account replied: *Fired? More like arrested!* A feminist collective called Equality or Death started a petition for me to be removed from the newspaper and, ideally, the country, writing: *Although we do our utmost to stand with women at all times, we believe that the transparently inappropriate conduct of this reporter proves that ALL genders can be abused. As crusaders for equality, it's only right that we bring this egregious conduct to the attention of the editors who enabled her, with the hope that she will not be allowed to take advantage of sources or interviewees ever again. Justice for everyone or justice for no one!*

The *Guardian* published two think pieces, both uncomplimentary. The one that stayed at the top of their "most read" section for forty-eight hours was titled "Two Consenting Adults but a Power Balance That Was Way Off—A Tale as Old as Time." It started up another wave of torch carriers. To my work email, a man who called himself "Nietzsche Was Right" wrote:

I'd teach you a lesson about the place of femoids in this world but you're not even pretty enough to rape.

I cried on the phone to Ellie through the cold British night, wishing I was in her Brooklyn apartment at dusk instead, the light turning pink outside her window as people took their dogs up and down the sidewalk, oblivious to the hell that was unfolding for me in the digital world. I imagined myself curled up on her sofa while she stroked my back and told me everything would be fine. Jake would make us an oven pizza and say he never understood these intrajournalism controversies anyway. Things would feel normal, familiar, reassuring, and Joe would tell me I'd been an idiot but he loved me anyway, and that was that.

I checked into a two-star Holiday Inn in Kings Cross after Joe kicked me out of our apartment. It was a large and anonymous place, with low ceilings, sad breakfast buffets, and the sound of other people's children banging against the flimsy walls. After three nights, I checked out, called myself a taxi, and dialed Footsie's number while I waited for it outside.

"I don't have anywhere to go," I said when Footsie picked up, my voice breaking on the line. "Is there any way I could stay with you for a bit?" I didn't really give her the option to say no.

The cab pulled up outside a three-story townhouse in Highgate. At the end of the cobblestone road was a pub lit up in welcoming golden lights, and as I stepped out of the taxi with my overnight bag on my shoulder, I noticed Footsie's door had a knocker in the shape of a fox. She opened the door before I could use it and enveloped me in her arms, saying, "I just got off the phone with some people at the other magazines. Everyone thinks it ridiculous and will all blow over, darling. Let's get you inside."

When I followed her in, I was momentarily taken aback to see a bearded man with salt-and-pepper hair sitting at the kitchen table, finishing off a large bowl of pasta.

"This is my husband," Footsie said, "and if you hear some moody teenagers shuffling around, that'll be my two stepkids. Bill, this is Natasha—she's just staying with us 'til she sorts out that disaster of a lease." She ushered me upstairs and said quietly as we climbed the carpeted steps, "No need for him to know all the sordid details."

I'd imagined Footsie's house as chaotic, filled to the brim with neon curiosities, but instead it was understated and classy, with polished wood floors and subtle rugs in neutral colors. The guest bedroom was beautifully appointed, with an oversize Jo Malone candle on the windowsill and an antique nightstand. "Make yourself at home," she said, giving me another hug.

"You have a really beautiful place," I said, with the last I could muster of my own voice.

"Oh, you know." She wrinkled her nose. "My husband does the comms for some awful dictatorial regimes so those kids can go to private school and we can live in luxury. I felt a bit terrible about it for a long time, to be honest, like I should do something to counterbalance the negative energy he was putting out into the universe. So most of *my* salary goes to this wonderful charity in Switzerland we set up to empower female refugees. And that has some favorable tax implications, of course."

When she'd gone back downstairs to her pasta-eating, dictator-consorting husband (her third?), I put my bag down and wondered what the fuck I was going to do next. I'd brought my laptop along, but I was afraid to open it; I couldn't imagine ever opening it again. I had four pairs of underwear with me that I'd already worn and was onto my final clean T-shirt, but felt too embarrassed to inquire about laundry facilities. I ended up padding quietly into the ensuite bathroom after everyone had gone to bed and washing my bras and underpants with hand soap in the sink, hanging them up to dry in my room on the end of the bed's footboard.

When I woke up the next day to the sound of birdsong—Actual birdsong, in London. Was Highgate another world?—the depression hit. It crushed me under its weight and pushed me back under the blankets. I kept the curtains closed and didn't look at my phone, knowing it could be filled with text messages from people who either loved or hated me now. When I did finally check it, it was to see whether Joe had sent anything, or called, which he hadn't—and then I threw it onto the carpeted floor without bothering with the missed calls and concerned texts from Mom and Ellie still languishing in cyberspace.

At noon, Footsie knocked tentatively on the door and said, "Everything okay in there, Tash? Just letting you know I'm popping out to a lunch meeting but I'll be back later on. Let me know if you need anything."

The days started blurring together. Footsie would stop by in the mornings before she left for the day, then I'd hear her depart. The husband seemed to be out of the house before I awoke. The stepkids had their own routines: one would get out of the house as early as humanly possible, sometimes even before the sun rose, and the other would slope out in the early afternoon. Once they'd all left, I would shuffle down to their clean, open-plan kitchen like an eighteenth-century invalid and make myself toast with cheese or eat some pickles out of the jar. I piled plates with incompatible foods and then slunk back off to my lair to eat them in half darkness, sometimes accompanied by a disgusting mug of Nescafé instant coffee floating purposelessly in boiling water.

I stopped showering. The clean panties stayed plastered to the footboard while I wandered around in the same clothes, day after day. I was aware that I smelled and started to revel in it. My crotch and my underarms itched, and I developed a rash that radiated out from my left armpit and into the crease of my boob. I wondered vaguely about flesh-eating bacteria. Did that kind of thing exist in England? How long did you have to abstain from cleaning yourself to find out?

I lost count of how long it had been that I'd sequestered myself in Footsie's guest room. I didn't answer calls from my mother, who'd found out about my now internationally recognized career suicide via her best friends' online children. At one point, Miriam texted me in desperation: *Can you at least let me know you're alive? Mom's going crazy over here,* and I replied with a vague allusion to staying with friends and being very busy. I only got one call from the office, which I was surprised about. It came from the generic main number rather than anyone's cell, so I guessed it was an HR manager. I didn't pick it up.

It was fourteen days later—something I only realized in retrospect—when Footsie started knocking on the door and wouldn't go away. It was the late evening; I knew that because I'd watched the slant of light underneath the curtains cycle through the usual colors and then fade to a navy blue just as the streetlamp outside flickered on, but it could've been any day of the week. She knocked politely at first, but then she kept going, getting more insistent. "Natasha," she said, "I don't want to invade your privacy but I'm going to open the door. I'm worried for your health."

I waited an interminably long time for her to leave until I realized that she wouldn't. So I slowly got out of the bed, pulling my leggings away from my ass cheeks, and stepped tentatively toward the other side of the room like a fetid baby deer.

"Oh, Tash," she said, when I cracked the door. "Look, I know it's hard. I know it's really hard right now." She wasn't dressed in any of her signature colors; she'd clearly washed her face for the night and peeled off the fake eyelashes, scrubbed away the foundation, and carefully removed the coral lipstick. Her face was lined and blotchy, and the bags under her eyes were obvious. She had a weirdly shaped forehead that I could see now because her hair was pulled back, creased at the sides and unnaturally stretched in the middle. I guessed her most recent Botox had partially worn off. Standing in the hallway in black jogging pants and an ill-fitting gray shirt, she didn't look anywhere near as imposing as she'd been in my head, but diminutive, almost delicate.

"I'm okay," I mumbled, which was demonstrably not true.

"I'm so sorry," she said, pressing her hands to her eyes like she was getting a migraine. "I'm really sorry, Tashie. I had to call your editor in chief—everyone's been looking for you, it's all just concern. Listen, they're sending you back to New York. This is the best possible thing for you, sweetheart, okay? I told them, you know, she can't be expected to attend any ridiculous meetings right now, she just needs to heal. I've got you a great little premium economy flight back to the States for tomorrow. Don't worry about it—air miles. You should be with your family right now, you know? This really is for the best. And let's think about taking a shower before then."

The betrayal hit me on a delay, like my emotional reflexes had been dulled by repeated assaults. When I was at my lowest point, she'd spoken about me to BR. BR, of all people. Then I looked her in the eye and said, with the kind of derision I'd rarely ever deployed against anyone, "Wow. Thanks a bunch."

To my surprise, her eyes filled with tears. "You know I only want the best for you," she said. "Look, this is just a little speed bump. It's all going to work out. I'll print out your flight details and put them under the door, and I'll book you a taxi for eleven."

It was late already; realistically, I had no chance of finding somewhere else to stay in London tonight. She'd decided to ambush me, to tell me what was happening at the last minute so there was no room for escape. Real nice, Footsie.

Back in the room, I texted Ellie, the only person I'd been in regular touch with since the article was published: *Footsie's kicking me out.*

Ah. Well, you had to leave sometime, Tash.

I just can't believe this. She acted like she's offering me a safe space and now she's throwing me out into the streets. I'll probably get torn apart by ravenous cat-owning keyboard warriors before I get to the airport anyway. I didn't even know if I was joking.

Don't catastrophize. Most people don't remember your name, if they even registered it to start. At most, it's a weird thing that happened on the internet that some people discussed over dinner a couple of weeks ago.

I had to shut down all my social media accounts, El. It's a deluge. Everyone is still so, so angry.

Look. It's easy to feel like everyone's out to get you when a couple hundred people are shouting online, but have some perspective.

I threw a sweatshirt and a pair of jeans into my Spartan suitcase with force. I wasn't about to be talked into *perspective* by anyone. *At the end of the day, a woman will always choose a man over another woman,* I wrote, my thumbs flying across my phone screen. *Everyone's a feminist until they get in line with the patriarchy.*

Tasha, with all due respect, what the fuck are you talking about? This woman took you into her home and protected you. Did you think you could stay in her guest room forever?

She didn't have to tell BR where I was and effectively get me deported.

So you were going to disappear into the British wilderness forever? Become a hermit on a deserted Scottish island?

I just needed some more time.

That isn't some random woman's prerogative, Tash. She probably had people on the phone asking if you were safe. Your colleagues at the paper might have been scared for you.

Scared for me?

You know what I mean.

No, go on. Spell it out for me.

Never mind. Tbh, I'm relieved that you're coming home. You don't sound like you're coping very well. I'm looking forward to seeing you, ok?

When I finally left the guest room the next morning, without cleaning up—the surfaces littered with molding rinds of cheese and mugs of solidified coffee, the floor covered in discarded makeup-removal wipes that I'd used on my first day, the curtains and windows still closed and the smell of my body odor sealed in—Footsie was downstairs, waiting for me.

"I really am sorry," she said, again a little tearfully, and she touched my shoulder gently with her hand as I barged past her, out the door, and into the cab. From the corner of my eye, I saw her standing at her beautiful doorway wearing one of her signature acid-green blazers with a faux-fur trim in pink, watching with concern as the car pulled away and made its way past the little pub and down the cobblestone street. *Fuck you*, I thought. *The sisterhood doesn't exist.*

NINE

ON MY WAY BACK TO THE ROCKAWAYS, STILL PROCESSING THE MEET-
ing with BR and the audience team, I treated myself by taking a
look at the latest text message from Zach. *Sure. Call tonight around
8?* I "liked" the message to affirm that the time worked.

I stopped by the GREAT BREKFEST bodega on my way back from
the train for supplies, and once home, made pasta with tomato
sauce and spinach in a pan, my signature dish and coincidentally
the only thing I knew how to cook. I played music through my
phone speaker and sang along until the next-door neighbor banged
on the wall. I took a shower, lathering my hair luxuriously, then
plucked my eyebrows in front of the bathroom mirror, pretending I
was conducting a YouTube beauty tutorial to pass the time. *See, it's
important to section off the brows and then take little hairs from each
side carefully, like this. Remember, you can take more off but you can't
put it back on!* It made the process of painfully removing parts of
myself in the name of vanity a little more bearable.

At eight, I waited on the sofa, my phone placed with careful
reverence on the coffee table in front of me like a goblet fresh
with Jesus's transubstantiated blood. He didn't call. Ten minutes
passed, then fifteen. I cracked at 8:20, texted him: *Oh hey, you still
free for that call?* like I'd only just realized myself that we were supposed to chat, no big deal.

Sure, he replied instantly. *Aren't you calling me?* He wanted me
to be the instigator? Why? Was this some sort of mind game? I

gave it a couple of minutes—I could plausibly be talking to another friend, or wiping down my kitchen counters, or finishing a chapter of a book, or any other activity that meant I wasn't obsessed with him and how he'd respond to me—then hit his number. It rang three times, then he picked up.

"Hey!" I could hear a train running in the background.

"Hey, hey!" I said, then instantly regretted it. What was I, a host on an after-school special? Then I quickly added, "How are you?" to cover up my embarrassment.

"Yeah, how are you?" he said, which obviously wasn't an answer. "Listen, thanks so much for stepping in with this apartment thing. I had something lined up but then—well, you know, friend drama, whatever, things fell through. So I really appreciate it."

"Oh. No problem," I said. I'd thought we might catch up a bit before he cut to the chase, but I guess we were only talking logistics. "So when are you heading to the city?"

"Next week, actually," he said.

"Wow, so soon!"

"Yeah. Yeah, very soon. Family stuff, really. My mom's kind of sick—my dad needs support. Think I'm gonna be up and down from their place a lot, but I said to them, you know, I'm not moving back to Yonkers in my midthirties. Maybe give it ten years. And I'm a city person so . . . Well, I got myself a soulless job but I'm looking to still do a lot of the arts stuff when I get down there from Boston." He delivered all this in a flattened tone, the same kind you might use if you were talking to a primary care physician about intermittent hemorrhoids.

"Great. Great." I paused and then added, "So my place . . . Well, I just moved in. It's a little basic, but there's a guest bedroom and a large enough living space outside the kitchen and it's near the beach. Not a selling point right now but it will be great in a couple of months."

"Oh yeah, for sure. Fourth of July at the beach will be sick." He said that, too, in a monotone, like it was uncool to be enthusiastic.

I thought about the idea of having friends over for the holiday and felt, again, like jumping off my balcony. I'd rather spend the entire summer in my bedroom with the blinds closed than have to socialize with the group who'd known me and Joe as a couple. But I guess for most normal people, the idea of summertime drinks by the ocean was pretty appealing. And Zach might come with his own set of friends with whom I could slowly ingratiate myself.

"So, I'm visiting family in Massachusetts at the end of next week," I said. "But I could let you in some weekday, get you settled in, then leave you to spend the weekend here by yourself."

"Oh, yeah. That would be ideal, actually."

"How's Tuesday?" All I had on Tuesday was a meeting with the editor of the local paper who I'd written on LinkedIn. Since I hoped to have my ego massaged by people at a lowlier publication who'd be desperate for an international reporter to come on board, I thought I'd be in an ideal mental state to welcome Zach.

"Um." I could hear him opening a door and stepping inside somewhere, away from the ambient noise of the street. The door clicked shut behind him and the background was silent. "Wednesday would be better for me."

"Great!" I could hear my blood in my ears. "Wednesday it is. I'll send the address."

"Perfect. Hey, thanks again, Nat. You're a good friend." He was the only one who called me Nat, and I took a pathetic pride in it, like he'd made me his own.

"You too," I said, then realized that made no sense in context and flushed red for the whole load of nobody who could see me.

"Yeah . . . cool. So, see you soon. Bye." He hung up, and I was fully alone again. I sat, slightly sweaty, in the growing gloom of dusk. Then I got up and started washing the tomato sauce out of my dinner bowl. *Zach was coming. The prodigal boyfriend would finally return, just in time to rescue me from perpetual spinsterhood.* I was like the spunky heroine of a Jane Austen novel, poised on the brink of good luck, finally. Maybe this is how it was always meant to be.

.   .   .

THAT NIGHT, I LAY IN BED AND MASTURBATED TO THE IMAGE OF Zach turning up with his bags and seeing me for the first time in four years. "Wow," he said in my fantasy. "You look . . . Well, I don't mean to be inappropriate, but you look incredible."

"How would that be inappropriate?" I laughed, calm and collected, and pointed toward the kitchen. "Coffee or tea?"

"Oh, tea," he said, and that surprised me. I was dressed in a cute outfit that accentuated my curves, which were more pronounced in the fantasy, and I saw him sneak a peek at my butt while I stood at the stove. I half turned and looked him in the eye, raising an eyebrow as if to say, *Tea, really?*

"Yeah," he said, sighing. "You know, ever since my mom got sick, I've tried to stay off the ultracaffeinated stuff. It gives me anxiety."

I walked over with our mugs and sat beside him on the sofa, putting an arm around his shoulder. "I know it's been a long time," I said. "I hope seeing me isn't too much of an emotional strain after everything that's happened with your family."

"No," he said. "Actually, it's exactly what I need. I haven't been intimate with someone in a more than a year. When you're going through something like that, all meaning sort of falls away, you know?"

"I know," I said, stroking his hair back from his face. "God, I know."

We lay on the sofa together, clinging to each other, and I could feel our respective sadnesses cresting and falling like waves in the ocean. "Isn't it kind of cool that we have each other?" I whispered into his ear, and he said, "It's the best thing I could've asked for."

Then he kissed me. I knew we shouldn't do anything, and that I was kind of taking advantage of his vulnerability, but I kissed him back anyway. He was on top of me on the sofa, and I could feel his erection through his jeans. "We should take it slow," I whispered.

"I don't know if I can," he whispered back.

Then I was on my knees, unzipping his jeans as he moaned. When I started going down on him, he made a strangled noise in his throat and said, "Oh God . . . that feels so good . . . Nat, please, you're gonna make me come."

"What's so wrong about that?" I said, but I stopped for a moment and pulled my skirt up so I could sit on his rock-hard cock. We were so close, breathing each other's air, each of us so much better in bed than we had been when we'd last fucked.

"You're so fucking hot," he said, as I moved up and down on him. In the fantasy, we came together and I watched him orgasm from up close, his face uninhibited and lost in ecstasy; in my bed alone, I came with that picture at the forefront of my mind. I was so close to him that our foreheads were touching. I imagined him leaning his head against my chest as I felt the spasms in his cock slow to a stop inside me.

I wondered what it would be like if we were so spontaneous and hot for each other that I ended up pregnant. It would be like a movie. One day, Joe would move back to Brooklyn and he'd pass us in Prospect Park, Zach pushing the stroller while I jogged beside him and the baby, getting back into shape after the birth. My stomach would already be washboard flat and my boobs would be perky.

"Natasha, hey," Joe would say quietly, looking down at the baby. Maybe he'd be with two of our friends who had abandoned me after the divorce. Unable to help themselves, they'd get on their knees and start cooing over the adorable kid.

"Hey," I'd say with a little smile. Zach would lean over the stroller and offer his hand, introducing himself, looking at me like: *Who even is this dude?*

"Oh, this is Joe," I'd say, like he could be anyone.

"You said your ex didn't want kids," Joe would mutter quietly.

I'd shrug lightly, unencumbered by emotional baggage. I'd been through so much since the divorce, and having a baby had made me realize how petty journalism was and how stupid the whole controversy around my article had been. I worked at an arts magazine, where Zach was the designer. I'd moved on.

"I guess a lot of us don't know what we want when we're young," I'd say. "All I can say is that he's a wonderful father now."

Joe, polite, would nod and step away, and Zach would tell him that we should all get coffee sometime. Then I'd raise one hand in a goodbye, and Joe would return the favor, and things would end like that: Hollywoodesque, poignant but perfect.

When we rounded the corner, I'd whisper to Zach that that was the man I used to be married to, and we definitely *shouldn't* get coffee sometime, and he'd go, "Oh! Right! Ha, wow, listen to my dumb ass asking your ex-husband for coffee." We'd laugh conspiratorially; I'd briefly lean my head into the muscular space just underneath his shoulder. The baby would clap her hands and giggle.

ON TUESDAY, I TOOK THE TRAIN, THEN A BUS, TO A COWORKING SPACE in the Navy Yard where I'd agreed to meet the editor of the local paper. On the way, I flicked through its latest edition, which I'd procured for free from a box at the side of the road. "Community-Led Efforts Transform Vacant Lots into Local Co-op!" announced the front page. An image of the co-op (featuring four-dollar peaches from a sustainable farm in Bed-Stuy) was proudly displayed alongside the headline. Two pages in: "New Progressive Curriculum at PS 137 Reverses Decades of Racism by Spotlighting Black Heroes." *Yeah*, I thought. *That'll do it. A New York City borough solved racism with this one easy trick!*

At the building, I texted the editor and he came down to meet me by the elevator. He was ghostly Celtic white, with blond hair styled to look artfully unkempt.

"Natasha Bailey!" he said, in the tone one might reserve for saying "Mr. President!" on Inauguration Day, and energetically stuck out his hand.

"Max!" I said, because I'd forgotten his last name, and shook it.

"Come up, come up." He pressed his finger to a screen that called the elevator and we entered it together. It was surprisingly small. Our shoulders almost touched, an intimacy that was so unexpected that neither of us spoke for an awkward two minutes until the elevator doors reopened on the fourth floor.

"So," he said when we emerged into normal space again, "tell me why you decided to reach out."

The publication rented one floor of labyrinthine space, where most of the real estate comprised hanging baskets of plastic trailing plants and glass-doored meeting rooms with exposed brickwork. It was an aesthetic that would've been considered cutting-edge in 2010; so would the paper.

"Oh," I said, thinking about the meeting with BR, Bryce Taylor, and Eliza, "you know, just . . . looking for new challenges."

He nodded that quick, certain nod that established men in their fifties do, and continued walking without speaking. I supposed he wanted to hear something complimentary.

"Actually," I said, "to tell you the truth, I was in a particularly uninspiring meeting at work. Don't get me wrong—I love where I am—but we were discussing next steps and . . . well, they're so eager for me to take on a managerial role these days, and in many ways it makes sense, but I'm more of an on-the-ground person, someone who cares about drawing attention to injustice and the real reasons we all went into journalism."

I wasn't delivering what he wanted and I could tell. We zipped through the corridors until we ended up at a meeting room about as small as the elevator, where he sat down on one side of a tiny table and motioned for me to take a seat at the other. The door shut behind me with a quiet click; my back was rubbing against exposed brick. I could feel myself turning pink as I spoke, so I decided to pivot: "So I thought to myself, you know, where can I go that really preserves that for me? And honestly, you know, to tell the truth . . ." *Stop saying you're telling the truth, it sounds suspicious.* "I left work and saw your paper in the box by the subway, and I was just, I don't know, *inspired* to take one because of the headline."

"That's great!" His smile was unwavering, though I could tell he wasn't exactly taken by me. "Which headline?"

"Oh . . ." I gestured around with my hands. "I don't remember it exactly, to tell you the truth." *To tell you the truth, to tell you the truth.* "But it was just one of those that really makes you remember why you got into journalism, you know? Like, something that speaks about . . . advocacy and worthiness and . . . well, I know I said social justice before but it really is so important to expose corruption and . . . speak truth to power."

"So important," he echoed. He was looking down at his phone now, visibly bored.

"And I've worked on a lot of that stuff in the past!" I said, louder, in a sad attempt to claw back his attention. "I don't know if you've read any of my work on NYCHA and how so many of the residents were being completely ignored by the city, or I can send you my piece from a few years ago about the immigrant-led effort to transform Flushing into an international foodie destination."

"Yeah, do that," he said, looking up briefly from his phone and smiling again. "So let's go through some ideas for what you might write if you did join us. Just hypothetically speaking."

"Oh . . . right . . . of course." Stupidly, I hadn't imagined it would come to this, and had nothing prepared. Instead of being cornered in a small, brick-lined room like a convict in a nineteenth-century jail cell, I'd thought he might take me to a roastery nearby, buy me an expensive coffee, and tell me about how flattered he was that I'd even considered working for a publication like his. I mean, he edited a *freemium*, for God's sake. "Well, I have a lot of ideas," I continued, "but of course, I probably shouldn't share all of them, because, well, they might be considered the intellectual property of my paper, ha-ha . . ."

He looked at me like I was talking complete nonsense, which I was. I scanned my brain for literally any idea, but all I could think of was "Is THIS the Woman Hunter Biden Doesn't Want You to Know About?" and "Mayor of California Town Embezzled Money, Says He Stored It 'Where the Sun Don't Shine' in Bombshell Testimony." Luckily, I was saved by a redheaded woman with French braids tapping on the glass door then opening it almost immediately. It opened inward, so Max had to move his chair a couple of inches to allow her to pop her head in. The table was now cutting into my thighs.

"Max," she said quietly, "just wanted to run something by you." Then she looked at me and said, "Hi, Natasha. We heard you were coming in."

Who's we? I thought, but said, "Oh, hi. Natasha Bailey." Then I remembered she'd already said my name and felt like an idiot.

"Can it wait?" said Max. "I'm just getting into the good stuff with Natasha."

She gave him a look and said, "Not really," then brought her phone screen right up into his face. We were all frozen in place there for an agonizing thirty seconds; me against the wall, tapping my foot nervously against the leg of the chair; the woman with braids hovering over Max with her phone in front of his face and her finger marking something she wanted him to see; Max, stockstill, his eyes running across the screen and his smile slowly dissipating as they did.

"Thanks, Gwen," he said eventually, and she nodded and left without another word.

"As I was saying," I began, but he cut in: "I don't think there's going to be space for you at this publication, actually."

"Ah," I said. "Well, I thought this was just a . . . casual coffee, anyway." We were in a tug-of-war for my pride, and my palms were bleeding.

"Have you seen this before?" He tapped something into his phone, turned the screen around, and showed my swimmer article being tweeted out from my paper's account. Before I'd left my apartment that morning, I'd quietly gone into the system and edited some of the most offensive wording, hoping that nobody would notice. I could tell, as the blood drained to my feet, what must have happened instead: The system had marked it as a new article after the edits, and then automatically tweeted it. Hundreds of retweets and comments were stacking up again: *Can't BELIEVE this paper has the AUDACITY to market this one again!*; *This BETTER be a joke, omg*; *For anyone at risk of being retraumatized by the platforming of a groomer, I suggest you unfollow THIS account immediately.*

"Yes," I said slowly, "I have."

"I have to say," said Max, "this is my bad. I knew about the story, of course, but I presumed the writer wasn't . . . Well, I would've Googled you ahead of time, but it's been pretty busy around here covering the antigentrification initiative and the protests against Drag Queen Story Time at the Brooklyn Library."

"No, I probably should have . . . led with that," I said, as if I didn't have a massive vested interest in doing the opposite. Behind Max, I could see that Gwen was back again, hovering outside the door.

"I'm sure you're a nice enough person, Natasha," Max said, "but we have to be very careful. We get some financial support from the city, and everyone who works here has to get through a very thorough vetting process."

"Absolutely," I said. "I respect that."

"And the great thing is," he added, "that your own newspaper has elected to keep you around. But fundamentally, we're grown-ups here, you know?"

I nodded and swallowed. There was a painfully long silence, then I said, "Should I show myself out?"

"Oh, there's no need to do that!" he said. I looked up hopefully as he clicked open the door again. "It's a complicated floor plan. Gwen can show you to the exit."

WEDNESDAY—THE DAY OF ZACH'S ARRIVAL—CAME AROUND, AND I woke up with a faint sense of impending doom after a dream that I was giving birth to an enormous, ugly, screaming child. It turned out that the labor pains were stomach cramps from the tacos I'd ordered the night before and the screaming was coming from the kid across the hall, but the dream stayed with me as I ran around the apartment cleaning and vacuuming and moving things around so they would look pleasing to Zach's eye.

He didn't turn up until two o'clock, the middle of a shift for me, even though he'd said lunchtime. When the buzzer rang, I was drafting a news piece proclaiming that "opinions are divided" about a man who'd vowed on TikTok that he would never date a Republican. Some of the people with divided opinions had started circulating the man's address and encouraging people to turn up at his house "to show him what our Second Amendment rights look like."

As I waited for Zach to come up the stairs—the tiny steel elevator was out of service again—I crossed and uncrossed my legs under the table, antsy. Eventually, I heard his footsteps outside and his unobtrusive knock, and I got up slowly, so as not to look desperate.

"Oh, it's you!" I said when I opened the door, as if I'd opened it for some completely different, cooler reason, like maybe to go to an underground rave and drop some acid or visit one of my multiple friends with benefits.

"Hey," he said, dipping his head in greeting. He had an oversize hiking-style backpack instead of a normal suitcase. "Good to see you."

"Yeah . . . Long time no see . . ." Stupid clichés cycled through my head as I stepped back and let him into the living room. He set his backpack down on the couch without asking.

The last time I'd seen him, I'd been "picking up some things" from his apartment after our breakup with a vastly obvious ulterior motive. Of course, we'd ended up having sex. I'd suggested we try anal to show him what he might be missing—then, in the aftermath, I'd cried and told him how much I was going to miss him and that he was a good person. Afterward, I'd sent him a long text praising him for dumping me, telling him that I knew he could fight his demons (mild, trendily nihilistic depression) and that I "believed in him." His reply had been mortifyingly succinct: *Yeah, same :)*.

Six months later, when I'd just met Joe, Zach had popped up one more time in my texts. *Hey, I should've treated you better. Just thinking about it. No ulterior motive, despite the hour, I promise.* Sent at 3:06 a.m. Three nights later came the phone call. I'd kept him on the line for a while, savoring the moment, then wheeled out my one-line victory speech: "I have a boyfriend now." Back when saying that made me so fucking smug. I'd wished him well before hanging up.

Then it had been the usual stuff. Likes on social media, a funny comment here and there. Once, while Joe and I were living in London, I'd taken a picture of the cover of an artsy European magazine in a corner shop and texted it to him, feeling worldly. *Saw this and thought of you.* His reply: *heh, that does look up my alley. Hope you're well.*

Now I'd manifested him in my living room, the same way I'd manifested my terrible job. There's something so tantalizing about returning to someone who treated you like shit, like you can right a great historical wrong simply by existing in front of them. I was almost gleeful.

I offered him a coffee; he accepted; it gave me something to do with my hands. The chemistry was not as forthcoming as it had been in my fantasy, and I felt embarrassed enough about it that I had to turn away. As I stood in the kitchen, my back to him, I asked, "So what are you most excited about doing now that you're back here?" Declaring that New York was dead, he'd moved to Boston not long after we broke up, for that mysterious "arts job" that hadn't worked out. A lot of his pronouncements about New York—stuff I hadn't remotely agreed with—had come out of my mouth, like his opinions were a sexually transmitted disease. I'd said them when I was high on coke at the awards ceremony with Footsie Dalmatian, and I'd included them in my "Goodbye to New York" essay. I had no idea why.

"Yeah, well, like I said when we talked, not much. My mom's not doing great," he said.

"Oh yeah. Sorry."

"No, it's fine. And, you know, she got the diagnosis such a long time ago. It's kind of hard to believe that it might be running its course."

Even when Zach and I had been together—or not together, in his view—his mother was sick. She'd been given a terminal diagnosis two years before I even met him. Then followed one experimental trial after the other, the drugs eking out tiny bits of time, a bolstered immune response here and a genetically targeted vaccine there. Everything worked, until it didn't.

"They say it always comes as a surprise," I said, even though I had no idea if it was true. Who were they? Did they say that?

"Yeah. Also, you know . . . it was the right time to move. There was stuff in Boston it was probably best to leave behind." He gave a humorless little laugh, and I understood that he'd screwed over some naïve Bostonian girl the way he'd screwed me over, and now he was running away. I didn't want to dig any deeper, because this wasn't part of the Sad Boy fantasy I'd built for him, in which he'd become a sensitive artiste who'd almost entirely renounced sex after ending things with me. Ideally, his lovers of choice since then had been middle-aged divorcées he brought back to his place to "learn from." They were experienced in bed, sure, but also weepy and sagging at the joints, cellulite-ridden under a bad light. When we finally slept together again, he'd remember my small but perky breasts and my tight, muscular thighs and feel like he was coming home, but in a hot way.

"Sounds tough," I said.

"Yeah." He sighed while unzipping his bag. "It is what it is."

I made the coffee and served it in an I ♥ NY mug I'd bought from a vendor on the Brooklyn Bridge when my mother was visiting and wanted to get a magnet for Miriam. That was back when being performatively ironic in front of my mother was one of my favorite hobbies, like I was stretching out the distance between us by making everything she did seem passé. *I'm your daughter, but I've already lapped you in this.* Maybe I did need therapy.

"Welcome back," I said, placing the mug in his hands with ceremony, but he didn't even glance at its insignia, instead just raising his eyebrows slightly in thanks.

"So I'll probably need the room for three months or so," he said. "The rent can't be that high on a place like this, right?"

I kept the smile pasted on my face through the insult. "No," I said. "Much less than you'd pay in Bushwick or Greenpoint, that's for sure. I'd be happy if you can chip in a thousand a month—if you need to stay longer than a couple weeks." It was way below what I should have been charging to cover half the mortgage.

"Oh, great." He nodded like he thought that was all it was worth anyway. "That works for me. And I won't bother you, you know—happy to keep to myself."

"Of course," I said, "but it'd be nice to actually hang out after all this time. And you've been through so much." I paused. Was I going to do it? I was going to do it. I leaned in and said, "Would you like a hug?" As I did, I positioned myself on the sofa beside him, my arms half outstretched, my face arranged in the way I always used to arrange it for him: slightly coy, slightly concerned—part matriarch, part coquette.

He looked back at me, and I remembered the time I'd come home from work and he'd gently unhooked my bra in the hallway, the way he'd kissed my neck and then carried me as I wrapped my legs around him into the bedroom of his shared apartment, the way we'd kept quiet so his roommate wouldn't hear our muffled moans.

"I'm good, thanks," he said.

TEN

I FLEW BACK TO NANTUCKET FOR MIRIAM'S BIRTHDAY AND, APPAR-
ently, my own mental health. ("If she can't rely on her own sister
to take a one-hour flight on her *birthday*, then who *can* she rely on,
Natasha? Besides, I think you need your family right now.") A fine
mist of rain had already settled in the crevices of our sweaters and
shoes, but the deck was warm under Mom's newly acquired heat
lamp. I promised myself I wouldn't mention Zach.

"You're taking the divorce very well, all things considered," said
Mom, apropos of nothing, while pouring me a glass of natural rosé.

"Thanks for bringing it up right away," I said.

"Oh, come on, you know I don't mean it like that. I'm just glad
you seem a little brightened up." Mom took a sip of her first glass
of wine, condensation clouding the side. "Anyway. Isn't this nice?
Just the three girls together. And my Miriam Rachel another year
older—I can hardly believe it." We clinked glasses. I didn't know if
Mom was drinking more or less these days; I couldn't even really
bring myself to ask my sister.

"Last time you were here, Natasha," Mom continued, warming
to her theme, "we really were a bit worried about you. Weren't we,
Miri? Pretty concerned."

"Oh, I don't know . . ." Miriam avoided my gaze, fixing her eyes
over Mom's shoulder at a sparrow landing in the birdhouse.

"No, I mean, you should be grateful you have relatives who
care," Mom continued. I could tell the forecast for this conversation

was mixed, with strong possibilities of soul-sapping hail. "You've been down and out, just like a lot of people in this world. We're here, and we have your back. And we also have the right to tell you when you're behaving like an asshole." She leaned forward on her wooden garden chair and gave me a playful shove, which I didn't yield to. I hated this game.

"Anyway," said Miriam, seeming to sense the atmospheric disturbance, "how do you like New York these days, Tash? Does it feel different after your time in London?"

"The same as I liked it before," I said. "It hasn't changed." Then I wondered if I was being a bit prickly and added, "Having the new apartment, it's really . . . nice. The area is only going to grow in popularity. And it's great to have my feet on the ground, to feel like I've put down some roots, you know?" I was just cycling through aphorisms that had no bearing on my actual experience, but whatever. Maybe one day I'd believe the apartment was a good decision and "putting down roots" was something I cared about.

"Miriam's thinking of moving there," said Mom with a big grin, refilling her glass. Miri had a shy smile on her face.

"What?" I blinked in a deliberate show of confusion.

"Yes, well, don't look so flustered!" Mom said. "She's hardly the first twentysomething to have her head turned by the Big Apple."

"Yeah, no, I get that," I said, taking a cautious sip of wine, savoring the tannins. "I just . . . Do you have a job?"

Miriam shrugged lightly, her delicate shoulders outlined by a fitted cyan sweater that looked suspiciously like cashmere. "Not yet. But I think you kind of need to *be there* to get the good opportunities, right? Like, there's no point trying to find a job in New York from Nantucket."

"I mean . . . I guess." I felt like I'd been ambushed, but I knew it was foolish to act like I owned New York City. *It's her birthday, it's her birthday.* "I can help you with your résumé if you like."

"Mrs. Downey from the flower show said she has a cousin who could get her an internship at a marketing agency," said Mom.

"We all had a talk about it, actually. She came for dinner, and, you know, one thing led to another."

"You can't stay in my apartment," I said, without letting my mother finish.

There was a short silence. "I didn't think I would anyway," said Miriam eventually. "I would ideally live somewhere a little more . . . you know."

I know what, Miriam? I felt like saying. Instead, I went with: "So, you float around Nantucket for years after dropping out of school and now you get an internship in the big city? That's a pretty cool way in. Wouldn't have spent so much time working my ass off if I knew there were shortcuts."

"Natasha," Mom said in a warning tone, but I held up my hand and continued: "No, no, I'm making a point here. You *know* how much I worked for that job—keeping up my GPA, all those extracurriculars, then the years paying my dues in journalism. Late nights, early mornings, twenty-four-hour shifts—"

"Yeah, and then you fucked it all up!" said Miriam, flushing red.

"Girls, girls!" Mom cut in, but I could tell from her face that she was loving the drama. "Listen, Tash, none of this detracts from your many achievements."

Miriam was getting up to leave.

"Sit down," I said. "Sit down, okay?"

"I don't get why you can never let anything be about me," Miri muttered. "Not even on the one day of the year—"

"Listen, Miriam." I put my glass down and leaned across the table. "You think I enjoy being the center of attention? You think I like emails telling me that being raped would teach me a lesson?" I saw the microsecond in which the word "raped" caused ripples of shock across Mom's and Miriam's faces before they restored themselves to guarded impassivity, and I felt the thrill of power. "You think I enjoy having lost literally everything I built? And all my friends? Believe me, all I want is for someone else to take the limelight. Step right up! What I object to—although not as much as you think—is when my little sister, who didn't do *any* of the years of toil I poured in, suddenly gets handed my life by Mom as if it's a fun little birthday present."

"It's not like that and you know it." Mom put her hand on top of mine, but I pulled it out quickly. "No one's saying Miriam's becoming a big-shot journalist like you. She just wants the chance to move to New York and try out a job—like basically every young person on this island! Where do you think all her friends went?"

"Mom, I don't think you understand," I said, restraining myself, and then all three of us sat at the table, avoiding one another's gaze. I was near tears, and Miriam was too.

"I always just wish you two girls would get along," Mom began, but Miri cut in—"Oh, will you *stop it* with that"—in an impressively venomous way. Unfortunately for her, it was just venomous enough to make our mother switch sides.

"You know, Miriam," she said, taking a gulp of wine, "your sister does have a point. And it's better to acknowledge that—"

"Jesus Christ." Miriam was out of her chair again, ready to storm back inside.

"It's better to acknowledge that," Mom continued, louder now, "than to pretend that things have been perfectly equal all the time. But it doesn't mean—"

"I'm tired of this," said Miri. "I'm an adult. I can do what I want. I don't need permission from you to do it, Mom, and Natasha, I *especially* don't need permission from you." She walked into the house and slammed the back door behind her.

"Real mature," I yelled after her. "Real testament to your *adult character* there."

"Hey," said Mom, leaning over the table to talk in a quieter voice to me. "Let's cut it out. Between you and me, she's been like this all week. She always gets this way around her birthday."

"Well, she can afford to sit around and be ruled by her emotions," I said, still mad. "It's not like she has to get up for work in the morning."

"That may be true, but it's not very nice."

"Oh, I stopped caring about being *very nice* a very long time ago." I downed my rosé and poured myself another glass; Mom grabbed the bottle and served herself the last bit. "Anyway," I added, emboldened by the alcohol, "who's going to pay her rent?"

Mom looked down and I could see she really didn't want to tell me. Then she looked up again and said, "You chose what you chose with *your* life. Don't take it out on Miri."

"I see. So Miri, who wants to live somewhere a *little bit more . . . you know* in New York, gets what she wants," I said. "Can I have you pay my rent in a better part of the city? Because if that's what's on the table—"

"Tash. I've been more than fair with you. More than fair. And let's not forget you *own* your place." Mom paused, then continued. "Anyway, you never know. It could be nice for you to have her around. Sisterly nights on the town . . ."

"Ah, I see now. Miri is actually living for free in New York City for *my* benefit."

"You have a real talent for making everything into a negative." I could see from Mom's face that she was tipsy now, and if I wasn't careful we'd be speeding past Generalization Town and hitting the end of the line at Personality Assassination Cove.

I thought about Miriam's directionless life, how she worshipped at the altar of the basic bitch in a room filled with cosmetics that said things like "Nama-Stay in Bed" and "I Can't Adult Today" on them. Somehow she was going to leapfrog over me, get herself an apartment on a fruit street in Brooklyn Heights and probably marry some banker looking for a low-ambition girl to make his sellout life more bearable. I'd be the sad aunt traveling to their upstate second home for the holidays while their perfect, mermaid-haired children got chased around by an expensive nanny. Every advantage I had had over anyone else was slowly being eroded.

"Look, I'm sorry." Mom leaned in, suddenly performatively contrite. "You know, living with your sister all this time has been . . . trying. She wants everything but she doesn't want to work for it. And I know you'll say I shouldn't say this, but she's a lot like her father. He seemed like something at some point but then he wasn't. A talented young man, yes, with big dreams, but ultimately *lazy*. I knew he'd take one look at a baby and faint backward, you know? Just a"—she gesticulated like she was trying to find a word in her head, then settled on—"a big flaccid jellyfish of a man!"

Her phrasing was so absurd and vaguely sexual that I started to laugh, then she caught my eye and we both broke into ridiculous, tipsy cackling. It continued until I was doubled over and she was resting her head on her hands over the table, laughing and laughing and laughing. It was that kind of borderline hysteria we'd engaged in outside Dr. Reese's office, the kind that erupts into the air like oil after you dig down too far into psychologically unhealthy depths.

"More wine?" said Mom.

"Sure! But I need to pee first," I said, and followed her inside, where she went to the kitchen and I walked in the opposite direction to the bathroom. Miriam was inside, cross-legged on the sofa with a face that told me she'd heard everything we'd said.

"I knew *she* was like that," she hissed at me as I made my way down the hall, "but I thought better of *you*."

I looked back at her, pink-faced. "Oh come on," I said. "We were only kidding around." I realized I was drunk; I hadn't eaten anything since early in the morning, when I'd arrived at JFK for my flight to Nantucket.

"Come join us outside again! Please? I traveled all this way to see you!" I added, and I knew I was taking on the role of our mother, the inebriated, inappropriate one who acted like anyone she'd deliberately offended was just uptight, oversensitive, or petulant. In this moment, Mom and I were a team, but I couldn't quite track exactly how it had happened.

"Yeah, no thanks," Miri said, and went up the stairs to her room. I heard her shut her door quietly behind her with the resignation of someone who knew exactly what this family was like.

IN THE MORNING, MIRIAM KNOCKED ON MY HALF-OPEN DOOR WITH an outstretched elbow, a mug of coffee in each hand. "I think . . . we shouldn't let Mom come between us," she said haltingly, clutching her caffeinated olive branch.

"I guess that makes sense," I replied. I let her inside and she crawled into bed beside me like we were kids on a Saturday morning again. Because of our age difference, Miriam had always been the "baby sister" rather than a partner in crime, but it wasn't a dynamic I always minded. I'd used her as my judgment-free pass into juvenile antics, for instance, a shield against growing up. On a trip to Disney World when she was six and I was twelve, I'd enjoyed pretending I also believed Mickey Mouse wasn't just a guy in a costume, and I'd gone on all the little kids' rides with glee. During weekends at home, I'd sit with her under a blanket on the couch and watch pleasantly mind-numbing cartoons when my friends were concerning themselves with interpersonal dramas involving boys. I didn't lose my virginity until I was twenty-two, lagging behind my peers but staying right on track with my much younger sister.

"I didn't think me moving to New York would upset you," Miri said, leaning against the headboard and blowing cautiously on her own cup of coffee. She had her silky hair tied back in two braids, while mine was matted and would soon require painful disentanglement with a brush.

"It doesn't, really," I said and shrugged. "I don't know. It's not my place to tell you what to do. I just hope you're making the right decision."

"What else am I going to do?" she asked, then, in a low voice, added, "Stay here with Mom?" We caught each other's eyes and I got the message.

When we were younger and Mom had one of her episodes—usually after a drunken fight with a short-term boyfriend—I'd stay in my bedroom, reading or painting my nails, and do my best to block it out. But then, inevitably, I'd hear my sister's halting footsteps outside my door and be drawn out onto the upstairs landing.

One particularly loud one happened just before Christmas when Miri was ten and I was sixteen. I was navigating teenage relationships and imagining my future at college; Miriam was up past her bedtime in cartoon pajamas. When Mom yelled, "And that's why that bitch left you *way before me!*" Miriam and I both leaned over the banisters, glimpsing only the shadow play of a domestic drama happening in the kitchen.

"What are they fighting about *now?*" Miri asked me, wide-eyed and pink-cheeked, a smear of toothpaste dried at the side of her mouth.

I shrugged. "Why do you even care?" I was thinking about Louis Dayton, prom dresses, whether Lisa had really been fingered by her older boyfriend during a free period.

"Why do you not?" she said, and I could tell she wanted more from me—or probably actually wanted whatever she couldn't get from our mother. I wasn't interested in giving it to her though.

The fight continued below until eventually the latest boyfriend's voice said, "Fuck this," the shadows became figures, and the front door slammed. We watched Mom melodramatically back up against the wall and then sink down to her knees on the carpet before beginning to sob loudly.

"Go to bed," I hissed to Miri.

"No," she said, padding toward the stairs in her chipmunk slippers. "I want to check on Mommy."

I sighed and then grabbed her by the pajama sleeve. "I said go to bed," I whispered. "Listen . . . you'll get in trouble. It's way past your bedtime. I'll go down, okay?"

"Okay, but *will* you?"

"I will."

She stood tentatively in the hallway for a moment or two, but after I raised my eyebrows meaningfully at her and pointed at her bedroom door, she went back to bed. I stayed on the landing for a minute or two, watching Mom wipe her tears on the back of her hand before gathering herself and walking toward the kitchen, toward another bottle of wine. Then, weighing each step so I could make sure Miri wouldn't hear me, I retreated back to my own bedroom.

Now, with Miriam in my bed, her face looked so unchanged from that night that I could hardly believe any time had passed. Her expressions hadn't become more guarded with age.

"She's not . . . sick, is she?" I said after a pause, because I wanted reassurance that it wasn't our responsibility to talk about Mom's problems with alcohol or the way she conducted herself. Miri was the watchman these days; I was a remote employee at best.

"No," said Miriam lightly, pulling one of her hair elastics out and then rebraiding one side. Her skin was so opaque, like she'd been drawn in a studio; mine showed layers of blemishes and sun damage, burst capillaries and the shadows of teenage acne. I felt a fresh swell of injustice that she'd had everything easier than me, but I wrestled it down.

"She's just a bit of an asshole," Miriam concluded, smiling at me in a knowing way.

"I guess," I said, setting my coffee on the nightstand. *An asshole who keeps you in golden handcuffs.* "But she's our asshole. Does that matter?"

Miri shrugged. "I guess. We could all get breakfast?"

WE BROUGHT MOM COFFEE FROM THE POT MIRIAM HAD MADE AND talked about how we'd never let anything come between us again, making the same promises we'd made many times before. Mom was slightly hungover and a little irritable but cheered up when we suggested a walk downtown. I poured her coffee into a thermos and the three of us navigated the short distance to Main Street, with Mom stopping to talk to neighbors about their empty flower baskets every so often.

"The daffodils will soon be out," she kept saying, while nudging my shoulder. "Next time you come, they'll be all along here. Do you remember?" It annoyed me but not justifiably.

Miriam insisted on getting herself a giant chocolate chip cookie from the bakery on the corner. As she did the usual back-and-forth with the guy behind the open-air counter—"I don't know where you put it," he said, as he put her latest baked good into a greaseproof bag. "It's all in my big toe," she joked in a folksy kind of way.—I leaned on the side of the building and zoned out while Mom talked about the town's Fourth of July preparations, already being made months in advance. The bakery had a decal promising FRESHLY MADE, JUST FOR YOU! on its side, which struck me as a particularly egregious example of a barefaced lie. Then I considered that the thought was funny in a sardonic way—the kind of humor that appealed to Zach—so I pulled out my phone and texted him: *Hey, how are you settling in? Just saw this piece of aggressive capitalist doublespeak in Nantucket and thought you might appreciate it.* I attached a picture of the bakery sign.

"You're texting a boy," said Mom, smiling knowingly at me.

"I'm not," I said, shoving my phone back into my pocket. I'd said too much to her about Zach, and now I was worried I might jinx it. But then my phone buzzed and I couldn't resist extricating it to read his reply: *lol. You've gone high concept.*

His instant response meant that he'd dropped whatever he was doing to type. But something about his tone bothered me. It was like he hadn't quite understood what I was saying or didn't want to enter into a conversation, not even answering my question about settling in. Was the speed of his reply a sign of wanting to mollify me as soon as possible so he could get back to something or someone more scintillating than me?

That kind of advertising primes you to live in an unreal world, I typed, then I looked at what I'd written and deleted it. What was I

doing, writing an academic thesis? I remembered something I'd
been told by a friend who did stand-up gigs in Brooklyn: *If you have
to explain the joke, the problem isn't the audience; it's your material.* I'd
had one chance to look witty and I'd screwed it up. His reply didn't
invite more.

Then my phone buzzed again. *Settling in great thanks. Been on
the balcony—surprisingly nice out there. Put a chair out there, hope
you don't mind. Tried the bodega—10/10 egg n cheese. Hope yr enjoying the island.* It was slightly impersonal, but undeniably comprised
multiple sentences. I imagined Zach leaving through the apartment door, going down the concrete steps and out into the street,
standing at the deli counter in the bodega, sitting on a bench on the
boardwalk overlooking the sea as he pensively chewed an egg and
cheese sandwich. I inserted myself into the image for a moment,
conjuring up a weekend in the future where I might wave at him
casually as I left the building, catch up to him, take a seat beside
him. When the weather got warmer, we could sit there in the early
morning and watch college kids lug their coolers of pineapple White
Claw down to the beach, and that's when I'd tell him about my ill-
fated marriage. He'd talk me through the final days of his mother's
illness. We'd bond. We'd get closer. We'd take it slow.

"Hey, do you want a bite of my cookie?" said Miriam, skipping
away from the bakery with her hippie-ish dress billowing softly behind her like she was in a commercial for J. fucking Crew.

"No, thanks," I said.

"Tasha's distracted," said Mom in a singsong voice.

"No I'm not." As I stuffed my phone back into my pocket, I could
feel my cheeks getting slightly pink and willed my overstimulated
blood vessels to calm, stop showing me up in front of my family.

"She's texting a *boy*," Mom continued, laughing, "and taking
photos of the *bakery*. Are you planning on bringing someone home
with you, Tashie?"

"Wow, I really can't do anything around here without an audience, huh?" I said.

"She'll tell us in her own good time," said Miriam in a deliberately loud, teacherly voice.

Mom laughed as we continued on down the street, and Miri whispered in my ear, "Tell me everything when we get home."

ON MY LAST NIGHT IN NANTUCKET, THE NEIGHBORS CAME OVER FOR dinner. They'd just moved into the blue house next door after the previous occupant had been transferred to an old folks' home by a son with dollar signs in his eyes.

"They're lesbians," Mom informed me in a confidential tone, while peeling shrimp for a paella. "I just want them to feel welcome." The island wasn't exactly a hotspot of homophobia, and almost every house on the street installed rainbow flags on their porches during Pride Month, but it was important to her to think of herself as a bastion of liberal sensibilities, so I did her a kindness by shutting up.

Sasha and Liz were the kind of functional, early-forties couple that puts observers at instant ease. Sasha, who was very short and very extroverted and had a pixie cut, bounced around the kitchen, chopping strawberries for dessert and sweeping errant grains of rice from the countertop with her hand while Mom stirred the paella.

"You don't have to do that, Sasha, please, sit down," Mom said, but I could tell she was enjoying it.

Liz, who was larger and dressed in a colorful kaftan, sat at the table sedately and watched Sasha dance around the kitchen with a gentle expression. "She's always like this in a new place," she told me, pouring me a glass from the bottle of red wine in the middle of the table. "Really it's just an excuse to get a look inside other people's cabinets."

"I heard that!" Sasha said.

"Don't pretend like it isn't true, then," Liz shot back, and winked at me.

"It's not what you think," said Sasha, turning and leaning her elbows on the kitchen island so she was facing me and Liz. "I just love interior design. I'm always looking for excuses to get Liz to let me run wild in that kitchen. Ever since we bought the place, I've just thought—well, no offense to the previous owner, but there's a lot we could do in there."

"It's *fine*," said Liz, shaking her head but smiling.

"Sure, it's fine, but am I okay with fine? Or am I aiming for *exceptional*?" Sasha twirled back around in the kitchen and pointed to one of Mom's favorite features, a wine cabinet sunk into the floor. It had cost a lot to install but she'd been convinced by a salesman one summer. "*This* is exceptional."

"I'll think about it," was Liz's response, friendly but firm. I could tell they were playing roles for us, bouncing off each other a little, putting on a show of conflict that would never progress past friendly banter. *What are we like? Old ball and chain!* Joe and I had occasionally done this act at friends' houses as well, so secure in our partnership that we could joke about marital rifts as if they were as likely as a lightning strike.

When we'd finished prepping the paella, Liz got up to help Sasha grab the cutlery, and I scrolled idly through social media on my phone. People's images and videos cycled past: Ellie and Jake in Prospect Park with Charlotte Louisa in a stroller; a college friend coming to the end of a marathon; a reporter colleague sharing a feature she'd written about women in South America launching an art collective. Then I saw it, in the background of an Instagram story posted by a friend we'd made in London: Joe, the man I'd once stood up with in front of a hundred people and pledged to spend the rest of my life with, sitting at a picnic table in a pub in Islington, his arm around a pretty girl in sunglasses. I knew what that arm meant.

"Not very sociable," said Miriam over my shoulder, arriving in the kitchen after spending the hour of food prep doing her hair in her room. She'd styled it into effortless-looking waves and outlined her eyes in a subtle, shimmery brown.

I turned my phone over and put it on the table. "Not very respectful of people's privacy," I shot back.

"As if I care about you creeping at your ex-boyfriend or whatever," she said. I stuck out a leg to kick her but she'd already bounced over to say an overenthusiastic hello to the neighbors. Under the harsh light of the stove, where Liz was calmly putting down the pan they'd used for melting sugar, I saw Miriam throw her arms around Sasha and Sasha reciprocate. How were they all such good friends? They'd only just moved in! I sat at the table watching them, feeling like the ghost at the feast.

WHEN WE SAT DOWN TO DINNER, MIRI ANNOUNCED SHE WAS GOING on a date later that evening.

"Not with the ice cream boy?" said Sasha.

"No," said Miriam, who'd clearly shared more about her love life with the neighbors than with me. "This one's with the boat guy."

"I can't keep up," said Liz.

"Oh, I've stopped trying," said Mom, serving her a dollop of paella with a gigantic wooden serving spoon. "It's these dating apps—people nowadays pick out boyfriends and girlfriends like pieces of candy. It leads to a crisis of commitment."

"Hot take, Mom," said Miriam, rolling her eyes.

Sasha made a valiant attempt to redirect the conversation, cutting in with: "Do you have a partner, Natasha?" *Perfect.*

"I actually got married a year and a half ago," I said, keeping my eyes on my food. "I met him on an app too. And he told me after our second date that he wanted to marry me. No crisis of commitment there."

Liz inclined her head toward her shoulder, fixed me kindly with her dark eyes. "How romantic."

"Yeah," I said. "I mean, he was pretty romantic in general. On our first anniversary, we spent the day winning arcade prizes at Coney Island and he proposed on the beach."

"Plenty of beaches around here—just a hint!" said Sasha, elbowing Liz playfully.

"Everyone said we wouldn't last," I continued, ignoring her, picking compulsively at the psychic wound. "They told us not to do every-thing so fast, but relocating to London was much easier as a married couple. And we were happy." Mom had tried to talk me out of getting married after knowing him for only a couple of years, but I'd thought she was just jealous I'd found a man willing to walk me down the aisle when all she'd done was find men willing to knock her up and leave. I hadn't put it quite like that when I said it out loud, obviously.

"People!" said Sasha, throwing up her arms and gesturing to the sky. Liz laughed and rolled her eyes and took mixed salad onto her plate from a large serving bowl.

"And what's he up to at the moment?" said Liz. Over her shoulder, Miriam was staring at me with an accusing gaze.

"Oh, we're divorced," I said. "I mean, the final papers haven't come through yet but everything's been agreed. Turns out transat-lantic relationship breakdowns are complicated." There was an un-comfortable silence with which I felt compelled to fill: "He has a new girlfriend."

"Oh. What a bastard. I'm sorry." Liz leaned out a large, soft arm to rest on my shoulder.

"It's not what you think," said Mom, finishing off her glass with a ceremonious swig. "She cheated on him."

Liz slowly retracted her arm and looked at the floor.

I MADE IT THROUGH THE REST OF DINNER, BUT AFTER WE'D SAID goodbye at the door to Sasha and Liz, I gave Mom a look that said I was no longer speaking to her and went upstairs.

"Natasha, don't ruin a nice evening by being oversensitive!" she yelled after me, but I didn't reply.

The next morning, I ordered a cab to take me to the airport early, when I knew she and Miriam would still be nursing their hangovers. My flight wasn't till the late afternoon, but I was done with their bullshit. Then I paced around the small building, bored and irritated, taking tiny bites out of a stale croissant I'd bought from the only store that was open.

When I boarded the plane a few hours later, my phone buzzed. I hoped it was Zach, but it was my mother, full of righteous self-pity: *I am by no means a perfect mom and I'm sorry I can't be one for you. But I try my best.* I thought about replying: *Well, your best clearly isn't good enough,* but instead I turned my phone to airplane mode.

As we rose through the clouds on our initial ascent, I considered whether "I try my best" was even remotely true. It seemed to me that despite her single parenthood, Mom had been pretty lucky in life: she'd got what she wanted, time and time again, without having to compromise. Doing your best usually entailed some hardship or sacrifice. And she'd always seemed a little put out by my happiness with Joe, and a little bit happy when it all went wrong. "He seems very . . . closed off," she'd say to me after each Nantucket visit, during which she would inevitably try to entice him into an argument about politics or child-rearing, and he'd placidly respond that he could "see her point" and "didn't feel strongly either way." Yes, Joe always took the path of least resistance. By the end of the flight, I wasn't convinced Mom had done her best; in fact, I was pretty sure she'd spent a lot of time during my childhood and adulthood doing her absolute worst.

When I walked out onto the concourse at JFK, she texted again: *You & Miri are the joys of my life. Without you, I would have nothing.* It was a guilt trip with the sole aim of provoking a reaction, but I had a disturbing thought: she was right. Perhaps you aren't supposed to be disturbed by statements like that. Perhaps they're supposed to give you warm fuzzies, rather than grip you by the throat. Maybe Mom's inputs were fine but my outputs were wrong. Maybe life had been really hard for her, and she'd made the best of it because she loved us. What was the truth? Sometimes I felt like a scuba diver hit by a wave, thrown off course in the middle of the ocean, with no way of knowing which way was up and which way was down.

ELEVEN

WHEN I OPENED THE DOOR, THE FIRST THING I NOTICED WAS THAT the apartment was a mess. Dotted around the kitchen and living room were deli wrappers and unwashed bowls, and Zach was sitting on the sofa under a blanket I didn't recognize, a laptop balanced on his knees.

He looked up from his phone without surprise when I walked in and said, with a half smile, "I was just reading about your controversy."

"Oh yeah?" I said uneasily. For a moment I thought he meant my dinner with Sasha and Liz, but then I realized he obviously meant the newsworthy controversy, the "reporter disgraces herself in front of the whole world then gets dumped by her husband" controversy, not a minor family drama.

"Yeah," he said, extending his toes along the sofa. "I guess it never really hit my radar in Boston."

The idea that anyone in the world might not have read every detail of my humiliation in stark and gory detail was alien to me. I walked down the street assuming that most of the passersby held views on my life, few of them sympathetic. The response on social media had been so overwhelming that I'd concluded it must have reached people in the billions, and certainly included all the ones I'd ever slept with. To comfort myself while the storm was still ongoing, I had lain in bed thinking about North Korea: nice, isolated North Korea, where people couldn't access the internet as we knew it.

North Koreans were probably tending to fields and strolling around cities, cooking dinner in their houses or watching bootlegged movies on thumb drives passed across the border while casting furtive glances over their shoulders for informers, and none of them were thinking about me and my divorce and my feature-length confession of an inappropriate dalliance with a beloved British athlete. At one point during my sequestered two weeks in Footsie Dalmatian's Highgate townhouse, I'd Googled flights to Pyongyang. You could get there pretty easily via Beijing, but you had to fly Air Koryo, an airline that exclusively used repurposed Russian aircraft from the Soviet era. I'd decided against it.

Yet here was Zach acting like he'd been living a completely normal life within the borders of the United States without any knowledge of my disgrace at all. He had acquaintances who were extremely online. He had an internet connection himself. He even had a couple of social media accounts. Did this mean redemption was possible?

Zach was fully smiling at me now, like the whole thing was a big joke. His hair had been different when we were together; these days, it was shorter, especially at the sides, and tucked behind his ears. I'd loved being able to run his longer hair through my fingers, but I had to admit it looked better this way. I registered the shallow lines around his eyes that hadn't been there five years ago. Everyone was getting older. Time was so close to running out.

Then I looked back at him with seriousness and said, "You know, in some ways that whole thing kind of . . . destroyed my life."

He shrugged, as if he didn't think that could really be true. Then he set his laptop gently down on the coffee table and said, "I didn't know you were married."

"Yeah? Well, I'm not anymore."

"Feels like an important interlude, though."

"I guess." The sun was setting and it was getting darker in the room, but neither of us made any move to turn on a light besides the screen of the computer. I both liked and disliked how he referred to my marriage as an "interlude." It downplayed its importance, of

course, but it also suggested that something better, more conse-
quential, had happened before and would happen after it.

"Honestly, Zach," I said, moving to perch on the arm of the
sofa, and I savored saying his name for a second: it felt strangely
intimate. "I don't know why I got married in the first place. He was
great, and I felt like I was living in a rom-com, and it all seemed so
easy and so different from anything I'd ever known. And everyone
kept saying, *You'll know it's right when it's easy.* And I forgot that I'm
the one who always makes things hard. I didn't take any responsibility, I didn't make any changes, and I kind of just thought he'd
save me and change me and protect me from all the stupid shit in
my head. And he didn't."

That was a lot. I knew it definitely, probably, likely qualified as
"intense" and "too much." The problem was that ever since I lost
Joe to my own idiocy and Ellie to her new baby, I had had nowhere
to put the weird parts of myself. Useless information leaked out of
my every orifice.

Zach held my gaze for a couple seconds, like he was considering whether to share something with me, then said, "No, yeah. I
hear you." *That's it?* Then, after a few seconds: "Hey, did you ever
do your Myers-Briggs Type?"

I rolled my eyes. "Yes, I've been bored on the internet before."

"Just thought it could provide some insight. I found that it
helped me a lot."

"Myers-Briggs is astrology for men," I said.

"Sounds like something a Sagittarius would say."

"Ha-ha." I rolled my eyes, but in a way that said I was okay with
the teasing. I wasn't even a Sagittarius. "You know, a lot of people
have told me a lot of different things would help me in the months
since my life collapsed. Therapy. Sound baths. Crypto. A particularly
vicious game of pickleball with my mother and her retiree friends."

"And did any of them work?"

"No, I don't think so. Brenna *killed* me on the court. And I'm
now officially long on Dogecoin, but I don't feel any different. I

suppose therapy papered over a few cracks, if I'm being generous to the backwater psychotherapist my mother found."

He laughed. "Therapy is such a scam. You *can't* say Myers-Briggs is astrology if you think microaggressions and gaslighting are real."

"I can't, huh?"

"Imagine trying to explain the concept of gaslighting to a medieval peasant. They'd think you were completely insane."

"Well, they were probably pretty busy dying from the plague or lack of adequate sanitation."

"Exactly! They had to work out pretty fast what their real priorities were. I honestly think our overactive brains come up with this shit just to entertain us because we're not out chasing lions anymore."

"I feel like the lions might've been chasing us, to be honest."

He laughed. "Fair enough. Antelope, then. Once upon a time, we'd be fashioning spears and hunting for the tribe. These days, we sit in our hermetically sealed dollar-making chambers and come up with terms for why someone annoyed us. It's honestly kind of ironic hearing about microaggressions so often from people who commit macroaggressions against human society on a daily basis just by living the way they do."

"I guess." Did I?

"Just try the Myers-Briggs thing. To satiate my curiosity." *Zach was curious about me, huh?* "Besides, at the point where you're being creamed by retirees on the pickleball court, what else do you have to lose?"

"Don't overdo the flattery. I can barely take it."

"Oh come on, what do you want me to say? That you're miles more intelligent than most people in the world and so much of the criticism aimed at you is rooted in jealousy? You've heard all that from a thousand guys like me." I hadn't, of course, and even though some sensible part of me recognized this as a fuckboy tactic, I flushed briefly at his implication that men routinely fell over themselves to compliment me. In our entire marriage, once the wedding day was in the rearview mirror, I don't think Joe—routinely lovely, ever-so-slightly self-involved Joe—had even so much as told me he liked my shirt. He wasn't needy and insecurely attached like me; he was undemonstrative, steady, straightforward, the son of a guy who quietly went out to buy the halloumi. Before I could respond to Zach, he added: "You know, I don't think I realized how much I missed this."

I breathed into the suddenly still air. *Was it all going to be this easy?* It had escalated quickly from a conversational stroll around the park to a tightrope walk without a safety net.

"Me either," I said, and then, when he didn't immediately fill the next pause, I ventured: "I think there are a lot of scenarios in which we might've worked out."

"Unless you come out as an ESTP," he said, elbowing me playfully. "Then we'll know we never would have worked in *any* time line. We'd have zero in common—except our dynamite sexual chemistry, of course."

Our dynamite sexual chemistry. He remembered.

"Hey, come on," I said. "What about the time line where we're the last two people on Earth?" I heard the sentence hang lamely in the air as soon as I'd said it.

He played along, though, in a clear act of generosity. "We'd probably have become infertile from the nuclear apocalypse that precipitated that situation. Or we'd have scores of kids who'd then have kids with one another and die out within a few generations due to inbreeding."

"You never know. Inbreeding works both ways. They might end up with some supertraits."

He raised his eyebrows. "Look at you going to bat for incest."

"Zach! Jesus Christ!" I took the opportunity to shove his arm playfully—since he'd broken the seal by elbowing me—and he grabbed my hand and looked into my eyes a little too long before he shoved me back. There was a silence while I smiled back at him and a multitude of possibilities stretched out before us.

Then he said, "Anyway," and got up to start unpacking a box in the guest bedroom doorway. I watched him move around the living room, rearranging his shoes onto my shoe rack by the entrance, hanging his coat up next to mine on the front door. After a couple of minutes, as the street and the ocean view outside receded into a dark blue, I got up and turned on the overhead light.

"How's your mom?" I said eventually.

He shrugged. "Not great. I saw her this weekend. Her skin is kind of yellow and she's itching all over."

"My God." I had a visceral reaction, like I did when people started describing their children's head lice. I wanted to scratch my own arm but realized how that would look. "I didn't . . . know that was one of the symptoms."

"The cancer's metastasized to her liver," he said. "And they found a small mass on her brain. In some ways, the liver failure taking her before the neurological stuff would be a blessing. I don't really want to see her at the point where she doesn't recognize me. But I think we'll probably get a combination of both."

"That's so cruel," I said. "I'm sorry." I had completely and utterly fucked up this conversation by bringing up his mother, and I knew it. Any semblance of romance had been sucked out of the air like I'd opened the escape door on an airplane forty thousand feet up.

"People deal with all sorts of things," he said, his gaze fixed on the kitchen alcove.

"Well, yes," I said. "Shitty things happen to everyone, but some are shittier than others."

"I think Confucius said that."

"Oh, it's a central tenet of ancient Chinese philosophy."

He caught my eye for a moment and I tried very, very hard not to have a sex flashback. Maybe I could bring it all back around? My mind cycled through the most inappropriate memories and fantasies it could possibly create in response, and I broke the pattern of thought by asking him, "Do you want some tea?"

.   •   •

I GOT AN EMAIL FROM BR SAYING THAT "ALL EMPLOYEES SHOULD BE present in the midtown office on Monday for an exciting announcement," so I made my way in, being sure to time it to arrive at the beginning of my shift. As I went through the metal meat grinder exit at Penn Station, a well-dressed man released a great globule of saliva right onto my shoe. I glanced down as the spittle separated into little transparent bubbles and then ran down the side of my foot, and he looked at my frozen face for a microsecond, then continued walking as if nothing had happened.

BR's "exciting announcement" turned out to be a list of new hires, culminating in the arrival of a man about my age who would now be "our big ideas guy on the ground, second only to the editor in chief, so everybody make sure you say hi!"

"That guy," said Eliza from the audience team into my ear, "just got fired from the *Journal* for trying to feel up an intern."

"You can't be serious," I whispered back. She just gave me a raised eyebrow and a nod as she turned to head back to the bank of desks where they crunched numbers all day.

"Natasha! Great to see you here!" said BR, as I was setting my laptop down on one of the hot desks assigned to the news team. "Why don't you come in and meet Willem?" Like all of BR's questions, it was rhetorical. He was already marching purposefully around the corner toward his glass box, and it was clear I was expected to follow him.

Inside BR's office, Willem the intern toucher stuck his hand out to me and introduced himself as "Willem, not William."

"Like Dafoe," I said.

He grinned, revealing yellow incisors. "Exactly! Here's a cultured lady, huh?" I elected not to respond.

"Willem's had a bit of trouble lately," said BR, taking a seat behind his desk. "I don't think it's a secret to say that, is it, Will? We're all friends in here."

"Oh sure, we're all friends!" Willem repeated in his booming voice. He had a beat-up old laptop perched in front of him on one end of BR's desk, and it was covered in stickers. One said MY WIFE IS IN THE PTA and another said MY PRONOUNS ARE BEER/HUNTING.

"Just some BS from an intern," said BR. "One of those he-said, she-said kind of things."

"Oh, it's not even really about that," said Willem confidently. "I think they just wanted to get rid of the old guard. New editor comes in, she's got some new ideas, she has a few friends she wants in the top jobs. Up came an opportunity to get rid of ol' Willem and"—he cocked an imaginary gun at me and fired—"pow!"

"What happened to the intern?" I asked.

BR and Willem looked at each other. "Like I said," Willem commented with a smile still pasted on his wide face, "a lot of people got reshuffled."

"That's not what we're here to discuss, anyway. Just a bit of background for you," said BR impatiently. He entered his password to unfreeze the screen on his computer, then turned it so both Willem and I could see a moving line graph. I realized after a second that it represented the website's number of readers per minute. "This line here needs to be going up. And as you can see, it's tracking down. I think that together you two can work on some solutions."

"I worked on the breaking news side for a while," said Willem, turning his chair to face me, close enough that his knee was touching the side of mine. "What I've really learned is that getting things out *with speed* matters. Something happens in this big ol' country of ours and bang! Right out there!" He clapped his hands for effect, because apparently he communicated most effectively through onomatopoeia.

I nodded. He was literally describing how news works. I was willing to bet he was making at least a hundred thousand dollars more than I was.

"Rapid response, that's where it's at," he continued enthusiastically. Now he was clicking his fingers. "Swift and opinionated—every possible angle. What I'd love you to do is start reaching out to those people who are affected by the stories. Supreme Court overturns some Second Amendment legislation? Get right on the phone to that guy, you know, the Parkland dad who never shuts up. Get him talking about how he thinks about his dead kid every day."

BR was watching Willem speak, utterly rapt. I subtly shifted my chair back.

"Say some transgender cheerleader gets in a fight about a bathroom or whatever. Just getting right out there, getting some LGBTXYZ character on camera with a rainbow flag tied around their ass—supereffective. Faces to stories. Video content at the top of every page. Maybe little graphs that move. That's the stuff that really pulls people in."

"These are really great ideas, Willem," said BR, with stunning sincerity. "Natasha, are you writing them down?"

"Don't worry," I said. "I'll remember them."

"We should send people on little getaways as well," Willem continued. "Say, maybe get someone sitting in the viewing room watching someone getting executed. One of those really grisly ones, with the gas chamber and everything. They do that shit in Tennessee, right? Like, show the world how barbaric it is. I can see it now: 'Genocide in America.' What a headline. Other stuff—oh! Basketball! We should send people out to all the NBA games."

"I think the sports reporters already do that," I said.

"Oh, sure. Of course. But also get them on the ground looking for celebrities. Say Jay-Z turns up with one of those cute kids, get someone in to try to talk to them. Ask them what it's like to have a famous daddy. See if they've ever actually been to Brooklyn."

"I think they have security," I said.

"Well, we're just throwing ideas around."

"See, this is what we've been missing!" said BR, wheeling

around in his chair. His eyes were positively shining. "Ideas! The idea man! This is the energy I want to feel in every room!"

"Right. And if anyone asks about Willem's . . . controversy," I said. "Not saying you're a bad guy or anything, Will, and I know there's two sides to every story. It's just, I imagine people might see things. On social, I mean. I just would want to know how to address that."

"So he got MeToo-ed," said BR, and he and Willem both laughed. "It's a rite of passage these days, right? You both have seen a little trouble in the past couple of years. You know, the reason I wanted you to meet Will was because he gave me a whole new perspective on your little predicament, Natasha. And he was the one who said to me—what did you say, Will?"

"I said: Come on, man, this is what equal rights looks like!" said Willem, his hands in the air and his palms open, before they both collapsed in laughter.

"Yeah," I said, biting my lip. "Yeah."

"Oh, relax, Natasha." BR leaned over his desk and gave me a little punch on the arm. I jumped back reflexively then tried to cover it with a fake, shoulder-shaking laugh. "You're a liberal, aren't you?" he continued. "Liberals are all about rehabilitation! And we're talking about a young girl, quite a naïve one, who really wanted a raise and a promotion and also, you know, didn't know everything about the fast-paced nature of the newsroom. A kid who'd been fed all sorts of stuff by college professors and didn't have the tools to navigate real-world stuff. It wasn't her *fault*, though. It's nobody's fault. She'll have a great career ahead of her too! What I'm trying to say is: This isn't Harvey Weinstein we're talking about."

"God, I hope not!" said Willem, still chuckling. "I don't think I'm ready for Rikers."

"He has good ideas and that's what counts." BR emphasized each word by gently tapping his desk with a closed fist. Then he stood up and said, "Thanks for coming by!" which was clearly my cue to leave.

As they led me to the door, Willem stuck out his hand and I reciprocated automatically, then died another tiny death inside at my own hypocrisy. He still had the biggest fucking smile on his face. He'd probably never once spent a night lying in bed, staring at the ceiling, and wondering whether he should leave society behind and commit to perpetual hermitage.

"We're going to work great together," he said, closing his other hand over mine. Then he let go and shouted after me as I walked back into the newsroom, "You and me, just two misunderstood hacks in a whole media machine gone retarded!"

Eliza and the rest of the audience team stared.

"You know, you're not supposed to say that word anymore," one of the lowlier audience reporters said, glaring at me as I continued back to my desk, as if by mere proximity to Willem I was now co-signing his assholery.

"Thanks for the memo," I said through gritted teeth.

BY LUNCHTIME, I'D ALREADY WRITTEN UP A STORY ABOUT AN eighteen-year-old Disney star getting secretly married to his long-term boyfriend and received a call from his apoplectic agent on my personal cell. "You parasites love preying on children, don't you?" she yelled. "You think it's funny to out this kid to his family and all of his fans? If he kills himself, it'll be on you. Take some responsibility!"

"Marriage documents are public," I said, as I'd been trained to do. "Take it up with the courthouse."

"A document in the courthouse doesn't require an outing in the mainstream media," said the woman. "I hope this haunts you." Then she hung up on me.

If you're done with that one, messaged the editor, *there's some kid in Vermont who's going to Switzerland for assisted suicide. Super sad story—some kind of unknown disease that causes him excruciating pain every waking moment. Cld you get on the phone with him and ask if he'd write a piece for us before he leaves?*

Before he leaves to kill himself?

Well, if you wanna put it like that. Personally I don't judge him.

Don't you think he'll be prioritizing time with his family?

He did a Reddit AMA last wk. Clearly passionate about it. If it was me I think I'd want to raise awareness of the issue.

Ok, I guess I can look him up.

The thing you've gotta realize, Tash, is that most ppl are really happy to hear they've got mainstream media interest. It validates them.

Haha. Yeah I guess.

Everyone's an attention whore at heart ;)

I went down to the cafeteria and bought myself a premixed sweet potato salad with feta and walnuts. Through the window, I watched people dressed in suits jostling for space with tourists on the sidewalk outside. A dark-skinned nanny dragged two white kids along with one hand and steered a stroller around the people gawking at the Empire State Building with the other. I had the sudden need to be outside with them, in the emerging spring heat that would, within a few short weeks, create a humid summer swamp. I wanted to be another anonymous person in the madding crowd.

I ditched my empty salad container and walked down to Hudson Yards, taking Thirty-Fourth Street all the way to the river until the pinecone of the Vessel rose up to my left. Hudson Yards was such a weird place, a shiny square populated with eye-wateringly expensive stores like Cartier and Rolex while food trucks sold cash-only tacos outside. Who came here? Russian tourists, the few moneyed New Yorkers who actually chose to live in midtown, money launderers? Who bought a Rolex on their lunch break?

As I rounded the corner toward the Vessel, I remembered a local blog I'd read about a young woman with postpartum psychosis who jumped off the top of it. Her father had shared videos of them singing together a few days before she killed herself, him holding the new baby under one arm and her strumming a guitar. It was obvious they were close. The father had been so angry with the architect of the Vessel and the people who had allowed it to be built. Because of the way it was designed, there were no safety nets underneath the lookout points, no bars that could prevent people from climbing over. The designer was a British man who'd said at a press conference when it opened that he hoped the Vessel would "bring people together." I didn't think it was fair to hold him responsible for the yearslong struggles of the young woman who'd used his structure as a suicide aid. But I understood the searing, angry grief of the father and the way it sprayed out in every direction like so many Kalashnikov bullets, looking for some innocent body to rip apart. Sometimes I felt overwhelmed by news stories like that; everyone was damaged and no one was a winner. *Get a grip, Natasha*, I thought to myself.

I turned around at the High Line and started walking back toward the office, passing the Megabus stops and the people lining up to board. Each city was announced by a smiling cartoon man in a yellow uniform: Baltimore, Buffalo, Toronto, Philadelphia, Washington. A woman with a little girl leaned against the bus as a man helped her stuff a plastic-wrapped suitcase inside the cargo hold. I wondered what her life was like and why she wasn't at work on a Monday afternoon, why she was traveling to Philadelphia instead. Maybe she didn't have a job and was just visiting family. Maybe her life was simple, oriented around the needs of her little girl and perhaps the competing needs of her parents. Some Mondays they'd go down to Philly to get cheesesteak with Grandpa, others they'd get ice cream in Brooklyn and eat it in the park. Their lives were fluid and natural. She didn't churn out tragedy porn for a newspaper by day and inspect her exes' social media accounts at night. If she met someone like Willem, she'd probably laugh, then shrug, rather than experiencing an existential crisis.

As I made my way back up Thirty-Fourth Street and my office building came into view, I imagined going home to Zach tonight. "Everything okay?" he'd say from the spare room, as I sighed dramatically and put my bag down just inside the door.

"Yeah. Just a crappy day," I'd say, and he'd come out with a curious look on his face, but I'd wave a hand and say, "Don't worry about it."

"I'm a *little* worried," he'd say softly, still standing there. "Do you want to come in here and hang out?"

"I'd rather just sit in the living room," I'd say, fussing with my coat, not realizing what he was implying. So he'd smile a little and come over, and as I was gasping with the relief of pulling my heels off, he'd sit close enough to me to make a point. I'd look up and say, "Zach," and he'd say, "What? You had a shitty day." I'd let him kiss me, not with lots of tongue but softly and gently, just to get my attention, and I'd end up moving slowly toward him and lying on top of him, feeling him get hard as we made out with more energy.

"We probably shouldn't," I said in the fantasy, starting to get up, but he grabbed me and pulled me back down, his hand sliding up my thigh and then expertly searching out my clit under my skirt.

"Wow, you're better at this than I remembered," I said, my face pressed against his, and he said, "So are you," with a devastatingly sexy raise of his eyebrow.

Then he picked me up and carried me to the balcony, bending me over in my work clothes. I was so wet I barely even registered him sliding himself inside me, only felt it when he thrust hard into me and I went careering against the shaky railings, grabbing on with both hands in front of me to steady myself.

"People will see," I said, but he whispered in my ear, "Who cares?" and as his fingers connected with my clit again, I found that I didn't. People on the street walked past without looking up, and on the beach, I could see a group of achingly hot people in bikinis and board shorts sharing a pack of beers. As we continued—and neither us could stop from making noise—the group looked up at us and a couple of them realized what we were doing, made sly eye contact with me. One of the guys mouthed, "That's hot."

When we came, we came together, and the group on the beach had now given up any pretense of talking to one another and instead burst into applause. Zach brushed my sweaty hair away from my ear and said, "Well, that was one hell of a welcome to the neighborhood," then I turned around, and he kissed me deeply and carried me inside. We slept in the IKEA bed I'd put in his room, and when we woke up in the middle of the night we fucked again, but this time slowly and romantically, looking into each other's eyes, connecting our past to our future together, recognizing each other as two formerly bad people who had become good in the face of a whole load of Confucian shittiness.

But when I got home from the newsroom after hassling a dying teen for a sound bite, my feet tired from standing for forty minutes on the train, the apartment was dark and silent, and Zach didn't come home until I had given up waiting and gone to bed.

TWELVE

I TEXTED ELLIE: *HOW'S THE BABE?*

Oh hello stranger, she messaged back. *She's fine. How are you?*

I'm okay. I thought about all the things I wanted to say to her and knew she deserved to hear: *Sorry I was a clueless idiot who tried to vie for your attention with your newborn baby; thanks for taking care of me when my whole life fell apart and possibly still is; I don't know how I'll repay you, and a lot of that guilt makes me feel inexplicably angry at you; your life is going how I imagined mine might go and clearly I can't deal with that fact like a mature adult who's supposed to know how to handle disappointment and understand context.* Instead, I wrote: *My sister's moving to NYC.*

There was a pause where I could see she was typing, then not, then typing again. Maybe she was weighing up how to phrase her reply without upsetting me. Or maybe she was so used to my negativity and histrionics that she wanted to choose her words extra carefully. "That's Tash," she'd say knowingly to Jake as they passed the baby between them. "No parade un-rained on."

After a minute, her reply came through: *Interesting development! Wine this week to discuss, if you don't mind mixing your drinks with babies? Might have to be near my place if you don't mind, since I'm now officially a member of the Park Slope Stroller Mafia.*

Sure, I texted back. *I've got a day off on Friday. Meet at the bar on Union around 5?*

I thought about Ellie and Jake's comfortable apartment in Park Slope with the hardwood floors and the extra room made up as a sad beige nursery for Charlotte Louisa. They were sure to graduate to a nice, boring suburban house within a couple of years, the kind with Bavarian-style wood paneling, a grassy yard, and a shed that could be done up as a man cave. Jake would commute in to work on the train or in a sensible, reliable Volvo, and Ellie would work part time from home through her second pregnancy, because, hello, Charlotte Louisa needs a sibling! Soon enough they'd be swallowed whole by the American Dream, indistinguishable from their parents and their parents' parents and everyone else's parents' parents. They'd live in a neighborhood that was 98 percent white and stick a Black Lives Matter sign on their perfectly manicured lawn, and Jake would keep on doing his job at the bank, advising businesses that contributed to the economic inequality that most impacted people of color. Charlotte Louisa and her little brother or sister would go to a "good school," and every time I went to visit, Ellie and I would sit out on the deck, a safe distance away from the automatic sprinklers, and she'd talk to me about how her mom is "so good with the kids," how she "takes them every weekend," how their relationship now functions on another level, parent-to-parent. The sound of Charlotte Louisa screaming with joy as Ellie's mom engaged her in some dumb game would be heard from inside the house every now and then. Jake would bring us ice cubes for our homemade cocktails. They'd start to think about installing a "small but functional" pool in the backyard.

ZACH SPENT A FULL NIGHT AWAY FROM THE APARTMENT AND RE-turned the following evening with dark circles under his eyes.

"One of my friends from Boston was on a panel about alternative architecture at that new venue in Sunset Park," he said. "He begged me to come, and you know, fuck it. About twenty people turned up. Obviously not great, but it made the acoustics of the place really powerful. I asked him a question about Elon Musk building a colony on Mars after what he did to the Social Network Formerly Known as Twitter." He gave a hard little laugh. "Like, can we trust a proto-oligarch to build intergalactic architecture that responds to this moment in history? Or are we basically sleepwalking toward the destruction of the entire human race because we keep rewarding rich white men with more rich whiteness?"

"Big question," I said, because I couldn't think of what else to say. "How did he respond?" I'd just finished an online shift and closed my laptop; my brain was full of "Man Accused of Leaving 'Dirty Bomb' Outside Supreme Court Justice's House Could Be Antifa" and "Voice-over Actress for New 'Dora the Explorer' Movie Posts 'Shockingly' Revealing Pics."

"He said that Elon Musk is already a perfectly formed example of performance art, which is radical creativity in a completely different form," Zach said, smiling. "That's probably the only answer."

"I feel increasingly like every public figure is performance art," I said, running with the theme and hoping I was getting it right. "Politicians, celebrities, news anchors . . . I'm kind of waiting for one of them to pull back the curtain and reveal that we all had to live through the past five years in the name of their artistic experiment, but now we can go back to our real lives."

"Surely you, as a representative of the mainstream media, would know if that were the case?" he said.

"All I can say is that we need to change the subject because their eyes are everywhere," I joked. "Hey, want to order some Thai food?" I said it like it had occurred to me in the moment, totally casual, normal.

"I'd love nothing more," he said, collapsing back into the couch. "God, I'm exhausted." After turning up to cheerlead for the radical architecture panel, he'd ended up going to a cocktail bar on the Lower East Side, he told me, then to a club in Bed-Stuy, then back to his friend's place, where he crashed before getting up to work in midtown the next morning. "Sadly, it's the kind of itinerary that's only possible with the help of some nose candy," he added. I didn't want to say, *You're on the wrong side of your thirties now, Zach,* or, *How does propping up the illegal drug market count as challenging our late-capitalist environment and bettering the lives of the downtrodden workers?* or, *How many privileged white guys does it take to call out other privileged white guys on a panel in Sunset Park?* but I thought them. He'd turned thirty-seven just before he left Boston. I'd seen the party on Instagram. What I actually said: "Well, you've been on a veritable tour of New York City."

"Yep, all I need to do now is visit the Bronx Zoo and take the Staten Island Ferry and I'll have managed all five boroughs in under forty-eight hours."

"You know, I've never actually been on the ferry," I said, opening a takeout app on my phone and sitting beside him on the sofa. His arms were spread out so wide that his hand almost touched my head. He didn't retract his fingers when they briefly connected with my hair.

"Wait," he said. "You've *never* been to Staten Island?"

"Never."

"That's *wild!*"

"Well, I didn't grow up here," I said, "and I've never had any particular reason to go."

"Me and my high school friends used to get the ferry back and forth when we had nothing else to do," he said. "We'd take the bus into the city and spend the day on the water for free. It was a good place to get a beer underage too."

I imagined teenage Zach and his friends boarding the ferry in lower Manhattan, sending the oldest-looking one, with his wispy mustache, to order beers from the ship's bar, sharing the drinks with the group as they passed the Statue of Liberty.

"What did you do when you got there?" I said.

"Oh." He thought for a moment. "Not much. Got some pizza, I think. There's probably some kind of Pete Davidson heritage tour now."

I gave him a charitable laugh and then held my phone screen

up to his face so he could see the menu. We got red curries with pineapple and shrimp, sticky rice, and some spring rolls with sweet chili sauce to share. It reminded me of when we used to order in from bed during weekends where we'd alternate between sex and eating, a low-key bacchanal all our own. He'd leap up when the door buzzed and throw on his underwear, or sometimes my bathrobe, to grab the bag from the delivery guy.

When the food arrived, I set it down on the table and brought bowls and plates in from the kitchen. "Choose your weapon," I said, proffering forks and spoons, and he took one of each, which I branded "controversial."

"Well, I'm a controversial kind of guy," he said, but sardonically, like he was quoting someone else. Then, as I spooned out curry and divided up pineapple pieces onto my plate, he said, "So, any plans for the weekend?"

"Not too many," I said. "I'm having a drink with my friend Ellie—maybe you remember her?"

"Ellie and Jake!" he said. "Yeah. Totally."

"Yep, Ellie and Jake. Believe it or not, they just had a baby."

"Together?"

His shock was so unexpected that I started to laugh. "Yes, together! They're real, actual adult human beings now. They're *parents*."

"Wow." He shook his head, skewered a spring roll with his fork, and dipped it liberally in sauce. "Imagine having a baby."

"How do you think we all got here?"

"Yes, I'm aware of how the human reproductive system works." He gave me a little nudge with his shoulder to show that he was joking. I felt it all the way through my body. "I just can't really imagine . . . I guess a lot of people you know end up going on to these incredibly conventional lives in their thirties. White picket fence, baby, reading up on local schools before they move somewhere, all that stuff I thought our generation might've left behind."

"Well," I said, feeling suddenly defensive on Ellie's part, "someone has to do it."

"Sure, sure. And no judgment. I've just been thinking a lot about overpopulation these days. A few of my friends are in the radical child-free space . . . There are other ways to live your life, is all I'm saying."

Even though I'd always imagined having kids myself, I found Zach's perspective seductive. What if Ellie and Jake were just prisoners of an old-fashioned ideal that was quickly becoming irrelevant? What if, by accident, I'd wandered into the best way to live, the most *responsible* way to live, on a dying planet increasingly governed by fascists? What if, instead of being left behind, I was enlightened, unencumbered, with space to think about technological and sociological solutions to our current moment of crisis rather than zombie-shuffling toward the apocalypse with a baby's greedy mouth on my tit?

"I guess you just end up losing sight of how to live differently," I said. "It feels like everyone around me is capitulating to a certain kind of lifestyle now. Before you know it, all your formerly progressive friends are going up to Maine in the summer and skiing in Vermont all winter. Carbon copies of Mom and Dad. Once you reach the tipping point and it's the majority of your social circle, maybe you just become that way by osmosis?"

"It's certainly a danger."

"But I don't feel like replacing all my friends, you know?" I couldn't exactly afford to be socially picky these days either. I said it pleadingly, then cringed at the way it came out.

"Well, you don't have to do that," said Zach mildly. "I'm friends with all sorts of assholes. One of my college friends is the son of a Saudi billionaire who's presumed to have thrown a couple of dissenters off balconies in Europe. But he gets it, you know? He does the work. Fundamentally, that's what you have to look out for." I guessed that if Zach managed to retain ideological purity while hanging out with the children of state-sponsored murderers, then maybe I could at least stay friends with Ellie and Jake.

"Yeah," I said, though my heart wasn't fully in it now I'd heard myself beg him for permission to keep my own friends. "I mean, it's cool to think about the possibility of not just living that standard life. Existing outside the expected parameters. Something like that, anyway."

"Listen, Ellie was always fun," said Zach, noticing the trailing off of my enthusiasm. "I didn't mean to insult your friend or anything."

"No, no," I said. "I was just . . . considering what you said."

"You and I are similar, I think," he said. I turned my head to look at him but he kept his eyes fixed on the wall.

"In terms of what?" I said, fishing.

"Oh, I don't know," he said. "I'm talking nonsense. Don't listen to me. I've been awake for basically two days straight."

I guess I'd asked for too much. We finished our Thai food and I cleaned up the mess, wiping up chili sauce from the coffee table with a wet dish towel, piling up the plates and cutlery and then sliding them into the mini dishwasher. I was enjoying myself, performing the role of housewife, reassuring him that I could look after him if he needed it.

When I sat back down again, I said, "Did you see your mom yesterday?"

"Oh yeah." His eyes were closed now, his head lolling back against the sofa cushion. "I did. Right before the panel, actually. I don't know. You get used to hearing an endless succession of bad news."

"Right."

"My brother said she didn't recognize him the other day. There was a bile duct infection, then a sepsis scare. No one can keep on top of all the pills. Antibiotics and more antibiotics, bacteria creeping in to take advantage of a weakening body. It's all very unrelentingly grim, as you can imagine."

"I don't know how you cope with it," I said, reaching out a hand, but stopped before I could place it on his shoulder.

He opened one eye and looked at me. "Nobody gets a choice," he said. "You cope with what you're given. And people lose their parents in all sorts of ways. I was saying to my friend Aileen, you know, her dad was killed in 9/11—no one would know what to choose if they were asked. Slow and painful with time to say goodbye, or quick and painless for you and traumatic for everybody else? Losing your parents is a universal experience. It's just details after that."

I thought about my mom and how I hadn't texted her back after leaving Nantucket without saying goodbye. Maybe keeping up the animosity wasn't worth it, I thought. Had I really thought she'd change after all this time? Maybe all we could do was love each other and accept that everyone has their flaws. Also, *who the fuck was Aileen?*

"You're being so strong," I tried, but Zach just shrugged like I'd missed the point and extended himself fully on the couch, blocking my ability to sit by him. I got up and gave the table a final wipe, then went to the bathroom. As I brushed my teeth, I made eye contact with myself for so long in the mirror that I began to disassociate. I thought about that poem by Carol Ann Duffy that one of my college professors had loved and I hated: "Small Female Skull." When I came back into the living room, Zach was asleep, his mouth partly open and his right arm cushioning his head, a blanket half covering his legs.

I walked over quietly under the guise of turning off the big lamp beside him. Then I reached out my hand, slowly, and stroked his arm. His face moved a little in his sleep, but he didn't resist; he even murmured a little. I crawled onto the other side of the sofa and pulled the blanket over myself too, leaning awkwardly over him so we were almost side by side. I felt the regular rise and fall of his chest, the warmth of his back through his shirt. My heart was beating so fast I could hear it in my ears, competing with the passing siren of an emergency vehicle outside.

When he moved his leg and looked like he was trying to turn over, I carefully pulled away and arranged the blanket over him again. As I did, my fingers hovered momentarily over his cheek. Was it safe to kiss him, like we'd kissed so many times before, this one just an innocent goodnight? As I leaned further over him, I could smell his breath: a mixture of curry spices and stale alcohol, an undertone of mint-flavored chewing gum. I imagined him the night before, deeply sad, sipping an old-fashioned in a speakeasy on the Lower East Side, and I wished I'd been there to wrap my arms around him and comfort him, to take him home to safety. I leaned down further and kissed him demurely on the cheek, like I was an eighteenth-century admirer and he was a tragic young woman I'd caught in a consumptive faint. I was aware how pathetic this was, but I did it anyway.

He didn't move as my lips connected with his cheek, and I didn't either, staying there seconds longer than I should have. With the lamp off, the lights of the ambulance outside made a mirror-ball effect across the room. Then I slowly rose and went to my room.

ON OUR FIRST WEEKEND IN LONDON, I'D BOOKED A TABLE FOR ME and Joe at an obscenely expensive restaurant called the Ugly Mould Tavern, which a Substack written by a food critic (who'd recently "parted ways" with the newspaper where she'd worked for more than four decades due to a "difference of opinion over identity politics") had touted as "a haven for molecular gastronomy." We couldn't really afford it—no one could—but I wanted to Instagram the theatrically smoking cocktails, and I liked the idea of marking the occasion of our transatlantic move with suitable aplomb.

I spent about an hour washing and drying my hair in preparation for going out, using an unnecessary amount of styling cream and an overpriced straightener made by a company that was known for its vacuum cleaners. It wasn't clear to me what hair straighteners and vacuum cleaners had in common, but the world had accepted they were natural bedfellows, and this was back when I was aligned with the world rather than at war with it. I squeezed myself into a pair of celebrity-endorsed shapewear compression shorts and a push-up bra, stuck on some fake eyelashes with glue, and watched a tutorial about how to contour my nose with various shades of eyeshadow. Then I emerged, triumphant, from the bedroom.

Joe was standing in the hallway waiting for me. His hair was still wet from the shower, and he was dressed in a comfortable shirt and the chinos he wore every other day.

"Ready?" he asked pleasantly as I made my entrance.

"Yep." I stood in position for a few seconds, waiting for a comment.

"Great! Should I bring keys or do you have yours?" He was already turning toward the door and pulling on his own jacket.

"Do you think I look nice?" I blurted out.

He turned back to me. "What?"

"Just . . . do you think I look nice?"

"Of course! You always do. The Uber's seven minutes away, it looks like . . ." He was already staring back at his phone, fiddling with the unfamiliar lock on the apartment door.

We made our way down to the street and settled in the back of a Volkswagen Polo that smelled like seventeen layers of cigarette smoke. After five minutes of silence as we traversed the streets of Hackney, Joe realized I was upset.

"Everything okay?" he asked, in the tone of forced levity he used when he knew it wasn't.

"I think you could stand to be a little more romantic, or . . . appreciative." I kept my eyes fixed on the window.

"What do you mean? I'm really grateful you booked the restaurant."

"I meant *of me.*"

A few seconds passed; I could almost hear the cogs turning in his head. Then he said, "Oh, I'm sorry. I thought you did that dressing-up stuff for you."

"Well, I don't. I mean, I do. But also . . . it would just be nice if you said I was hot once in a while, you know?"

"That doesn't exactly sound like the height of romance, to be honest."

"Or beautiful, then." I suddenly felt overwhelmed with sadness that he hadn't said I was beautiful tonight—perhaps had *never* even said it—even though I hadn't known until that moment that it was what I'd wanted. Could I really expect that of Joe, a man who got me a "really good" set of kitchen knives for my last birthday? When I'd told Miri about that particular gift, she'd looked at me with genuine concern and said, "Is he trying to send you a message?"

"I'm sorry, Tash," said Joe, putting a hand on my stupidly stockinged knee. "I can be a bit clueless sometimes. I guess I didn't get the memo."

"As usual," I said under my breath, and I childishly moved my knee away from his palm.

"Tash? I didn't catch that." Did I really want to do this? The driver turned a little too fast onto a busy street where students staggered toward club nights and raves in high heels and sneakers, and I decided I did.

"*As usual*," I said, louder. "I think I'm allowed to ask for validation sometimes. It can't always be visa logistics and coding and serial killer birthday presents."

"Serial killer . . ." I could see him sounding it out to himself, confused. It had been a while since my birthday. "Oh, you mean the knives?"

"Yes, Joe." I sighed audibly. "I mean the knives."

"Well, I'm not sure what quality tools have to do with how you look tonight, but you do look beautiful. And if you don't want any more kitchen items for presents, consider that information recorded."

"You know," I said, as the car pulled up to the curb across from the restaurant, "there's something to be said for reaffirming your love every once in a while."

He shook his head. "I don't get it, Tash. You *know* how much I love you. What's there to reaffirm?"

"Forget it. Let's just enjoy the dinner." I got out of the cab and slammed the door with one hand while adjusting my bunched-up shapewear with the other.

THIRTEEN

ON FRIDAY, ELLIE NAVIGATED CHARLOTTE LOUISA'S STROLLER INTO the wine bar around the corner from her apartment while the waiters joked with her about whether the baby counted as an underage drinker, and even allowed her to park up right by the table. She had such an easy way of communicating with the world. Her whole demeanor announced *I have nothing to hide*, and people responded to that.

"Do you think you'll ever call her Charlie?" I asked. Everyone was still calling the baby Charlotte Louisa, including me, like proximity to the womb imbued a person with extra authority. I remembered how my mother had done that when my sister was born too; for the first two years she was always Miriam and often Miriam Rachel. I guess parents like to say the names they chose out loud. In London, there was always some obnoxious parent on the Tube with a kid dressed in a straw boater hat, knee-high socks, and a sweater that told everyone she went to St. Martha's Very Expensive School for Special Little Girls and Boys, who loved to yell after her, "Oh goodness, Penelope Rose, *will you* come here rather than running ahead of me and Sebastian?" I openly rolled my eyes when I saw those types, striving to let them know how much everybody judged them for being utterly unbearable. At work, we referred to them as "yummy mummies" and called their urban SUVs that powered up and down the Kings Road "Chelsea tractors." The dads escaped our ire because they never even appeared on the street with their children, presumably busy punching numbers and snorting coke at the top of a skyscraper in Canary Wharf for twenty hours a day instead.

Ellie shrugged at the question. "I don't think so. I mean, I'm not a *huge* fan of Charlie. If she really doesn't like the full thing, we were thinking maybe Lottie."

"That's cute," I said, without feeling.

"You never know though," Ellie said, perusing the menu with her eyes. "It's not like you can control these things. My parents wanted me to be a Beth."

We ordered a bottle of rosé for the table and it felt so nice, so normal, to be able to sit with someone and share something made for two. Ellie chose a crisp bottle from Austria, eschewing the French and California wines that the waiter urged us toward. "We don't like sweet," she said firmly, setting her very white teeth in a firm line.

I'd hoped I might be able to hold Charlotte Louisa, maybe snap a photo for social media of me looking like a grown-up, but she slept in the stroller's bassinet the entire time we were at the table, and Ellie told me we couldn't wake her up. So instead I reminded myself that cosplaying motherhood was lame anyway, and that this was all part of the stuffy, traditional ideal that I had opted out of.

"Me and Zach are getting along really well," I said, holding my cold glass against my bottom lip.

Ellie shook her head. "I still can't believe you moved him in."

"It isn't like that, El. He has agency."

"You know what I mean. There are plenty of men in New York, Tash—literally thousands of them."

"It's well known that the stats aren't in women's favor in this city," I said. "And that three-quarters of the single men are undatable."

"Those are numbers made up by people marketing either new apps or sex bots," she said. "Are you really telling me you're pursuing your shitty ex-boyfriend out of fear?"

"Pursuing my shitty ex-boyfriend?" I said. "Do you really think I'm that pathetic?"

She wasn't taking the bait. "I don't know, Natasha. *Are* you?"

"Look, if you must know . . ." I turned my eyes away, took time topping up my glass from the bottle in the middle of the table, while I readied myself to embellish. "It's more like the other way around. He's taken a bit of an interest in . . . reconnecting."

Ellie was silent for a couple of beats, then she said flatly, "Go on."

"Well, the other night we had dinner. His suggestion," I said, my eyes still on the table in front of me. "We ended up talking basically all night. He shared a lot of stuff about his mom—it's a real tragedy, you know, and I think it's made him reassess his priorities. Nothing *happened* happened, but we did end up falling asleep on the couch together." I was stretching the truth, admittedly, but it felt inevitable enough that it might as well be true.

Ellie's expression remained skeptical. "In like, a friendly way, or . . . ?"

"Well." I shrugged like *no big deal.* "It's hard to know, isn't it? I didn't want to push it. I mean, at the end of the day, it's a vulnerable time for him." I couldn't help but add a magnanimous flair to my lie.

Ellie made a little, almost imperceptible, facial movement, sipped her wine, and said, "Huh."

"Look, I know you—justifiably—are not Zach's biggest fan," I said.

"The emotionally unavailable fuckboy who used polyamory as a weapon?" she said. "Now, come on. I like him as much as the next manipulative narcissist."

"See, this is what I'm talking about," I said. "And why I can't really share any of this with you unless you're willing to forget what he was like when he was in his *twenties—*"

"Thirty-one."

"—and give him a chance now that we've all grown up a little bit."

Ellie sighed like she'd just gotten some bad news and bit her lip. The waiter came over to ask if we needed anything, and she waved him away. Then she said, "Okay. I can deal with it. If he's really changed. You know all I care about is that you're happy."

"I know that," I said. "And I appreciate it. Just trust me that I've got this. It's been really nice, actually."

After we finished the bottle, we each ordered an Aperol spritz to round off the evening and picked at a charcuterie and cheese board so we didn't get too drunk. By that time, I'd really warmed to my theme, and started talking about how I, as his roommate, would probably be the first person to see Zach after his mother's death, and so I had to prepare myself to deal with that huge responsibility. What was I supposed to do, I asked her, if he wanted me to go to the funeral?

"I don't know if I should," I said. "I mean, I've only met his parents once, in passing."

Ellie sipped meaningfully on her straw. "Just make sure you do what's appropriate," she said, then, "*Fuck*. There's a special place in hell for the person who invented paper straws."

"But think of the turtles with plastic around their necks."

"Trust me, I think of them all the time, and the way in which Big Oil has convinced us all that it's my fault rather than corporate greed."

"Me and Zach were talking about this, actually," I said, sensing an opening. "How to change the status quo when you're no longer a student. You know, now that we're in our thirties and we have a bit more money and power, how do we preserve our radical selves?"

"I'll let you know if I find the time." Ellie leaned over to take a good look at sleeping Charlotte Louisa in the stroller, then straightened up again.

"Well," I said, "that's just it, isn't it? There's an inevitable treadmill to a certain kind of life that squeezes the radical thought out of you. White-picket-fence suburbia. Summers in Maine, winters in Vermont . . ."

"Treadmills don't go anywhere, Tash."

"You know what I mean. Assembly line, whatever."

Ellie popped an ice cube into her mouth, chewed on it in a way that set my teeth on edge, then said slowly, "I think there's a real arrogance in saying a nice family life is the worst thing you can possibly imagine. I mean, it's an incredibly privileged thing to roll your eyes at people living comfortably. You have to have come from wealth in the first place to get a kick out of rejecting it."

"That's not true at all," I said. "Look at . . ." I tried to think of someone relevant and of-the-moment who had lived through a difficult, working-class childhood and still come out against suburban boringness, but the alcohol had slowed my brain, so I settled on, "Kurt Cobain."

"Kurt Cobain?" She raised an eyebrow. "It really worked out for him, huh?"

"Yes, Ellie, I think Kurt Cobain shot himself in the head because he realized he was wrong about suburbia."

"That's not what I was saying and you know it." She was smiling at me fondly, like, *Natasha's having one of her episodes again.* "Besides, I'm pretty sure Kurt Cobain had a wife and a baby. Pretty conventional. For all you know, if he'd just found an antidepressant that worked for him, he might've ended up as the president of the HOA."

I was too irritated to find it funny. "I know I fucked up my life," I said. "But maybe it gave me some perspective."

She sighed. "All right. All right. But look, Natasha. Homeless shelters are filled with people who would kill for soul-sucking suburban boredom. Do you honestly think SNAP recipients who struggle to make ends meet are doing it to be edgy?"

"Now you're making me sound like an idiot."

"I can't *make you sound* any kind of way." She waved a hand toward the waiter, like this conversation wasn't even worth her full attention, then turned back to me. "Have you been spending too much time with Zach, perhaps? The revolutionary from the two-million-dollar McMansion in Scarsdale?" I looked at the ground, and she gave me a playful nudge, adding to my humiliation. "Did he also tell you his favorite book is *American Psycho*?"

"You think I can't form my own opinions."

"That's not it at all. Your opinions are fresh and interesting and well-informed . . . when they're your own."

The waiter skirted past our table, deftly dumped a bill to the side, and I picked it up and examined it thoroughly so I didn't have to say anything.

"Tash, criticizing that kind of life is a rite of passage for people who grew up comfortable, and they all end up wealthy again anyway. Trust me—it's not the parents living in nice houses with front yards for their kids who are destroying the world. It's Big Oil and plastic straws all over again."

I thought: *How can you be so sure?* But out loud, I said: "I guess. Whatever, I'm bored of this conversation."

JAKE CAME BY THE BAR AS WE WERE SETTLING UP. HE PUSHED CHAR-lotte Louisa in her stroller while Ellie and I weaved up and down the sidewalk, and she said, "God, it's so nice to be drunk again." Her tolerance was so much lower than it had been before she was pregnant, and nothing compared to when we used to do beer-and-shot combos in dive bars before hitting the clubs, where we knew men would buy us drinks for the rest of the night. Ellie once brought home a hedge-fund guy who'd sampled so much of the Bollinger and premium Grey Goose he'd bought for the table that he collapsed, facedown, in our dirty kitchen before they could even get to the bedroom. We laughed and went to bed, and when we woke up in the morning, he was gone.

That wasn't long after we'd graduated, before Zach or Jake or Joe, when there was no urgency around dating, and we felt like we held all the cards during our interactions with men: we were young, hot, mostly unencumbered, and, crucially, poor, so when they bought our drinks we made sure to act grateful for about five minutes. Really, we wanted to get fucked up more than we wanted to get fucked, but we understood we were entering into a transaction.

Jake and Ellie insisted I stay over at their place because of the weekend subway delays, and I didn't argue. Their second bedroom would become Charlotte Louisa's before too long, but right now the crib was in their room and the nursery still had a twin bed in it with pristine sheets, just waiting for visitors.

"My mom has been staying here," said Ellie, fussing with the pillows. "But the sheets are clean. And hey! We can have brunch in the morning."

I settled into the clean, fresh-smelling bed. The pillowcases had a calming odor of pine and I nestled my face into them, imagining I was back in Nantucket during one of my mother's better periods. By the light of an IKEA lamp, I scrolled through the text messages I'd missed while we were out: one from Miriam saying *just call Mom please will you she's going crazy I can't believe I always have to do this with you two* that I mentally marked as a to-do for tomorrow, and one—I couldn't help but feel it, the zing of adrenaline that he'd reached out to me first—from Zach. I hovered over the message with my finger for a few seconds, then opened it and read: *Used some of the $$ on your laundry card—will pay you back tomorrow. T-shirt emergency!*

No problem, I replied, then, emboldened by the alcohol: *Did I ever tell you I almost moved to North Korea?*

I lay there in the quieting apartment waiting for him to reply, listening to Charlotte Louisa fuss and Jake mumbling some soothing words to her, then the floor creaking a little as Ellie got into bed. Just as I was sure I wouldn't hear back from Zach, he replied: *Happens to the best of us.*

> *For real. I thought it would be a good way to escape the shame of divorcing my husband.*

> *Wow. They really did a number on you.*

I guess you could say that. I tried to think of a way to prolong the conversation. *How are the Rockaways tonight?*

Windy! Lot of creaking.

Oh yeah. The building does that. I find it kinda cozy tho.

Yeah I appreciate it. Connects me to my material sur-
roundings lol. Assume you're spending the night elsewhere?

I elected to keep some semblance of mystique. *Just at a friend's.*
We had a bit too much to drink.

Gotcha.

Not like that. I'm very much in the spare room. As soon as I'd
typed it, I regretted ruining the mystique. Would it have killed me
to allow him to think of me as desirable? My need to reassure him
had ruined my ability to put a proper strategy into play.

There was a pause again, and then: *Won't interrupt your fun any*
longer. Goodnight!

Dammit. I took the only Cool Girl option: *Night!* and turned
out the light. Another opportunity missed.

I WOKE IN THE MORNING TO THE SMELL OF COFFEE. JAKE HAD AL-
ready delivered a mug to Ellie, who was still in bed, and he poured one
for me when I padded into the kitchen. "Thought that might smoke
you out," he said, gesturing toward the brewing pot with a wink.

"Morning, Tash!" Ellie yelled out from her bedroom, the door
propped open. Charlotte Louisa was snuggled up against her boob,
making weird little noises. "Hope she didn't wake you during the
night."

"I didn't hear anything," I said truthfully, and set myself down
at the bench table by the large window in their breakfast nook. It
was only seven o'clock. I guess they got up early on weekends now.

Jake started beating eggs in a bowl and pouring oil into a fry-ing pan for brunch—though at this hour, it was breakfast. As he and Ellie fussed around the house, picking up mugs and Charlotte Louisa's burping towels and talking about refilling the diaper supply and going on a walk around the park with a stop at the place that sold Jake's favorite coffee beans, I luxuriated in the normalcy. It felt like I was borrowing somebody's life. When Jake presented me with a plate of scrambled eggs and avocado with a side of bacon and a slice of liberally buttered toast, I could have cried.

"Tasha's hanging out with Zach again, *apparently*," said Ellie, giving Jake a look as she balanced Charlotte Louisa at her shoulder.

"Seriously?" Jake looked at me for confirmation, and I nodded while loading up a forkful of scrambled eggs, striving to keep my features straight.

"Yes," I said, "and Ellie has agreed to be nice about it."

"I am being nice," said Ellie, handing Charlotte Louisa to Jake so she could eat. "What do you think, Jake?"

"I know better than to comment on women's love lives," Jake said diplomatically. Holding Charlotte Louisa with one hand, he popped a piece of crispy bacon into his mouth with the other and added, "Mmm, that's good."

"Trust me," I said. "He's changed a lot in the past five years. Maybe you'll see him again soon and get to judge for yourself."

"Well, I'd like that," said Ellie, clearly in a conciliatory mood.

I imagined the four of us—even the five of us, with Charlotte Louisa—at a trivia night, Zach getting all the arts questions right, Ellie laughing at herself for knowing all the terrible songs in the Top 40. Zach would hold Charlotte Louisa and admit she was very cute, "Even to an antinatalist." Ellie and Jake would go back to their apartment, and Zach and I would go back to ours. He'd wind his fingers through mine on the train.

I thought about how he'd texted me about the laundry card the night before. He hadn't needed to tell me that. It was in no way urgent. He could've easily mentioned it to me when I got home. What did that say about him?

FOURTEEN

I STAYED AT ELLIE AND JAKE'S UNTIL THE EARLY EVENING—THE DAY ebbed away as I grabbed diapers, made sandwiches, wiped down surfaces, held Charlotte Louisa while each of them showered, all of which I bore stoically even though they weren't exactly forthcoming with their gratitude—then, when I reached my limits of exhaustion, I headed home. "Zach might be waiting," I told them kindly, so they didn't have to know how much life force their baby had sapped from me.

When I got off the train in the Rockaways, I called my mother. She picked up on the second ring and sounded like she was outside. "Oh, hello Tash. I've just been potting some of the herbs Sasha and Liz gave me for the garden."

"That's great," I said. "I'm sorry you haven't heard from me for a while."

"Sure. I know you've been through an emotional time," she said, "but you don't have to take it all out on me."

I bit my lip. "I think we'll have to agree to disagree on why we weren't speaking."

"Well, I think that's right. Water under the bridge. Hey, it's beautiful on the island right now. Hope you're planning your next visit."

"Yeah," I said. "Soon."

"Maybe you should come in a couple of weeks, and then you can help Miriam move. She's all ready to go, you know. She's found herself two nice roommates in Brooklyn—the same area as your friend Ellie, I think."

"Oh right. Great." I tried to disguise any note of hurt in my voice.

"So is anything good happening for you right now? Let's focus on the positives."

Although I hated the idea of being coached in mental well-being by someone who sank a bottle of wine a night, I'd been looking forward to her asking.

"Well, I do have *some* good news," I said.

"Ooh!" I could hear her running water in the background; I imagined her pulling off her gardening gloves, rinsing her hands in the sink, her eyes on the new herbal section of the deck garden. "Tell me everything!"

"There's not much to tell," I said, coyly. "But Zach and I have been getting a little . . . closer lately."

"Oh, I knew it. I *knew* it. You two always had a spark!"

"We did, yeah, we did." I was grinning like an idiot now as I made my way past the GREAT BREKFEST bodega. I walked past my building onto the boardwalk, looking out at the sea. It was much colder down here than it had been in Brooklyn, and the wind created goose bumps on my arms. On the streets around Ellie and Jake's, where the concrete sucked up the heat of the day and spat it back out again, it had been pretty temperate; springtime reached Park Slope and its bankers and marketing professionals before the rest of us peasants.

"So go on, how did it happen?" Mom prompted.

"Oh, it's not *happened* so much as . . . happening." I approached the chained-up public restrooms, turned around, and began walking the other way again. The sea slapped the shore in the background. "You know, we've been having a lot of long talks, coffees, dinners, things like that. And it feels like there could be a natural progression there. But I've already decided that I'd want to take it super slow." Okay, there hadn't been an *abundance* of long talks or dinners. But if Zach and I did end up getting back together, I'd need to have Mom prepared, or she'd only embarrass me.

"Great idea. You don't want to throw yourself into anything too fast after Joe. But at the same time, I have to admit I was afraid for you, Tash. I was scared, thinking about your *time of life* and everything and your opportunities—I mean, by the time I was your age I'd had two children."

"You almost went an entire week without reminding me too."

"Don't take it the wrong way. It's just because I love and care for you. I meant it when I said you and Miri are my everything, because you know, Tashie, if anything happened to either of you, *anything . . .*"

"Let's stay on track here," I said. "No big tragedy has befallen either of us."

"Oh, I know. I *know.* But this is wonderful news. It's just what you deserved—a beautiful springtime romance!"

"Well, I don't know about that." But I was allowing myself to be carried away, letting myself believe in it. "I have to be cautious. Things went south between me and Zach before, so . . ."

"Oh, but you were so young. What were you, midtwenties? It's different now. And I remember when you brought him home that weekend in the summer—he was such a polite young man. Really helpful and nice company. Certainly someone I could get on board with as a son-in-law. In fact, if you must know, I always thought he was better looking than Joe."

"That's . . . I don't know, Mom, that's not really what this is about," I said, taking my second turn on the boardwalk back toward the restrooms again.

"I know it's not what it's about," she said, a smile in her voice. "But it certainly helps, don't you think?"

"Well," I said, looking out to sea, "there's no denying that it *helps.*"

BY THE TIME I'D HUNG UP WITH MY MOTHER AND GOTTEN BACK TO my building, I'd agreed to fly to Nantucket in a couple of weeks and return to New York with Miriam in tow, ready to slot her right into her new life. I still assumed she'd walk into some easy situation as some rich guy's hired uterus, but I didn't feel as bad about it. When I envisioned my future with Zach, I saw it as more bohemian than Miri and her new guy's life anyway. We'd be the creative counterpoint to her traditional conformity. Where she'd have a succession of beautiful kids, Zach and I would do a lot of traveling, maybe eventually have one baby when we were in our early forties and looking for a new challenge. Mom would be thrilled for us both.

When I walked into the apartment, I could hear Zach moving around in his room, so I called out, "The cavalry has arrived!" then immediately blushed at my own idiocy. *What the hell was that?*

He came out into the living area and raised one hand in greeting. "Oh hey, you're back. How was your night?"

Think like the newspaper: Leave an abyss of intrigue. "It was nice. How about yours?"

"Can't say I did that much. Tried out a new brewery in East Williamsburg, got some Chinese food."

"They're still opening new things in Williamsburg? I thought it reached maximum capacity when they moved in the Whole Foods."

"Hey, when I was growing up, it was basically a no-go zone. Then it had its glory days when I was young and sprightly, and I still cling to them, okay? Give an old man a break." He made his way to the kitchen with an empty glass and turned on the faucet. "Those were some halcyon days, when the streets were full of indie guys trying to make a living off their art and music, long before all the yoga teachers with liberal arts degrees moved in to open their studios with their daddies' money."

"The mayor must urgently address the yoga-teacher-with-liberal-arts-degree-to-Williamsburg pipeline," I said, joining in the joke, but it struck me that his characterization of the neighborhood's journey from cutting edge to passé was kind of naïve and also kind of sexist. I reminded myself not to get wound up.

Zach drained his glass of water quickly, refilled it and drained it again. I raised an eyebrow. "Overindulged at the brewery, huh?"

He shook his head. "Nah. Just thirsty. How's work?"

That seemed like a clear distraction technique to me, but I pretended I didn't notice. "Oh, not bad. The planet's burning and fossil fuels are running out, fascist despots are rehabbing their image on reality TV, ninety-pound influencers give calorie-counting tips to anorexic kids and call it wellness. The usual."

"Didn't you used to be an actual reporter?"

I resisted the urge to take the insult as an insult and continued blithely: "Yeah. Before I kind of . . . well, you know. And back then I did do more meaningful work—going out on interviews, speaking to politicians, writing human-interest stories that got a lot of traction and caused genuine debate. Or at least, I thought it was meaningful at the time. Now that the newsroom looks how it does, I don't know. It's changed a lot in the past few years—or maybe I'm just noticing what I didn't notice before."

"Never see how the sausage is made."

"Right. And you know, the people who churn out crap all day alongside me don't think much of the reporters doing actual journalism either. They think they're precious and overhyped and, well, expendable. Going by most metrics, they'd be correct." I sat down on the sofa and started picking at a piece of material coming loose from one of the cushions. It was brand new and already unraveling. I felt for it. "The newspaper could get by with just the news-churn people and none of the actual reporters, but not the other way around. Everybody knows that, and it creates . . . tensions."

"Missing the days in your ivory tower when everybody used to fawn all over you?"

"It's not like that," I said. *Don't take the bait. Don't look like you care too much.* "I'm just talking about a general trend, you know? In the industry."

"Sure." He sat down on the other end of the couch and peered at me over his glass. "Anyway, I didn't mean to annoy you."

"Hey, you're not annoying me," I said, forcing myself to be pliable, agreeable, unflappable. "How's *your* job, anyway?"

"Gloriously simple." He stretched luxuriously and then leaned back with his arms behind his head. "I turn up, I input data, I wander around Bryant Park on my lunch break, I clock out, I leave. No homework, no discussion, no office politics. I don't know why people don't do this their entire working lives."

I shrugged. "Some of them do."

"Oh, yeah, I know. But not like . . . educated people."

"Sure. I guess a lot of people want a career rather than a job. But maybe it's time to reimagine that."

"It's *absolutely* time to reimagine that!" He looked at me like I'd just hit on something he'd been thinking for years but hadn't been able to put into words. It felt good. "Everyone sleepwalking into *careers* with their college degrees, thinking they have to make their parents happy, playing status games, always trying to live up to society's expectations. But the whole *point* is to make you feel inadequate! The whole point is to suck up all your time so you don't have the resources to think deeply about the way late capitalism has ravaged our communities and left us with basically nothing. Every stupid little white-collar worker marching through the revolving doors to the big shiny office, hoping they can afford the rising cost of their Xanax refill to get themselves through the day, is contributing to this nightmare of a situation."

"Well, some of those people probably just want to pay off their student loans," I said.

"This is about what happens when we serve our wealthy overlords *willingly*, though, you know?" He rubbed his right hand across his face. "I *know* how this makes me sound, but, my God, once you buy into the career lie, you're basically neutered."

He's going through a tough time, I thought. *The least you can do is give him a win.* "You're right," I said out loud. "You're absolutely right." There was something kind of sexual about acquiescing to his point of view, allowing him to fill me up with his opinions, without stopping to wonder if what he was saying was nuanced or right or good. Maybe he was helping me. Maybe he had all the answers. Maybe the yoga teachers of Williamsburg were deconstructing the socialist utopia, foam brick by foam brick, and they had to be stopped.

"I suppose I'm not being completely fair," he said after a pause. *So you can't even agree with me when I say you're right?* "I really do admire people who can live that kind of life, on some level. It's a way to maintain personal happiness in the hell that is corporate America. And I respect cultivating your own joy in the arid plains, you know? You can't fault the people who heard about the American Dream and believed it was real any more than you can fault kids for believing in Santa Claus. I *wish* I could make it work for me. But personally, climbing the ladder, doing the nine-to-five—it would drive me insane. My brain's not built that way."

I looked at him. "You mean like mine?"

He stretched out a leg languidly. "Not exactly. I just mean like everybody's."

"Oh, I see. You're not like the other boys."

He laughed mildly. "I'd just rather disconnect money from what I care about. It's cleaner that way."

"I'll have you know I'm changing the world with my silly little career," I said, smiling like it was all a big joke to me: my ambitions, my working life, my prestigious college degree that I worked so hard for.

"One young swimmer at a time?"

I felt it like a shiv to the kidneys, but on the outside I kept smiling and said, "Careful."

"Oh, I'm careful." He got up and took a Diet Coke out of the fridge. The Diet Coke I'd picked up from the bodega a couple of days earlier on my way back from the office and been looking forward to enjoying on the balcony. He caught me looking at the can, raised it, and said, "Cheers."

"Cheers," I said flatly. I looked down at my phone as he gulped the soda. Apple News was serving up an article from my own paper as a suggested read: "Are You Being Poisoned by Your Own Apartment?" I clicked on it and scrolled quickly to the bottom, where I found that the real thing I needed to worry about was lead piping in my building, not spurious assertions about my life's work from an ex-boyfriend. The site suggested I continue on to "Did a Feud Between Tom Hanks and Mister Rogers Once Explode into Violence? Bombshell Video Inside!" but I didn't have the mental energy to watch a video clip, so I locked my phone and put it down.

"I'm glad you're interested in this stuff, Nat," Zach said from the kitchen. "Some people . . . I mean, you can never get everyone on board." Was he talking about a girl? It felt like it. I could see he was facing the window, and presumed he was wistfully studying the facades of buildings and bodegas while ruminating on a relationship that failed because the girl wasn't radical enough. *And where did that lead you, Zach? Back to me.*

"You never can," I agreed. "But maybe one day, enough people . . ."

"Oh, I've given up on that." He gave a short laugh as he sauntered back out toward the sofa again. "America's done. The sooner we accept that, the better. But I have high hopes for Canada." Could I live in Canada with Zach? I already had a pretty good pair of snow boots and a down jacket. I could get into snow shoveling as an exercise routine, for the liberal-socialist-anti-late-capitalism cause; for my last realistic chance at romance; for him.

"Well, you just let me know when you're ready to leave and I'll brush up on my French," I said.

ZACH HAD SOME LEFTOVER CHINESE FOOD FROM THE NIGHT BEFORE that he heated up in the microwave and allowed me to share, and we talked for a while about Ellie and Jake again. "I'm happy for them, seriously," he said, gesticulating with a piece of chicken on the end of his fork. "I know I was less than charitable about babies the other day. But I was just being an asshole."

"You? Never!" I said, laughing, and he elbowed me.

I told him I was going to book my flights for my trip to Nantucket in a couple of weeks and that my sister was coming back with me. He didn't seem to remember meeting Miriam, and I didn't push it. Then he said, "Hey, this might sound a little crazy—"

"—but the moon landings were faked by the CIA?"

"Very funny. But for real, there's a ferry to Nantucket from midtown. It's, like, half the price of the plane and an awesome experience. I have a friend who swears by it."

"Really?" I polished off the chicken and rice, and then added, "Somehow I've never heard of it."

"Seriously. You have to try it. Bring me your laptop." Here we were, together, making plans! I went into my bedroom, grabbed my computer, confirmed I didn't have any inappropriate tabs open, and then put it on the coffee table in front of us. He directed me to the ferry website and watched over my shoulder as I booked it, repeating, "Honestly, you won't regret it," until I said, "Your enthusiasm is now getting into 'hired someone to push me off the side of the boat' territory, I hope you know."

"Well, I was going to pretend I was getting a cut of the ticket, but you got me."

It was going well, so well that I saw an opening. "Hey, maybe one day we can get the boat together."

He cut through a gelatinous shrimp dumpling with his fork and, without looking up, said, "Oh yeah. Maybe," in a pleasant, noncommittal way, as if I'd said, *When we've colonized other planets, we should do some space tourism.* But that "yeah, maybe" was all I needed for now.

When the food was gone, I gathered up the boxes and threw them out, then went to the bathroom to wash sauce off my hands. Standing under the harsh light, I thought how I looked particularly nice today. My hair wasn't as frizzy as usual; my anemic winter pallor was giving way to a healthier spring glow. The freckles on my cheeks were becoming a little darker in a flirty kind of way. I'd experimented with an eye shadow that had a slight shimmer, and it actually looked good. Zach probably thought I looked better than I did when we first met.

Then, as I lazily surveyed the rest of the small bathroom, I saw it. Perched on the side of the tub was a "no white marks" deodorant with a picture of a woman's dress on it. The scent was peach blossom and lavender. I was an aloe girl. It wasn't mine.

I walked back out into the living room, holding up the small plastic stick. "Is this yours?" I said, a tightness in my chest.

Zach was reclining on the sofa, his feet dangling off the edge, playing with his phone. He looked up, squinted to see what I was holding, then sat up a little and said, "Ah. No."

"Well, it's not mine," I said, my tone clipped.

"Damn. I'm sorry about that. I had someone over last night, but I didn't mean to clutter up your space. Feel free to chuck it into my room."

I looked down at the deodorant and up at him again. "No, it's fine," I said, and placed it back in the bathroom but in a more prominent spot, its treacherous face glaring out at me from under the mirror. I felt like I'd been punched in the chest. In front of the mirror again, I took two deep breaths and swallowed.

"Hey—was it not okay for me to have someone over?" Zach said when I reemerged.

"It's cool." I couldn't look at him. "I just didn't expect it."

"I mean . . . you were away for the night."

"Yeah. For sure."

"I'd never leave a stranger alone in your apartment, just to be clear. I even closed your bedroom door."

"You know what, Zach? That is *great* to know," I snapped, and then realized I needed to get away from him before I said something really stupid. I marched back over to the door, grabbed my keys off the side table, and started pulling on my shoes. "Want anything from the bodega?"

He was lying down on the sofa again now, back on his phone. "No, thanks."

"Cool." I slammed the door as I left—I couldn't help it—and marched down the concrete stairs with purpose. Near the exit to the building, I kicked the hard tiles on the side of the lobby wall. They were unrelenting and I hurt my toe. *Fuck.*

It was dark and windy outside and the few people on the streets were hurrying back home, clutching their jackets closer to themselves. I went down to the sparsely lit boardwalk and then onto the beach, toward the crashing waves, through the thick sand. It wasn't a long walk to the ocean edge; I realized the tide was coming in. I felt like I needed to reconnect to reality, to get the image of Zach and another woman out of my head, to delete the scenes now playing in my mind of him touching her, wanting her, coming inside her while I lay in Ellie and Jake's guest room, texting him like an ignorant little fool, thinking he wanted to end our conversation quickly because he was jealous rather than the truth: he was busy with someone more interesting, more attractive, probably younger, definitely not damaged goods.

I dodged the yellowing scum at the shallowest edges of the sea, knelt down, and picked up a handful of black seaweed. It was less slimy than I'd imagined it would be, and its dark nodules ran satisfyingly through my fingers as I let each strand fall from my right hand. Then I bent down to pick up more, dropping a handful and then throwing it onto the sand inches away. I knew I looked like a madwoman, but the action soothed me. The seaweed was so cold that it numbed the ends of my fingers, and when water dripped down onto my pants and the end of my shirt, I started to shiver. Compulsively, I bent down again and plunged both hands into a huge mound of it, pulling the long tendrils out with my fingers and examining them briefly before flinging them back down. A few droplets of seawater sprayed up, catching me on the cheek and the lip, and I tasted salt.

Then there was a man behind me on the beach, jogging in my direction. I looked back hopefully: *Zach?* But it was just some guy with a dachshund on a leash and a worried look on his face.

"What are you doing?" he said, with a Spanish accent.

"I'm walking," I said, because that was the only explanation I could think of. He shook his head and gestured forcefully at the ocean.

"Get back to the boardwalk. Sea's coming in fast. Idiot!" Then he walked off, shaking his head, dragging his dachshund after him.

"Hey! Don't call me an idiot!" I shouted when he was too far away to hear. *Cowardly.* I dropped my last handful of seaweed and started to retreat. The cold air on my damp clothes and in the parts of my shoes that had been invaded by sand felt good, then neutral, then bad. Little pieces of grit began to irritate my toes as I navigated back from the shoreline.

As I stepped onto the boardwalk and began stamping the sand off my shoes, I saw that Mrs. Konstantin—Olinka—had been watching me, clutching her ugly little dog. She was dressed in a waterproof coat and a colorful headscarf, and the dog was wearing a quilted jacket in the same vibrant colors, an absurd coordinating couple.

I planned to ignore her and continue down the boardwalk in the direction of home, but she spoke as I passed so I turned to look at her. Her face was only partially illuminated by the orange streetlamp above us.

"What?" I said.

"You're a crazy girl," she said, shaking her head, but she was smiling.

"Fine," I said, under my breath, then, louder: "Fine! But at least I cared when I thought you were *dead*!"

She shrank away for a moment and a gust of wind blew across the sand, then she started to laugh. I stood there, incredulous. She didn't stop.

"I'm not the crazy one," I said eventually.

"Listen, girl—" she said.

"Natasha."

"Okay, listen, Natasha. When I came to this country, Putin was on throne for twenty-five years. I walked seventeen miles over border with Estonia under heavy fire, carrying dog in a Walmart bag. American government sets me up in this building by the beach in New York City and I sell coffee on the boardwalk in summer and I'm happy. You see what I mean? Happy."

"Yeah? Well, good for you." I was starting to feel a little guilty.

"You should try harder to be happy."

"Happiness isn't a choice, you know," I said, rubbing the side of my face where some saltwater still remained.

"Silly girl. Of course it is." I looked into her face: it was lined and weathered, and her lipstick was a bizarre shade of purple that didn't complement her pallor. Her pale hair, the remnants of ginger speckled in with white, was matted around her face.

"No offense, but you don't know anything about me," I said, "so you probably shouldn't be doling out advice."

"Ah, you remind me of myself," she said. Fucking fantastic. Of course I do. Funny how CEOs and models never say that to me, but a batshit old woman falls over herself to let me know.

"I have to go," I said, like I'd just stopped for a bit of seaweed calibration on my way to something important, and stalked off back toward the building, feeling her eyes on my back the entire time.

ON SUNDAY MORNING, WHEN I CAME INTO THE LIVING ROOM AND logged on to work my monthly weekend shift, Zach had already left the apartment. I was glad that I didn't have to face him. I could already tell it was a day that I wasn't going to change out of my pajamas.

Almost immediately, someone pinged me on the newspaper's internal messaging system: *How about this?* Attached was a link to a bottom-feeder celebrity gossip site that claimed "Former Miss Brazil Is PANSEXUAL, Might Marry a SEX DOLL!!" I looked at the details of the account, and sure enough, it was Willem the intern toucher. Even though he'd struggled to adjust to the modern era morally, he seemed to have managed it technologically. He'd set his name as "willEM" and his avatar as the Robert Downey Jr. incarnation of Iron Man.

Interesting, I wrote back, because I couldn't really think of what else to say. The story was based on rampant speculation from an unnamed "source" that had posted spurious claims on a subreddit. Did he really think this was newsworthy, or even verifiable? Or was the interest all because she was hot? Were we now publishing articles solely so teenage boys and middle-aged men could salivate over the idea of a woman in a swimsuit who once won some bullshit beauty pageant having sex with an inanimate object? I felt like asking him if he knew there was actual porn on the internet these days but considered that if he hadn't already worked it out, I didn't need to be the one to tell him.

I'll add it to your list, he replied.

Great! Will look into.

A few minutes later, he messaged again. *Been thinking about that meeting we had with the ol' editor in chief. I thought it went well, no?*

I tried to be as noncommittal as possible. *Yeah, totally.* I wasn't ready to be "felt-up female colleague number two" in the supporting cast of Willem's life.

We've got access to this new service that shows us where readers go once they've read our stuff. He sent another link, this time to a site called Clicksmax, followed by some login details. *Why don't you give it a go?*

I scrolled through Clicksmax for a few seconds, taking in its offerings: audience insights, tailor-made reports telling you what your readers "really want," analyses of cookies that follow people around the internet logging the content they "love best." It didn't feel particularly revolutionary.

This is a very, very powerful tool that could be a game changer for the company, wrote Willem.

Oh yeah. It looks super helpful.

Why don't you build a report with Clicksmax this afternoon and send it across to our friend in the big office? Great way to show your worth and it's v easy to do—but don't worry, I won't tell him that ;)

Great! I'll see if I can find the time.

This is where news is headed so def worth it!!

I wrote up the pansexual Brazilian story, scouring Instagram for photos of the woman onstage at Miss World wearing a swimsuit and a ridiculous tiara. I ignored the ones of her in sweatpants taking her toddler out strawberry picking or lounging on the sofa with her husband. Then I went back to Clicksmax, scrolling through graphs and promises about "learning more than you could possibly have ever imagined about the desires and needs of your users." At one point, the cheery cartoon people who cavorted around their moving graphs referred to the nondigital world as "meatspace" and encouraged users to "leverage your human capital."

Willem was right about one thing: it was easy to use Clicksmax to make a professional-looking report that served up numbers and pie charts about "where to direct resources next." By looking at what our paper's regular online readers did after they read one of our stories, the algorithm created recommendations about what topics editors and writers should focus on next. My own report—which I titled "Natasha's Recommendations"—said that over the next six months, we should "level up" on content about the TV show *My 600-lb. Life* and anything in the "surprise pregnancy genre." As an example of the latter, Clicksmax helpfully provided two recent examples: a Facebook post about a college student who'd given birth on the toilet while getting ready for a night out; and a local news report about a woman who was touted as a "modern-day Mamma Mia" because she had three candidates for the father of her baby, none of whom wanted to take a paternity test. Both items had gotten an unusual amount of user engagement.

Under "level down," Clicksmax suggested we publish fewer articles about infrastructure policy and the Supreme Court, as well as "content related to Asia." It cited a recent article by our China reporter that talked about the possibility of labor camps being built near Mongolia, and that hadn't generated much buzz on social media. Clicksmax considered the piece "highly level-downable."

I put a couple of finishing touches on the report and then sat in front of it for twenty minutes, doubting myself. Would BR really take kindly to these recommendations? Could they seriously help to resurrect my disgraced career? Eventually, I took a screenshot of the report, which I sent to Willem with a note: *Does this look all right to you?* Look at me, taking professional advice from a pervert.

His reply came quickly: *I think that's more than all right. That's fantastic! Let's go NATASHA!* To accompany his message, he sent me a gif of Jim and Pam from *The Office* high-fiving each other. Despite myself, I smiled.

FIFTEEN

A COUPLE OF DAYS AFTER I LEARNED THAT HE'D SNUCK A WOMAN into our home, I bumped into Zach in the kitchen. He was dressed in boxer shorts and a T-shirt, disheveled from sleep and slow with morning vulnerability. I couldn't be mad at him anymore. As I watched him move sluggishly around the kitchen, reaching up for a slice of bread from the cabinet, dropping it into the toaster, then fiddling with the dials, I felt a compulsion to reach out and stroke the dark hair on his arms, or to sink my teeth into his shoulder.

"Do you want to talk about it?" I asked.

He looked back at me. "About what?"

TWO WEEKS LATER, I TOOK THE BOAT TO NANTUCKET. I FELT GOOD about my decision as I lined up in the sunshine in midtown with fifty or so other people to board, then found myself a seat on the top deck outside. The early afternoon light was perfect, and as we departed just after noon, I snapped a burst of photos of the Manhattan skyline and sent one to Zach: *Pretty good views from the boat!*

Told you it was worth it, he replied.

Things between us had been a little more formal since I'd found the anonymous woman's deodorant. She hadn't been back, so that was one thing. He'd never even told me her name. I was grateful that it seemed like she hadn't really meant anything.

As the ferry maneuvered its way around the curves of the East River and eventually onto the open sea, I texted Ellie: *Things with Zach feel complicated.*

It took her a few minutes to get back to me, during which I paced the deck, placing my hands on the metal guardrails and leaning over so I could get a glimpse of the Statue of Liberty. When I returned to my seat and checked my phone, she'd replied: *Yeah? I guess that was inevitable.* She added a few seconds later, presumably for diplomacy's sake: *It's not your fault. Remaining platonic might've always been the better option.* I imagined her rocking Charlotte Louisa in a bouncer with one foot, then turning to Jake and saying, "Well, no surprises here. Natasha's screwed up again." I hated how she spoke to me like I'd never been in a relationship before, like I hadn't been through an entire marriage. She thought her version was the only version.

It might be a little early to decide nothing will come of it, I typed back. *He's just been super distracted. Probably family stuff.* I paused then added: *He had a girl over the other night.* That part was hard to admit.

> *Honestly? Sounds like the same old Zach. At least now you know.*

I bristled. *Or maybe we've all changed and we just need some time. Not everyone needs a family portrait and a lifetime of monogamy.*

> *Hard not to read that like you're implying something.*

You're being too sensitive. It felt like I'd regained the upper hand, and it felt good. I took another lap of the boat and then, when it seemed like she wouldn't reply, added: *I'm on a boat right now. Zach recommended I take it back to my mom's to see what it's like.*

Oh cool! Doesn't that take a long time?

Yeah, about 5 hours. But no airport hassle and there's a bar onboard.

That sounds great!

For sure. I thought about ordering myself a beer. *It's a nice way to travel. Would be better with some company tho! Maybe you guys will come in the future. Or Zach!*

You never know.

It'd be weird reintroducing him to my mom tho lol.

Well let's take this one day at a time.

I leaned back into my seat and thought about how cautious Ellie was about my life, like I was a dangerous animal who might devour everything in sight if given even a glimpse of it. Was I too much for everyone? Had I always been?

The boat was great for a couple of hours, until the late afternoon began to set in and the sea blasted a chill along the top deck. I rubbed my arms, but the goose bumps kept reforming even under my coat sleeves. By sunset, everyone had gone inside, and I reluctantly joined them after thirty minutes of pretending to myself that I was having a great time.

Downstairs, everything stank of stale beer, and a man and woman leaned against the back of the bar, talking. There was a long line for each of the bathrooms, one of which smelled powerfully of urine. All the seats were already occupied by people who'd come inside earlier and sensibly found a spot on this level, and as I stood in the corner on the carpeted floor, I got a direct view of a kid screaming at his mom that he'd had "enough of the boat" before proceeding to vomit all over her lap.

I watched this mom, who looked about my age or younger, calmly get up and ask the guy behind the bar for some napkins. As she walked, brown chunks of spew undulated down her skirt and some of the liquid dripped onto the floor, almost hitting her shoe. The smell combined powerfully with the piss stink from the toilet, and I began to feel hot and shaky and conscious of the boat's motion. So I sat on the steps leading up to the top deck, trying to catch a whiff of fresh air, and attempted to convince myself I was comfortable while the metal grooves cut into my ass cheeks.

When the ferry finally pulled into the Nantucket terminal at seven thirty, after an interminably long stop at Martha's Vineyard, Mom was waiting for me, standing next to the car with her arms folded across her chest.

"Well, that was a stupid idea," she said as I made my way down to the parking lot under the sparse streetlights, kissed her hello on the cheek, then chucked my duffel bag into the trunk. "I've been waiting here for over an hour."

"Have a sense of adventure, Mom," I said. "I liked it."

WE DROVE PAST THE HIGH SCHOOL ON OUR WAY HOME, ITS FLOOD-lights illuminating a newly built outdoor basketball court and an expanded science building. On the court, some kids were tossing a ball around in a lackluster manner. I assumed they were actu-ally there to pass around furtive drinks that they'd brought in their backpacks, the way I'd done on spring nights with my classmates before we all grew up and moved away.

"Remember all those times I'd come pick you up from school and then drop you at Louis Dayton's?" Mom said. "You were so into him." Louis Dayton was my first-ever boyfriend, a passable, middle-of-the-road guy who was on the JV track team. I wasn't cool or good-looking enough to tempt an athletic superstar, but I'd accepted his advances, mainly because I wanted some nominal sexual experience before I left for college. He'd shoved three dirty fingers inside me on his mother's sofa while we "hung out" after school. I'd told him it felt good and then wondered what all the fuss was about.

"You never dropped me at Louis Dayton's or anywhere," I said to Mom. "I drove myself."

"Are you kidding me? I spent so many years trucking you back and forth between extracurriculars, friends' houses, parties . . ."

"That was Miri."

"You've never been able to accept that I did anything for you." She shook her head and sighed. "Anyway, who do you think got you that car?"

As soon as we reached home, Mom poured herself a glass of wine from a half-empty bottle and downed it. When I told her I was sticking with water, she decided to go to bed. Miri came home a half hour later, fresh from another date, dressed in loose-fitting jeans and a web of loose threads that I guess passed for a shirt these days. Presumably only Sasha next door would know which guy she'd been out with.

Miriam heard Mom walking around her en suite bathroom upstairs and put her finger on her lips, signaling to me to wait until the coast was fully clear. When we heard the sag of Mom's mattress and the click of her bedside lamp, we nodded to each other and began to talk freely.

"How was it?" I asked, raising an eyebrow.

"Oh, fine." She dismissed the question, but I could see from the look on her face that it had gone well. It was almost nine, late enough for me to suspect they'd gone back to his place after dinner.

"What about when you move to New York?" I asked. "You don't mind leaving him behind?"

"It's not like I'm moving to Australia," she said. "He can visit anytime."

"You'll find someone else in New York anyway," I said. I was kind of trying to get a rise out of her—her easy-breezy confidence when it came to dating rankled me—but instead she just lifted one shoulder and said, "Maybe," before filling the kettle and setting it on the stove.

"Tea? This one gives you a flat stomach." She opened a cupboard and shook a little bag of something called Skinny Tea at me.

"No, thanks. And let me see those ingredients. You're always falling for the dumbest things."

"And you're always criticizing everything I do. It's *healthy*." She chucked me the bag nevertheless and I ran my eyes down the ingredients, shaking my head. Cranberry, ginger root, rosebuds, "detoxifying ground chia seeds." At least it wasn't meth.

"Did you buy this from an infomercial?"

"Yes, because it's 1995." She held her hand over the steaming kettle to test if it was boiling yet, then, at the first sign of a whistle, took it off the stove and poured herself a large mug, adding two Skinny Tea bags. "If you must know, I saw it on Instagram." She looked at me meaningfully before I could open my mouth. "*Don't* laugh. Just try to actually be the bigger person for once."

"For once!" I said with a hollow laugh, but I elected not to say more. I wasn't here to fight. We sat in a comfortable silence as she sipped the tea, and I looked at a framed painting of two dogs on a beach that I hadn't noticed before in the living room. It was a saccharine scene, with the dogs bounding off down the sand, a woman and man following hand in hand behind them, dressed in coats and scarves. I recognized it as one of Mom's creations; she must've liked it enough to keep it. For a moment, it made me a little sad that this was what our mother came up with when left alone with her imagination. She'd been to *art school*, for God's sake. The whole scene made me feel on a primal level that she was desperately lonely.

"Do you ever think about your father?" Miri asked suddenly.

I looked at her in surprise. "Stan the Russian?"

She rolled her eyes. "No, the local Catholic priest."

I shrugged. "Not really." I'd been through a phase in my teenage years when I'd idealized Stan. I'd imagined finding him one day on a construction site in LA—I'd been toying with the idea of becoming a celebrity reporter at the time—and him reacting with excitement and emotion when I said, "It's me, your daughter." He would look exactly like me, with my pale Siberian skin, my strong, thick legs and my slightly upturned eyes. On him, I'd see how the features I was so critical of on myself could be kind of charming. He'd tell me he'd lit a candle every year on my birthday, a single tear trailing down his angular face. He'd hoped that one day I'd contact him, because Mom never left an address or a phone number before she and her swelling belly disappeared into the ether. I snapped out of that by the time I was twenty-two. If Stan even knew he had a daughter, and even if by some miracle I tracked him down, he'd probably scarper as soon as he caught sight of me: "Sorry, girlie, nothing personal, but I don't want to be on the hook for eighteen years of unpaid child support!"

"I think about mine all the time." Miri laid out her willowy forearms on the kitchen island and picked at a bug bite on the inside of one. "Ezekiel." She said his name as if she were a sailor's widow clutching her handkerchief to her chest. Mom had only ever called him Zeke.

"I don't want to burst your bubble," I said, "but you know he's probably an asshole too, right?"

She looked at me with innocent affront. "How could you possibly know that?"

"Well, first of all, he's not here." I gestured at the house, the garden, the island. "Second of all, Mom has a habit of choosing horrible men."

"That's not entirely true. She has a habit of scaring off decent men, too."

I smiled at that and plopped onto the sofa. "Fair enough. I'll give you that."

"I just feel like . . ." Miri looked down at her inner elbow again, avoiding my gaze. "I don't know. You know who you are. You have a calling. You wrote for the middle school student paper when you were twelve and now you work for an international newsroom—"

"Look how that turned out."

"Let me finish. You've done so much more with your life. And I don't even know who I am or what I'm doing. I have no identity."

I looked at her standing barefoot on the tiled kitchen floor, a pendant light illuminating her artfully messy topknot and that ridiculous nonshirt. She looked so childlike, so defenseless, so exposed. Through the male gaze, she was basically perfect. I guess I was too used to looking at her in that way.

"I never imagine you having crises like this," I said. "You always seem to find life so easy."

"I don't find any of this easy," she said, shaking her head. Her failed attempts at college had looked like they meant nothing to me. She'd gotten jobs on the island with a click of her fingers and found new boyfriends and maneuvered expertly around our mother. I hadn't really thought about the other side of those college failures, and the jobs or men she'd held for a few months, then lost before moving on: the silent car rides home with Mom, boxes full of posters and bedclothes and college textbooks rattling around in the trunk; the humiliating conversations with managers of seafood restaurants that catered to loud men in pastel chinos and loud shirts; the inevitable blowoffs from guys on dating apps who lost interest when her whimsical shtick stopped working for them.

"Hey," I said, getting up from my seat and walking around the kitchen island to her. "We have each other. That's a big part of both of our identities, right? Our sisterhood? And it's better than some glorified sperm donor you've never even met. You know what Mom says, for all her flaws. We're three girls together."

"Sure." She smiled a little sadly. "Do you think you might be able to . . . look out for me in New York?"

"Oh God, Miri." I rolled my eyes and pulled her in for a hug. "I've been looking out for you your whole life."

Miri looked back at me unsurely. "But will you *now*?"

"Of course, you idiot. You'll be trying to get rid of me before you know it." I sighed and tried to muss her topknot, but she pulled away. I retracted my hand, smiling at her knee-jerk vanity. And I envied the way she could easily ask for help, the way it cost her nothing to admit that she craved being looked after, and to accept that looking-after when it was offered.

"Okay, make me one of those stupid teas," I said. "And let me get your read on how things are going with my new roommate."

"This is Zach? Tell me everything," she said, grabbing another mug and filling it with boiling water. "Are you going to get back together? Mom can't stop talking about it."

MIRI AND I HEADED TO THE AIRPORT TOGETHER, EACH DRAGGING two large suitcases filled with her clothes, and Mom packed an extra lunch bag for her as if she were a kid, complete with cheese sandwiches with the crusts cut off.

"It makes me so happy to see my girls supporting each other," she said as she idled the car to drop us at the door.

I hugged her and breathed in the smell of the herbs on the porch, rose shower gel, soil from the garden. "You should come and visit us next time," I said, without enthusiasm, because it felt like the right thing to say in the moment.

"I will!" she said, clinging to me a little too tightly. "Maybe next month? Or the one after?"

"Well, let's wait and see how Miri feels with work," I said, anxiety building in my throat.

The night before, Mom had made a lasagna with the aged cheddar I loved from the obnoxious farm-to-table store down the road, and we'd sat on the deck under the glow of the heat lamp, sipping on light lagers with slices of lime. I could tell she was making an effort, like she thought she was marking a momentous occasion; at one point, during a slightly fantastical conversation about everything Miriam was going to achieve in her internship, she even got teary. By the end of the night, both of them were acting like my sister was weeks away from the C-suite. I bit my tongue.

On the plane, Miri pulled out her phone and started watching an episode of some documentary about cheerleaders through the in-flight entertainment system. "Hey, look," she said, half an hour into it, elbowing me in the ribs. "You're in this!"

"What?" I'd been staring out the window, playing my sad house music at full volume.

Miri had paused the documentary on her screen and was pointing to it with a slender, manicured finger. "I'm telling you! It's you!"

I leaned over and looked closer at the phone screen as she rewound the ten-second clip. First, a picture of a young girl in a yellow cheerleading outfit flashed up on the screen; immediately after, a familiar-looking headline popped up, reading "Gruesome Injuries of Cheerleader Whose Head Was Found in a Tote Bag Finally Revealed by Police." The article had been written a month prior, but I didn't even remember publishing it, much less typing the words; it was so similar to all the others I'd done on the boners-for-gore conveyor belt. Underneath the headline was my byline and a tiny picture of my face that had been taken on my first day as a reporter. I smiled out of the screen with radiant new-job energy, like I'd murdered the poor cheerleader with my own hands.

SIXTEEN

MIRIAM INSISTED THAT SHE WANTED TO SPEND HER FIRST NIGHT IN New York in my apartment, so we shared a cab from the airport and got in late. Zach was in the living room, watching a John Mulaney stand-up special on his laptop.

"We met a long time ago, right? I barely recognized you," he said when Miriam gave him a little wave, and he offered her his hand in a show of formality that I thought was a bit over the top.

"Careful, Zach," I said, dragging Miriam's suitcase into my bedroom. "You're showing your age."

Miri changed into pajamas in my room, pointing at the living room to ask whether it was okay to hang out in there with Zach. I shrugged like nothing about Zach was a big deal to me—*why would it be a big deal to me?*—and we joined him on the sofa, where John Mulaney was now joking about the problems inherent in having a baby with another celebrity. It was not relatable content.

"He's about the only comedian left I can stand to watch," Zach said to Miri rather than to me.

"Oh, I don't really follow comedy," she replied unselfconsciously.

"You're not missing much," said Zach, his eyes trained on the screen. "I hate to be one of those idiots who rails against cancel culture, but it does feel like everything's gotten so sanitized these days. Comedy peaked in the nineties."

"Seriously?" I said. "The *nineties*?"

"Nat's always making fun of me when I say stuff like that," said Zach, rolling his eyes at Miri like they were united in some sort of conspiracy of fun against me, the opinion tyrant. "But in the nineties we had creative freedom, you know? In 1997, the Prodigy had an internationally successful hit with 'Smack My Bitch Up.'" He slapped his hand on the side of the couch as if this fact revealed a fundamental truth that had been staring us in the face all along. Miri flinched.

"Yes," I ventured. "But is that . . . good?"

"What? The ability to say the offensive? Fostering a creative environment in which it's permitted to push boundaries?"

"I just . . . I don't know if it's that boundary pushing, you know? Like was misogyny that unusual in 1997?"

"I guess it comes down to this: Would you rather live in a society obsessed with culture wars, where the left is eating itself and no progressive politician can answer the question, 'Is health care a human right?' in public, or would you rather live in a society where people can write songs about smacking bitches?"

I nodded my head slowly and nudged my shoe into the carpet. Maybe if I kept at it for long enough, the moment for answering would pass.

"Yeah," I said eventually. "Yeah. That is the question."

"I'm pretty tired," said Miri.

MY SISTER KICKED ME AND STOLE THE COVERS ALL NIGHT, WAKING me more than once. Eventually I couldn't get back to sleep at all. Instead, I lay there remembering a summer camping trip on which we'd had to share a tent, and I'd ended up punching her in the jaw in retaliation. We were kids then, and I didn't do any damage except to Miriam's feelings. She'd run crying to Mom, obviously, who had rewarded her for snitching with a chocolate bar.

Now I listened to the wind rattling the windowpanes and the creak of Olinka's feet above me in a badly constructed building in the Rockaways while Miriam snored softly and shuffled around the bed, her body giving off so much heat. Truth be told, the issue wasn't just her: I'd forgotten what it was like sleeping in the same space as someone else, having to think about what my face looked like when I turned around with my mouth open, not having the freedom to extend my limbs wherever I wanted. Maybe this wasn't what I wanted. Maybe it was worth staying permanently single to have an undisturbed bed.

In the morning, we got up and took a Lyft to Brooklyn, where I met Miriam's roommates, then helped her organize her clothes in her new closet and rearrange some furniture she'd inherited from the former inhabitant of the room. We unpacked a boxed-up mattress she'd ordered to the place and pulled it out, watching it inflate as it filled the bedroom with its plasticky smell.

"You know that's full of toxins," said one of Miri's new roommates, Amira, standing in the doorframe. "You should open a window."

"Thanks for the tip," I said a little sarcastically, and cracked the window an inch. She probably didn't deserve my tone; I was just underslept.

At lunchtime, we sat around a small, round table with Amira and the other roommate, who'd brought in a mezze platter from the Turkish takeout place down the block. They divided up pita breads and vine leaves with expert precision and said no to the beers we'd brought along as a house offering.

When I left, Miri hugged me hard with her bony little arms and said, "I'll see you soon, right?"

"Of course," I said. "And remember, Ellie lives just down the block. I can set you up on a coffee date if you want."

It was the kind of offer I'd have scorned in her position, like it was an implication I couldn't look after myself. I would never have wanted someone six years older than me who I'd maybe met once to check in on how I was doing in a new city. But Miri nodded eagerly and said, "I would love that."

"Okay, sure," I told her, giving her a last little pat on the shoulder.

On my way home on the subway, I texted Ellie: *Miri's just moved to the area. She's kinda nervous about NYC, having a real job, living without my mom looking after her, etc. I said you might take her for coffee.*

Some people were really pathetic.

IT TOOK ELLIE A COUPLE OF WEEKS TO SET UP A COFFEE DATE WITH Miriam because Charlotte Louisa wasn't sleeping properly, and she and Jake had decided to attend a "sleep regression class" at some bougie pediatrician's office in downtown Manhattan.

Is CL old enough to regress in anything? I messaged her when she told me. *She was quite literally born yesterday.*

It's all relative, Ellie replied. *At this point she's spent about two-thirds of her life sleeping and one-third of it screaming.*

Honestly, hard relate.

Ha ha. Getting the OBGYN to check out my vagina stitches has been high up on my glamorous to-do list as well, so I may as well do that while I'm in Manhattan.

Oh man. How are things doing down there?

My taint feels like a fucking war zone but according to Jake's non-expert eye, everything looks normal.

So you guys are going at it again?

Absolutely not. Maybe a bit of freshman-level fooling around when he's lucky. But mainly I'm just getting him to inspect my perineal stitches in the shower. It's very sexy.

In some niche communities I'm sure that's considered a kink.

Then maybe they can throw me some cash on Only-
Fans. God knows I need it for diapers.

AND SO THREE WEEKS MELTED AWAY WHILE MY BEST FRIEND TOOK
classes on how to sleep like a baby and my sister "coped remarkably"—
according to my mother—with living her new life in the greatest
city in the world, rent-free. I met up with Ellie again when springtime had properly set in. We sat outside a coffeehouse on Fifth in
Park Slope, Charlotte Louisa parked and sleeping while Ellie and
I perched on outdoor tables in the sunshine. Every few minutes,
Ellie fussed around with the hood of the bassinet, mumbling about
how babies can't wear sunscreen.

"Humans really need to get it together," I said. "The Gowanus
Canal is radioactive and the citywide water system is contaminated
with crustaceans, but we haven't evolved to tolerate a bit of zinc
yet? How can we possibly hope to survive the inevitable nuclear
holocaust?"

"Tell me about it," Ellie said, but her mouth was a thin line.
Maybe she didn't love my apocalyptic vision of the future when
she'd just had a baby who might have to live through it; maybe she
wanted a bit more googly-eyed adoration from me around Charlotte
Louisa. I knew I was a little less interested in the baby than Ellie had
hoped I would be. I smiled at her when she cooed in Ellie or Jake's
lap, but I wasn't interested in hearing about her sleep cycles or wake
windows, and I'd never said she made me want to have kids myself.
She was an impediment to my life, really. That was the brutal truth.

The barista brought me out an iced coffee while Ellie sipped
on some green tea concoction and said no to sharing a blueberry
muffin.

"Are you on a diet?" I said, deploying that judgmental inflection women were allowed to use with their friends now that
body positivity was mainstream. In the nineties—the feted era of
"Smack My Bitch Up"—it was all "Are you really going to have that

whole burger?" and shaming your friends into calorie-counting. These days, it was imperative to tell off your pals if they acted like they might be considering deliberately losing weight. *Pile on the pounds for the cause, goddammit.* Social media hypocrites in Spandex navigated this new terrain by waxing lyrical about "doing this for my mental health" while subsisting on celery and Pelotons. Meanwhile, the rest of us had to get fat or be accused of not being liberal.

"Not exactly," she said in answer to the diet question, looking down into her green tea. "I'm just trying to stay healthy this summer, you know? Pregnancy can take a lot out of you."

"I guess," I said. "But make sure you don't starve yourself." *Make sure you don't get thin while having the perfect life as well.*

"So, Miriam," said Ellie quickly.

I dug my nails into the top of the muffin, extracted a handful of dough-covered blueberries, and nodded. "Thank you for meeting with her."

"No, I mean, it was nice! She's a sweet girl. Just as shy as she was at your graduation. Little older, though, obviously."

"She hasn't grown up much since then. Emotionally, I mean."

"Oh, I thought she seemed levelheaded. She just seemed a bit nervous about living in the city. That's normal."

I shook my head. "She's totally unequipped for all this, really, isn't she?"

"I wouldn't say that. She was doing some research about the place she's interning at, had some stuff written down about what she wanted to do there. She had a little planner—I thought it was sweet. There's no reason she can't make a success of it this time."

"You don't know Miri the way I do," I said, shoveling another handful of muffin into my mouth. "She's always enthusiastic at the start. And then as soon as she hits a bump in the road, everything falls apart. She doesn't have staying power." My mother's ghost rose in the background.

"Tash, be a little more generous," said Ellie, reaching back over into the bassinet to rearrange Charlotte Louisa's blanket. "She can

stand to muddle her way through this, even make a few mistakes—
she's still in her twenties."

I couldn't help but think: *What the hell is that supposed to mean?*

A BURST OF HOT WEATHER HIT WITHOUT WARNING AT THE END OF
May and the air went from thin, tentative, and changeable to humid
as hell within twenty-four hours. My hair became so uncontrollable
that I resorted to using gel to try to flatten flyaways. Miri, of course,
simply sported professional-looking beach waves without any dis-
cernible effort.

On the first weekend of true heat, a little over a month after
she'd made her move to New York City, I took her to a champagne
bar in Williamsburg and we shared happy-hour oysters on ice at a
table on the street corner. That conversation with Zach about the
neighborhood going to hell had made me realize how much I'd
missed the bar, one of my old haunts from before London.

"This is so great," Miri kept saying, gazing wide-eyed at the
waiters in vintage New Orleans–style getups. "Do you come here all
the time?"

"No," I said with a little laugh. "Just special occasions."

"And this occasion is?"

"Officially welcoming you to the city." We touched glasses in
acknowledgment of the moment, and she talked about the people
she'd met at her internship. She kept looking around at the polished
surroundings and the generic storefronts of Lululemon, Urban Out-
fitters, Madewell. The fake water tower at the top of the Williamsburg Hotel was beginning to light up; I could imagine the hordes of
tourists already lining up outside to spend a timed ninety minutes
sipping twenty-five-dollar cocktails on a rock-hard barstool while re-
garding the view.

"It's really different here from where I am," Miri said. "And definitely from where you live."

"I guess," I said, shrugging. "I mean, most people barely consider
Williamsburg part of Brooklyn anymore. It's basically Manhattan."

"You're so right," she said, "it's awesome." I was a little affronted by her enthusiasm. It was supposed to be an insult.

As our conversation continued, it became obvious that the reason Miri was enjoying her internship so far had less to do with any work being done by the company and more to do with her manager, Dan.

"Remember you're not there for an office romance. Especially not with your manager," I said, after about fifteen minutes of her soliloquizing about how Dan looked in a fitted shirt.

She blushed and poked at an oyster shell with her finger. "It's not like that."

"You've had a few false starts, so you really need to concentrate on work now," I added, warming to my theme. She was better than me at letting things go; she merely nodded and took another sip of champagne.

"How's *your* work?" she asked after a pause.

"Oh, I don't know. It's a dying industry."

"But do you think you'll stay on the breaking news team or maybe . . . you might get a promotion?" She said it like she was innocently asking about progression, when what she really meant was: *Maybe you'll get back to where you were before the screwup.*

A week earlier, the whole staff had been called into the midtown office for a long presentation about the company's stellar performance. Record profits, helped along by the sale of customer data to various advertising companies, were touted triumphantly by BR. The breaking news team, he said, would be expanding. The on-the-ground reporting team would be "streamlined." Reality TV and crime were doing well for us. We were going to concentrate less on publishing content from Asia.

After the meeting, Willem had given me an overfamiliar pat on the arm—not quite sleazy, but not exactly *not* sleazy—and said, "You know he couldn't have done that presentation without your insights. You should drop into his office later and remind him."

It went against every fiber in my body, but I surmised that Willem would follow up with me if I didn't. So before I'd finished my shift, I'd forced myself to go around to BR's glass box, where I'd knocked once and been waved in while he finished up a phone call. Then I'd pulled the words out of the greasiest bit of my dying soul: "Cool presentation earlier."

"Oh! Yes! Really fantastic stuff, isn't it? Great news for your team especially." BR gave an abrupt little nod at the end of every sentence.

"Yeah, about that." I'd looked down at my hands and then back up at him. "I wondered if there was any chance in the future of me . . . moving away from the breaking news desk and back into the on-the-ground reporting team?" BR's expression didn't exactly scream "enthusiastic," so I quickly added, "I understand if you don't want to send me abroad again. I understand the notion of consequences. And I know you weren't a fan of my subscription model idea. But I do think I could be really effective as an internal affairs reporter here in New York. I've been following a few big issues in the city, and there's so much to dig into, like the man who died outside the homeless shelter in East New York because they wouldn't allow his dog inside, and that foster-care case where the children—"

"Natasha," BR said gently, putting his clasped hands down on the table. "I don't know if you took from that presentation what you were supposed to."

I looked back at him, silent.

"The breaking news team is *growing*," he continued. "The reporters-at-large are being *streamlined*. This is what the future of the newsroom looks like. You're in exactly the right place for fantastic opportunities."

"I get that," I said, "and the last thing I'd want is to seem ungrateful. But there's something to be said for professional fulfillment. And you know, I've won awards for my feature writing and my long-form work. I was pulling in new readers with my investigations."

"You're making far more money for the company now than you ever did before. Those speedy news nuggets are what really get people sharing. And shares mean ads seen, partnerships made, wheels turning, happy board members. Revenue."

"I understand, but when I was in the reporting team, I really helped with the branding—"

"Natasha, Natasha." BR put his fingers to his eyes and massaged his pressure points before bringing them back down. "We all appreciated that—seven years ago. But now we *have* an established brand. It's just a case of business prioritization—all that boring stuff I have to think about while everybody else has fun."

"Sure." I knew how far I could push the issue. "Well, thanks for your time anyway."

"If you maximize your output times on breaking news, you could be in for a raise as soon as next year," BR said as I got up from my chair. "And you know, *everyone* has priorities. I have priorities, the CEO has priorities, the board has them, the advertising team has them. As a woman in your midthirties, I'm guessing you might have some priorities outside of work too—family priorities, perhaps." He smiled. "And I want you to know that we celebrate that. That's nothing to be ashamed of. Maybe look to them for now."

When I'd left the office that day, I hadn't even felt angry, just numb.

Now I looked across the table at Miri and thought about what she'd say if she knew all of this was waiting for her in a few short years. I did her the favor of not saying it. She deserved to proceed with blessed naïvety, just as she did with everything else.

"I'm not looking to join the reporting team again," I said. "All that running around, chasing leads, interviewing assholes, never knowing if a story is going to get killed . . . I'm just at a stage of my life where it's so much better that I know what I'm doing day-to-day, and I have some security while I deal with doing up the apartment and finalizing the divorce and everything else."

"Oh. Yeah. Absolutely." Miri nodded so many times that I thought she might fall off her chair. *You're not convincing anybody, Miri*, I thought, but I was kind of touched by the effort.

As we finished off our oysters, squeezing lemon slices and spooning on a vinegary solution, the Friday afternoon warning siren sounded throughout the neighborhood. I raised a hand to the waiter and pointed to my glass for a refill, then I realized that Miri was looking at me across the table with genuine fear.

"What is that?" she asked. "Is there a hurricane?"

"Oh!" I laughed, watching calm pedestrians traversing the streets of Williamsburg in the golden light without a care in the world. "No, no. That's just the Shabbat siren—the Hasidic community sounds it to warn one another about the sun setting. It's so they can get home before the light goes. You mainly hear it in Williamsburg and Crown Heights."

I'd gotten used to living with the siren, the areas where you could discern the thin line of the eruv above the houses and the Hasidic families who walked through the local parks in groups. We lived parallel lives. The women with shiny wigs, long sleeves, below-the-knee skirts, and pantyhose even in the heat and men with long payos and black hats had surprised me when I'd first moved from WASPy Nantucket. But after years of living in New York, the yellow school buses with Hebrew on the side barely registered with me, though I often watched the large families—kids directing other kids, young teens pushing their toddler siblings in double strollers, the mothers hanging behind with a kindergartner in each hand to chat with one another—and wondered about their lives. I'd envied the way everything seemed so simple and communal: on Shabbat, you made the food and lit the candles of your ancestors, and everyone you knew turned up to share it with you. Your parents carefully selected a suitor, with an eye on good looks and high intelligence, and none of the young men had slept around or declared themselves "ethically nonmonogamous." And you popped out your kids early while your body could still bounce back, all the while relying on the support of a family that put no pressure on you to succeed in a career. Nobody expected you to "have it all," that toxic phrase we'd all agreed had destroyed so many women's lives but also hadn't honestly disavowed. I knew what Ellie would say: *Tash, you're losing yourself in a fantasy that's both culturally insensitive and ridiculously reductive. You have to bring yourself back down to Earth.* I hated how she lived rent-free in my head. She always took the sensible line, the zoomed-out perspective—but maybe I was just a bit braver, a bit more open-minded than her.

"If they don't get home by sunset, what happens?" said Miri, as we watched two young Hasidic men in white shirts and long black jackets making their way at a leisurely pace past the restaurant and back toward the buildings where they lived.

"They incur God's wrath, I presume," I said. I watched another couple of men head down the street opposite, averting their eyes from us. I got the feeling they always made it home well before the evening closed in. There's something to be said for not pushing your luck.

SEVENTEEN

Woman Sparks Debate with the Most "Bridezilla"
Demand Ever

Fox News Host Spars with Man Who "Spiritually
Identifies" as a Raccoon

Woman Sparks Debate by Having First Child at Age 47

Do You have "Political Depression"? TikTok Says Yes

Woman Sparks Debate after Wearing Box Braids on
the Catwalk

Inside the Wreckage of Grisly Plane Crash Where 8
Died and 2 Maimed for Life

Woman Sparks Debate by Claiming Boyfriend Should
Cook and Clean "Because of the Patriarchy"

Man Banned from Restaurant After Claiming
"Ancestral Right" to Wear the Confederate Flag

Woman Sparks Debate by Refusing to Give Her
"Begging" Child a Sibling

.　　.　　.

I CLOSED MY LAPTOP ON A THURSDAY NIGHT AT THE KITCHEN TABLE in June and said to Zach, who was sitting on the couch in the living room, "Is data entry as soul-destroying as this stuff?"

"Nope! It's beautifully predictable," he responded without missing a beat.

I sighed. "If only breaking news was that way."

"What's the latest?"

"Well, the last piece I wrote was about a woman wearing a sports bra to her local church in Kansas. Apparently the pastor fainted. But then he had some kind of visitation from the Holy Spirit, so maybe it was all worth it for him."

"That counts as breaking news these days?"

"Oh, everything does," I said. "I mean, as long as it's happened within about forty-eight hours and is getting talked about online."

"Sounds . . . honest."

"For sure. And I'm apparently stuck on this side of it forever. Because of one dumb screwup."

"Not ideal."

"Nope." I went to the fridge, extracted a beer I didn't recognize but assumed was communal, and held another up in his eyeline, offering it to him. He nodded and I opened the two cans and placed one in front of him before retreating back to my desk space.

"No one demoted Hunter S. Thompson for fucking people and getting high while he was reporting, by the way," I said, taking a long swig of lager. "He got a cult following and a book deal instead."

Zach raised his beer in my direction and took a sip. A strand of his hair had started falling artfully across his forehead. His arms were starting to tan, too, and today he was wearing an absurdly neon tank that somehow looked great against them. *Why did he have to look good in everything?* I tried to imagine him in something deeply unflattering, an outfit that would surely make him look ridiculous, like a pair of baggy overalls with an eyebrow piercing and black eyeliner, but somehow, even in the cruelest depths of my imagination, he made it work. *Fuck.*

"Do you think it's a bad thing that the mainstream media is failing?" he asked, placing his beer carefully in front of him. "I can see the advantages."

"Okay, Donald Trump."

"No, I mean it though. Is hearing this crap day in, day out doing something to our collective psyche? Maybe it's why everyone walks around so on edge all the time. Wars that we'd never know about, people's miseries that we share in though we've never met them, pets killed and kids dying of mysterious diseases . . ."

"The alternative is burying your head in the sand," I said, a little irritably.

"If you want to call it that. Personally, I stopped reading the news years ago, and I've found it's done a lot for my mental health."

"Well, I don't exactly have that option," I retorted. We sat in silence for a moment while I debated whether to ask him if he really thought entering numbers into spreadsheets for anonymous companies was bringing us any closer to fully automated luxury communism than writing up articles about fainting priests. My better nature won out and I bit my tongue.

"You don't have to take it personally," said Zach mildly. "I mean, if I recall correctly, you have your own misgivings about the industry. And if you can't remove your own interests from a political debate—"

"It's not that, Zach," I said and sighed. "Look, I don't even know why I'm defending this bullshit. If you haven't already noticed, I absolutely fucking hate my job."

He leaned back in his chair, spreading his legs out a little, and smiled. I imagined climbing on top of him, extracting his dick from his zipper with one hand, pulling him inside me as he gasped. Then he said in a self-satisfied kind of way, "Ah. Well, that makes more sense. And it certainly makes me respect you a lot more."

I felt an electric jolt that started at my throat and ended in my vagina. *Zach respected me.*

"The system's broken," I said, trying to keep it casual, but I could feel my cheeks flushing. "I guess we just have to sit tight and wait for the revolution."

"Or we can perpetrate it ourselves," Zach added, turning the can around in his hands. It was an eye-wateringly expensive beer from a microbrewery in Greenpoint.

I raised an eyebrow and said jokingly, "Didn't you go to a private liberal arts college? You'd be first up against the wall."

"In which case, I better enjoy life while I can." He raised the can and threw back a more substantial amount of beer. "You know, Gen Z doesn't even drink alcohol. They've eliminated every vice we fell for. I have high hopes for them, from a revolutionary perspective."

"As someone who works with Gen Z on a regular basis," I said, "I'm not as optimistic. All I see is a sea of yerba mate–drinking assholes in flared jeans pushing out the same cynical content as the millennials."

"Hmm." Zach used one foot to push off his shoe, then did the same with the other. "You know, yerba mate is a traditional South American ingredient. Just because it's been appropriated by a few young Americans doesn't mean it's for assholes."

"Well, we're not in Uruguay right now, are we? Context matters. They're assholes." I was doubling down now, irritated at his constant nitpicking.

"What makes them assholes isn't what they drink; it's what they write. If they had any backbone, they'd be publishing a hundred articles a day about the epidemic of missing Indigenous women in this country."

"I mean . . . it's not because they don't want to. If stories about missing Indigenous women were raking in audience numbers, it'd be different. But the public is very clearly telling us what they want. And so that's what we write."

He looked at me. "That's how your news team decides what to publish? Shouldn't it be the other way around?"

"Readers show us what they want through their search behavior, and we produce content for them," I said. "Isn't it a bit paternalistic and elitist to decide their opinions don't matter?"

Zach cleared his throat and smiled, but the smile didn't reach his eyes. "I don't know. Are we having an argument?"

"I'd call it a robust discussion." *What are you doing for the missing Indigenous women?* I thought, but I decided not to say it. Instead, I added: "And I know that you, of all people, can take it."

He accepted the compliment and said quietly, "Sure can." Then, after a beat: "Hey, I was thinking we should throw a party."

"Here?" I looked around at the bare-bones living room, the little square of kitchen, the dark bedrooms, and I thought about the way our downstairs neighbors hit the ceiling with a broom if I walked around in heels. This wasn't exactly the first venue I'd choose to host an event.

"Yeah, I mean like for the Fourth of July. Remember we talked about it when I first moved in? It'd be fun." He pointed toward the beach. "We could start it out there, bring out a cooler and a couple of umbrellas or something, maybe a sound system. Invite some friends, colleagues, whatever. And if it's still going into the night, maybe come back here."

I thought about it. "I guess that wouldn't be awful." The Fourth was three weeks away. Was that enough time to pull together enough people so I wouldn't look like a social pariah in front of Zach?

"There's that effusive, spontaneous energy she's known for!" he quipped, and I rolled my eyes.

"I was just thinking through the logistics," I said. "Like the neighbors, the police, all of that."

"It's the Fourth of July. Literal explosions with gunpowder are encouraged. I'm sure the neighbors can deal with a few extra footsteps and one or two people on the balcony."

Though I'd been to a grand total of zero parties since London, I could feel myself coming around to this idea. Zach asking if we could host something together undeniably counted as a domestic collaboration. Maybe he'd ask me if I wanted to get back together over a hard seltzer on the sand, as the sea gently lapped the shore and Ellie and Jake introduced a giggling Charlotte Louisa to a couple of Zach's high school friends. "I know it took me a while," he'd say, "but I didn't want to bring it up right when I moved in. For one thing, I thought it was important that we take it slow this time. For another, I wanted to play it cool." He'd wink and I'd give him a little shove then pull him close, slipping my tongue deep in his mouth, and then he'd push me back onto the sand and people around would start drunkenly whooping and cheering and shouting "Get a room!" Just as they did, the first fireworks would pop overhead.

"Let's do it," I said. "I think we can make it work."

"Victory!" He raised his arms in the air like he was coming in first at the end of an Olympic sprint. For a microsecond I thought about the swimmer, about how he'd never celebrated when he'd won a race but instead stayed still in the pool, a mischievous grin on his face. I pushed that memory back down into the annals.

Instead: "You really had your heart set on that party," I said, laughing.

"Yeah, well. Gotta have something to look forward to. Or at least something that feels normal. Especially with everything going on."

"Right," I said, nodding. "It sounds so tough." Updates on Zach's mother came sporadically, and I tried not to force them.

"The bad news keeps on coming at a hundred miles an hour. Probably like working on a breaking news desk, actually," he said, avoiding my gaze. "Tumors are growing in these nodules along my mother's spine. She's on a lot of morphine. It's at the point of full-scale invasion."

"Gosh. Poor woman." I imagined Zach's mother, yellow from

liver damage, and her back serrated, like a sickly stegosaurus. She and I had met just once when Zach and I were dating, sort of by accident—he was leaving lunch with her and meeting up with me afterward. If he and I did work out as a couple, surely the fact of our having connected would bring him some comfort, even if she couldn't be present at the wedding. *If* I decided to get married again—and he'd really have to convince me.

"Yeah. That's an understatement, really," Zach said, in response to my woefully inadequate words of comfort. "I think we're approaching the end of the road. My brother's coming back from his globally destructive job in Texas this week, and my sister's actually deigning to leave her gated community on Long Island. They're like the horsemen of the apocalypse—when they start moving, you know shit's getting serious."

"I'm guessing you guys haven't magically become closer in the past few years."

"Not at all. I mean, my sister can be all right but . . ." He trailed off and I watched his gaze run along the walls, the ceiling, and back again.

"I hate to ask," I said, "but do you have a sense of when—"

His eyes still trained on the walls, he cut in without emotion: "They think it's days, not weeks."

AFTER TWO MONTHS ON THE JOB IN LONDON, I HAD INTERVIEWED A female member of Parliament who had been so horrible to me that I'd cried. I'd been imbued with the excitement of the newly arrived expat, bright-eyed and bushy-tailed like a trash panda with ideas above its station. I'd bounded down to her office, repeating in my head: *Britain's youngest female MP, big on social media, Pakistani dad who used to be a bus driver, England's answer to AOC.* I knocked on her door and then entered with a stupid grin, drawing out my "Hi!" like she was going to hug me or something. She'd just nodded from her seated position on a green leather chair and told me, with a brisk smile that didn't meet her eyes, to go ahead and sit down too.

Every question I'd asked her was batted back to me with a challenge. I'd wanted to know how she felt about the "England's answer to AOC" moniker; it was a phrase that had been mentioned in a couple of profiles. She told me Americans are desperate to make everything about them, that Britain was a complex country with a long history, and maybe I should do my reading.

"Oh . . . I did," I said, caught off guard, and she immediately snapped back, "Well, what reading did you do?" leaving me unable to pluck the title of even a single nonfiction book from my frozen mind. I'd prepared for political repartee and brushed up on the voting practices in the House of Commons, but I hadn't been expecting to be challenged on my syllabus.

Eventually, to my great shame, I'd stuttered out: "Well, I know Harry Potter isn't exactly an accurate portrayal of British life but . . ."

"No, it isn't," she interrupted. "If you look on my website, there's a reading list for people who are just getting into politics."

The humiliation didn't end there. She told me Americans are natural puritans, that our rollback of abortion rights was proof of it, that a bunch of evangelical white people had left Europe a few hundred years ago in search of a new land where they could institute a repressive, theocratic regime. "Which, of course, they've finally managed to do," she said, then added, "but at the beginning it was mainly about killing off the natives." She described how my home country was a cesspit of child sacrifice by gunfire and *Hunger Games*–style health care and medieval, racist capital punishment, and any self-respecting American would publicly renounce their nationality as soon as they reached adulthood. "I assume you came here looking for a better future?" she asked, finally, before I'd gotten a word in.

"I . . . might go home one day. You know, just because of my family," I said meekly.

She nodded and gave me a humorless smile. I'd kept it together while I wobbled in my work heels down the long, carpeted Westminster halls and out into the cloudy street, and waited until I was on the Tube to cry. As I wiped tears messily away from my cheeks, allowing my mascara to bleed liberally, a man about ten years older than me had leaned over and passed me a tissue.

Back at home, in our creaky, Victorian flat with single-glazed windows and a mouse infestation no one seemed to think was a big deal, I stomped around and ranted at a sympathetic Joe. "They think they have no problems! None! The way they talk about it, you'd think it was a fucking utopian paradise, rather than a failed experiment in democracy run by people who are yet to discover modern orthodontics!"

Joe laughed and shook his head, told me to forget about the stupid bitch.

"Hey, that's misogynistic," I said, and he apologized: "I was just trying to back you up!"

"I know," I said. "I'm sorry. I'm just sick and tired of this European exceptionalism. They're just a bunch of passive-aggressive, neo-colonial, low-energy, chinless, bad-toothed monarchists!" I kicked the bottom cabinet with my slippered foot and did a dumb-voice impression of a man we'd had a conversation with at a restaurant two weeks earlier: "'American culture? *That's* an oxymoron!' It's enough to make me want to sign up for the goddamn Tea Party!"

Joe was shaking with silent laughter by then; he always seemed to find my outbursts comical. He only laughed when he could tell that I was half joking though. He knew how to read a room.

"Now, now, I'll have you know the United Kingdom has one excellent resource that no other country can possibly match," he said, in a fake aristocratic British accent.

"Which is?" I replied, playing along, my own voice sliding into Cockney.

"The cuisine, of course!" Joe threw up his arms. "Black pudding! Spotted dick! Scotch eggs! Mushy peas!"

"Deep-fried haggis!" I joined in, to which he replied, "Well, *that* would be a delicacy!" and then continued rattling off culinary crimes: blood sausage, tripe and onions, shepherd's pie, toad-in-the-hole.

By the time he'd finished, I was lying on the stained linoleum floor laughing so hard that my sides hurt, begging him to stop.

I think we fell asleep on the sofa together that night, curled up under the overpriced cashmere blanket I'd bought from a friendly woman at Broadway Market. I imagine we'd probably watched some familiar, unchallenging sitcom to take my mind off the adoring profile of the politician I'd have to start drafting the next day. My head would have rested on Joe's shoulder; he would have put one arm around me and let the other one go numb from lack of circulation. He was always charitable like that, though he did sometimes complain about it the next morning.

There was no Joe to comfort me after a bad day of work now. Most likely he waited for his new girlfriend to come home and rubbed her shoulders the same way he once rubbed mine, cooked her spaghetti and salmon with cream cheese (his specialty), performed spontaneous comedy routines to cheer her up while he danced around the kitchen with a spatula. He was thousands of miles away, still living our expat dream with a shiny new non-spousal visa, and it was all my fault.

EIGHTEEN

FOUR DAYS AFTER WE CONCEIVED THE FOURTH OF JULY PARTY, I WAS working in a coffee shop when a new editor for the lifestyle section messaged me.

> *Hey! I was just reading all about the swimmer stuff.*

My matcha latte stuck in my throat. *Hi*, I wrote back. *Yeah, it was rough.*

> *That really affected your mental health, right?*

Did I even know this person? I looked at her thumbnail photo—a red-haired woman pictured with a tabby cat balanced on her shoulders and a laughing man behind her. I definitely hadn't ever met her in person. *I guess*, I replied.

> *Omg forgive me. I forget sometimes that not everyone is discussing mental health all day and night lol! But obvs on lifestyle, we think about it so often.*

Sure. No harm done! I ground my molars together, sending a shooting pain through the right side of my jaw.

> *I was just thinking . . . would you be up for working thru your trauma on the page?*

In what way?

*Like, writing a lifestyle piece about the before and after.
How it affected yr mental health, what you did to come back
from it, etc etc. There's so much discussion right now about
how writing about yr biggest mistake can be life-changing.*

And sharing it with millions of people?

Wasn't it already public?

I made a concerted effort to unclench my jaw and took a breath.
*I just don't know if that would work for me. I think it's a great idea but
maybe for someone else?*

*Yeeeahhh. It's just, like, no one else has really done any-
thing like that.*

*I'm sure you'll find someone. I think . . . it just feels too meta for
me. Too inside baseball for the average reader. Could it be more like a
listicle for more minor mistakes everyday people would make?* I was
grasping at straws.

*No, honestly, I think there's still big interest!! Lots of traf-
fic still incoming from yr original article, according to Bryce.*

Well, that was great to know. *I don't think that traffic is a load of
adoring fans, unfortunately,* I wrote. *So the piece that you're suggesting
feels like adding fuel to the fire.*

Bryce was pretty sure.

I started typing: *Well, why don't you tell Bryce that I said,* but
then my phone began to ring. I looked at the vibrating handset like

it was an alien; who the hell makes phone calls apart from bots and CIA agents these days? Apparently, Zach did.

"Natasha Bailey, professional clickbait generator—what's your latest tragedy?" I said, minimizing the internal messaging app on my laptop.

"Hey," he said. "My mom died last night."

"Oh, shit."

"Yeah."

I looked around the coffee shop with its whitewashed, industrial walls and its hanging plants and felt guilty about even being there. Why did I have to make that stupid joke? I hadn't been concerned when Zach hadn't come home the night before; I thought he'd just be back late. I hadn't connected the dots and realized what his absence might mean.

"Do you want me to come and get you?" I said.

"No, no." I could hear that he was walking down a hallway or a street, people's conversations rising up and then quieting in the background. "There will be a funeral and everything; I've got to help make some arrangements. Dad's a bit out of it right now. Understandably."

"And you?"

"I'm as okay as anyone can be in the circumstances. I'm doing the whole fifties housewife thing of throwing myself into domestic details and occasionally taking a Valium. There's something so surreal about negotiating sandwich fillings with caterers and inviting people to wear yellow to the service while your mother's body lies in a freezer. Everyone keeps calling it a celebration of life and telling me how great the flower arrangement looks on a solid oak coffin."

I thought about the toxic positivity of it all, the aggressive demand for something photogenic at a time of overwhelming grief. These days, no one was allowed the quiet dignity of black clothes and closed curtains and a prolonged retreat from society, much less open weeping and a cathartic throwing of oneself into the open grave. It was such a shame.

"I can be there, any day, whatever time, if you need any help. And I'll definitely be at the funeral," I said. Emotion rose in my throat. I knew that now the call had come, I would answer it; I would stand up and be counted; I would do what was good and righteous. I would call in sick to work if necessary—hell, I'd tell them I had to take compassionate leave.

"That's kind," he said, "but I think we've got it under control. In fact, between my brother and my sister, I think we might have a too-many-cooks scenario."

"Got it," I said. "Then consider me there for silent support only."

"I really appreciate that, Nat," he said. "But listen, I don't want to ruin your day. Funerals aren't exactly a laugh a minute. And it's a long trip from Queens. I couldn't ask that of you."

"I totally get it," I said. *You don't have to be so strong. It's clear you want me to know about your pain.*

I wondered then whether his sex drive might be impacted by the grief. How long would I have to wait until it recovered and I could ethically make a move? Would it count as taking advantage if *he* wanted to fuck away the pain? If we were at the wake together, my hand on the small of his back, my freshly washed and blow-dried hair spilling out onto his shoulder as I leaned on him slightly, he might feel an urgency to prove to the universe that he was still alive. While aunts and uncles dabbed at the corners of their eyes and talked in low voices, I imagined us stepping outside, him looking into my eyes so intensely that my voice would catch in my throat. As we leaned against the back wall of the funeral home, accidentally trampling soil and flowers, he'd hitch up my yellow skirt and pick me up with his muscular arms, his gaze never leaving mine. Would it be a transgression to do it, to bite his lip till it bled so nobody inside could hear us? Or would it be strangely beautiful, one of those movie-worthy moments that said so much about sex and death and love and human perseverance?

. . .

A COUPLE DAYS LATER, AT THE END OF AN IN-OFFICE SHIFT, I TOOK the subway to Soho to shop for a yellow dress. It was a fine line I'd have to walk: obviously I had to look attractive enough that family and friends remembered me afterward, but also demure enough to be respectful. I wandered around H&M, then Zara, holding yellow fabrics to my face in the open mirrors so I could check which shade complemented my skin tone. Neon yellow was out: insensitively loud. Soft, pastel yellows washed me out, and it helped no one if I turned up looking worse than the person in the coffin. It felt like an orangey, sunflower-type yellow was best in terms of playing up my eyes.

After an hour or so, I decided on a bridesmaid-style dress I found in Anthropologie that had a long, flowing skirt and a high enough neck to be church-ready. The skirt was covered in tiny white flowers that I found charming. As I lined up at the register to pay, I texted Zach: *Hey, when's the funeral?*

It took him a few minutes to text back, during which time I had paid and exited the store. I was on the street, headed toward the nearest subway and squinting in the sunlight when I got his reply: *Oh. I didn't know you really wanted to come.*

I was a little affronted. But then I'd heard before that grief can do things to your memory. *Well, you invited me,* I replied, hoping that would get us back on track. Isn't that what he meant when he said he wanted me for silent support? He'd told me all the funeral details, called me specifically to tell me his mother had died. If that wasn't tantamount to an invitation, then I didn't know what was.

I was on the platform waiting for the train when I got his response. *Like I said, it's just a lot of travel, family politics, etc. You'd barely see me anyway.*

But who will be there for you? I clutched the cardboard bag containing the yellow dress tightly as I typed. I was just thinking of him.

Plenty of people? he answered immediately, with the damning question mark, as if to say that much was obvious.

I'd thought about the funeral ever since I saw that image of the bag marked CYTOTOXIC. I just thought that maybe he'd want me there, as an old friend, as someone he could trust. I would turn up at his childhood home—finally seeing it, because I'd never gotten the chance when we dated the first time around—and clasp his father by the hand, saying, "Brian, I'm so sorry about Mary." I would say her name bravely, even though it was uncomfortable, and Zach's father would receive it like a blessing. Everyone else had danced around the wording, had refused to say her name since she'd died and had instead dealt in euphemisms: *I'm sorry about what happened, I'm sorry for your loss.*

"Thank you," he would say, holding my hand close to his heart.

Then I'd drive Zach to the church early in his car—he wouldn't be able to take the wheel himself because his hands were shaking—and we'd sit outside while he gathered himself and I gave him a pep talk.

"The worst day of your life has already happened," I would say. "This is just one hour."

I'd carry a delicate bouquet of flowers to set down next to the coffin, and I'd touch Zach's hand lightly but lovingly as he wiped away a tear during the beautiful service. He'd give a short, sweet eulogy about how his mother had been his guiding light and the foundation for all his future adventures, and when he stood up to deliver it he'd glance at me briefly because I'd given him strength that day. He'd tell me afterward that none of his other friends had stepped up in the way I had, without even expecting a thank-you.

And now he was taking all of that from me.

NINETEEN

I GOT A CAR EARLY IN THE MORNING. I'D GOOGLED THE OBITUARY, found it on the funeral home's website, and called to confirm the timing of the service. This was old hat for me—I'd done it hundreds of times before on the news desk when someone died an especially tragic, especially marketable death, and I had to confirm it. Zach had wanted to minimize my inconvenience, and that was sweet, but I didn't feel like it was right for me to stay home. I'd been raised to be compassionate and thoughtful, not to abandon a friend during his time of need.

The funeral was set for 10:00 a.m. at a small church in Yonkers, and the family were asking for donations to a cancer research charity in lieu of flowers. I pondered that as a man named Vijay drove me in his Honda Civic inland from Rockaway Beach, across the Jamaica Bay Wildlife Refuge with the sea on either side, through heavy traffic around the airport, and then up through Queens over the Whitestone Bridge and across the Bronx to Yonkers. How were you supposed to communicate that you'd given that money to charity? Did they take it on faith? Did you leave a little card by the gravestone with the details of your donation? Was there a wedding-style table set aside for cards and gifts? I'd clicked through to the charity's site but then left without donating anything, confused about the protocol.

The journey took much longer than I'd anticipated, and by the time we got close to the church, I'd been in the car for over an hour.

It was long enough for the caffeine from my morning black coffee to have worn off, and my confidence was beginning to wane. But I was wearing the yellow dress, just like Zach had asked. The important thing was to be there for a person when they were at their lowest point, when they didn't even know what they wanted themselves.

Vijay dropped me off a street away from the church, gesturing to the road ahead. "I can't go any farther than here," he said. "Traffic."

"That's fine," I replied. "Thank you so much." And I got out of the car, wishing him a nice day while at the same time deciding that I would only tip him 10 percent. If he couldn't go the extra mile for me, I couldn't go the extra mile for him.

I walked down the road and up to the entrance of the white church, where two women were fussing around a large flower arrangement that spelled out the word "MOM." *Tacky. I bet his brother chose that.* A small group of people dressed in yellow were standing outside, talking to one another in low voices, but the hearse hadn't arrived, and it was clear most family members hadn't either. I hung back, watching the door of the church and judging the outfits of the arriving guests: *Lemon-colored pants and a polo shirt, really? It's not a kindergarten graduation.*

After about ten minutes, I saw it: a long black car making its slow way up the miniature driveway from the street, followed by a limousine. One middle-aged woman gasped dramatically and held a tissue to her mouth when she caught sight of the vehicles, and a companion she'd been standing with put a reassuring hand on her shoulder. "She's in a better place, Linda," I heard the friend say, as though that solved everything.

I couldn't decide if I had made a terrible, intrusive mistake or if I was committing an admirably unselfish act. The possibility that it was the former made me increasingly anxious. My heart hammered in my ears as I watched the doors of the limousine open and a slightly stooped, ashen-faced man stagger out of one side, supported by a woman around my age who was wearing lots of makeup and a yellow peplum dress. Zach's sister and father, presumably. I couldn't see the other side very well because it was obscured by the church door, but I saw two pairs of men's shoes emerge and then the backs of two heads. One belonged unmistakably to Zach; the other man, I assumed, was his brother.

I had the compulsion to call out to him but I didn't. Instead, I watched the brother hold a hand up to some of the gathered people in a weak hello, while Zach put his head down and proceeded into the church without looking at anyone. The sister made sure the father was properly upright and then joined who I presumed were her husband and two kids in the doorway, and they all went in together. I thought about Zach, alone, and almost stepped forward. But then the other guests began entering in groups, and music started up inside, and the moment had passed.

I stepped closer to the church entrance from my position on the path as groups of people walked in, and eventually got so close that they had to stream around me on their way inside. Standing sentinel at the doorway was the pastor, who was greeting the mourners with a practiced kind of smile that conveyed welcoming consolation. Beside the pastor was one of the women whom I'd seen helping with the MOM arrangement, and then, after a few seconds, I noticed them both notice me. The pastor whispered something in her ear. She nodded professionally and then came toward me.

My field of vision was widening and narrowing, and my palms were sweating. I tried to swallow but it felt like my trachea had expanded inside my throat and my saliva was sticking to the inside. It wasn't the time to have a panic attack. It was the time to be strong for Zach.

When the woman reached me, she put a gentle hand on my elbow and said, "Are you here for the funeral?"

I looked at her with widened eyes, unable to communicate because I couldn't force enough air through my vocal cords. My autonomic system was failing me.

"Are you a member of the family?" she asked. "I know days like today are very hard."

I managed to shake my head and force out a few hoarse words. "Honestly," I said, "I was just . . . visiting."

She looked at me searchingly. "Perhaps you don't feel like everyone would welcome you here?" she said even more quietly, lowering her head closer to mine like we were sharing a secret.

"It's not that." I swallowed and began backing away. "Thank you for your help. Really. I don't need anything. I'm just going to go. Thank you."

She stood staring at me in the space I'd just vacated, clearly wondering whether she should pursue me or let me go, as I continued taking backward steps.

"Thank you again," I said, and started walking quickly through the small cemetery. When I reached the other side, I turned back one more time to see the woman conversing with the pastor. Were they talking about me? I held up my hand in a weak wave to make it clear that I wasn't returning and then took off faster, communicating internally to my feet so they wouldn't stop: *left foot, right foot, left foot, right foot.* I heard the heavy footsteps of pallbearers arranging themselves beside the coffin at the back of the hearse. The music from inside the church got louder. I turned the corner onto the sidewalk and carried on.

AT BRUNCH WITH ELLIE AND MIRIAM THAT FRIDAY, I WAS SUBDUED. We'd agreed to meet at an Israeli place in Park Slope since we all had the day off work, and to my annoyance, they both seemed familiar with the restaurant when I got there.

"Yeah, I came here with my roommates," said Miri, when I arrived. "The halloumi shakshuka is to *die* for."

"I know!" said Ellie. "Jake always says you just can't do better."

"Okay, okay, Brooklynites," I said, shaking my head and taking a seat.

"You're an honorary Brooklynite, right? The Rockaways are just, like, south *south* Brooklyn," said Miri, putting an arm around my upper back, which I delicately shook off. Now she was condescending to me about where I fit into the New York City hierarchy? Me, who'd lived in Brooklyn before she'd even managed to drop out of college the first time?

We ordered an assortment of appetizers and endured a five-minute monologue from Ellie about how wonderful it was to be out without Charlotte Louisa and how much of a goddamn saint Jake was to take care of his own daughter while she went out for a single meal. *He's a co-parent, not a Purple Heart recipient,* I felt like saying, but I didn't because I'm a good friend.

Dan at work had asked out Miri, which had immediately annihilated her crush on him. "I just kind of liked it better when I admired him from afar," she said, wrinkling her nose. "Do you know the feeling?"

"Sure," said Ellie. "That's how I like to keep things with Timothée Chalamet."

Miriam laughed in an open, unguarded way that I hadn't seen in a while. Then she turned to me and said: "Anyway, Tash, tell us about *your* love life."

"Oh, come on," I said, but the smile crept onto my face. Miri was smiling back at me encouragingly, but I could see in the corner of my eye that Ellie was watching me with a weird expression, like she was holding something back.

"If you're talking about Zach, I'm really happy with the pace of how it's going," I said. "We spend so much quality time together, thanks to the apartment. It's made me realize it really was worth buying it, even if I don't know every new restaurant on the block in Brooklyn." A less-than-subtle dig, but neither of them reacted. "Anyway, I don't want to jump into bed with just anyone anymore. I did enough of that in my twenties."

"Ew, okay, that's TMI for me," said Miri, and dramatically downed her mimosa.

"Well, you came along for girl time, so it's girl time," Ellie said, laughing, but I saw the concern was still in her eyes.

"Moving *swiftly on* in case of sisterly embarrassment," I continued,

"I feel positive about this whole thing. But I won't lie and say everything's been great lately. For one thing, Zach's mom died last week."

Miri gasped and held her hand to her mouth like she was in a play. Her childish histrionics had always annoyed me, but this time I was grateful that they were lubricating the conversation.

"Yeah," I said, looking down at my plate. "So sad."

"Man, I'm sorry, Tash," said Ellie. "That's really tough."

"Yeah, it's been *so* tough for him. And . . . well, this one's hard for me to admit. But Zach asked me not to go to the funeral."

Ellie and Miriam both went silent, just as a waiter appeared with a plate of pita bread and assorted dips. As he arranged labneh and harissa on the table between us, I offered an excuse on Zach's behalf: "Maybe he just doesn't want the first time I meet his entire family to be the same day that everyone's there to mourn his mother's death. Which I totally understand."

"No, yeah, that's understandable." Miri tore off a piece of warm pita and dipped it in some labneh and olive oil.

"I get it, I do get it," I said. "But a part of me finds it hurtful."

Ellie nodded, then asked in a slightly combative tone, "What about it is hurtful, exactly? You're just friends, aren't you?"

I looked at her, then down at the table. "You're right, I'm making it all about myself."

"No, but I'm being serious. I think it's a good idea to investigate what part of this has triggered your distress. Because, you know, it's obvious this *has* upset you."

"I suppose . . . I just wanted to be part of his support network, you know? I wanted him to know that he could lean on me. And this feels like a rejection of that," I said, taking a careful sip of my spice-rimmed Bloody Mary.

"I get that," said Miri.

Ellie shook her head. "I don't, to be honest. But we don't all have to be on the same page about this."

"No," I said. "We don't. But listen—I appreciate your input." I suddenly felt like I might start to cry.

AFTER WE FINISHED OUR *TO-DIE-FOR* SHAKSHUKAS, ELLIE WENT home to feed Charlotte Louisa and I took a leisurely walk toward the park with my sister. She linked arms with me as we soaked up the sun, and it was that perfect kind of day New York occasionally produces, warm enough to feel like summer but not hot enough to make a turn for the oppressive.

"It's the Hasidic people again," Miri said, pointing toward the Shabbat Bus, which passed by on its regular circuit around Grand Army Plaza on Fridays, playing upbeat music.

"Yeah," I said. "A lot of them live around here."

"It's so cool."

"You think everything in New York is *so cool*."

"So what if I do? You want me to be jaded?" She gave me a teasing poke, and I gave her a little shove in return.

As we continued down the sidewalk, I could see two groups of youngish teens ahead—one of young boys and one of young girls—all dressed in traditional ultra-Orthodox garb. They were each firing the same question at passersby: "Are you Jewish? Are you Jewish? Are you Jewish?"

Miri looked at me. "What are they doing?"

I shrugged. "Beats me. But it's pretty common, I've seen groups like this do it every Friday."

She nodded slowly and we continued on, stopping outside an overpriced ice cream store at one point to order from the window. As Miri hesitated in front of the menu, two of the girls, dressed in long-sleeved shirts and long skirts, came up to us and very politely and quietly asked, "Excuse me, are you Jewish?"

"No," I said at the same time as Miriam said, "Yes." I looked at her with warning eyes, but she was deliberately avoiding my gaze.

The girl who had asked her was smiling shyly from ear to ear.

"Did you know it's Shabbat tonight?" she asked, pulling a little paper bag out of a stash in her other hand. "Have you ever observed it before?"

"Miriam," I said, "come on."

"No, *you* come on." Miri gave me a sharp look then went back to the girl and said, "No, I've never observed it. But I've been meaning to."

The girl looked at her other two companions and clapped her hands in excitement. "This is so wonderful! What's your name?"

"Miriam."

"A beautiful Jewish name! One of my sisters is called Miriam."

"She is?" Miri was blushing, like she was seriously flattered by the idea that a stranger's sister shared her name.

"Yes! I'm Sarah—and this is Tovah and Chava." The girl indicated her two friends, who smiled and nodded at us while still hanging a couple steps behind.

"Great to meet you," said Miriam sincerely. "What are you guys doing out here?"

"We give out candles to people like you so that you can share in the joy of Shabbat," said Sarah, and I could tell she was beginning a spiel she'd previously memorized. "See these little candles here? You just light them when the sun goes down—tonight the time is 8:27 p.m. We wrote it on the box, too, so you don't forget. It's very important you light them then, before full darkness."

Miriam was taking the little bag with the candles in them and nodding. "I will, I will."

"Great! And then," Sarah continued, "while you light the candles, you can say the prayer in Hebrew. It's written down on this pamphlet here. Do you know any Hebrew?"

"Sadly, I don't," Miri replied, sounding sorry.

"But that's okay! The words are phonetic. You don't have to be able to read the alphabet. This is where you start." Sarah patted Miri's hand quickly as she gestured to the candles and the pamphlet, then added, "Even if you've been off the derech, it's never too late to come home."

"Thank you *so* much." Miriam put her hands together in front of her and held the little bag with reverence, and Sarah, Tovah, and Chava copied her gesture and smiled back at her. "I've been doing so much finding myself lately, and this . . . this helps a lot."

"It's never too late to start," ventured Tovah, who was a little younger than the other two. Then they started off down the sidewalk again, back on their journey to find Jewish New Yorkers before sunset.

Miri immediately launched into a speech at a hundred miles per hour about how she'd finally found a community, and I rolled my eyes and pushed her toward the ice cream window. "Just order your dessert," I said. "That whole thing was weird."

"What's weird about learning about your own cultural identity?" she asked, clearly annoyed. "Maybe you're just jealous."

I sighed. "Ellie was right. You are naïve."

"When did she say that?"

"Not today. But that's what she actually thinks of you, if you want to know the truth. And it's a pretty good assessment."

Miri looked like she'd been slapped. "I didn't know you guys talked like that about me."

"We don't—much—but let's be honest. The two of us know a bit more about the world than you do. And you've essentially proved our point, haven't you? Now you're moving up here, confusing people by claiming you're something you're not . . . It's borderline inappropriate, Miri. You're not Jewish. It's a matrilineal religion. Our mother was in the church choir!"

She turned her head away from me and looked back in the direction of Sarah, Tovah, and Chava, who had stopped to talk among themselves after a number of unsuccessful efforts to engage other passersby. What did she think they were going to do, save her from her evil sister?

"Do you think Mom was even telling the truth about your dad?" I said, determined to make her see my point. "Ezekiel probably doesn't even exist! It's just some story she made up to make us both feel better about her having sex with so many guys bareback."

She recoiled and muttered, "That's disgusting," then added, "I'm sorry if it makes you mad that I'm interested in exploring my identity. That I care about who I really am."

"It's not *who you are*, Miriam. Who you are is a college dropout whose mother pays her rent. Who you are is a vanilla-pudding girl from Massachusetts with good hair and nothing in your head!"

Miri started to cry, and I could see Sarah, Tovah, and Chava looking over, their attention piqued by the rising volume of my voice.

"She's not even Jewish!" I yelled over to them, and the quiet one winced.

"You think you can police who every single person in the world is and how they react to you, Natasha," said Miri, quickly wiping her tears away as they fell. "And you can't. It doesn't make you better tearing other people down!"

"Trust me, I don't want to police you, Miri. I don't want to be responsible for you at all. But all my life I've had to make up for your mistakes, go out and get the big job so you can screw around walking dogs and painting pictures and Mom will still have someone to brag about to the neighbors on a Saturday night."

"Oh please, you think you're worth bragging about?" Miri forced out a humorless little laugh. "You know what I thought when I went out for coffee with Ellie? I thought: This is what a big sister is supposed to be like! A married woman with a baby who lives in a normal neighborhood—not some fucked-up sex offender who lives in a creepy apartment building by the sea!"

"Right. Fine. I'm leaving." I threw my ice cream cone into the gutter and started walking away. I wasn't going to be spoken to this way by someone that much younger than me, with that little experience in the world—my own baby sister! When I turned back around briefly, I saw Miriam had joined the three Hasidic girls, who seemed to be comforting her.

"You're living in a fucking fantasy world!" I shouted toward them all. Little Tovah shook her head in the distance.

TWENTY

MY NEXT NEWS SHIFT WAS TWO DAYS AFTER MY FIGHT WITH MIRIAM, on a Sunday, which usually meant a quiet one. When I logged on, however, I found that the usual news editor had been replaced by Willem, who announced in our group messaging channel that he'd decided to "oversee today's shift, to get a feel for what needs to change."

There was an email waiting for me in my inbox sent by Eliza from the audience team. It was weirdly fawning, talking about an investigative article I'd written three years prior about a little boy who'd fallen out of a window in a badly maintained building in Flatbush, where slumlords were packing desperate undocumented immigrants five to a room. It was a story that had haunted me for a long time after writing it, the kind where the pain of the people involved is so raw that it becomes permanently woven into your own emotional tapestry. The landlord had gone to prison eventually, but the police investigation—prompted mainly by the article— had also led to the deportation and forced separation of multiple Colombian families. Eliza had written in her email:

> When you talked about the mom of the boy who fell— how she had all the Christmas presents ready? And then she went and gave them to the food bank on Christmas Eve? I cried, I actually cried.

She wanted to let me know that they were going to resell the article across the newspaper's social channels, along with "other high-quality evergreen content." I wanted to reply: *Are you in a position to judge quality, Eliza? Didn't you graduate eighteen months ago?* but I didn't. After all, she liked my piece, and it was gratifying to see anyone enjoying my journalism these days.

It was hard, perched in front of my laptop watching the cards pile up, to cling to the memories of my glory days of reporting. I didn't know if doing so was good or bad for my mental health. A year before I'd moved to London, I'd scored an interview with a former Supreme Court justice whom I'd particularly admired before she stood down, and had flown to San Francisco to conduct it. She'd folded a dish towel in a no-nonsense way while we were standing in her cavernous kitchen and said, "Don't be dumb enough to think you can't do everything I did." I didn't think much of the phrase—she'd said a slew of much more specific and interesting things while we sat opposite each other at her farmhouse table, sharing homemade bread and jam—but I'd included the line in my profile, and BR had seized upon it. He insisted it was "emblematic of everything women need to hear today." After the interview went viral, the newspaper had produced a line of mugs and T-shirts featuring the quote for subscriber holiday gifts. Joe had rolled up one of the T-shirts and put it in my Christmas stocking.

But now there was aggregation, there were cards to be filled out, there was Willem. *This has gotta be up your alley*, he messaged me a few minutes after I'd signed in, with a link to an article on Fox News about two Democrats disagreeing about abortion rights during a congressional hearing. "Pro-Life Democrat Viciously Attacked by Her Own Party—Then Driven Out of Town by Far-Left Rioters," the headline said. *This is what Willem thought was "up my alley"?*

I sat down to read the article and watch the associated videos, and concluded that two female members of Congress had had a normal exchange of opinions. Later, the one who opposed abortion had left a restaurant after pro-choice protesters stood on the sidewalk outside with signs saying KEEP YOUR ROSARIES OFF MY OVARIES and IF I WANTED THE GOVERNMENT IN MY WOMB, I'D FUCK A SENATOR.

I don't know if this story is as exciting as we think it is, I replied to Willem. *The debate feels like business as usual on the Hill, as is someone leaving a restaurant thru the back door to avoid a couple of protesters.*

I'm sure with the benefit of your big brain we can spice it up a bit, he replied. *Has intimidation by left-wing mob gone too far if a sitting member of Congress can't even eat a burger in peace?*

In my apartment, where I was sitting at the coffee table with the balcony door propped open in lieu of turning on the AC, I laughed out loud. Then I messaged him back: *Left-wing mob? Come on.*

Hey, I'm trying to be fair to all sides here.

Shouldn't we put things in slightly more neutral terms though?

We're a news publication, Natasha! And that means giving people what they want! He sent an emoji of a little face that winked then laughed in a friendly manner, followed by a gif of a news anchor from the 1976 film *Network* yelling: "Give the people what they want!" The fact that he was able to do a satirical meta-analysis of his own absurd position was somehow more unnerving than if he was a straight-up fascist.

Haha, I said, and closed the Fox News article. *But what about the piece about the dog who got that disastrous haircut? That feels like a fun one we should get out sooner rather than later.*

LOVE that one. But still think you should pick up our left-wing mobsters first ;)

Hey now. That guy wasn't even a licensed dog groomer! Social media's going crazy over it. I don't want to neglect a story with such good traffic potential.

For sure. It'll take you 20 seconds to write up after you've done the restaurant one.

I sat in front of my screen for a few minutes, looking at the message as if the words might warp themselves into less offensive ones. I really didn't want my name on this culture wars stuff, especially considering I might one day have the opportunity to interview one of these women. I decided to play my last card: *It seems like a complex story tho. Maybe I should hand it over to the politics team?*

He came back with the worst of all possible answers: *Got time for a quick call?* As soon as I read it, my cell began to ring.

"Willem, hi," I said in my at-work voice, pressing the phone painfully hard against my ear.

"Tasha! I always find it's best to talk these things out on the phone, you know? So much nuance gets lost otherwise."

"Totally."

"So, listen. Since I trust you, I may as well let you know about my little promotion."

"Oh," I said. "Congratulations."

"I said *little*. So, you know, I'm not replacing our dear leader or anything." He laughed in a way that implied he *would* be replacing BR within a year if he had anything to do with it. "But I will be taking the reins on news. For too long, everything's been sort of fragmented—breaking news, news analysis, political news . . . you know. There's really no need for everything to be separate. Now, I'm not one to toot my own horn, but I know a thing or two about news operations, which is why I've been taking the time to oversee each section these past few weeks."

"Sure," I said, without emotion. "Makes sense." As if I cared about his personal machinations. All I knew was that he had more power now and was trying to intimidate me with his ability to accrue even more. I got up from my makeshift desk and began to pace the apartment, coming to a stop at the window above the kitchen sink where I could rest my eyes on someone folding their laundry in the building opposite mine.

"I've always liked you, Natasha," Willem continued. "I know you're not one to push back unnecessarily against good ideas. That's why it's so important for us to continue on the same page."

"Sure. I hear you."

"I just want to make sure I'm coming across clearly when I communicate with you. Because once this is announced—and my deputy is in place—there are going to be some awesome opportunities in the newsroom. You could be in line for a raise. Probably not a new role just yet, but definitely a little more cash."

"There's a deputy position?"

"Oh—yes, technically, but it's going to be someone I'm bringing in from my old job. It's all going to be modeled on a structure I know works really well. Maybe we'll offer some financial incentives behind all that traffic you've been working hard on generating. I hope you're excited."

"Of course," I said, with resignation.

"And, you know, inevitably, when there's a regime change, some people don't like it, they find they don't fit into the new structure, and then they find themselves without a job. I hate that about our industry—heck, I've been on the wrong side of it! But it happens."

"Right."

There was a silence on the line, and I was about to ask if he was still there when he said, "Anyway, it's been great to catch up, Natasha. Looking forward to seeing your take on the political mob story. You always bring a fresh perspective!"

He hung up without saying goodbye.

A couple of hours later, I was still officially "working on" the article when my inbox dinged with a new email. I assumed it was a press release or a blanket email to global staff about food left in the London office's refrigerator or someone in Sydney having a baby. But when I clicked back to my inbox, I was surprised to see the name of the sender: Footsie Dalmatian.

Dearest Tash,

I hope you're doing wonderfully these days. I hope you
do realise now that everything I did was absolutely with
your welfare in mind. I spoke with your lovely editor in
chief recently and he mentioned you're settling into your
new role back in NYC really well, which is truly fantastic, and I also wanted to discuss an additional idea with
you if you're game to hear it. I don't know if you might
have possibly got a new phone number but I tried . . .

The shame and the image of the guest room rose up again;
I minimized Outlook and shoved that memory right back down
where I kept questions about my biological father and whether my
mother would ever stop drinking. I looked at the time and did the
math: it was midnight in the UK. Maybe the fact that she'd introduced me to the swimmer weighed on Footsie's mind when she
was sitting late at night at the kitchen island in her big house on the
cobblestoned street, writing up vignettes about the London Fashion Week A/W collections or sorting out her and her husband's
taxes so the sullen stepkids could continue at their eye-wateringly
expensive schools.

I held my palm over my phone and tapped my fingers, my eyes
on the couch in the living room. Should I reply to Footsie's email?
I decided not to. Like many people, she talked a good talk, but the
truth was that she probably had nothing of value to offer me now—
and even if she did, she wouldn't be willing to give it.

IN BED THAT NIGHT, ON MY FINAL PERUSAL OF SOCIAL MEDIA, I TOOK
a look at the early Olympics coverage. The swimmer's moment was
finally here, and his online fans were more hyped up than ever.
There was a meme circulating that showed a zoomed-in photo of his
head, blue-and-white Team GB swim cap, and wide, white-toothed
smile on display. He was doing a thumbs-up motion to the cam-

era. WIN GOLD. BANG CHICKS was emblazoned across the image in red writing, I presume intended somewhat ironically. In the background of the image, a row of young women could be seen pressing their faces against a plexiglass separation panel, waving. A couple were holding placards decorated with illegible scribbles. One had her hands in the air—was she making a heart sign with her fingers?

I Googled the swimmer's name and "interview" and clicked on the first link. On a news site, under a headline about his world-record-breaking times in the 100-meter freestyle, there was a video clip of him coming out of the pool, glistening, his strong arms leading his comparatively lean legs. He was gesturing at one of his coaches for a towel in a practiced, entitled way that I didn't recognize. Then the video cut to a press conference he'd given a few minutes later, a large mic in front of his face and camera flashes every few seconds illuminating the scene.

"Yeah, I worked very hard this past year and, you know, it's great to see your work pay off, especially when you're up against such incredible competitors," he was saying. He spoke much more confidently than I was used to, with that edge of boredom famous people often seemed to have when they reel off their achievements for the umpteenth time.

At the very end, one of the reporters in the press scrum could be heard jumping in to say, "And your personal life has been the source of some fascination, especially since—"

"I really don't have time for any of that. It's just teenage fantasy stuff." He kept the smile on his face, delivered the line calmly before walking off with a practiced-looking ease. Before disappearing into the corridors leading to the Olympic Village, he stopped to give one final wave to his screaming fans. *Fully media trained*, I thought to myself. *You've come a long way already. You'll never be that naïve again.*

"Well, Tom, I guess that was all he had time for," said a host to her compatriot as the video transferred back to a TV studio. "There we have it—not just a record-breaking swimmer in no fewer than

three separate races, but also a *very* impressive dancer, as any fol-
lower of his TikTok knows all too well."

WHEN MY MOTHER CALLED ON MONDAY, I BALANCED THE PHONE ON
the kitchen sideboard on speaker while I stirred some linguine
and waited for her to spit out that she was calling on Miri's behalf.
Eventually, after a long update about the plants on the deck and
some kind of petition she was putting together with Sasha and Liz
to try to stop the erecting of a beach restaurant in a spot where the
endangered seabirds nested every year, she slipped it in: "And how
are you getting along with your sister?"

I poured the pasta and boiling water into a strainer I'd positioned in the sink and said, "She told you, then."

"Told me what exactly?"

"That we had a fight."

"Miriam didn't put it quite like that, but yes."

"Let me guess. She said I ran over a puppy, sacrificed her first-
born son to Satanists, and punched her in the face."

"Natasha. You're not ten years old anymore."

"Oh, I'm quite aware of that, Mom, thank you very much." I
poured some canned tomatoes and spinach into the still-warm pan
and stirred in some cream to make a sauce for the pasta. "You already had kids when you were my age."

"You said some quite cruel things to her, you know, Tash. She's
in a sensitive place right now."

"She's having her rent covered by her mother and doing a part-
time internship while I pay a mortgage and finalize a divorce, and
she's the one in the sensitive place. Got it." I shook the spinach
leaves in the pan and placed the lid on top to make them wilt faster.

"You're always *comparing yourself* to her. But she's six years
younger. And you're two very different people."

"That wasn't me comparing us," I said lightly, but I could feel
myself getting dragged into a you-started-it fight with her already.
"It was just me stating the facts."

"I just want you girls to get along, for the three of us to be a team. Ever since I was pregnant with Miri, and you'd put your pudgy little hand on my stomach . . ."

"Yeah, yeah, yeah, I got it. I don't have time for the greatest hits today." I transferred the strained pasta into a bowl and then poured the sauce and spinach on top of it. Truthfully, I had no plans for the rest of the day and, with Zach out of the house, all the time in the world. But that didn't mean I wanted to be treated to a repeat performance of the Martyred Mother and her Endless Quest for Unity.

"Listen," said Mom. "It wasn't just for her benefit that I helped Miri move to New York, if you must know. I thought having her nearby would help keep you on the straight and narrow. We both did."

I froze, my fork suspended in the air above my pasta. "You two discussed this?"

"It all just fell together at the right time. But it was a consideration. So maybe you need to give her a chance. Even if she does want to . . . go to a synagogue or whatever she's doing right now."

"I don't know what to say," I said. "I feel really . . . violated." At the very least, I felt nauseated about the whole thing.

"Oh, don't be so dramatic. People care about you. So what?"

I WENT OUT ONTO THE BOARDWALK TO CLEAR MY HEAD AND TRY TO work out if I was justified in feeling angry at Mom and Miri, angry at their plotting, angry at their concern, angry at their sympathy. It was an overcast day and a strong wind blew intermittently, throwing open my light Zara jacket, which I'd lugged across the ocean twice. It wasn't even remotely fashionable anymore, but I could never quite bring myself to throw it away.

The wind had blown a few isolated strands of seaweed onto the boardwalk and I prodded them with the toe of one sneaker as I walked along the slats. I thought about the Atlantic Ocean, extending up past the mansions on the East End of Long Island; transformed into a thrashing, black mass on the shores of Newfoundland; settling only slightly as it reached Ireland; becoming sedate again on beaches in Portugal and the south of France. The same waves that crashed on Brighton Beach in Brooklyn would wash up at the Brighton Beach you reached by the fast train from Victoriain London. Thousands of miles away, this sea touched the place where Joe and I had walked on a day trip from Hackney, kicking the pebbles along the shore and wondering aloud to each other whether England would ever produce a beach-worthy day. It was August, but we'd been wearing jeans and sweaters. Defiant against the weather, I'd bought us soft serves from an ice cream truck that played nursery rhymes at a semioffensive volume. Joe had taken the cone from me and said, "Oh, I didn't really feel like ice cream, but sure, thanks." When we finished our treats and he tried to take my hand, I'd curled my fingers inward and turned away. *Couldn't you have just pretended you did feel like it, for once?* But if I said it out loud, I knew what he'd reply: *You don't have to take honesty like aggression, Tash. Sometimes a thing is just a thing, not a thing with bells on.* Sure, *he* didn't have to take honesty like aggression. Not with a family like his.

Ten minutes down the Rockaway boardwalk, an old woman was standing with a makeshift coffee cart—less the newsstand type that you'd see in Manhattan, more the style of a child's lemonade stand. A handmade sign affixed to the foldout table said OLINKA'S COFFEE, $2.50. CHEAPEST IN ROCKAWAY. PROBABLY SAME QUALITY AS ANYWHERE ELSE. I smiled a little at the unabashed honesty of the advertisement and then I realized, as the woman's face came into clear view, that it was Mrs. Konstantin.

"It's true," she said, tapping the sign, obviously having noticed I was looking.

"I don't doubt it," I replied, but my eyes still involuntarily flickered toward the storefront behind her, where a sullen man sold various items in a cavernous space: Adirondack chairs, beach umbrellas, fresh juice, bouncy balls, homemade tacos, and, according to a chalkboard, COFFEE @ $3.

"You're a person who needs proof," said Olinka, smiling like she'd caught me in the act.

"Just the habits of a journalist. We're natural skeptics," I said, and I peeled three dollars out of my pocket. Coffee on the boardwalk sounded fine. What else was I going to do, change into my bathing suit and swim in the ocean?

"Tips are welcome, by the way," Olinka said as she took my money and gestured toward an empty jar to her left side. Her accent sounded different; maybe she'd been practicing her English with patrons.

"You should put a few bills in the jar," I said. "People usually do that to give the illusion they get frequent tips. It's good for shaming customers into doing the same."

"Oh, it is?" She seemed like she was making fun of me, but I plowed on.

"Well, I assume it is. I don't work in the industry."

"No." She shook her head. "What kind of reporting do you do?"

"I'm not really in the mood to talk."

"I could tell." She handed me the cup of coffee and I warmed my hands on its Styrofoam sides. But she was persistent: "It's news reporting?"

"I told you I wasn't in the mood to talk."

"I'm interested. You have shame for what you do? You go through famous people's trash, maybe?"

"No." Despite myself, I laughed. "Not even as interesting as that. Have you been practicing your American accent? Or at least your American style of interrogation?"

"Ukrainians are direct." She held my gaze. "Journalists don't usually live out here."

I rolled my eyes. "That's right. I'm a shitty journalist, so I'm in exile."

"Exile can be good for the soul." She breathed in the sea air and looked so thoroughly satisfied with herself that it made me feel off-kilter. *How can you be so happy? You make your money hawking hot drinks for pocket change on a boardwalk. You live alone and clearly don't own a hairbrush.*

She continued to smile at me while I sipped my coffee and poisoned the atmosphere with my thoughts, and her sedateness had a way of making me feel the full force of my own toxicity. Then I felt bad that I'd thought that stuff about the hairbrush, so I asked politely, "When did you decide to open a coffee stand?"

"It's an easy living," she said, shrugging. "Americans love coffee."

"Do you miss Ukraine?"

"Sometimes. But it's a good life here. And I left a terrible ex-lover behind in my country. Nasty man. Only interested in one thing. Better off here by myself with the coffee and the dog."

I couldn't help it—I laughed out loud. Then I put my hand over my mouth and said, "Sorry. Sorry—I just . . ."

"Couldn't imagine old lady like me having lovers? Don't worry about it. It's natural. People your age have to think they're the only ones who ever got into relationships. But you know, a long time ago, I was with a terrible man. I couldn't admit what he was doing to me because my family would've taken . . . decisive action. I had a real job once—not *journalism* job, but job with a desk. You make compromises. Then the war happened."

I took my first long gulp of the bad coffee and felt grit in my mouth as I held her gaze. Granules mixed with boiling water. I suppressed the urge to spit it out. Then I said, "Hey, you want to grab some lunch?"

IN A DINER TWO STREETS IN FROM THE BOARDWALK (OLINKA HAD unfolded another handwritten sign from her backpack and taped it to her stand: ON BREAK. BACK SOON FOR MORE CHEAP, ORDINARY COFFEE!), we took a red vinyl booth next to the window. I'd offered to go to the Ukrainian place a little farther down the boardwalk, but she said her family didn't see eye-to-eye with the manager's family, and it was better to go to an American diner, "where there are no politics." "Not all of us like one another, you know," she added.

Olinka ordered shrimp and grits and I chose eggs Benedict, which turned out to be way beyond the culinary capacities of the line cook on duty. I picked at the gray solution pooled at the top of the underdone eggs and flaked the dry biscuit underneath with my fork while Olinka told me that she'd worked at a fairground in rural Ukraine, where they'd gotten half-starved animals from soon-to-be-defunct zoos shipped over by Russian human traffickers doing a side gig. They had a jaguar that had almost taken her arm off. She pulled up her sleeve and showed me the scar, a mess of purple and white tissue crisscrossed over itself. She took opiates to help with the pain, she added. Then one night, she'd lain in bed listening to the sad lowing of the baby bears taken from their mothers and the frustrated grunts of the jaguar who should have been out controlling the deer population in grasslands and savannas across Central America but was instead confined to a cage only large enough for pacing and eating rabbits and roadkill. She decided she had to escape, and she packed her bags and left before the morning. She opened the animals' cages on her way out too.

"Now tell me the real story," I said. "Enough *Life of Pi* shit."

She shrugged. "It's not an interesting story, really. It's normal. Bad boyfriend, judgmental family, addiction, complications from the war. Jaguars make it a little more exciting. So tell me yours."

And then the information leakage happened again, and, as I ritualistically massacred the sad corpse of the eggs Benedict and then ordered another bad coffee to satiate myself instead, I told her everything in sordid detail: the swimmer in the pub, the way Joe looked at me like he loved me but hardly ever said it, the terrible writing in the terrible feature and the terrible day I published it, the phone call with BR, the demotion, the poor excuse for reporting I now did while hunched over a work-owned laptop in a depressing apartment I thought I deserved, the people at work I looked down on and the ones who looked down on me (sometimes the same people), the naïve sister I couldn't help hurting, the mother who hadn't bequeathed me any healthy coping mechanisms, the chase for the sunset as I attempted to get my life back on track before my thirties disappeared and left me—according to most societal metrics and Leonardo DiCaprio—a worthless shell of a woman.

"No offense," I added, slightly guiltily.

"None taken," said Olinka, who'd polished off her shrimp and grits with the pragmatic voraciousness of someone who never took food for granted.

"Basically, I'm aware I'm not a very nice person right now," I said, "especially to people who have been kinder to me than I deserve." I paused, then added, "My best friend had a baby."

Olinka nodded. "That's a big milestone." That accent was definitely different. It sounded American. It sounded . . . southern? The skeptical reporter in me rose again, suspicious, but I told her to give me a minute.

"Yeah, and I . . . barely acknowledged it," I continued. "In fact, I kind of made it all about myself."

"Perhaps you've been busy with keeping your head above water."

"Maybe. I don't know. I'm not drowning, exactly, but I'm not . . . floating."

We called over the teenage server who'd spent most of the afternoon leaning over the counter glumly, and he delivered the check to our table like it was his last will and testament. I insisted on paying, and Olinka did, too, and eventually we agreed that I would cover the bill and she would leave the tip in cash. As she got a handful of dollars together, she told me, with her eyes on the rapidly emptying beach outside the window, that she was dying: "I went to urgent care a few months ago. They referred me for tests. Heart failure. It's not much of a surprise."

"Gosh, Olinka," I said. "I'm sorry." It was the first time I'd said her name out loud.

"That's why it's better off that we didn't become friends," she said. My first reaction was to tell her that she didn't need to protect me—that I wasn't afraid of knowing someone who was dying—when I realized that I hadn't exactly given her reason to think that my friendship would be beneficial to her either. I was a self-centered ass with a complicated past and present, and probably the last person she wanted around during her final weeks on Earth.

"I get that," I said. "But acquaintances can enjoy a coffee together now and then."

As we walked back toward the coffee stand, I tried to tell Olinka more about Zach, but she was visibly uninterested. I could tell she was looking around at the few passersby with their sleeves pulled down and hats that helped protect their eyes from the sand that got whipped up every time the wind blew, scrutinizing their faces and ignoring most of my hopeful narrative. Cruising for potential customers, maybe. It made me feel a little foolish.

"He doesn't sound like much of a solution," she said eventually. "What do you need some guy for anyway?"

"Like I said. Not all of us can be recluses selling coffee on the beach. There's room for one of you in the Rockaways, maximum."

"I told you I'm dying. There's an imminent vacancy."

I laughed. "That's dark." We reached her coffee cart, and she got to work setting up a new pot on her portable hot-plate and re-folding the piece of paper that had declared herself on break. I understood from the way she got to work, swift and businesslike, that she was done with me for the day.

"One thing I've been wondering," I said before I left. "When you saw me by the water a few weeks ago, why did you laugh at me?"

The answer came without hesitation: "Because you were entertaining."

"Come on."

"Well, also, like I said, you reminded me of myself."

"Don't take this the wrong way, but I'm not sure that's a good thing."

She shrugged. "You're mixed up right now. That much is clear to anyone who gets within twenty feet of you. But being mixed up isn't a crime, so long as you don't become totally untethered." The coffee began to simmer. "Trust me," she added, as she took a dirty-looking dishcloth to the mug she drank her own coffee from.

"You can always start again. Your generation forgets that. You are unforgiving, mostly to yourselves."

I kicked the bottom of the stand and looked at the ground. "I had a lot going for me before, you know? I don't know if I want to start over."

"Well." She folded her arms across her chest. "Maybe that's the problem."

"Are you really from Ukraine?" I asked, but she started busying herself with extracting a stack of Styrofoam cups from some plastic wrapping and didn't meet my eye again.

TWENTY-ONE

ZACH CAME HOME AFTER MY LUNCH WITH OLINKA. I'D BEEN KEEP-
ing an eye on his social media and saw him post a thread about
his mom's death and everything she'd "stood for." It ended with:
"Most of all, what my mom would say to you if you're worried about
what to do during this tense political moment is this: CALL YOUR
ELECTED OFFICIALS!" with a link to a registration form.

So true, replied someone whose handle was NotHere4ur
Compliments. *This is what she would have wanted! Rest in power!*

How the fuck do you know what she would have wanted? I felt
like replying, but I didn't.

Zach had texted me to let me know he was on his way back, so I
made a special effort to clean the apartment and make it look inviting. I bought a couple of subtly scented candles on Amazon and lit
them on the windowsill in the living room and made sure the sofa
cushions were fluffy. I set out three of my more culturally relevant
books on the coffee table (*Annie Leibovitz: The Big Ones, How the
World Stays Caffeinated,* and *From Tamagotchis to Totalitarianism:
A Y2K Retrospective*) and scrubbed the scum off the side of the
kitchen sink, then pulled the hair out of the shower drain with
my bare hands before checking the bathroom tiles for signs of residual cockroaches, like brown smear marks or droppings. Then I
plugged in a diffuser that promised scents of "grass and linen," and
sat down with my laptop open in front of me so it would look like
I was casually working when he walked in.

He'd only been gone for eight days, but when he came through the door, I thought he looked thinner and paler.

"Hey," he said, "I checked the mailbox," and chucked a letter at me.

That disoriented me a little. "Hey," I said, putting the letter on the coffee table beside me. "Thanks. How have you been?"

"About the same as anyone else who's just lost a parent."

"Of course," I said. "I didn't mean to imply . . ."

"No, no, you're fine." He walked into the kitchen alcove and poured himself a glass of water, sipped it, then stood at the sink and looked out the window. *It's okay. Take a breath*, I told myself. *He just needs time*. I picked up the letter he'd given me and started tearing a line along the top of it with my nail, then slowly extracted a number of papers inside. It was clearly important, because the envelope had a hard cardboard back and DO NOT BEND written in red letters on the front. The only other time I'd received anything like that was when I'd been sent my diploma after graduation.

As I slowly began to extract the small stack of papers, it became obvious what it was: *New York State Decree of Divorce*. Underneath the bold letters was a lot of legalese that detailed how Joe and I had agreed to divide our assets and go our separate ways. Behind those papers was another, shorter letter titled "Certificate of Divorce" that, my lawyer wrote on a sticky note attached, "is a less detailed document, good for showing anyone who might need to know the basics of the dissolution of your marriage—banks, landlords, etc."

So it was done, not with a bang but a whimper. Without any further contact and with no court date or climactic speech in front of a judge, my legal relationship with Joe had been dissolved like salt in water. I thought about whether the documentation would have reached him in London by now; whether he was also sitting on a sofa with an envelope on his lap, staring into the middle distance and feeling the muffled thump of the very end. Probably not. In a few days' time, it would get delivered by Royal Mail and he'd know what it was immediately from the return address. His lawyer might have called to congratulate him, or to let him know everything had been signed and was on its way. He was more organized than me, more on top of mail and bank statements and pretty much everything else in his life. He'd take a quick peek inside the envelope to confirm its contents, then file it away in case he needed it in the future before going out for a celebratory dinner with his new girlfriend. I imagined them sharing a bottle of champagne inside the cavernous wine bar on the South Bank we'd liked to visit on weekends, him winking and saying to her, "Today's the first day of the rest of our lives."

"Hey, at least there's *some* good news in this household!" I said, holding up the papers, as Zach emerged from the kitchen.

He looked back at me with some confusion then made his way to the couch, squinted at the bold lettering, and said, "Does that mean it's final?"

"Yep! Whew, what a journey." I stuffed the papers haphazardly back inside the envelope and threw it into the space under the coffee table. Zach remained silent, perching carefully at the other end of the couch, and I realized my casual comparison might have hit the wrong note.

"That was too much, wasn't it?" I said. "I didn't mean to minimize your pain. Obviously it doesn't hold a candle to what you've been through."

"No, it's not that. Sorry. My brain just feels like it's moving through sludge at the moment. I think I'm just not reacting to things as quickly."

"I understand." I moved the tiniest amount closer to him and said, "Do you want to talk about your mom?"

He shook his head. "Not really. I've just had a week and a half of people constantly coming at me with their memories and . . . I dunno, I feel like I need a bit of a break or I'll go insane."

"Of course." We sat in silence for a few minutes, and then I added, "I've read that sometimes, after someone very sick dies, the person who's been looking after them can feel a sense of relief."

"I'm sorry to repeat myself, but I really don't want to talk about it."

I felt a little stung by that, but I said, again, "Of course," and we went on sitting in silence. Below us, five stories down on the sidewalk, a gaggle of teenagers coming home from school were shouting at one another about whether they wanted to get Wendy's; their voices carried across the bare streets and up to a window I'd cracked open. I noticed the confluence of smells in the room properly for the first time—the "grass and linen" diffuser mingling in the air with the ginger and cranberry Amazon candles—and realized the whole apartment reeked of a sickly and synthetic odor. Why did I always mess everything up?

After a while, Zach got up from the couch and said, "I think I'm just going to chill in my room for a while."

"Go for it," I said, like it meant nothing to me, and I kept typing as though I were working, when actually I was cycling through personality quizzes and Googling travel destinations I could never afford. Anything to distract myself from physically grabbing him and pulling him into the embrace I knew he needed.

An hour and a half passed. I'd found out which sandwich filling suited my "summer personality," which K-pop star would be my ideal life partner, and what my period blood said about me. I'd read at least fifteen separate Wikipedia pages about extremely rare and fatal genetic disorders that are only discovered at birth. And I'd perused an entire forum about family annihilators, populated with tale after tale of middle-aged men slaughtering their wives and children in their sleep. Yes, I felt a little better about my life again. But was Zach ever going to speak to me?

His door was slightly ajar, so I got up and knocked softly. "Can I come in?" I asked.

"Oh, hey." He was on the bed in the evening light, and he propped himself up on his elbows as I poked my head around the door. "I'm not doing anything interesting, I'm afraid."

"Do you feel like takeout, maybe?"

"I ate before I got back here. My sister insisted on feeding her little bro."

"Ah, nice." I thought about him sitting across from his well-groomed sister, with her carefully applied makeup and her probable hair extensions. I found it a little suspect that she'd managed to make herself look so good for the funeral. What was she trying to prove?

"You know, I'm not that hungry either," I said. "But I have another idea." I went to the kitchen and put the kettle on the stove, reached for the box of ginger tea bags from the cabinet above.

When I got back to his bedroom with a steaming mug of ginger tea in each hand, I saw he'd closed the door. I used my foot to tap the bottom of it a couple times, then, when he didn't answer, I did a more insistent knock with my knee.

After a few seconds, he came to the door and opened it again, standing in the doorframe so I couldn't see past him into the room this time. "What is it?" He didn't sound annoyed, exactly, more weary.

"I made you some tea," I said, holding up the mug in my left hand.

"Oh. That's kind. Thanks very much." He extended a hand for it, but I held it—gently—just out of his reach.

"I thought we could drink them together," I said.

"Honestly, Nat, I need some time to myself tonight. I appreciate the tea, though."

I continued standing at the door, a smile pasted on my face, slightly shaking my head. "Do you think you should be alone right now?"

He stretched out a long arm to support himself against the frame. "Are you . . . ? Listen, Nat, I'm getting a bit of a weird vibe."

"Wow," I said, taking a step back. "I was just trying to be supportive."

"Sure. I hope you're not getting something out of this," he said, with a cruel inflection, and I recoiled and went to sit back on the sofa. He might as well have punched me in the face.

I heard him sigh loudly, and then, after a minute, he walked over to join me. I felt it like a little victory kick in my stomach.

"Listen, I'm sorry," he said, taking a seat at the far end of the couch. "I'm just . . . well, I'm not entirely myself right now."

"No, of course, of course." I shuffled over and started gently stroking his shoulder, and he allowed himself to be touched. I dared to move close enough that I could reach around and lightly run my fingers up and down his arm, feeling his body heat through his skin, tracing my nails along the little hairs. I wanted to grab him and hold him to me, refuse to let him go. But instead I stayed like that, restrained, lending him my comforting touch while he breathed irregularly beside me into the silence. After a minute or two, he sighed again, but not like how he'd sighed when he was in his bedroom doorway. Instead, it sounded like he was relaxing into it, accepting me.

"There now, isn't that better?" I whispered and pulled him a little nearer. I thought I felt an inch of resistance, but then he allowed me to bring him into an embrace. It was still dead quiet in the room, but I was now close enough to feel his heart beating—or was it mine? Through the rectangle of the glass balcony door, I could see a real show of a sunset being put on for us: pinks and yellows streaked across a collection of cotton-like cumulus clouds. *It was so perfect.* I turned my head toward Zach and—despite myself, despite everything—leaned in for a kiss.

Instantly, he moved away, pushing me a little at the shoulder as he did so. We looked at each other in mutual shock.

"I'm just going to pretend that never happened," he said after a moment and rose quickly from the couch, leaving his mug of tea on the table. He went directly to his bedroom, closed the door quietly behind him, and then I heard him twist the lock for the very first time.

I looked at the two mugs in front of me and felt a deeper sadness than I'd felt in months. They seemed so emblematic of the domestic bliss I thought Zach and I could create after our respective tragedies. I imagined him coming back out, slowly, holding my hand in his cupped palms like I was the most precious thing in the world, and then kissing me softly, chastely, with a closed mouth. In his bed, we'd wrap our limbs around each other and feel grateful for the fact that we'd found love in a world that was so desperately cruel so much of the time.

It wasn't going to happen—at least not tonight.

I stayed in the living room for a while, though, giving him a chance to reemerge, taking occasional sips of my tea. Then I went to the kitchen alcove and washed both of the mugs in the sink before going back to my own room and lying down on the bed in the early darkness. What was the point in staying awake any longer? I slid under the sheets I hadn't bothered washing once since I'd moved in and breathed in my own scent, made more potent by the excretions of bacteria and minuscule insects living on the accumulation of my dead skin and sweat. I held the comforter to my face and turned over into the fetal position, and then the tears started to come hot and thick, creating a pool of water on my pillow by my head.

The night he'd found out about the swimmer, Joe had come into our bed in our London apartment, where I'd been lying in the same pose. As soon as he'd heard about the article, he'd asked me, in the kitchen, if there was any truth to it. He was so hurt, so open, so unlike me. I couldn't lie to him.

We'd had an argument then, and it was clear that he thought I should get out of his space, at least temporarily. But by that time, it was late and I had nowhere to go, so he'd told me he would sleep on the sofa, and I'd crept back to our room. I still thought maybe it wasn't the end, not the real end. Then, in the early hours of the morning, there he was.

"Are you awake?" he whispered, as he clambered between the sheets beside me, and I nodded in the pale orange light of a streetlamp that always illuminated our bedroom from the outside. He said nothing, just lay on his back beside me with his hands behind his head.

I moved toward him in the bed and tentatively rested my head on his chest. "I know it'll take you a lot to forgive me," I said, inhaling him, feeling the familiar swell of his chest and stomach and shoulders under his T-shirt, my arm reaching out for his hand and, when he wouldn't connect with my fingers, stopping to rest on his bicep instead.

We lay like that for a long time, like it was any other night. Then I felt his tears dropping into my hair. One slid down my face and onto my chin.

"Why'd you do it?" he said eventually, in a strangled voice. "I don't . . . I just want to understand." That was the first time he asked.

I moved up the bed so we were lying face-to-face, his nose against mine, his breath on my cheek. I could feel the solidity of his body, the movement of his blood, the aliveness of him under the surface. This strange intimacy that I'd built with one person, the sharing of bodily fluids and the knowledge of each physical and mental detail, felt like being let in on a cosmic secret. It was unbearable to me that I might not have access to this person—this whole person in its psychological and corporeal completeness, with the brain and heart and arms and legs and penis and vocal cords I associated with love and pleasure and reassurance—ever again. It just couldn't be true.

"I don't know," I said. "It was nothing. Please. I'll make it right. I'll never do anything like this, ever again. Please, Joe."

It was a lie, because of course I knew, but the reasons were so small as to be insulting. It was a tale as old as time: my life was barreling toward duty and obligation like a cannonball in a video game, and I was racing on top, trying to grab as many gold coins as I could before I hit the end of the track. I wasn't unhappy. I wasn't out of my mind. I didn't even think my husband—my docile, loving, quietly loyal husband—would ever find out. I was just dumb, and scared, and stupidly complacent.

He turned and moved onto his side, and when I tried to put my arms around him, he pushed them gently but firmly away. So I gave up and moved onto my back, watching the pattern of the streetlights on the ceiling, listening to the occasional hushed conversations of people making their way home after a long night out.

It wasn't until the morning that he told me I had to leave.

TWENTY-TWO

BY THE END OF JUNE, I WAS SPENDING ALMOST ALL MY TIME ON THE balcony, letting the sea breeze blow around the apartment.

"Summer is when this place really comes into its own," I said to Zach, who just nodded without saying anything and went to his room to turn on his own AC unit with the door closed. We hadn't been speaking much.

Ellie texted me on the final Sunday of the month, while I was sitting on a deck chair I'd bought from one of the seasonal beach shops on the boardwalk. I opened the message and saw it featured a picture of Charlotte Louisa smiling, reaching up for the camera. *She officially laughs at my jokes now!* said the accompanying text.

My heart! I messaged back. *How is she SO adorable!* Then I leaned against the balcony rail to snap a picture that made it look like I had a better view of the ocean than I really did. *Current view from the apartment—not too shabby!* I added. Was I using too many exclamation marks? Did it make me look manic? I scanned the message again before deciding it was just Ellie and it didn't matter too much.

I saw Miri the other day, Ellie replied. So this was her ulterior motive.

Usually I only have to deal with my mother being a flying monkey for my sister, I wrote back. Now she was spoiling my summer vibe—after I'd taken the time to make myself an iced coffee and a grilled cheese for my afternoon relaxation too.

You're jumping to conclusions. She just said you two hadn't spoken in a while.

So why are you telling me?

Because I thought maybe we could all get brunch together again?

I sat there bouncing my phone in my hand, considering how well she'd played this. Then I replied: *No thanks.*

She's your sister, Tash. And she just moved here.

I'm aware. I thought about how I was digging my heels in and reconsidered the situation. Was I really that angry at Miri? I could barely remember what she'd done to make me mad by now, and so much had happened since then. I suppose I didn't have to keep up the resentment. *She pissed me off,* I continued, *but I guess it doesn't matter that much. I'll text her.*

Okay, great! Really glad to hear that.

And can I tempt you back to the Rockaways soon? I promise my place isn't as much of an oppressive hellhole when the sun's shining.

I'm willing to give it another chance if you can do the same for Miriam.

Deal.

I put down my phone, took a bite of my grilled cheese, and sighed. A string of molten cheddar stuck to my chin, and I used my nail to pry it off and deposit it back into my mouth. Then I fixed my eyes on the section of the ocean I could make out through the other buildings, took a long sip of the bitter coffee and let its energy course through me.

I picked up my phone again.

> *Hey. Let's stop being dumb to each other.*

Miri replied within seconds. *Yes please!*

> *Are you ever going to come back to my apartment?*

> *You haven't invited me!*

> *Consider this an invitation.*

> *Awesome! I have plans all week but maybe Thursday would work? Spend the Fourth together?* Well, look at that—my little sister had a busier New York City social calendar than I did.

Sure. No prob if you're too busy to see me, I replied. I knew I was being petulant.

> *Or I could rearrange some stuff and come a night after work if you want?*

> *No, honestly the Fourth is fine.*

> *No, no, I want to come sooner! I need my sisterly one-on-one time! How about Tuesday?*

> *Tuesday works, I guess.*

> *Cool! And then I'll get to meet Zak properly too. I can't wait!!*

I decided to let her misspelling of Zach's name slide, but I subtly pointed it out by including the correct spelling in my next message. *Yeah Zach is looking forward to getting to know you too. But tbh he's been a bit weird these days. Think his mom's death has made him a little crazy. Probably better that we meet outside the house for now.*

Aw man. It's so hard for him. It's so great he has you there, tho, so you can help him thru it!

Yeah. I guess that is the silver lining.

THE NEXT DAY, I CAME HOME FROM A SHIFT AT THE OFFICE AND heard shrieks of laughter before I even turned my key in the door. I unlocked it to find Zach in the apartment with three other people, a girl and two other guys. They were stretched out across my sofa and rug, the girl extending her long limbs across the couch to rest on Zach's lap at the other end. He didn't seem to mind, and in fact was balancing one of her sandaled feet in his hand, bouncing it up and down in a familiar way.

"Hey, Nat!" said Zach, in a voice I'd never heard him use before, a formal tone for company.

"Oh, hey," I said cautiously, putting my bag down by the door.

"We're just having a couple of beers," said Zach, and one of his male friends, who'd been sitting on the floor, poked his thumb toward the fridge and said, "Can I get you one?"

I gave him a thin smile and said, "No, thanks," while the girl moved her head upside-down to look at me, twisting herself into an absurdly gymnastic position rather than merely turning her shoulder. She was achingly pretty, with tanned skin covered in light freckles and her hair in a messy, thick braid. As I got closer, I saw that her oversize T-shirt said BOSTON'S BEST OYSTER FARM across it and was thrown on above a pair of tiny denim shorts. When she repositioned herself on the sofa, I saw her ass cheeks.

"Hey!" she said, flashing me her white teeth. "I'm Dominique."

"Natasha," I said, holding up a hand.

"I'm glad you're here actually," said Zach to me, letting go of Dominique's foot and pointing to his other two friends, who were sitting on the floor at the other end of the coffee table. "This unwashed hippie over here is Jim. And *this* is Arlo. We went to elementary school together, can you believe it?"

"How sweet," I said without enthusiasm.

"Yeah. And then he followed me to Boston. Clearly obsessed with me—but can you blame him? I've been meaning to introduce you two for ages. Arlo works in media too."

"Oh, you do?" I crouched on the carpet, since apparently the sofa was taken. "Where?"

"The *Post*," Arlo responded, smiling and rolling his eyes. He had a kind face but was objectively ugly, with a pronounced underbite and long, unbrushed blond hair. "And before you say anything, I know. But I just moved back to the city, and it pays the bills."

"No, no, I wasn't going to say anything," I said, disarmed by his friendly candor. "Zach probably told you that my company gets all its stories off far-right conspiracy networks in the name of traffic, so."

"God, tell me about it. Do you also have interminably long meetings about audience calibration?"

"Absolutely. They're culling as many writers as they can in sacrifice to the traffic gods."

"You know, I don't even have my own socials. Apparently that's a problem. But I mean, isn't social media just a virtue-signaling cesspit for people who pretend to hate capitalism to promote their GoFundMes?"

I laughed out loud. "Have they at least made you sign up to Clicksmax?"

"Clicksmax!" Arlo threw his head back and laughed. "Finally somebody else who understands that tool of Satan!"

"Oh my God, *yes*," I said, but then I turned to Zach, Dominique, and Jim, and saw that they looked confused. "Sorry, maybe this is a little inside baseball for the other kids at the table."

"No, no, don't let us interrupt," said Zach, looking oddly triumphant. "In fact, Dom and Jim and I have something very important to discuss among ourselves."

"Oh God, what's it gonna be?" said Dominique, kicking her feet in a childlike way.

"You *know* what it is!" Zach picked up her foot again and tugged on it. I didn't know if I'd ever seen him this animated. "Come on, come on, Dom, you're gonna get it—look at me!" He leaned over and looked in her eyes intensely, and the smile on his face grew wider and wider.

Then Dominique—*Dom*—clapped her hand over her mouth and started to laugh, and said, "Mr. O'Leary!" and immediately she, Zach, and Jim collapsed into renewed laughter. Arlo shook his head at them but he was smiling.

"*I swear to you all my mother's from Dublin!*" said Dominique in a bad imitation of an Irish accent, and Jim began to laugh so hard that he collapsed on the rug.

"And he wouldn't even let us into the bar in the end," said Arlo in a quieter voice, shaking his head, which made Dominique shriek again.

"Too good. Too good," Zach said and took a long sip of his beer.

Then Arlo turned to me and said, "Sorry, Natasha. This is just what happens when three idiots come invade your apartment. I won't even insult your intelligence by trying to relate the story."

I wanted to run to my room, slam the door, put my headphones on, and never see any of them again. But that option was worse than staying out here, I knew: lying under my comforter in my darkened room, trying not to hear Dominique's laughter, Zach pulling her closer with each joke, putting his finger on his lips to quiet her shrieking, all on the couch I'd picked out with my ex-husband. Yes, that would be too much to bear.

So instead I said, "Are you kidding? I'm just glad Zach's finally brought home some friends," and went into the kitchen to get myself that beer after all. If I had to endure this evening, I'd need alcohol.

I took a deliberately long time selecting and opening a beer, then pouring it into a glass, hoping they could get all their private jokes out of their systems by the time I returned. But when I emerged, Zach was doing the stupid Irish accent and the other guy was saying, "But the *best* thing was his commitment to the lie. *My mother milked three hundred cows every morning in under thirty minutes!*"

"So, are you coming to our Fourth of July party?" I interrupted, setting myself cross-legged on the carpet and placing my beer on the coffee table.

They shut up and looked at me.

"There's a party?" Dominique said eventually, looking to Zach for confirmation.

"Yeah, actually," he said, after a beat. "Just a little gathering."

Dominique already had her phone out, presumably scrolling through her calendar to make sure she didn't have any better plans in place that she'd already forgotten about. "And it's on the actual Fourth? This Thursday?"

"The very same."

"Yeah, we decided we needed to throw a big one because we're massive patriots," I said, deadpan, hoping to elicit a laugh, but they all just looked at me with confusion on their faces. I added, "I'm kidding," then they nodded and Arlo gave a generous little chuckle, which made the moment even more embarrassing.

"More like giving me something to feel normal about again," said Zach, before looking at Dom and adding, with a little half smile: "See, now you have to come."

"Well, I'm free *anyway*," she said, putting down her phone and saving me from further humiliation. God forbid I gain some rapport with this tight-knit little group. "Hey, Arlo, Jim, I *know* you don't have any plans."

"Who says I don't have friends lining up around the block to invite me to watch the fireworks?" said Jim, but then he winked at her and said, "Nah, you got me. I'm free as a bird." The whole group dynamic seemed to be based on low-level flirtation with Dominique, and she kept preening in expectation of it. It made me feel sick.

"Who have you invited, Nat?" said Zach suddenly, giving me a serious look.

"Oh, not many people." I waved my hand in a no-big-deal kind of way. Of course I hadn't invited anyone, partly because I had almost no one to invite, and partly because I didn't know whether we'd go ahead with the party after Zach's mother had died. He'd insisted on normalcy, though, and my heart had hurt—in a good way—at his stoicism. "My sister, maybe Ellie and Jake . . . some colleagues, probably."

"Cool!" said Zach brightly. "I have a couple work friends coming too. I might even mix some margaritas."

"Oh, don't, though," said Dominique. "Remember—I'm not even gonna say it, but you know—"

"Haven't you guys embarrassed me enough today?" said Jim, and they all began to laugh again.

I'd reached saturation point. I drained my beer and put the glass back on the table loudly enough that they all stopped to look at me. "Actually, I'm going to make it an early night," I said.

Dominique looked at the guys in turn, then said to me, "Will we be too loud out here?"

"No, no. Gosh, of course not." I didn't look at her as I got up and went back to the kitchen to put my glass in the sink. "I've just got a shift tomorrow . . . Arlo knows what it's like. Clicksmax calls! But it was *great* to meet you guys. And hey, I'll look forward to seeing you on the Fourth!"

"Yeah, see you then," said Jim, while Arlo gave me a small wave and a bit of an anxious look.

I went into my bedroom and closed the door quietly behind me. Where was Zach's mind these days? His moods had become so hard to read. I put my head in my hands and massaged my ears for a bit, distorting all sound like I was underwater. Then I sat back on my pillows and took three deep breaths. He was speaking to me again; that's all that mattered.

I INVITED MIRIAM TO THE FOURTH OF JULY PARTY WHILE WE SAT having happy hour drinks at a horseshoe bar in Fort Greene on Tuesday night. We were elbow-to-elbow with trust-fund kids, but this was apparently now one of Miriam's favorite places.

"That's in, like, two days," she said, licking the salt off the edge of her cocktail glass. "Couldn't you have mentioned it earlier?"

"Why, you got somewhere to be?"

"Actually, maybe. Dan from work is having a party and he lives in this big warehouse complex that his uncle bought in the seventies."

"I appreciate it must be really tough, deciding between your sister and the guy at work you've known for five minutes and who *you* turned down when he asked you out," I said, "but just let me know."

"Oh, Tash, don't be like that." She nudged me gently under the table with her high heel. She seemed to have acquired an expensive new wardrobe somehow. "You *know* I'll be at your party."

"All right, well, good." I finished off my cocktail and ordered another. As the waiter returned to place an old-fashioned with a comically large ice cube in front of me, the sad feline sound of an ambulance passed in the distance. Miriam twisted her head around, panic in her eyes.

"What's wrong?" I said.

"Nothing. Just . . . is that the Shabbat siren?"

"No, Miriam," I said flatly. "It's Tuesday."

"Right. I was just asking."

I looked at her in sudden disbelief, and she stared down at her napkin. "You're not seriously suggesting . . ."

"Well, what if one day I did observe Shabbat?"

I raised one eyebrow. "On a Friday, you mean?"

"Yes, on a Friday." She didn't take the bait. "Would that be so bad?"

"What if one day I did observe Shabbat? Would that be so bad?"

I balled up my napkin and leaned back in my seat a little. "Honestly, it would be kind of ridiculous. I know you're probably being coddled by all your new friends in the self-identify-as-a-dog-and-wear-a-tail world or whatever, but you *know* it deep down."

She shook her head and muttered, "That's so offensive." Then she said, louder, "I want you to know I've been exploring this seriously, okay? After we met Sarah at the park, she—she invited me to one of their Shabbat dinners with their group. The Chabad. They're really nice, you know. And not everyone there was Hasidic. There are varying levels of orthodoxy—"

"So you're an expert now, are you?"

"Compared to you, maybe."

I shook my head and sipped my old-fashioned. "You're not even Jewish," I said quietly. "And you're still carrying on with that Zeke fantasy. You can't seriously still think he's real. It's *so* clear Mom just can't remember every guy she was boning in the nineties."

"I do! I do think he's real! And stop talking about Mom like that! It's creepy."

"You had no interest in any kind of religion a couple of months ago," I said, "and now you're having dinner with people who have dedicated their whole lives to studying the Torah. It's all just a game to you."

"Stop getting offended on behalf of people you don't even know! The people who've hosted me are *welcoming*." She took another sip of her cocktail and added, "If you can't be nice about any of it, then maybe you should just stop bringing it up altogether. It's not your place."

"Not my place, really? If you're buying into this, you're deluded and I'm worried about you. Maybe you stayed on that stupid little island with Mom for too long and it messed with your head."

We sat for a long time without talking before Miri said, almost under her breath, "You just don't want anyone to have anything now that you have nothing."

"I have nothing? Well, that's news to me." I gave a hollow,

unconvincing laugh. "I'm sorry for trying to disabuse you of a damaging fantasy, but sometimes you have to be cruel to be kind."

She got up and walked outside, and after a few minutes I realized she wasn't coming back, so I got the check and paid it. Outside the bar, I found her sucking on a menthol vape like a pacifier. That was a new habit she'd failed to mention.

"Why do we have to get into an argument basically every time we hang out?" she said when I came to stand beside her.

"I don't know. Maybe because you can't face real life."

"This *is* my real life, Tash! It's not the same as yours, but there's room for different kinds of lives in this city, you know!"

"You've been in New York for a microsecond, so don't tell me what there's room for," I said. But hearing the words come out of my mouth, I knew I didn't really want a rerun of the scene outside the park. I leaned against the wall of the bar, kicking the brickwork behind me with my shoe. I needed to smooth this over, and I needed her to be there on the Fourth of July, or else I'd look like the friendless loser that I was in front of Zach.

After I'd given myself a few breaths to calm down, I said, "Look, Miriam, I just don't want you getting mixed up in something you don't understand."

"I understand it fine. It's you who doesn't understand. Or maybe you're just scared that I'm getting my own life, or that I'm finding parts of myself that have nothing to do with you and Mom."

"Yeah, sure. You're right, Miri." I felt defeated. I watched the people milling past: tourists on their way to meet friends, wealthy students whose parents paid for their apartments, thirtysomethings who lived here on their six-figure paychecks. The bar was filling up behind us.

"What do I know?" I said in a different voice, as I watched my sister blow out another puff of flavored smoke and then put the vape away. "Maybe I'm just scared."

She looked at me like she couldn't tell whether I was being

serious. Well, she'd have no luck scrutinizing my face, because I hardly knew myself. As we continued to people watch in the fading sun, I said to her, "Let me try it," and she extracted the vape slowly then balanced it in my outstretched hand.

"Thanks," I said quietly, and inhaled then breathed out. The vapor curled into the air in front of me and disappeared.

WHEN I LOGGED INTO WORK THE FOLLOWING DAY, I HAD A PRIVATE message from Eliza on the audience team. *Hey.* Sent three hours earlier, no further details. That felt unusual.

Hey, I replied. *Sorry, I'm only just logging in.*

No problem. I just wanted to say goodbye.

Had Willem fired me and forgot to mention it? I saw the world lurch for a moment, then forced myself to breathe and write back: *What do you mean?*

I got fired today.

Ah, sweet relief. *Oh no! What happened?*

They said I was using ChatGPT to write the headlines.

Ah. I didn't know what else to add except: *Were you?* Then: *No judgment of course if you did! It's super busy around here and I know you've been dealing with like 100 headline/url requests per minute.*

No I wasn't.

Oh yeah. I didn't think you would. Was just checking.

I know some people do stuff like that, but I actually took my job really seriously.

I'm so sorry, Eliza. Genuinely. You don't even know if that's the real reason, you know? They might just be doing one of those team-shrinking things. "Streamlining."

Yeah, maybe. I'm honestly just so upset. I've been crying all morning.

Look, if there's one thing I've learned in this industry, it's that every single newspaper is desperate to hire audience analysts. You will find another job, no problem.

I guess. But this was a big break for me. And they told me when I interviewed that if I did really well on the audience team, they might let me move into reporting eventually.

Of course they did. *I'm not sure that ever would've happened anyway,* I said. *So don't beat yourself up.*

That's not exactly reassuring tbh. I have a journalism degree too, you know.

I never doubted that! I said, though I hadn't registered it at all. *You've got a great career ahead of you, whether or not you want to stay in the audience team or try your hand at reporting.*

Yeah. Maybe. I know it went wrong for you, but you were still super lucky. You got to do what you loved for a while.

You'll be lucky too. And you won't fuck it up like I did, I wrote, then changed "fuck" to "f" because I was worried the word might set off an alert in the internal messaging system.

I can tell what you think of our team and I don't even blame you. It's depressing.

Eliza. Don't spiral. You're going to be okay.

I was valedictorian of my graduating class in high school. I went to Cornell! And all I've done is help this industry go to the dogs.

Listen. What *I* did was wrong. What you did was neutral, dumb at best. Have you ever heard of the paperclip problem?

No. Should I?

Basically, it goes like this: Some form of AI kills off the whole of humanity without even meaning to. It's not evil or programmed for genocide. It's just programmed to make paperclips, without any other restraints imposed upon it. So one day, it realizes: If I move all the humans off a certain continent, then I'll have more space to build paperclip factories. So it does that, and millions of people are displaced. Then it realizes: If I kill all the humans on the planet, I'll have way more space for paperclips. So it ends up doing that. And all day, all night, forever, it works to do the job it was programmed for, by human beings, until there are literally no human beings left, and the world is filled with paperclips. It's not what anyone envisioned when they set up the AI, but it is logically consistent with what it was asked to do. Do you get what I'm saying?

Not really.

I'm saying that most of us here are type A people, honor roll students with big dreams. Most Likely to Succeeds. We turn up here ready to change the world. And then we get told to make paperclips.

TWENTY-THREE

AT LUNCHTIME ON THE FOURTH OF JULY, I WAS MIXING A HIGHLY
alcoholic punch to distribute into plastic bottles to take to the beach
when I heard muffled voices outside the front door. Zach was in the
shower, and no one except my sister was due to arrive for a couple
more hours, so I walked over carefully and pressed my ear to
the door, squinting like it might make me hear better. Through
the peephole, all I could see was the balding back of someone else's
head, so eventually I opened the door all the way, to give a look to
whoever was chitchatting right outside it.

Staring back at me in the hallway were Miri—who had promised to come over early and help with food and drinks—and the man
who lived across from Olinka, the one who held his hands up like
I had him at gunpoint every time I tried to talk to him. He was balancing an insulated bag under his arm and there was an unfamiliar-
to-me smile on his face. Miri was in the middle of a gesticulation
when the door opened, her hand in the air, a frozen grin on her face.

"Oh!" I said. "Hi!"

The man frowned and looked at the ground. "Hello."

"You two were getting to know each other, huh?" I said, jolly
as I could manage.

"We *were!*" said Miri, failing to pick up on any tension. "Jorge
was just telling me all about how his nephew is moving here from
Venezuela." She turned back to my neighbor. "Your family history
is just fascinating. So *moving.* I can't believe everything you went

through. And the way you managed to sponsor Luis after working so hard to make your catering business successful!" She turned back to me. "Did you know Jorge worked for *eighty hours* a week catering weddings with only two other coworkers? And he moved here on his own when he was a teenager, with fourteen dollars to his name? I mean, you've probably heard all of this before, Tash, but I just . . ." She shook her head. "I'm in so much awe."

"Your sister is a very nice person," Jorge said to me.

"*Super* nice," I said, without trying to disguise the sarcasm, and opened the door wider. "But we have a lot to do, so. Miri? Are you going to join me in the kitchen?"

"See you soon, Jorge," said Miri, and he gave her a jaunty wave. *What the fuck?* As he headed off back upstairs, I could see Miri was clutching a greasy paper with pastry remnants on it in her left hand.

"Arepas!" she said, when she saw me looking. "I'm guessing you have Jorge's arepas *all the time*, but I've only just had the privilege."

"All the time," I echoed, closing the door a little harder than usual behind us.

BY THE TIME PEOPLE BEGAN TO ARRIVE FOR THE PARTY A COUPLE OF hours later, Miri and I had loaded our spiked punch into bottles in a cooler and were ready to decamp to the beach.

"Zach!" I yelled toward his bedroom. "You coming?"

"I'll be there in a minute," he responded through the closed door. "You go ahead."

Down on the sand, as Miri and I set up chairs and a sheltering tent, I caught sight of Zach's three friends on the boardwalk. I held a hand up in greeting and they started to approach.

"How's everything going?" Dominique said, bouncing up to me and Miri on the sand. I thought I'd seen her give Arlo a little push toward me when they were back on the boardwalk, to which he'd shaken his head slightly. "Can I help with anything?"

"Not really," I said. "Maybe you can make this tent thing a bit more stable?"

"Got it!" She began to rearrange the tent in a surprisingly expert way, twisting it so that it was perfectly positioned to protect our chairs and towels from the ocean winds. "This is such a great idea," she added as she secured it with the weight of the cooler. I knew what she was doing: trying to act nice so as to fly under my radar while she staked a claim on Zach. She was acting like I'd never been to high school before.

"Hey," said Arlo, coming to kneel on the sand beside me. "Good to see you again." He was close enough that I could smell his breath, which wasn't fresh. Had he brushed his teeth that morning?

"Yeah, you too." I didn't want this guy latching on to me, so I employed the tactic I'd read about on internet forums: gray rocking. Be the gray rock in the interesting landscape. Actively repel unwanted people with your mundanity.

But then Zach appeared from farther along the boardwalk, and I couldn't be a gray rock anymore. I rose to go over to him, but Dominique and Jim snagged him first, and then Arlo stood in front of me in an obstructive manner and said, "Still hilariously unhappy at the newspaper?"

"I prefer to call it a vehicle for leveraging meatspace interest," I said while keeping my eye on Zach over his shoulder.

"You know, we're actually hiring over at the *Post* if you want me to put a good word in," he said.

"Oh . . . you know, I'm not sure I'm ready to change jobs right now," I said. "I might take a break from the whole twenty-four-seven newsroom thing in the future, spend some time freelancing or traveling . . ."

"Gotcha." He nodded so energetically that his entire body rocked. "We're actually also expanding our freelance budget." Although he was being nice, I sensed the sexual appetite underneath the friendliness, and it made me want to snap, *Just leave me alone.*

"Sure, I mean. I don't know. I can't see myself turning anything big around in the near future," I said instead. "I went through a lot of turmoil kind of recently . . ."

"Zach was saying," he said. "With your divorce and everything, right?"

I stopped for a moment and noticed everything that had previously been background noise: the sound of screaming children chasing one another along the shoreline, the Coast Guard's helicopter flying low overhead, the excited chatter of a bunch of teenage girls in neon bikinis and plastic flip-flops trading snacks, the dark waves of the Atlantic crashing into each other and receding. Then I said, "Yeah. Right. With my divorce."

"I'm sorry." He reached out and touched my arm gently. "I'm really sorry if bringing that up was inappropriate."

I looked down at my arm like it was an alien appendage, then said, "Really, it's fine." And I began to walk away, toward Zach and Dominique. I could see in the corner of my eye that Arlo looked a little confused, but then Miriam jumped in to pick up the dregs of the conversation, and I could hear it becoming animated again as I navigated back to the boardwalk.

"Hey," I said to Zach, unapologetically interrupting a lively back-and-forth he was having with Dominique. "Do you need anything from upstairs? I was thinking maybe we could do a final sweep together, grab extra supplies."

"Oh, I think we have enough." He smiled sedately, and I saw he already had an open can of IPA in his hand. He was wearing a white tank top and a short-sleeved open shirt with slightly too short shorts, and somehow, the whole thing worked. I tried not to look at the muscular tops of his thighs. Dominique was in a bikini top and a long, yellow skirt, a pale-pink bucket hat perched on her head. They looked like a still from the latest Wes Anderson movie. I remained a gray rock.

"Hey, I can come, Natasha," Dominique said kindly, "if you need someone to help carry anything."

"You're a guest," I said. "Just sit down and enjoy yourself. *We're* the ones hosting." I didn't mean to say the last part with an irritated edge, but I could tell from the look on her face that that's how

I'd delivered it. Her features rearranged themselves in involuntary surprise, and then she recovered, smiled, and said, "Yeah . . . sure . . . okay."

"Zach?" I said, a little more insistently, and gestured toward the street, but he shook his head and said, "Nah, Nat, really. I'm still greeting everyone." Another group was walking toward us on the sand and waving to him: the promised friends from work. No surprise that everyone showed up for the guy whose mom just died.

"Alright." Feeling spurned, I marched off toward our building. I couldn't think of anything I needed from the apartment; I'd just felt like we needed a moment alone, so we could start this evening off on a good foot, propel it back toward the romantic scenario I'd imagined when we first planned it. But I guess he didn't care about that—and now I'd made such a big deal about going upstairs, I had to do it.

My flip-flops stuck to loose rocks as I walked on the sidewalk, and the metal door of the entrance seared the skin of my hand as I pushed it open. *Whatever. He'd have to talk to me eventually.*

INSIDE THE APARTMENT, WHOSE SHADES WE'D CLOSED TO KEEP IT from overheating, it was dark. It took a minute for my eyes to adjust.

I latched the door behind me and walked into the middle of the living room, keeping an eye on the balcony to my right. I couldn't see the boardwalk or the beach from there without leaning, so I knew no one down there would be able to see me either.

I took quiet steps toward Zach's bedroom as though afraid of waking someone. Maybe one day I wouldn't have to be so furtive, wouldn't have to feel like I was crossing a boundary. Right now, I just needed to live life on fast-forward for a moment.

As I pushed open the door, I breathed in the smell of Zach: deodorant, the residual tang of feet, the pair of sweaty jeans he wore most days, which were hanging over the back of a chair. His bed was haphazardly made, the comforter thrown over the pillows in a casual manner, and the rest of the room was as sparsely decorated as I'd left it for him when he moved in. His suitcase was still propped up in one corner like he might pack up and leave at any moment—but his clean clothes were inside the small set of drawers I'd placed by his bed, and as I pulled the top drawer open, I saw that he had a good array of freshly laundered underwear. I ran my fingers over the boxer shorts and briefs, appreciating the different materials of the tighter underwear for working out and the roomier boxers for casual wear. I wondered where he kept his dirty laundry, the sets of underwear already marked by his scent, the ones that had been close to the most intimate parts of his body.

As I continued running my hand around in the top drawer, I hit on what I thought was a tube of ointment. For a moment, I worried it was going to be something deeply unsexy like hemorrhoid medication, but then I picked it up and realized it was a half-used container of lube. I thought about him lying in the bedroom opposite mine, touching himself, caressing his balls, stroking his growing cock, thoughts racing through his mind. I saw him lying on his back, his eyes closed, trying to keep quiet as he came in a hot, syrupy river all over his stomach and hands. When I'd fooled around with my college boyfriend in our dorm, he'd once come so hard that his semen hit the wall behind us and then made a viscous trail down it as we laughed in astonishment. I imagined the power of Zach's orgasm being similar, radiating through him in pleasurable waves and then being made physical in a gushing white projectile. I'd lick it off my fingers while looking into his eyes. *All this time*, I thought, as I held the tube in my hand, *I could've been doing it for you.*

I squeezed a small drop of the lube onto my fingers and lay down on the badly made bed, my mind still on Zach's clandestine masturbation sessions. I made lazy circles on my clit with my finger as I thought about walking in on him accidentally when he was touching himself in the shower. His rock-hard dick would be in his hand, and he'd be all embarrassed.

"Jesus, Nat, I'm so sorry," he'd say. "I should've locked the door."

"Don't apologize," I'd say, moving toward him, and he'd look at me a little self-consciously but he'd continue touching himself, unable to stop.

Then my phone began to ring. I opened my eyes, saw Ellie's name on the screen, and sent the call to voicemail. She'd texted to say she was on her way only twenty minutes ago—she couldn't be here. But then she called again, and the vibration became too hard to ignore.

I sighed and picked up. "Hello?"

"Hey! So where are you? We just got off the train."

"Oh hey. Great! We're just on the sand next to the burrito place, two minutes off the boardwalk. The group with the big white tent. Zach's down there; I'm just . . . finishing up some stuff inside."

"Well, it'd be great if we could drop by your place first. I think Charlotte might need a diaper change. Unless the guy next to us on the train had some kind of bowel issue."

That ended my alone time. "Sure. You've got the address. Just buzz when you get here and I'll let you up."

"Perfect. We're three streets away. See you soon!"

I got up off the bed, put the lid back on the lube, and slid it into the back of Zach's top drawer again. Then I put the comforter back in its prior position before making my way to the refrigerator so I could plausibly say I'd been gathering more beers and ice. When the buzzer rang just a few minutes later, I had pulled myself together.

AFTER CHARLOTTE LOUISA'S DIAPER CHANGE AND AN EPISODE WITH wet wipes that I hoped never to repeat, I went back down to the beach with Ellie and Jake and settled them inside the shade of the tent with the baby.

"Aww, a baby!" said Dominique, and came over to grab Charlotte Louisa's chubby little fingers and pinch her cheeks.

"Hey, you two dress the same," said Zach, pointing at Charlotte Louisa's yellow sundress, and Dominique rolled her eyes and leaned her head on his shoulder.

"Stop it," she said, and I had to look away.

"This is what I imagined living in the Rockaways would be like," I said to Jake, sliding off my shoes and burying my toes in the warm sand. "I'm so glad it's finally summer."

"Yeah, it's something else," he said with a complacent smile. To me, Jake was so familiar that he was basically sexless. I tried to imagine wanting to fuck him, couldn't do it; tried to envision Ellie climbing on top of him, out of her mind with lust, and riding him to completion, but I couldn't do that either. It felt incestuous.

"It's so much better now that you've decorated your place a bit and the weather has turned," said Ellie. "I'm willing to admit I judged it a little too soon."

"No, you were right." I shrugged and grabbed a bottle of the moonshine cocktail Miri and I had made from the cooler. "It was horrible in the winter." It wasn't true that I'd imagined idyllic ocean scenes like this when I'd bought the place; instead, it had been an act of self-punishment. But that was easier to say than the truth.

There was a shark warning along Long Island extending to Rockaway Beach, so red flags were positioned at points along the sand, and lifeguards kept blowing whistles at anyone who tried to wade into the sea beyond their ankles. A small plane passed overhead pulling a banner that said DRINK BILL'S ORGANIC HARD SELTZER! WHY NOT? and I laughed.

"That's the most halfhearted advertising I've ever seen in my life," I said to Jake—it reminded me of Olinka's "ORDINARY COFFEE"—but when I turned my head I realized he was no longer listening to me and had started helping Ellie wrestle Charlotte Louisa into a rashguard that covered her arms and legs.

"What?" he asked, but I just shook my head and said, "Don't worry about it." I took a long drink of moonshine and let the welcome effects of the alcohol course through me: the heady relaxation and the slight cramp in my lower limbs. Then I pulled my sunglasses down over my eyes and sat back for a moment. The sun was shining. People were talking. Zach was here. Life was good.

After I'd finished my first cocktail, I got up and walked over to Zach, who was leaning against the boardwalk railings and distributing sunblock over the tops of his ears.

"Hey," I said.

"How's it going?"

"Pretty good, actually." I copied his lean and we looked out toward the ocean together.

"Do you remember that Fourth of July when you came to Nantucket?" I asked him.

He took a sip from his can. "Oh, yeah . . . vaguely."

I did a casual little laugh. "You weren't that impressed, if I recall."

He looked at me for a moment, in an unapologetic manner, then said, "I wasn't?"

"I'm not sure. Maybe you were in a bad place."

He shrugged. "It's perfectly possible." He took another swig and then said, "Anyway, we were young."

This seemed like the perfect opening for a longer conversation about our current friendship and where it might go, but as soon as he'd said that, he got up and walked down the boardwalk to the trash, ditched his empty beer, and didn't return. Instead, he wandered up the beach to say hi to Ellie, Jake, and Miri, who were now all gathered together in the shade of the tent sharing a bag of Doritos.

When we'd visited Nantucket, back in those early days, Zach had been coolly scathing about pretty much everything—"All the idyllic trappings of small-town America," he'd said, with an edge, as we passed flag-bedecked storefronts and kids' lemonade stands—and the more I saw my childhood through his eyes, the more I hated it.

"Sorry if it all seemed a bit . . . family values," I'd said, because he spent the entire day watching the fire trucks spray kids with hoses along Main Street with a sardonic little half-smile on his face. I didn't actually understand what had put him on the offensive, why he couldn't just immerse himself and enjoy it a little for once. It wasn't like all the people he knew in New York were watching.

"Fourth of July was a weird one for me and my family," he'd replied in what I presumed was supposed to be an explanation for his mood. "My mom always insisted on hosting this *big* cookout, and it was the only time I really saw my aunts and uncles from her side of the family. My cousins would come over and shoot at our light fixtures with pellet guns and drag our dog into the pool by the neck. My dad would yell at my mom about coming from a hillbilly family."

I laughed, but that evidently wasn't the right reaction. He looked at me a little reproachfully.

"Sorry," I said. "It does sound like chaos. But I mean, in some ways . . . fun chaos?"

"You don't really see what I mean," he said. "The class system in this country can be really cruel."

"Right. But you grew up pretty wealthy."

"That's not really the point. Poverty creates generational trauma, you know? Just knowing what my mom went through— you know, three siblings to a room in a trailer, hurricane alarms, rural schools with no curriculum and no access to funding—it makes all the America the Great stuff feel really hollow on a day like today."

I struggled to understand his point. As far as I knew, he'd only visited his mother's hometown in the south a handful of times. "Your dad speaking to your mom like that about her family must have really hurt," I tried.

"It did," he said. "Because, those kids with pellet guns and dirt bikes? They didn't know any better. Can we really hold them to the same standards?"

We walked along in silence for a bit until I ventured, "But . . . if we don't then isn't it a little problematic? Just playing devil's advocate."

He looked back at me reproachfully. "I don't mean this in a bad way, but you've never had a dad around, so you're not going to get how it feels. Parent against parent. Being torn down the middle like that."

I thought about my biological father, a Russian immigrant who worked in construction. Might he not have something to say about generational trauma and poverty, about the American Dream? But it was true I'd never known him. I hadn't wanted to go toe-to-toe with the fragile male ego that evening, so I just said, "In a way, yeah, you're right." I was still saying that to him now.

THEN I WAS BACK IN THE APARTMENT AND FOUR OF US WERE crammed on the balcony, watching the last of the sunset. Someone had opened all the curtains, and Arlo had his arm around the small of my back.

"It's so cool that you lived abroad," he was saying. "I've always wanted to try that."

"I wouldn't recommend England," I replied. "They think we're a nation of gun-toting fascists who put our dogs on Prozac, and they let you know it at pretty much every opportunity."

"I think I'd find that hilarious," he said. "Maybe I could set myself up as London's first canine psychiatrist."

"Well, maybe you'd like it there," I said. "Personally, I'm never going back." And I went to the kitchen to get myself a light beer and escape any further conversation with him.

Then it was dark, and I was on the sofa with Dominique. Our knees were touching.

"Natasha, my girl," she was saying, "I just love how you always tell the truth."

"It's a blessing and a curse," I said.

"No, no, always a blessing," she said and put her head on my shoulder in the same way she'd put her head on Zach's earlier, and I could tell she was drunk too.

Then someone was knocking on the front door, and when

I got up and opened it, it was a middle-aged guy I'd never seen before.

"Yeah, I'm your neighbor to the left," he said. "I'm sorry, but the music is just way too loud."

"I'm sorry," I said. "We'll turn it down."

"I'm surprised you didn't do that when we were knocking on the wall."

"We didn't hear," I said, and he was still standing there, so I repeated, "We'll turn it down." When he didn't move, I added, "Did you want to come in?" and he exhaled in an irritated way and stalked back off to his apartment.

"It's the Fourth of July!" Dominique, who'd appeared at my shoulder, yelled after him. As I closed the door, she said, "What a loser. Like, I could understand, but it's the *Fourth*. People know what that means."

"Totally," I said, and I was going to head toward the balcony, where I could see the silhouettes of two figures in the darkness, but she grabbed my arm and said, "Hey! You're not getting away that easy. Let's do shots!"

Then we were in the kitchen with Arlo and Jim, and Dominique was pouring tequila and cutting the single lemon in our fridge into pieces with a dull knife. "To Mr. O'Leary!" said Jim, as we knocked back the shots, and now I didn't see the reference as exclusionary but instead as an invitation, so I said, "Long live Mr. O'Leary!" with them as I swallowed and ended up laughing until I was coughing.

Then it was fully dark outside, and inside the apartment only the standing lamp beside the sofa and a light in Zach's bedroom were on. Dominique, Arlo, and Jim were sitting on the floor, playing some card game I'd never heard of. I was standing to the side of the couch, watching a couple from Zach's work have a heated debate about whether it was okay to use your roommate's Adderall. "At the end of the day," a girl with red hair was saying, "what does a doctor know about my state of mind that I don't know myself? It's subjective by definition."

And then I felt a wave of nausea wash over me and realized I needed some air. I staggered toward the balcony and saw the same silhouettes from an hour earlier were still there. As I got closer I could see they were kissing, and when I was a couple of feet from them I could see that they weren't just silhouettes, but they were two people I knew. It was Zach and Miri.

And then Miriam was breaking away and I was walking toward them and we were all on the balcony together, the music spilling out into the night after us and fireworks still periodically exploding from gardens and street corners below. I couldn't hear myself think. I couldn't say anything. I leaned back because my vision was swimming, and then I went back inside, physical sickness and anger swirling inside me.

And then Miri and I were sitting outside the apartment, on the cold concrete floor of the stairwell, and she was crying. She was such a fucking crybaby.

"It wasn't anything, I swear," she was saying. "I don't even like him!"

"I bring you to my home," I was saying, my head between my knees to keep from throwing up. "I bring you to my city, I introduce you to my friends."

"He was following me around all night," she was saying in a plaintive little voice, and her hand was gripping mine. "I swear, Tash, I swear. You have to believe me."

"Why would you even be out there alone with him?"

"I wasn't! I was by myself! I went out to text that guy Sarah introduced me to. I was trying to get away from him!"

"I saw what happened with my own eyes," I said, balling my hands into fists. "I saw how you were kissing him . . ."

"I didn't get what was happening! I pulled away! Tash, *please!*" She was outright sobbing now, and as I raised my head I saw snot running down her face onto her lip and eyeshadow and mascara smudged down one cheek.

"You *always* turn on the waterworks," I snapped.

"I'm so confused, Tash, seriously. I don't even know what's going on. He was following me everywhere, and I kept trying to get your attention, and that Dominique girl kept pulling you away . . . and I don't know. Honestly, he was being a little creepy. And I don't know, Tash, I don't know. I think you need to talk to him. Because I don't think he's going to get to the same place as you are."

I sat up fully then. "What do you mean?"

But she just shook her head and wiped her nose with her bare forearm. "I don't know. I just think you should talk to him."

I looked at my phone and saw it was one in the morning. The harsh stairwell lighting was giving me a headache. I got up and pushed the door to the apartment open and went inside to find Dominique, Arlo, Jim, and Zach all squashed together on the sofa in a little pile, legs over legs and arms over shoulders. They looked like they were having an intense conversation.

"What the *fuck*," I said, "were you thinking?"

Standing at my full height above them like that, I felt powerful. I staggered a little on one foot but righted myself, my eyes fixed on Zach as he looked at me with no emotion on his face.

"Natasha," said Dominique, quickly. "Natasha, come on, let's just—"

"Shut *up*," I said, and she fell quiet. Then I turned back to Zach. "You fucking monster," I said. "You disgusting piece of shit. After *everything* I've done for you—all the support, the apartment, the long talks, the funeral—and all the weird signals, and this *atmosphere* you've been projecting—are you *trying* to hurt me? Because even you must know that my own *sister*—"

"Natasha," said Zach, standing up so he was face-to-face with me but speaking dangerously quietly, and I thought in some back corner of my mind that that was the first time I'd heard him use my full first name. "What the hell are you talking about?"

"Don't pretend like you don't know," I said, holding his gaze. My voice shook, and I knew I sounded like I was losing it. I was also aware that everyone else in the apartment had gone completely silent, watching us with a kind of mesmerized horror.

"I really don't," he said, "and frankly, I think you've got a serious problem."

The room was moving, but it swayed in a predictable enough way that I could still keep my balance, like I was on a subway car pulling into a familiar station. I could hear myself breathing heavily with the effort, but I wasn't going to let him win.

"I'm glad your mom got sick," I said eventually, choosing my words carefully and injecting them with just the right amount of venom. "You know what? I'm glad she died. You deserved it."

Then there was noise again, and Miriam had come up behind me and taken my arm to pull me away, and Dominique was shooting me a look of disgust, and Arlo and Jim were leading Zach back to his bedroom while he was saying something to them like, "No, I should have known, I should have known . . ."

Then someone cut the music and slammed the balcony door shut.

Then it was the middle of the night, just before dawn, and Miriam was asleep in my bed next to me, and I was woken by the apartment door shutting in the darkness.

Then I was standing in the kitchen, and the white morning light was bouncing off the kitchen tiles and into my protesting eyes, and I was covered in sweat and trying to go through the motions of putting on a pot of coffee, and Miri was shaking her head and saying, "Tasha. It's empty. He's gone."

TWENTY-FOUR

TWO DAYS LATER, I WENT DOWN TO THE BOARDWALK TO GET A COFFEE from Olinka and was surprised to see she had a line, and that she'd expanded her repertoire to iced drinks. One man inexplicably dressed in a suit jacket and shirt paired with board shorts was screaming into his phone and gesturing to Olinka every thirty seconds that he wanted his iced coffee *stat*.

"Hey, Olinka," I said when I reached the front of the line. "I think I'm about to take some decisive action and I just wanted you to know."

She raised her eyebrows and handed me a drink while pointing with her other hand to the tip jar. "Okay," she said. "Destruction is fine, if you have a plan for what comes after."

"I don't have time to make a plan for after." I fondled the ice cubes through the plastic cup, aware I sounded a little unhinged.

"Natasha," she said, as I turned to walk away. "You know, where I'm from, the farmers burn the crops in their fields every other year. Makes the air pretty awful for a summer. But they do it so the soil is fertile again within a couple of seasons. It's good for replanting. Get my drift? It's a metaphor."

"Sorry. I'm a literal person."

She shook her head and gestured for the next customer in line—a beautiful woman in a pin-striped bathing suit—to come forward. "Okay, kiddo. Just think on it. One day you might get it—you never know."

I TOOK THE EXPRESS A TRAIN AND ARRIVED AT THE OFFICE BRIGHT and early for my shift, zipping through the cards with unusual speed.

Young Father Who Had a "Slight Headache" Dies
from Increasingly Common Brain-Eating
Bacteria

"Beautiful, Talented" College Student Mutilated at
Work After "Freak Accident" with a Meat Grinder: Pics
Released

Inside the Mansion of Silicon Valley's Latest Socialist
Hypocrite

Mysterious Signal Heard from as Far as 2,000
Galaxies Away "Sounds Deliberate," Says Radio
Enthusiast

Critics Say "Beauty Queen" Accused Billionaire
Boyfriend of Domestic Abuse "For Money"

Heartless: The Doctors Who Said My Baby Would
Never Walk

Hazmat Suits for Sale?: Prepare Yourself for This
Direct Hit from a Solar Storm

At lunchtime I bought a salad, brought it back to my hot desk, and opened my laptop. I'd made my decision.

SWIMSUIT MODEL DROWNS IN SEMEN AT WORLD'S LARGEST SEX PARTY

Byline: Natasha Bailey

An orgy of oiled-up fraternity brothers and sorority sisters ended in tragedy Tuesday when the lifeless body of a popular student was found on the grounds of Hotpeople University, a college that only admits the best-looking applicants. The former swimsuit model had last been seen eliciting a Japanese sex move known as "bukkake" from a group of male athletes. She reportedly had the largest breasts of any student ever accepted at the Ivy League–esque institution.

"It's ironic, really," said a tearful friend who wished to remain anonymous. "She drowned when she was most famous for promoting safe swim practices."

If you've read this far, you probably have already realized that this news story is complete fiction. It's twisted and morbidly titillating, like most of the junk we're now encouraged to pump out because an algorithm told us to. Make no mistake: this is disrespect for humanity on a corporate scale. What used to be a respected newspaper is now a cynical operation designed to make money from your basest human instincts. Please stop reading this bullshit and for the love of God don't click on any of the (many, many) surrounding ads, because that will only encourage them. From the outside, I know this looks like it might be a responsible news site delivering you an objective view of reality; but from inside the belly of the beast, it's a monster.

I'm writing this because I'm the only person who can—a disgraced former reporter and Public Enemy Number One on the internet. I stayed at the paper to try to resurrect my career because I made myself unemployable by going down on an interviewee one time. You'll be pleased to hear, since you're all such hardline moralists, that I lost my husband, my future, and pretty much every other chance at happiness in the process. The fact that you hate me, though, shouldn't mean that you ignore this message.

So many other people who work here feel the same way. I see it in their eyes and I hear it in their voices during "traffic" meetings. But they drag themselves out of bed every day and come to work producing content that furthers nefarious agendas and saps at their souls because they still believe in journalism. They proceed in the vain hope that, one day, they might become a Pulitzer Prize–winning reporter blowing an investigative case wide open. They've fooled themselves into thinking that they'll work on a story with global ramifications, spotlighting an issue that changes the world for the better. Management exploits this optimism by telling these reporters that they're "keeping the lights on" by copying stories from websites likely operated by Russian bots—stories that are waved through because the fact-checkers were considered "surplus to demand" years ago. But when all anyone is doing is keeping the lights on, what's left isn't a noble publication—it's an empty, brightly lit display case.

The truth is that the dream of doing good journalism is horrendously outdated. Budgets for original reporting are being slashed every year because of "the economy," but make no mistake: the money is there—it's just being pumped into recruiting and hiring more overpaid managers, more audience analysts, and more depressed news aggregators rewriting content they find on conspiracy-laden fringe websites. The only people who get to conduct investigations or high-level interviews are the children of celebrities or other moneyed freelancers with millions of online followers and a big financial safety net. Anyone who works in-house gets sucked into the aggregation machine.

The people in charge will tell you that their investors and their advertisers can't take the risk of sending someone to a war zone for a week just to see if they might get one story. It doesn't make economic sense. Reporting is being "streamlined," and people are being recalled from foreign countries because their work about refugee crises doesn't get as many clicks as stories about dead swimsuit models and culture wars. It's "not the nineties anymore." The C-level executives—none of whom have ever actually worked in a newsroom, by the way (I checked)—would prefer those people retrain in the art of directing more eyes toward advertising space. And they don't realize that destroying your own brand is its own risk.

I guess what I'm trying to say to the people up top is that I'm ready to gather the last shreds of my dignity around me and quit. And what I'm trying to say to you, the reader, is that you should look at everything—even this admittedly bitter essay, written by a former hack who lacks a growth mindset—with a skeptical eye. Because, like probably everything else you've read today, this is clickbait.

I hit publish and sent the link to the audience team, who approved the headline without reading the article and arranged for it to be tweeted out from all accounts within twenty minutes. It had a Facebook slot in an hour and would be part of an Instagram story then too. I could put it forward for a TikTok compilation this evening. The wheels kept grinding on.

I took my time powering down my laptop, sliding it into its protective pouch, and then into my leather purse. I took the elevator and walked out of the building at a leisurely pace, stepping briefly aside for an excited toddler closely pursued by a harried-looking man. Fetid steam rose from a drain somewhere in the middle of the road. The sidewalks were full of people who didn't know what I'd done.

Near the entrance to the subway, I stopped for a second beside an oversize trash can and a bus stop and looked back at the office tower I'd just exited. It didn't look like a place where lives were regularly upended. It just looked like any old, unremarkable place of business.

Then I carefully extricated my electronic newsroom pass from my pocket and, with a casual flick of the wrist, threw it into the trash.

TWENTY-FIVE

THE ROCKAWAY BULLETIN

BODY FOUND WAS LOCAL COFFEE MAKER, SAY POLICE

The body found washed up on a Lawrence shoreline yesterday has been identified as that of local Rockaway coffee stand operator Olinka Kovalenka, Nassau County police say. Officers had been alerted by an early morning dog walker that a woman was seen walking into the ocean near the boardwalk a week earlier. The temperatures that day were cold enough that hypothermia would have set in almost immediately, the Coast Guard said.

Local residents say Kovalenka's coffee cart was a staple on the boardwalk in recent years, but that she rarely spoke with customers, preferring to keep to herself. "She was pretty unfriendly," said the dog walker, who asked not to be named. "The one time I bought coffee from her, she asked me if I dressed like this deliberately. I found that rude."

A small funeral will be provided by Go As You Please Funeral Services. Go As You Please director

Martin Diaz said that Kovalenka had provided him free coffees on her way to and from the boardwalk with her cart. "She seemed interested in what we were doing," he said. "It's unusual, but it's appreciated."

Mr. Diaz added that his expectations for the service on Thursday were modest. "As far as I know, she had no family or close friends," he said. "But we'd still like to give her a proper send-off."

It's believed that Olinka Kovalenka was terminally ill. According to a source in her building, she left a note in her apartment for her building superintendent to find, saying she'd decided to "take matters into [her] own hands while [she] still could."

THE PLANE LURCHED IN THE RAIN AS IT BEGAN ITS DESCENT, AND the woman in the seat next to mine gripped our shared armrest for a moment. I shot her a sympathetic look. I remembered when a fear of turbulence had scared me out of traveling, and I felt a pang of empathy for her. Today, I was just enjoying the ride.

October was warm in New York, but it was cold where I was headed. I'd packed my two hard-shell suitcases full of raincoats and sweaters, waterproof boots and thick woolen socks. When Joe and I had set out for London, the contents of my luggage had been very similar—but this time, I turned up to the airport alone, struggling through the terminal with my luggage. It felt good to pull my own baggage, not to have to wait for anyone at the TSA checkpoint. Inside my head, it was quiet.

Back in the Rockaways, Miriam was preparing for her housewarming party with help from Ellie and Jake. I imagined them lighting candles and setting out bowls of chips and salsa, Miri carefully curating the playlist. It would be a sedate affair compared to the ill-fated party last held there. I'd left my sister in the care of my best friend, and I was confident they'd work it out together. Of course, Miri wouldn't actually need Ellie as much now that she had Etan.

Etan was Miri's age, but he'd already been married. His parents were Orthodox, but they "leaned modern," he'd told me, unconvincingly. Miri was still in Hebrew classes and due to complete her conversion in a few months' time. Their wedding was scheduled for next year, and their unofficial abode—to be made official after they were married—was my apartment in the Rockaways, far enough away from everyone they knew that no rumors could be confirmed. Miri had thought about tracking down her absent father to walk her down the aisle, but Mom had talked her out of it. She'd been ambivalent about the idea of helping plan a wedding for Miri so soon after my divorce. "You strike out on your own to live a bohemian lifestyle after generations of stifling tradition," she'd said, "and then your kids become addicted to marriage." Like she hadn't had a hand in that.

The article I'd written and published as my final goodbye to the newspaper had stayed on the site for twenty-seven minutes. By that time, it had been saved and screenshotted and reshared by millions of users. Reporters from other newspapers had started calling my cell, wanting to interview me so they could write their own pieces about the drama. Everything went viral. The snake ate its own tail, ad infinitum.

Someone at the *Washington Post* had asked me if I minded having my picture next to the article. "I hope you don't think we're doing the same thing, publishing pictures of pretty girls front and center to sell stories," he'd said amiably.

"Oh wow," I'd said. "Thanks for calling me pretty."

I'd thought Zach might be proud of me for flaming out of the capitalist hellhole mainstream media so spectacularly, but when I tried to text him, it didn't go through—he'd clearly blocked me—and when I went on all the usual social media sites, I found he'd blocked me there as well. He'd left nothing behind him when he moved out except the key, amputated from its companions on his keychain and left on the coffee table as the sole proof that he'd once been there.

When I checked my mail for the last time, in preparation for my second big move abroad, I'd found a folded-up note inside. NA-TASHA was written on the outside of the paper in clumsy block capitals with a familiar-looking black Sharpie. Standing in the lobby, my heart beating in my ear, I unfolded the paper. I'd seen the local reports in the *Rockaway Bulletin*. I'd noticed that Olinka's coffee cart no longer competed with the ice cream vendors and the guys who pulled furtive coolers of homemade cocktail mixes up and down the sand, mumbling, "Nutcrackers, nutcrackers, nutcrackers," out of the corners of their mouths. Her apartment had been quiet. But I'd assumed that, like last time, she might've just had a medical appointment.

> Sorry, had to go—bad news at the hospital & it just
> made sense. At least the jaguar didn't get me. My real
> name is Jaylene Wilson—look me up sometime. Feel
> free to use that however you want, the dead aren't
> precious. Thanks again for lunch—"Olinka"

I read it a few times, then I went upstairs to my almost-empty apartment, pulled open my laptop, and Googled "Jaylene Wilson." Page after page of hits loaded. A poster with a blurry photo of a much younger woman on the FBI website. A page on the National Missing and Unidentified Persons System. On YouTube, I clicked on a grainy video from a press conference twenty-seven years ago that had been uploaded by an internet sleuth. Policemen from a rural town in Oregon talked about "keeping our options open;" a set of teary-eyed parents sat to the side and a man identified as a brother leaned forward to the mic. The brother looked directly into the camera and pleaded, "Jaylene, whatever you've done or whatever's happened, it doesn't matter. Just please come home."

"At the very least," the father said, his lip overshadowed by a thick, untrimmed mustache, "can you let us know that you're okay?"

I followed the tranche of news reports to a local paper detailing an arrest: a boyfriend with prior convictions for domestic violence, circumstantial evidence, bloody clothes found in the drier, the ex-lover behind bars, a prison sentence that was ongoing. A lawyer saying, "My client maintains his innocence. Jaylene Wilson took off in the middle of the night and was never seen again." The jaguar in a cage.

A subreddit dedicated to conspiracy theories about where Jaylene ended up. A few sightings reported across the country, a few in a homeless neighborhood in California and a single one of a woman whose description sounded like Olinka getting out of a yellow cab in lower Manhattan a decade ago. A Reddit post that declared: "Much as we all love a mystery, it's safe to say that Occam's razor dictates Jaylene Wilson is dead." Five hundred upvotes, with a comment underneath that read: "She's clearly been dead for a very long time." Another: "There's been a definitive conviction in this case. End of story."

I thought about Olinka's stories about Ukraine. *I walked seventeen miles to cross the border with Estonia.* She'd said it with such conviction that I'd never thought about the fact that Estonia doesn't share a border with Ukraine. *I brought my dog over in a Walmart bag.* Walmart? Why hadn't I questioned that? And why would a Ukrainian woman, new to the country, have had strong enough views on Reaganomics to be muttering about them on my first day in the building? I thought about her shifting accent; the way she'd ordered shrimp and grits in the diner the day we discussed our respective pasts; the choice of the American diner over the Ukrainian restaurant, where it would've become clear she didn't speak the language. The day when I'd stormed out on Zach and gone to the beach, Olinka had told me Putin had been "on the throne for twenty-five years" when she'd moved to America. I'd been so tied up in my own history that I'd failed to pick up on the clues she was leaving for me everywhere.

Feel free to use that however you want, the dead aren't precious. I'd

carefully refolded the note and stuck it into my purse, before closing my laptop and packing it up for one last time in the Rockaways.

THE PLANE LURCHED ONCE MORE IN THE PREVAILING WINDS, AND
then, seconds later, the wheels slammed into the runway. We landed
reassuringly hard. The woman beside me pressed her white knuckles farther into the armrest and closed her eyes until we slowed to
a complete stop. I trained my eyes on the view outside, the moun-
tains rising up in the distance, the green fields on one side and the
built-up city on the other. I'd been promised that the air was clean.

Once we deplaned, I followed the crowd to the baggage carou-
sel, retrieved my suitcases, and took one in each hand. Immigra-
tion was fast and efficient, even though my American passport was
supposed to slow things down. Everything was gleaming white,
the windows wide and the billboards welcoming us into the country decorated with images of trees, lakes, chocolate fountains, and
friendly chefs holding fondue pots filled with bubbling cheese.

When I came out through customs under the NOTHING TO
DECLARE sign, I spotted someone waving from behind the lines
of drivers holding up names on white boards. Then Footsie Dalmatian ran toward me, holding out one hand to grab a suitcase,
embracing me with the other.

"I'm so glad to see you," she said, and she looked it. She was wearing a crisp, white dress cinched in the middle with a brown leather
belt, an absurdly large necklace displaying various gemstones, and
a neon-blue purse made of carpet material. "Welcome to Zurich!"

Footsie had a car in Switzerland that she used on the weekends, and she maneuvered it around disoriented tourists and out
onto the open road with ease. As I settled into the heated seat, she
talked nonstop about my new apartment and the job I'd start in a
couple weeks at her nonprofit for female refugees: "Like I said on
the phone, what you were really missing was a sense of *purpose*.
Anyway, as we grow in size, we really need an English speaker here
full time. And doing the publicity is just so easy, you know, because

the mission is one everyone can get on board with. Not that I'm saying"—she briefly looked away from the road a little nervously, studying my face—"that you *need* it to be easy."

"No, no," I said. "I didn't take offense." And I hadn't.

My new apartment was in the Old Town, a third-story walk-up that you entered from a cobbled side street. "You're walking distance to the lake," Footsie said proudly. "I'm so glad we bought this place before the housing market went crazy. Well, actually, it kind of was crazy when we bought it. But I suppose it sounds less quaint to say I'm so glad we could afford it. Anyway, you're going to love it here, I just know it."

Inside the ornate building, the doorman crouched down and picked up a suitcase in each hand like it was nothing at all, led us up the curving staircase, then dropped them in front of my new apartment door without a word. Footsie handed him a Swiss franc note and they nodded at each other.

"Oh, and the spare key?" she asked, then, "Uh . . . der Schlüssel?" He nodded, descended the stairs, then reappeared with a surprisingly small key that he deposited in her hand.

"As you can see, my German is wanting," Footsie said, giving me a wink. "You've really got to learn through immersion, in my opinion. We've got you a couple weeks of language classes just to help you through that tricky first month—Swiss German really is a different beast to what they speak in Munich or Frankfurt, or even Vienna, but you'll pick it up. You'll be fluent by the time I next see you, I bet! So here, go on, try it." She held out the key. I slid it into the lock obligingly and pushed the door open, and we walked together into an open-plan apartment whose large windows overlooked a small, picturesque square. The place was decorated mostly with instantly recognizable IKEA furniture: humanity had prayed for a global lingua franca, and the gods had given us Billy bookcases.

"See? The newest appliances. Everything in here." Footsie walked around the apartment with me, flicking on lights and tapping the stove and the microwave with her colorful fingernails. She even turned on the kitchen faucet and the garbage disposal for a few seconds to demonstrate how they worked.

"Thanks, Footsie," I said, after we'd made sure everything was present and operational. "I really do appreciate this."

"Oh, nonsense." She walked over to the wall of windows without looking at me. "I offered you a job and you took it. And I'm very, very glad you're here."

"Me too," I said. "I guess I better unpack. And I actually promised my mom I would call her as soon as I landed."

"Tell her you were delayed," said Footsie, with a smile. "I have a place to show you first. It's going to be your favorite coffee shop—not just in Zurich, but in the whole world. It's just round the corner and it dates back three hundred years. And my God, when you see it decorated in all those lights at Christmas—it's like an actual fairy tale. I don't know how these Swiss fuckers do it."

"All right," I said, slipping my wallet out of my backpack and into my pocket. The Old Town looked inviting in the afternoon light, and what else did I have to do anyway? These days, I had all the time and space in the world.

"Great!" Footsie picked up her neon purse again and slung it over her shoulder, ready to conquer Zurich with me. "Now make sure you lock your door behind you."

IT WAS ONLY AN HOUR AND A HALF AFTER MY RETURN FROM HOT chocolate with Footsie that my phone rang: my old American phone, lying on my nightstand, not the new Swiss iPhone Footsie had gifted me at the café. I grabbed it off the table, assuming it was my mother or Ellie. But no: the number was Unknown, with a UK country code. I picked up, thinking maybe Footsie's husband or one of her stepkids needed to get ahold of her and had this number.

"Hello, Natasha speaking," I heard myself say, overly formal.

"Hi," said a male voice. "So, I heard you quit your job." It was the same voice I'd traded hopes and dreams with a million years ago, a voice that had once told me it loved me and agreed to spend the rest of its life with me.

"Joe," I said.

"Well, yes."

I didn't know what to say, so all I managed was: "You got a new number."

"I did. A while ago now. You might have had something to do with that."

I sank down into a seated position at the end of the bed. "It's really nice to hear your voice again." I was measuring my words carefully, like a wrong move might scare him away.

"Yeah. Same. I mean, I didn't know if it would be but . . ."

"You were justified in wondering," I said quickly. "I was a complete asshole. Beyond that. There aren't even words for what I was. But God, Joe." My eyes were filling with tears. This wasn't supposed to be about me. I swallowed them back down.

"Yeah, you kind of were. But it's been over a year now. So, are you in the middle of lunch? I'm just walking home from the Tube. Late night at work." I imagined him traversing the streets of London, the Victorian homes leaning into each other like schoolgirls sharing secrets, the orange lights, the families sitting down in front of televisions behind large bay windows. Dirty escalators littered with Big Mac wrappers, advertisements for Maybelline lip gloss and Greggs sausage rolls, buses hissing past and announcing in a British female monotone: "Seventy-three to King's Cross Station."

"No, I'm not in New York," I said.

"Oh, are you at your mom's place?"

"Actually, I'm in Zurich."

"As in Switzerland?" He sounded surprised.

I laughed. "The very same."

"Wow. What are you doing there?"

"I just moved here." I looked at my suitcases, one splayed out on the floor and one standing neatly by the door. I'd brought so little with me; Footsie had taken care of almost everything I'd need. "I got a job. A non-media job."

"Well, I guess it makes sense that you don't work in the industry anymore. At least you can say you went out with a bang."

"Ha. Yeah."

I heard him walking down the street, passing a gaggle of kids who were shouting at one another about going to the corner shop for crisps. I had so much to say to him that I couldn't possibly get out the words. There was silence on the line for a moment before he said, as if he'd had to build up to it, "Have you been with anyone else?"

Absurdly, I felt myself blush, alone in the dusk of my new apartment. Joe wasn't the kind of man to force a moment to its crisis. This was clearly something he'd been waiting to find out for a long time. I thought of Zach, the Rockaways, Arlo, the silhouette of a boy I once liked kissing my sister during a drunken evening.

"No," I said. "Not even close."

He made a strangled little noise. "Wow. Yeah. I just . . . I always assumed there might've been someone else in the background, you know? Or that you'd move on quickly, at least."

"No. No, no." I paused. "Listen, Joe, I don't think I ever told you this explicitly—or at least without a thousand caveats—and I can't tell you how stupid I feel for just realizing it, but I'm so goddamn sorry. You have no idea." Two fat, selfish tears ran down my reddening cheeks, but I kept their existence out of my voice.

"It means a lot to hear you say that. Even if it took a while."

I took a second to steady myself, wiped another tear away with a flattened palm, then said, "Have *you* . . . been with anyone?" As if I hadn't known the answer.

There was a pause, then, "Yes."

"Ah."

"Yeah."

On the street below my apartment, a man and a woman stopped to open a door. I could hear them laughing together, the clink of wine bottles and groceries in plastic shopping bags. I imagined them making dinner in the kitchen next to mine, then falling asleep together on the sofa.

Joe's voice rose again. "I was actually calling because . . . well, I know people use social media a lot and everything, and it's a whole wide world of communications and miscommunications out there. And I didn't want you to find out through somebody else. I'm getting married again."

Of course he was. Of course. I mean, that made so much sense.

"Congratulations," I said weakly.

"Look, I'm not some cold, unfeeling jerk. I know that must be shitty to hear."

"No, I mean . . . it is and it isn't. But mostly it isn't. I'm happy for you. You deserve this."

"Yeah, well. It won't be right away. I've come to believe in the merits of a long engagement." Neither of us knew what to say, and I heard him force out an awkward, hollow little laugh. "So . . . second time's the charm, huh?"

"Totally."

Between us opened a chasm of friendly civility, the kind that separates exes who have truly moved on, so much more quietly devastating than the raw sadness and anger and regret of the divorce. That chasm would become a small artifact in the landscape of our respective lives, something to visit infrequently. But it existed as a marker on my emotional map now, and for that I had to be grateful.

"If you're ever in London," he started, and I recognized that he was trying to wrap up the conversation as politely as possible. "Well, I guess you're pretty close these days."

"Relatively, yes." I smiled into nothingness.

"Listen, Tash. I know you're not always . . . great with the emotional honesty stuff one hundred percent of the time." *God, Joe, you always were so generous*, I thought sincerely. "But I do feel like I need to say this to you, and I don't expect anything in return, so just humor me. I don't regret being in love with you. At all. I think we made a good go of it."

That final phrase, so Britishized, so emblematic of how he'd changed in the time we'd been apart, gave me a brief feeling of vertigo. This person who had existed inside my head for a year and a half was a separate being from me, had been out having different experiences—talking, working, meeting up with new friends. Falling in love.

"I agree," I said. "For what it's worth. And I think for a while I believed you were replaceable somehow, and now I know you're not, and that's very freeing."

He spoke quietly. "I hope you know you're not being replaced just because I'm moving on. You'll still always be . . . well. Special to me."

"That's kind, thank you."

I heard footsteps, the jangle of keys in a pocket. "Listen, I'm about to get to my house and it's probably best for Lydia not to hear all of this. But I'm glad we spoke, Tash. Stay in touch."

"Of course," I said, knowing that we wouldn't, knowing it was the last thing he wanted. Then, as if to add to the charade, like we'd see each other at a meeting tomorrow: "Have a great evening."

"Yeah," he said. "You, too." Already in his voice I heard the distraction of someone moving into a different subset of their neatly categorized life, preparing their face for a domestic life partner and dinner on the table by eight. The line went dead.

I sat in the stillness for a few minutes, the muffled words from someone else's TV the only sound. I felt adrift, but not capsized. My new life was a shoreline within reach. Joe was gone and never coming back. And I knew that love—real love—would eventually come back around again, as it always does, as predictable and thoughtless as the tides.

EPILOGUE

To: arlojosephs@nypost.com
From: natasha.olga.bailey@gmail.com
December 5

Hey Arlo,

Thanks so much for coming to the party at my place a few months ago, and sorry about my minor freak-out—tequila and I are not friends, I guess!

I know you said you had some colleagues at the *Post* who might be interested in seeing freelance pitches, and I have something that I hope might be worth mentioning to them! I'm living in Zurich these days, but I've been working on an investigative piece about a missing person case for a while now. Hopefully, it's got everything the *Post* might want—relationships gone awry, rural and urban poverty, medical tragedy, suicide, gory details, etc., etc.—so I thought it might be a good sell. I've attached full details here but this is basically how I imagined it:

Lying Woman Took on Immigrant Identity Before Mysterious Suicide

The *Post* can exclusively reveal, through the investigative efforts of Natasha Bailey (celebrated journalist known for "The Pelosi Question" and "NYCHAland: A Forgotten Desert for Human Compassion") that a woman posing as a Ukrainian refugee in the Rockaways was actually longtime missing American Jaylene Wilson.

Wilson—whose distraught family members had believed her to be dead—took advantage of Eastern European turmoil and passed herself off as an innocent refugee for years. Her story raises questions about who else might be living off New York's generous social safety net. With the subway becoming a no-go zone for anyone without a weapon and rumored "super-gangs" taking over the projects, can we really afford for naïve city officials to continue turning a blind eye to the state's de facto open-border policy?

Anyway, let me know. I think this one has the potential to be really big.

Best wishes,
Natasha

MY FINGER HOVERED OVER THE SEND BUTTON AS I TRIED TO SUM-mon up the nerve to click.

ACKNOWLEDGMENTS

THIS BOOK WOULD STILL JUST BE A WEIRD, DEVIANT MANUSCRIPT saved on my computer if not for my agent, Dan Mandel, a wise and tenacious and extremely funny man who championed it from day minus-one. And I am truly lucky to have worked to turn it into a reality with Emily Griffin at Harper Perennial, whose particular brand of unfailing kindness coupled with unfailing thoroughness makes for a dream editor.

I'm also indebted to my incredible publicists, Brittani Hilles and Isabel Banta; to Heather Drucker, again for working publicity magic; and to the intrepid copy editors Jane Cavolina and Suzette Lam, who continually kept me from making an ass of myself.

Thank you to Susan Shapiro, my friend, mentor, and book party thrower, the person who probably has the best literary karma in the whole world; and to Danielle Perez, for her invaluable guidance.

To my earliest readers—Rhiannon, my *Vagenda* blog cofounder whose linen closet I once lived inside; Clémence, who married me, but not in that way; Josie, the best-connected person in any city; and Madeline, who solved all my feline problems and many of my other problems—all of whom are talented writers whose work and whose friendship I have had the good fortune of enjoying over the years.

To Frances and Rema, who have known me since I was a ridiculous eighteen-year-old and who still fly round the world to see me, despite the fact that I have grown into a ridiculous thirty-five-year-old. Your endless moral support means more than you know.

To my parents, Lynne and Neil, who are both storytellers in their own way and who nurtured in me a love of creativity and a healthy skepticism of authority. I am truly lucky that neither of you ever so much as implied a woman can't do everything a man can.

To Milk and Pull in Bed-Stuy for keeping me caffeinated, even after my most challenging nights with the baby. My brain runs on your black coffee.

To my husband, Edmund, who read my multiple manuscripts in all their forms, who designed a Miro board setting out all the themes and characters so he could make sure he'd understood it right, who held the baby while I did edits and went to book parties, and who always, always stands in my corner. People throw around the phrase "my better half" a lot, but I don't know anyone who encapsulates it as well as you.

And finally, a shout-out to my baby son, who came in stage left, smashed up the scenery, rerigged the lighting, charmed the audience, and turned a two-person production into an ensemble piece. Mummy loves you, so very much. (And when you grow up and can actually read a book of this size, please skip over the sex parts.)

ABOUT THE AUTHOR

© The Independent

HOLLY BAXTER WAS BORN IN NEWCASTLE, ENGLAND, AND STUDIED AT University College London. She traveled to New York City in 2019 to report on the 2020 election, intending to stay for six months, and still lives in Brooklyn with her husband and baby son.

She has spent over a decade in journalism, writing and editing for publications including *The Independent, The Guardian, BuzzFeed, VICE, The New Statesman,* and *The Times.* She has also worked as a terrible barista and a passable Subway Sandwich Artist.

Clickbait is her debut novel. You can find her on Instagram @hawleybackster and on Twitter (no one calls it X, come on) @hollyb4xter.